W9-AKD-759

CHAPTER 1

"ALL I've learned about women is that whatever it is they want it's what I don't have," I said, to see what kind of rise it would get.

"Don't have it—never had it—can't get it," I added, a little portentously.

I was talking, as usual, mostly to hear myself talk. Declarations of that nature cut no ice with my companion, and I knew it. She was cradling a coffee cup in her hands and looking out the window of the restaurant. For all practical purposes, she was absent—a woman enjoying her coffee—but that was all right. It was Sunday noon, a time when almost everyone in Hollywood might be described as absent. Probably the health freaks were out, chasing one another around Westwood, but they didn't count. The true lotus-eaters were still in their mansions and bungalows, in the hazy hills, languid from all-night drinking, all-night doping, and all-night TV. Some few of them may even have got fucked, from what one hears, but I wouldn't bet on it. By noon they would have begun to grope around in their vast beds, flopping their limbs now and then, blank, spiritless, and slothlike, hoping the phone would ring and summon them back to life. Before the first phone call not many of them would be able to vouch for their own existence, but once the little bell begins to jingle they soon take heart. In an hour or two most of them will be up and about, ready to choke down some more lotus.

Jill kept looking out at the Sunset Strip, which was white with noon sunlight and a little blurry with smog. I pointed my fork at her, meaning to generalize further about the impossibilities of women, but before I could swallow the mouthful of blueberry pancake I was chewing she shifted her gaze abruptly and was looking me in the eye.

"If you stopped chasing rich girls you'd be better off," she said, as if that were the only sensible statement that could possibly be made about myself and the ladies, now and forevermore.

Well, I was always a sucker for dogmatic women. The absolute and unassailable confidence with which they deliver their judgments on human behavior charms me to my toes—the more so because I've noticed that it usually exists side by side with an almost total uncertainty as to how to proceed with their own lives. I like to think, though, that I've learned to conceal how charmed I am, appreciation being all too often mistaken for condescension, these days.

Unfortunately, my little efforts at concealment didn't work with Jill Peel. If her intuition could have been marketed, it would have put radar out of business within a week.

"Talking with you is more like boxing than talking," I said. "You're always coming at me with the jab." I heaved a dramatic sigh—it took as much breath as if I'd heaved a shot put.

Jill kept looking me in the eye, as was her wont.

"I guess you think you're grown up, just because you made a picture," I said. "I guess now you think you know as much as I do."

"Nope," she said. "I don't know half as much as you do. I just know that if you stopped chasing rich girls you'd be better off."

"It's just that they seem to pin all their hopes on pleasure," I said. "There's a heartbreaking simplicity in that that I can't resist. They know it won't save them, but they don't know where else to look. I find that very appealing."

"I think you chase them because they're usually better looking," she said casually. "I know you like to have philosophic reasons worked out for everything you do, but that doesn't mean I have to believe them."

She went back to looking out the window. Her coffee was too hot to drink, and the coffee cup almost too hot to hold, but the service at the restaurant was so compulsively good that whenever she set the cup down for a moment someone immediately filled it, making it hotter still.

The odd thing about Jill was that almost all her motions, inner as well as outer, were awkward. In appearance she was a neat, fine-boned woman, but about the only things she had ever learned to handle gracefully were the tools of her old trade: pen, pencil, and brush. She drew beautifully, but the confidence with which she drew only served to emphasize the difficulty she had just moving about normally in the world. The easy moves that other women make so naturally —like rising from bed, or picking up a magazine—just wouldn't come for Jill. Her eyes were the only feature that betrayed her real grace. Otherwise, she was awkward, and the awkwardness seemed to contribute to a kind of bluntness of spirit that she had never lost, and perhaps found necessary.

"That's not how I am," she often said, when someone got carried away and tried to overstate her merits. She wouldn't have it, and in fact was uncomfortable with what physical distinction she did possess. Her efforts to make herself plainer and ever plainer were the despair of her women friends. Instead of contriving to make the most of her looks, as any normal woman would, she contrived to make the least of them, as if that were the only honest thing to do. If she made the least of them, then no unwary man would be misled by dress or makeup or a particularly fetching hairstyle into falling in love with her. The thought that some man might start to love her because she had been able—temporarily and artificially—to give herself the appearance of beauty was an affront to her. She wouldn't have love if it appeared to be coming from that direction. Where love was concerned, her standards were severe, which was probably the reason she remained so unremittingly critical of me—her oldest, and, I guess, her closest friend.

Myself, I had no standards to speak of—it would never occur to me to apply a word like standards to a happenstance like love. Even less would it occur to me to look askance at beauty. I have managed to love all sorts of beautiful women: tall ones and short ones, dumb ones and smart ones, loyal Penelopes and faithless sluts. Jill has wasted god knows how many hours of her life getting me over various of them, all the while arguing, with impeccable logic and sometimes even wisdom, that there were better things I could do with my life.

There may be, but frankly I doubt it. My wife, a beautiful woman herself, felt I should write a great, or at least a good, novel, but instead of doing that I spent twenty-five happy years yakking with her. Then, offering no excuse except cancer, she died. After her death a great many people made suggestions as to what I could best do with my time, but for some reason I found their suggestions pallid. With Claudia gone, not there to be with, it seemed to me that chasing beautiful women was about the best thing left. I didn't start immediately, but when I did start I went at it with a will, if not precisely with a heart.

I suppose, if pressed, I might have to admit that beauty isn't everything, in women; but I admit that reluctantly, and I would still claim that there's a real sense in which—as some football coach said, in another context—it's the only thing. Having wrestled with it across many a fetid sheet, and having watched it vanish down many a driveway, I have to think that it offers at least as high a challenge as art. Of course, having little talent, I can't really claim to have felt the grip of the challenge of art, but it has been a long time since I have been totally free of the grip of womanly beauty, and even at that moment something inside me was being squeezed by the beauty of Jill Peel's eyes—a beauty that was still being directed out the window, at some fairly tawdry. real estate.

Watching her jiggle the coffee cup, I reached over and touched her wrist.

"Would you allow me to tell you something before you start lecturing me?" I asked. "A little later in life, when you're a world-famous director, you might find it visually useful."

She brightened at once. "Tell me," she said.

"Gosh you're cute when you're expectant," I said. "Do you suppose that's why I sit here doling out the hard-earned secrets of a lifetime, over these fucking pancakes?"

"Yes, that's exactly why," Jill said. "What might be visually useful?"

"The way women handle coffee cups," I said. "It's out of sight."

"Stop using those trendy expressions," she said.

"Pardon me. What I meant to say was that there is something supremely feminine about the way women handle coffee cups. It's quite delicate. In fact, it's exactly the way men would like women to handle their toys, if you know what I mean."

Jill blushed and set her coffee cup down.

"Aw," I said. "I was just making a scholarly point. It's not like you suddenly discovered a couple of testicles in your hand."

"I knew sex was all you ever thought about," she said. "I just forgot." But she grinned when she said it and the blush faded, until all that remained of it were some little speckles of color near her cheekbones. "Are you coming to New York with me or not?" she asked.

"If I come to New York with you, it will be for one reason," I said. "One reason only. You have to try and guess what my reason is."

"I don't want to guess," she said. "I just want you to come. I'm scared of all this."

She looked at me in the startling, direct way she had. I had been idly thinking of my reason and wasn't set for such a look—every time she hits me with one I have the sense that once again I've bumbled unexpectedly onto a moral battlefield. Was I really her friend or not? the look asked.

Of course I was her friend. I would have rushed off immediately to man any barricade she wanted manned. Still, from blueberry pancakes to a moral battlefield is an awkward move. I swallowed wrong and was forced to sputter for a bit.

"Of course I'll go," I said, when I could speak.

"Good, drink some water," Jill said firmly. "I didn't mean to make you choke. I just really want you to go with me. I don't know what might happen next."

Who does? I could have said, if I hadn't been dutifully drinking my water. An Asian waiter stood nearby, poised to refill my glass the moment it left my lips.

"Besides," Jill said, and stopped.

"Besides what?"

She gave a little shrug of embarrassment. "I'm not familiar with New York," she said, as if she were referring to a book —some classic she had neglected to read.

I wasn't familiar with New York either, to tell the truth, but of course I had no intention of telling my darling companion a truth of that sort. Why tell women the truth, anyway? No need to add to their advantages.

I cleared my throat, patted her hand, and summoned my most world-traveled voice. It was just an act, but it was our act, and there were times when we were both almost able to suspend our disbelief in me. At times I was almost able to convince us that I knew what I was talking about, although, for it to work, it was necessary not to say much. If I said anything complex, Jill would methodically pick my statement apart. I would make an ill-considered but grandiose statement and she would calmly reduce it to a rubble of illogic. Somehow or other we had proceeded in that way for a good many years—she was looking at me now, waiting for a grandiose statement, the fine little chisel ready in her mind.

"Say something, Joe," she said.

"Oh, well," I said. "I was just going to point out that it's different."

"What's different?"

"New York," I said. "I remember that much. New York is different from here."

"Oh. I thought you were going to say something," she said, and allowed the impatient Asian to pour her some more coffee.

CHAPTER 2

THE "all this" that Jill Peel was afraid of was nothing less than impending fame. In three days' time a picture she had directed would be premiered at the New York Film Festival. It was called *Womanly Ways*, and there was no doubt in my mind that it would make her famous, if only temporarily and for circumstantial reasons.

First among the circumstantial reasons was simply that she was a woman. The studios were tired of having the women's movement on their backs—even though, in their terms, its weight was not especially formidable. Several studios had been casting about rather timidly for some time, hoping to turn up a woman director they could more or less trust. Hollywood lives on rumor, and for several months rumors of which woman would land which directing plum kept certain segments of the populace agog. One heard talk of Shirley Clarke, of Eleanor Perry, even of Joan Didion. Obscure quantities were sometimes mentioned: Susan Sontag, two French women, and a Swedish documentarian. There were also some local candidates. Two very bright ladies had spent their lives in editing rooms, snipping and splicing, and a third was a highly competent casting director—any of the three would have been happy to be shoved behind a camera, but no executive quite had the nerve.

Somehow none of the obvious prospects worked out, and the talk gradually trailed off. Joan Didion preferred to write novels. Susan Sontag, Shirley Clarke, and Eleanor Perry proved difficult, each in her own way; it was generally agreed that they were all much too New Yorky. The French women talked too fast, and the Swedish documentarian didn't need Hollywood, or even want it. There were a couple of talented girls at U.C.L.A., but nobody was about to gamble on anyone young.

For practical purposes, that left Jill Peel. She had been in Hollywood so long that everyone assumed they knew her. Up until her hour came round she had been quietly making a name for herself as an art director, a craft she had arrived at by a somewhat circuitous route.

She had shown up in Hollywood in the late '50s, fresh out of high school, and immediately landed a job as an animator. When she wasn't animating she hung around U.C.L.A., auditing film classes, art classes, whatever. Three years later she had an Oscar, for an animated short called *Mr. Molecule*. The Oscar went to every head but hers. For the next few years every cartoon producer in town tried to hire her, and then to fuck her. I didn't know her well in those years, but I eventually found out a good deal about her ups and downs, which included an early marriage and a child she couldn't really cope with. Her second marriage, to a French cinematographer, was unlikely, but evidently it proved to be therapeutic. The cinematographer wanted to be a director, but in the long run he wasn't obsessed enough. They wrote several scripts together, none of which ever quite got made. In Europe, where they lived for a time, she began to work as a set designer, and while the two of them were in Sicily, doing a picture, he left her for a younger woman.

Jill came back to Hollywood, but not to cartoons. Henry Bennington, a stable older director with a lifetime of modest successes behind him (he got his Oscar in '56, for *Frosting on the Cake*), used her on a couple of good pictures and touted her highly to anyone who would listen. Out of nearly thirty pictures, Henry Bennington had only had about four flops, so people listened. From set designing it was a comparatively short step to art direction, although, unfortunately, Henry Bennington wasn't around to see Jill take it. His wife, never as stable as Henry, drove their car into an irrigation ditch south of Fresno, drowning them both.

Leon O'Reilly, of all people, helped Jill to an immediate Oscar nomination as an art director. Leon had just had a tragedy in his life: his faithful secretary, Juney, whose devotion to her boss would have been rare anywhere in the world except Hollywood—where all the best secretaries are bound to their bosses with ties of steel—had killed herself in a particularly foolish way. She jumped off an overpass on the Hollywood Freeway during rush hour, a way out that would usually at least have got her headlines. In her case the headlines were several days late, due to the fact that she landed on top of a trailer truck. The truck was carrying three bulldozers north to Alaska—Juney landed in the seat of one of them, broke her fat, devoted neck, died, and was not discovered until the trucks were well up into British Columbia.

That was the Hollywood of romance: a town where secretaries died for their bosses, one way or another. In a town with any story sense—much less any real respect for passion—Juney's story might have resulted in a good film. But in the town we all know, and more or less love, and continue to work in, it resulted in nothing.

Juney flung herself from the overpass because Leon, normally the most manageable of men and certainly the most predictable of producers, suddenly did something that no one—least of all Juney—would have predicted. He too had come to Hollywood in the '50s, straight from Harvard, and had not budged since. The wife he brought with him did budge, however. She found the level of taste in L.A. insupportable—I heard her use that very word, several times—so after a few years, during which I guess she satisfied herself that she had tried, she went back to Greenwich, Connecticut, where I imagine the level of taste must be terrific.

Leon survived her departure with the help of Juney, who spent the next thirteen or fourteen years taking very good care of him. A Swiss hotel would have had nothing on Juney when it comes to taking care, but there were limits to what one could do for Leon O'Reilly. His soul was no problem—Juney made it a home—but his body was something else. Perhaps his wife's departure shocked him into a state of dormancy that lasted fourteen years. If true, it was a state from which Juney—in appearance she was not unlike a sea cow—was simply not the person to release him.

At any rate, for several tranquil and productive years Leon was the straightest man in Hollywood. He didn't smoke, he drank nothing more deadly than an occasional brandy and soda, and he had no affairs. The eight or ten pictures he produced in those years were among the worst stinkers of their era, but somehow they made money. Then, just after making a highly profitable stinker called *Cloverleaf*—about the biggest, most awe-inspiring L.A. freeway wreck of all time, three hundred cars totally destroyed—Leon, as if jolted from a long sleep, opened his eyes and discovered beautiful girls. It occurred to him, one day, that he too might have a beautiful girl, and the minute this novel thought entered his head he reverted, as it were, to his roots. He flew straight home to Binghampton, Mass., and married a remarkably beautiful Boston deb named Elizabeth ("Betsy") Rousselet. A few days later, heartbroken, Juney dove onto the bulldozer.

Jill had always thought Leon O'Reilly an uptight Eastern creep—though when it came to uptightness she really had no room to talk, and she had grown up about as far west as you can get. (She was from Santa Maria, a nondescript little town a couple of hundred miles up the coast.) But Jill, like everyone else in Hollywood, loved Juney, a good-hearted woman who didn't mind that everyone in the industry knew she had a hopeless crush on a silly man. Juney was the archetypal studio secretary, a woman with no children, no hobbies, no boyfriends. Her life was Leon O'Reilly. The two of them worked almost around the clock, putting together his pictures—a quixotic pair, Leon the mad knight of Century City, Juney his faithful squire. What the rest of us took to be pretensions were to Juney grand visions, I guess.

Anyway, Betsy Rousselet was too much. Juney didn't bother adjusting. In a town filled with therapies of every description, she chose the simplest one.

A little later, when Leon asked Jill to be the art director on *Burning Deck*, Jill accepted, in memory of Juney. In the '60s, when Columbia was still over on Gower Street, she had had an office across the hall from Leon's, and she and Juney had taken their lunch breaks together.

"If Juney were alive, I'd turn him down in a minute," Jill said. "She'd understand. But I can't turn him down with her dead. I'll just do this one picture."

Burning Deck—the one picture—took off like it was headed for Mars. It was, as one might guess, about a fire on a ship: in this case, an oil barge in the Persian Gulf. It had terrorism; it had sex; Soraya, the former empress of Iran, played a bit part; and Al Pacino, the lead terrorist, got burned to a crisp fighting for his cause. America could be thought to be a nation of pyromaniacs from the way people flocked to that movie. In six months it had grossed $78 million, a record that stood for almost a year, until *Jaws* broke it. With one stroke, *Burning Deck* made three reputations: Leon's (it was by far his biggest winner), Jilly Legendre's (he directed it), and Bo Brimmer's. Bo, with exquisite timing, had escaped from Metro and become Head of Production at Universal the very week that Leon brought the project in.

None of this had much to do with Jill, not even the fact that the director she ended up working for had a first name so much like her own that the gossip columnists immediately tried to conjure up a romance between them. If there's one thing Hollywood adores, it's alliteration. While the picture was being shot, and for a few months after its release, all the smart magazines published rumors that Jill and Jilly were becoming—as they still love to put it—"more than friends."

In fact, Jill and Jilly got on admirably, but it was because they were both dead-serious professionals. Obsessive professionals, in fact. Jilly Legendre was an interesting filmmaker, and in this instance it didn't hurt any that he had close ties to the international jet set. Not only did he coax Soraya into performing, but he also persuaded an old family friend, Aristotle Onassis, to rent Universal an oil barge at a very cheap rate.

The picture was really Bo Brimmer's gamble. It cost a lot of money, and if it hadn't worked he would have probably been out on his ass. But what Leon O'Reilly had done, quite inadvertently, was bring together the two hardest working, most upwardly mobile young hustlers in Hollywood: Jilly, the French-Swiss-Creole aristocrat, who weighed in at the time at close to 300 poorly distributed pounds, and Bo, 115 pounds soaking wet, the former paperboy from Little Rock who still looked like a paperboy from Little Rock.

Lost in the shuffle, ironically, was Betsy Rousselet O'Reilly. She couldn't stand the Persian Gulf, nor the un-Bostonian groves of Holmby Hills. In less than a year she was back in the East. Poor Juney should have hung in there.

Jill, of course, did her usual thorough job. She probably should have had an Oscar for it, but the nod that year went to an aging Austrian art director named Bruno Himmel—an old drinking buddy of mine. Bruno had worked on a rather ham-handed remake of *King Solomon's Mines*, a case of misjudgment that cost Fox what everyone kindly hoped were its last shekels. It cost Bruno too: one night in the bush, drunk out of his skull and bored with listening to lions grunt, he wandered off to the equipment shed, got his feet tangled up, and fell into a pile of assegais, poking out one of his piercing blue eyes. I seem to have been the only person hardhearted enough to be disgruntled when the Academy rewarded this act of clumsiness with an Oscar, mostly because I know Bruno for the old pussy-hound that he is. With his snow-white hair, his European good health, and his raffish eye patch, he'll be lucky not to fuck his brains out.

In any case, when the studios finally concluded that there might be PR benefits to letting a woman direct, there was Jill. Her competence was one of the givens of the industry. She had one Oscar in her pocket, and, had it not been for a pile of assegais, would have had another. She was known to be stubborn, but then all directors were stubborn—none of them ever willingly submitted to the rule of reason.

What clinched it, though, was that Jill actually had something essential, over and above her undoubted talent: she had a produceable script. Jill and two actor friends, Pete Sweet and Anna Lyle, had done the script way back in the '60s, when the three of them had shared rent on a little beach house near Malibu. The script had been passed around Hollywood for so long that everyone had forgotten it existed—everyone, that is, except Lulu Dickey, the agent, and old Aaron Mondschiem, the patriarch of Paramount. In this case, Mr. Mond, as he liked to be called, was one step ahead of the redoubtable Lulu.

He bought the script and Jill and, what was most surprising, Pete Sweet and Anna Lyle, only a day or two before Lulu Dickey managed to suck the script out of her formidable memory. Her uncharacteristic delay in remembering it seems to have been caused by a troublesome boyfriend, a rock star named Digby Buttons, who kept overdosing every few weeks. Lulu was always in the papers, trailing along as Digby was wheeled into or out of one hospital after another. She was six feet three and crazy-looking—the scandal sheets just couldn't get enough of the two of them.

In this case, love proved bad for business, giving point, in fact, to one of Lulu's most famous statements, which was: "Fucking clouds the mind." She made the remark in an interview with *Women's Wear Daily*, when that paper chose to honor her ascendance as an agent. They broke precedent and ran it verbatim, without even putting in any little dashes. Since it brought her a degree or two more celebrity,

Lulu adopted the remark as her motto, and had it engraved on an ivory-and-gold plaque, which hung in her office.

In this case it didn't seem quite applicable, since Digby was known to be far too dopey to get it up, even if he hadn't been more gay than not. In fact, Lulu hated Jill and had thrown the script away years before—a rare professional slip. The minute she remembered it, without even bothering to steal a copy and reread it, she got on the phone to Bo Brimmer and offered him a package which included Jill to direct, Toole Peters (the hottest screenwriter in town) to do a rewrite, and Sherry Solaré to star. Since Sherry was one of the two immediately financeable female stars left, Bo was intrigued. He had never seen the script—it had been a forgotten hunk of paper before he even arrived in town—but he was ready to buy the package, contingent only upon something resembling producibility.

When Lulu found out, from Jill, that Aaron Mondschiem had just bought the script, she drove home and went into such a froth that two maids quit and Digby Buttons decided he'd rather live in a hospital. Then she calmed down, abandoned her hopes of a coup, and set about a salvage operation. Before the picture was even shot she had talked both Pete Sweet and Anna Lyle into dumping their agents and signing up with her. It was her way of covering the only bets that Mr. Mond had left uncovered.

Pete and Anna were both good actors whose careers had never been commensurate with their abilities. It's a common story in Hollywood—too common to dwell on. Mostly they did television work—spots on *Gunsmoke* and *Marcus Welby* and the like. A lot of it was done at Warners, so I bumped into them from time to time. Anna was a bosomy, slightly blowsy brunette with a permanently distracted expression and a considerable flair for comedy. If she had come along in the '50s, when she was slimmer, she might have made it to the level of Linda Darnell, or even Ann Sheridan, but probably she wouldn't have. Her features weren't quite good enough. Pete was a big, jowly guy with sorrowful eyes and a kind of slow, self-deprecating charm.

I'm sure they were excited that their script had finally

sold, and happy that they were going to get to act in it—still, Lulu Dickey's invitation must have been the real shocker. Anyone can finally luck into a picture, if they hang around long enough and keep working, but to be courted by Lulu was something else again. What it meant was that Lulu smelled a winner. Old Aaron smelled it too, and the scent had carried all the way to Bo Brimmer, over the hills in Studio City. How this could be, with the script unrevised in nearly a decade, an untried director at the helm, and not a frame shot, was a puzzle to all—but there it was. The three quickest noses in Hollywood had sniffed out *Womanly Ways*, and of the three, the old man's had been the quickest.

I was happy about the deal, myself, partly for Jill but mostly for Pete and Anna. They were members of Hollywood's oldest club: the ones who wait. They weren't has-beens, because they had never been. Three minutes on *The Waltons* or ten minutes in an overbudgeted Western shot in Old Tucson was what they thought of as good exposure. Only the most compulsive film buffs would have known their names: the kind of people who, in another sport, can tell you the batting average of every third baseman Detroit has ever had. Pete and Anna were just part of the Hollywood troops, camping in the canyons, moving out to the Valley and then back to Santa Monica, then back to the Valley again, getting married and divorced, fucked and fucked over, and, I would imagine, a little more strung out all the time. They were not in shape, like Jill, who had done nothing but work since she came to L.A. They had been waiting a long time, and with people like that you never know for sure what will happen, not until the cameras begin to roll.

Bo Brimmer, smart as he is, would never have cast them. Bo was too new to it all—he still worked in concepts. Old Aaron was different. People—and of course the press—liked to call him an old fox, an absurd delicacy on their part. That wheezing, sulking, malign old man, with the longest and for all I know the strongest jaw in America, was no fox. He was an old wolf, looking down from his floodlit lair atop Mulholland Drive at the city he had known since 1912. I like to think that old Aaron stayed up there, in those dry, unfashionable hills above the Hollywood Freeway, so he could see both directions, keep his eye on it all. His house was at the highest point in the hills, giving him a view of both the basin and the Valley.

His jaw was so long that if you were standing too close to him and he turned suddenly his chin could knock you down: I saw it happen, at a party in the '30s. The person he knocked down was a meek little character actor named Sweeney McCaffrey, whose temple was just on a level with Aaron's chin. He wouldn't help you up, either: in his view you shouldn't have been standing so close. He was the old wolf of the hills, and he cast Pete and Anna out of instinct—not an instinct about them, an instinct about Jill. He let her have her friends, knowing that if he did she'd make it work.

He was right, too. Under Jill's direction they both gave fine performances. Of course the fact that they had written the roles for themselves didn't hurt anything. *Womanly Ways* was about the wife of the world's most successful automobile dealer. Such a supersalesman actually exists, in California; for many years he has been an all-too-familiar figure to people who watch late movies on TV. Jill and Pete and Anna, after years of having this superenergetic figure interrupt their favorite flicks in order to prance up and down in front of thousands of new cars, finally stopped detesting him and began to be curious about him. Then Pete thought of a wonderfully grisly opening. The salesman frequently brought lions and elephants and other exotic beasts into his salesman act, and he also kept donkeys and ponies and goats and what-have-you so the kiddies could be kept amused while their parents were filling out credit forms. Pete's idea was to have one of the lions go berserk, maul the supersalesman for a while, then run off with a donkey in its mouth. All this would be happening on live TV, of course, and we would see it over the shoulder of the salesman's wife, alone in her huge bed in their home in the Palisades.

From that beginning—it was eventually discarded—grew a nice little script about fucked-over wives. Pete was the salesman, Anna his bedraggled, frenetic, resilient but ultimately desperate spouse. At the climax of the picture she comes to the car lot in disguise, buys a shiny new Chevy, and runs her husband down while he's doing a TV spot: the male chauvinist gets his just deserts. For my taste it was a trifle too pat, but then it wasn't my movie.

This being California, where no publicity can hurt you, they had no trouble persuading the very dealer who inspired the script to let them shoot on his car lot. When Jill showed me the rough cut, over at Paramount, I knew old Aaron had got a real bargain. It only cost a little over a million, about a third of what Sherry Solaré would have cost all by herself.

It was odd that Jill had become a director. For one thing, she had no vanity, and directors *need* vanity, the way fish need gills. For another, she had always seemed to treasure her solitude, yet directors have no solitude. They live amid a mob, like politicians. Finally, there was her excessive sense of responsibility. I wouldn't have thought she would want to be responsible for a million dollars of someone else's money—but I guess I was wrong. Maybe I didn't know her as well as I liked to think. She wasn't twenty-four any more—a lovely but introverted girl who really only liked to draw. She was thirty-seven, and faced with impending fame.

I, on the other hand, still seemed to be faced with a couple of unwavering gray eyes.

"What? I've forgotten the question," I said, stuffing my face.

"I think you've started living in the past," she said. "Half the time you don't keep up with what we're talking about."

"I could be living in the future," I said.

"If it's the future, then you're just thinking about screwing some rich girl," she said. "I guess that's why you agreed to go to New York. You probably have a few back there that you need to go see."

I decided to be honest, if only for the novelty.

"Honey, I haven't been to New York in twenty years," I said. "Why would anyone take *me* to New York. My last trip was to Point Barrow, Alaska, when we did *Igloo*. Several years before that I got to go to Argentina, because Tony Maury insisted on making *Gaucho's Gauntlet.*"

Even as I said it, it occurred to me that there *was* a disconsolate Betsy Rousselet O'Reilly, somewhere in that neck of the woods. We had had a couple of friendly chats.

"You didn't guess the real reason I agreed to go," I said. "I might as well tell you. It's because of *Variety.*"

Jill looked blank.

"I'm talking about the magazine *Variety,*" I said. "Not variety as in the spice of life. You know those little boxes they have in the magazine? The four categories that tell you who's going where: New York to L.A., L.A. to New York, U.S. to Europe, and Europe to U.S. I've never had my name in those little boxes. It seems little enough to ask in the way of recognition, considering that I've spent damn near my whole life in this industry. Maybe if I go with you I could even get it in twice, once under L.A. to New York, and once under New York to L.A., when we come back. I think that would be sort of romantic."

Jill was silent, looking at me. It was different when she was silent than when she was just quiet. Usually she was quiet—that was her manner, and I was very comfortable with it. But when she dropped from quiet to silent, something less comfortable went on. Her silence had a frequency all its own, one that I could never endure for very long. It was like one of those dog whistles that make a sound only dogs can hear—a sound that cracked eggs, or something. I was the egg Jill's silence usually cracked.

"Stop it," I said. "I was kidding. I was just kidding. I don't really care whether I get my name in *Variety* or not."

She shrugged that off. Accidentally, I had touched her sympathies. The thought that a lifelong drudge in the hemp mills had never had his name in the trade paper of the hemp industry cut her to the heart. A susceptibility to such small poignancies was one of her real assets as a director, but in day-to-day life such susceptibility had its drawbacks.

"You take things too seriously," I said. "I *would* get a kick out of seeing my name in one of those little lists, but it's no big deal. Half of me doesn't give a shit."

She sighed, disgustedly. At least it was a sound.

"The whole business makes me tired," she said. "I almost wish I hadn't made the picture."

Indeed, she looked tired—there were little dark circles under her eyes. She had the look of a woman who was tired of her life. I could understand it, too. Her life was demanding without being very exciting, and fatiguing but not particularly satisfying. Part of it was her fault, for taking things too seriously, as I had just said. It meant an unending sequence of moral tangles, a maddening snarl of ethical string. No matter how hard she tried, things never quite came right.

"The fun part of this movie is all over," she added, pursing her lips.

She was right about that. The awful tedium of publicity lay ahead of her. Only a few ego-kings enjoy that part of it.

"I'm going," I said. "I'm going. Cheer up. We'll have some fun. Just tell me where you're staying. Maybe I can get a room down the hall."

"At the Sherry-something," she said. "You can just have a room in my room. I believe I have a suite at my disposal."

"Come on," I said. "You've got to try and be conventional for a few days, for the sake of your picture. You can't go housing a bloated old type like me, no matter how big your suite is. I'm too old to be a gofer or a lover, and I'm not your father or your uncle. If I stay with you the press won't know what to make of things, and that's fatal. The press *must* know what to make of things. If I stay in your suite everybody will just think we're fucking, and how will that look?"

Jill brightened a little. She gave me a defiant look. "Oh, well," she said. "So what? If I'm a big director I guess I can be permitted a weakness for old farts with potbellies, can't I? Just forget about a room. The studio can take care of it."

"You're a naive child," I said. "I work for Warners, remember? This is a Paramount extravaganza. Just because you're about to make them millions doesn't mean they're going to want you treating your kooky friends to free hotel rooms."

Of course she disregarded my measured analysis of the situation vis-à-vis rooms. She glanced at me and made a disgusted little motion with her mouth. Then she went back to looking out at the Strip.

"You wouldn't stay in my room anyway," she said. "I know you. You want a room of your own, just in case you stumble over a debutante."

CHAPTER 3

WHEN it came to measured analysis, Jill was on a par with me. She had me cold on the room situation, as far as that went. What she probably didn't realize is that she had hit on the phrase that best describes my method with women—if it can be called a method. I stumble over them.

One of the reasons I still live in L.A. is because it literally teems with women. One can stumble and fall almost anywhere in L.A. and land on a woman. I've done it time and again, and often, if I'm lucky, I even stumble over ladies who haven't been in town too long. Ladies who have resided here for ten years or so I try not to stumble into—like other flora of the desert, those ladies will have grown thorns.

But when women first get to town the sun and the breeze and the relaxed, undemanding patter of Hollywood talk has a tranquilizing effect. Sometimes this effect lasts three or four years, interrupted only by periods of gnawing, puzzled loneliness. The gnawing and the puzzlement are apt to be especially pronounced if the lady comes here from the East —that's the American East—due to the level-of-taste factor. During these first years the nice, newly arrived women can be counted on to be extremely companionable, and on the whole I've done pretty well with them, thanks to my vulnerability and my obvious helplessness. Few women can resist helpless men: what a focus it gives them for their talents.

With that in mind, I've always studiously avoided learning how to do anything more complicated than making drinks. In the very old days I used to try and attract women by demonstrations of superiority, but all that got me was an occasional masochist. It was my beloved wife, Claudia, the serial queen, who convinced me that in the male inferiority is by far the more attractive quality.

I was broadly inferior to Claudia, but she adored me. She was an Olympic swimmer, for one thing. Her performance in the Olympics was overshadowed by Johnny Weissmuller's, and he went on to overshadow her in pictures too, but she could swing through the vines with the best of them; besides which, she could cook, decorate houses, grow flowers, and do a lot of other things. I couldn't touch her: not in talent, not in human ability, not even in spirit. By the time we met I had published a couple of thin, affected novels, given up, and was doing hack work around the studios, writing Westerns, jungle movies, serials, shorts, and propaganda pictures. It wasn't destroying my sensitive, artistic soul, either, because I didn't have one. I was just lucky enough to have found a craft I liked, at which I was reasonably competent. Claudia talked for a time about my writing a really good novel, but I think it was only because she liked to hope that I might someday grow up.

In the end I did grow up: as she was dying. Up until then it had been unnecessary, maybe even undesirable. I remained her roaring boy, lover, wayward son, whatever.

A year or two after her death, when I grudgingly went on to other ladies, I seldom, if ever, found that I needed to feign inferiority. In most cases, I *was* inferior. Of course I was smarter than a few of them, but that didn't help me much. Women know precisely where intelligence fits in the scale of human values. It may occasionally get you a meal, but it won't get you fucked. There are always more powerful factors at work, such as beauty and ugliness, dependence and independence, greed and need. I'm usually inferior in every visible way to the smart, expensive ladies I keep company with, and yet they continue to waft down upon me, one after another, like discarded garments.

It drives Jill mad. She doesn't understand what they see in me that they can't seem to see in their handsome, well-kept husbands.

But then I've never been sure that Jill has ever been attracted enough to have any understanding of attraction. She may not realize that passion is usually answering some important question. In the case of myself and women who are seemingly far too good for me, the question it answers is whether there is anything real except beauty and money. At least that's the question it answers for the ladies. For me the question is more like "What am I going to do without Claudia?" The ladies are only a temporary answer, but if you repeat a temporary answer often enough, it acquires a degree of permanency. And a degree is certainly all I expect.

The fact that these young women, with their trim ankles, high cheekbones, good educations, bright eyes, little bosoms, and expensive clothes, keep coming to my bungalow and often to my bed, despite the fact that I'm old, fat, often drunk, beneath them on the social scale, and in love with a dead woman, only increases Jill's impatience with her own sex. Their foolishness drives her up the wall, and my willingness to assist them in their obvious folly is a constant bone of contention between us.

Human unreason is Jill's *bête noire*, as I often point out. I think sometimes she doesn't know what heat there is in incongruity. I get a certain mileage out of incongruity, but in fact my success with women—modest as it is—is due to nothing more than a capacity for attention. This capacity is not mysterious, but it is rare, in a man. I like to think it is particularly rare in Los Angeles, but I really don't know that. It may be just as rare everywhere. Maybe the truth is that only men like myself, who have nothing else to do in life, can afford to pay serious attention to women.

The moment I realized I wasn't a real writer and thus had no important artistic task to perform, I became a serious ladies' man—although for twenty-five years I was a ladies' man with only one lady. I became a kind of Proust of women, with every tit and giggle tucked away in my memory somewhere. Claudia and I met at Republic, when I was writing an episode or two of the *Nyoka* serials she was in. We had breakfast together at Schwab's a few times, drove out to Santa Monica once or twice on Sunday, to see the waves, and from beginnings in no way original or even very intense found ourselves in a marriage that grew like a great book, filling twenty-five years with many thousands of elaborate and subtle details. They were not all happy details, of course. Some years were not all that well-written, one might say. Claudia had three affairs, for example, whereas my philandering, during the whole of the marriage, boiled down to a one-night stand in Carson City. But then no idyll is a great book, nor any great marriage an idyll.

I came away from her grave with a lot of memories, and with the ability to pay attention to women—an ability that's kept me in company ever since. It brought me Jill, for that matter. When she came to work at Warners, not long after her Oscar, she still looked like a girl who wasn't ready to leave junior high. I had known her slightly for several years, through Tony Maury, but only slightly. We didn't share the same weaknesses, which is how people usually make friends, in Hollywood or elsewhere.

Once she got to Warners, we soon developed a serious weakness for one another. It started, of course, with me being chivalrous. I kept noticing her in the commissary, a skinny girl with short hair, invariably wearing jeans, sneakers, and a jogger's sweat shirt. Just as invariably, she would be being pestered by three or four men.

Jill might not vary, but the men did. In my view they constituted a potpourri of the worst assholes on the lot, an eclectic mixture of would-be studs. Socially, they pretty well covered the spectrum, from grips and prop men and boom operators all the way up to perhaps the second level of executives. In fact, the first time I met Preston Sibley III he was pestering Jill, and him fresh off the plane from Locust Valley.

I took in the situation at a glance—as they used to say in the pulps—and the situation was that a lot of horses' asses were pestering the one creature in the world that they should have known they were not equipped to deal with: an intelligent woman. When pressed, I can be as impatient with my sex as Jill is with hers. It was obvious that none of the pesterers would have had the faintest idea what to do with her if they could have attracted her, but, perversely, they kept right at it, as if she were the only woman on the lot worth their time.

In those days she was far too shy and polite just to tell them to fuck off—she still is, as far as that goes—so her lunch hours at Warners consisted mostly of parrying unwanted sexual thrusts. It seemed to me to be a boring way to spend lunch, so I presumed on our mutual friendship with the infamous Tony Maury and began inserting myself at her table. Then I would either tell loud, labyrinthine stories about the old days, or launch into a little lecture about the latest serious book I had read reviews of—*The Origins of Totalitarianism*, perhaps—all this to the great annoyance of the would-be cocksmen.

To my surprise, Jill enjoyed my stories. She liked hearing about all those happy, hard-drinking boys I used to know, the fellows who would have made Hollywood great if they could have. More surprisingly, she enjoyed my little lectures too. Half the time she even went and read the damn books, and then came back and put me to shame, or at least forced me to bullshit rather skillfully. She was curious about everything, but particularly curious about people. *Why* did they do the things they did?

She seemed to think I might know, and in all likelihood I encouraged her to think so. There's nothing more tonic to an aging man than a bright, gray-eyed student who appears to be completely taken in by whatever false wisdom or learned nonsense he may feel like babbling.

This time it worked out well, though. By the time Jill realized that I was an old fraud, rather than Socrates, she loved me anyway and it didn't matter. Besides, the cocksmen soon decided that the prospect of fucking her wasn't worth having to listen to me—particularly since it was a remote prospect at best. In no time at all we had a table to ourselves, and I guess we still do.

"Remember our days at Warners?" I said, smiling.

"Sure," Jill said. "You drove off all my would-be boyfriends with your pontificating. Who knows what I missed because of you? I might have managed to want one of them, eventually."

"You had true respect for me in those days," I said. "You thought I knew everything about life."

"Yes," she said, shaking her head quickly, with some force. It was an old mannerism, that headshake, and meant that she was utterly convinced about something—as if fate were a long flight of stairs down which she could see to the very bottom. Meanwhile, she put her hand over her coffee cup, to discourage the lurking Oriental.

"Is that a floating yes?" I asked. "Are you affirming life, like Molly Bloom?"

"Yes, you do know everything about life," she said. "You just won't tell me very much at a time. It's your hook. If you told me everything you know, then I wouldn't need you any more, and I might go off and leave you. Then you'd be stuck with all your little friends. How would that be?"

"Well, I wouldn't have to think so hard at this hour on Sundays," I said. "This is a freakish conversation. Why can't we just talk about deals and box office, like normal people?"

"Let's go," she said. "I'm tired of guarding a coffee cup."

I reached for the check, but she was quicker. "I'm the one that's going to be rich," she said. "You can tip."

She was at the cash register, waiting none too patiently, when I finally unwedged myself from what had been our booth.

CHAPTER 4

OUTSIDE, we walked down Sunset Boulevard, toward La Brea. It was early November and cool enough that the smog looked milky in the hills. Jill walked along with her hands in the pockets of her jeans for a block or two. Then, abrupt and awkward as ever, she came over and tucked one arm in mine. She even put her cheek against my arm for a moment, like a girl come to Daddy.

"Maybe it will be a terrible flop," she said. "Maybe I've really wasted all that money."

I put my arm around her and we walked along for a time.

"I wonder how long it would take to walk to San Bernardino?" she asked.

I had nothing to say to that either. The concept of walking to San Bernardino was one no sane mind would admit.

"I think they all thought I was frigid," she said a little later.

"Who?"

"Those guys at Warners," she said. "Those boys you bored to death. I bet a lot of people still think that."

"What brought this on?"

"You did," she said. "I was fine until you pointed out that if I travel with anyone it's supposed to be a boyfriend. Where am I going to get a boyfriend, in two days' time?"

The way she said it struck me as so funny that I sat down on a bench at a bus stop, to laugh my fill. It embarrassed Jill. "Stop laughing," she said. It did no good. A car full of chicanos slowed down as they passed us, to take in the spectacle of a fat man laughing on a bench at a bus stop while a skinny woman in jeans looked at him helplessly. Finally Jill sat down by me on the bench.

"You have a perverse sense of humor," she said.

"I'm sorry," I said. "It was just the way you said it. That's your essence, or something."

She looked at me, as if perhaps suddenly mindful that I might have problems, too, and began to rub the back of my neck. "I don't have an essence," she said. "I used to, but I lost it. I could just sit here on this old bus bench forever, talking to you, and I'd be just as happy as I'll be otherwise."

I think I was laughing just to keep from crying, although at the moment it would have been hard to put a finger on what I might have had to cry about. Jill has a strange effect on me. Statements that are perfectly innocent, maybe just a little droll because of her odd way of putting things, turn out to be piercing in a lot of cases. I end up laughing too much. Of course it's just a sign that I'm slightly cracked, but that's no secret.

"You could get a boyfriend instantly, if you really want one," I said. "You're one of the most sought-after women in Hollywood."

She ignored me. "I would have been perfectly happy to go to New York if I could have had you stay with me," she said. "Of course that won't do because I might get in the way of some conquest. Far be it from me to ask you to do without a debutante for a whole week."

"All right, stop it," I said. "Debutantes are people, too."

"I apologize," she said. "I'm sure you're right. You if anyone should know."

She didn't say it nicely. In fact, there was an edge to the remark that I found intolerable.

"Don't talk like that to me," I said. "So what? I'm not the soul of convention, like yourself. You're so fucking proper you can't even take a simple trip without wondering whether some asshole will think badly of you because you don't have a boyfriend. Why do you always try to do what you think people expect of you?"

"Probably because I know I never can," she said. Her eyes cleared—they had darkened with hostility for a moment.

"What a screwy outlook you have," I said. "It's nobody's fucking business what you do. Do you really care what people think about your love life? If you do, you're not going about it right. The only suitable boyfriends for promising young female directors are rock stars, politicians, studio heads, and French photographers. Take your pick and get busy."

I have a wicked tongue, but then so does she.

Her eyes darkened again. "Perhaps I'll take Preston Sibley," she said. "He's a studio head. If I take him, maybe you'll get to keep his wife for a few more weeks."

She got up and walked across the Boulevard and up toward the hills. I got up and followed. Her house was up there, and mine too. She got about two blocks ahead of me and then went up a curving road, out of sight. I found her sitting on the pink steps of the little four-room bungalow she had lived in for the last several years. Her face was red but I didn't notice any tears.

"Terrible behavior on my part," I said. "On the Sabbath, too. I feel you deserve a refund on a breakfast."

"Shut up," she said. "Come on in."

Just as I stepped into her yard, a kid whizzed down past me on a skateboard. If he had hit me, at the speed he was going, it would have turned us to peanut butter. The kid had so much hair that, if he hadn't had on tie-dyes, I would have thought it was just a blond sheep dog skateboarding by. Then three bicyclists sliced down the street, their teeth clenched. I couldn't tell what sex they were: all I saw was teeth. Hollywood was waking up, just at the hour when I felt most in need of a nap.

I went in and lay down on the large white wicker couch that covered one wall of Jill's small living room. A while later, when I woke up, she was sitting across the room on a blue pillow, talking quietly on the telephone. Sunlight filled the room behind her, the only spacious room in the house. It was supposed to be a dining room, but Jill used it for a studio. Her drawing board was there, and piles of magazines, books, sketches, and scripts were arranged in neat stacks under the large windows.

A bloody Mary sat on a little teak coffee table, almost within reach of my hand. It had a large stick of celery in it. What a thoughtful woman she was. I demonstrated my own thoughtfulness by eating the stick of celery as loudly as possible. It was the only way to keep myself from eavesdropping on her conversation. In the light of my recent boorishness, such an effort seemed only fair.

I was mean to Jill because I couldn't afford to be mean to Page Sibley, wife of Preston Sibley III. Page had just about completed the Joe Percy tutorial in Real Life, and would soon go back to being a Beautiful Person. Real life wasn't going to last, which was the main reason I had been a little reluctant to accompany Jill to New York in the first place. Preston Sibley was going to New York for the Festival, even though he didn't have a picture in it. The Festival was an excuse to go east, and any excuse was good enough for Preston.

At the same time, he would not be likely to encourage Page to go, since the lover she had had before me lived there. He was one of America's better painters, and, like me, he was much too old for Page, herself a tawny twenty-five.

She hadn't been tawny before she married Preston and moved to L.A., but now she had that irresistible golden hue that is to be found only on women who happen to inhabit the tiny area of the earth's surface that lies between Wilshire Boulevard and the Bel Air Hotel. Examples of this extraordinary hue will sometimes occur as far afield as Westwood or even Santa Monica, in certain seasons, but those will seldom be the finest examples. Perfection, whether of leg, shoulder, upper arm, or midriff, will usually be confined to those living within the area specified: elsewhere the color is apt to be too light, evocative of wheat-germ breakfasts and an obsessive interest in health, or else too dark, meaning too much time spent on the beach.

Page lived about 400 yards from the Bel Air Hotel, and her skin was all you could ask for, when it came to skin. If her mind had been the equal of her skin, there would have been no stopping her—which is not to derogate her mind. She had a fair mind. Certainly it had picked mine clean in about six months. But her mind, as a mind, couldn't begin to compete with her skin as skin. Page was the Einstein of tawny young women, and I had been lucky to see as much of her as I had.

Preston Sibley didn't know about me—he would have had trouble believing it if he had—but he did know about her artist lover on the Upper West Side. Unfortunately for his marriage, Preston was the sort of producer who could not believe that his wife could be as interested in him as she would naturally be in any artist, however decrepit, repulsive, and foul. Obviously a woman like Page would prefer an artist to an executive—obviously to Preston, that is. It probably surprised the hell out of him when she broke it off with the artist and married him. He was a nice, sweet man, but if you tried to explain to him that an intelligent woman's instincts are invariably conservative, he wouldn't believe you.

He and Page had been married three or four years, but Preston didn't trust it yet. He wouldn't take Page back to the New York Film Festival, not if he could possibly get out of it. That could make for a very nice week, if I stayed in Hollywood; and it would probably mark the end of Page's little fling with me if I didn't. Page couldn't tolerate any mention of Jill, as it was, and she was hardly going to welcome the news that I had decided to accompany Jill to New

York in order to be a reassuring presence. Page didn't trust me any farther than Preston trusted her. If I told her I was going to New York because an old, old friend needed moral support, her scorn would know no bounds. Indeed, when I thought about it, I had so much to think about that a little eavesdropping could only be a welcome distraction.

However, Jill was too quick for me. "We'll just play it by ear, okay?" she was saying when I finished munching the celery. "You call me or something. Maybe we'll end up at the same party."

Then she put down the phone and silence fell. She sat on her pillow for a while, and I sipped my bloody Mary.

"That was Bo," she said finally.

"Those Southern boys can be persistent," I said. "The ones of them that aren't lazy fuck-ups. Old Bo does keep trying."

"I don't know why," she said. "It's ridiculous. Everyone knows he's in love with Jacqueline Bisset."

She was right—the whole world knew that, or at least that portion of the world that followed the sexual and emotional writhings of the movie colony, so-called. I have to admit that I follow these things fairly closely myself, being a lifelong gossip. Still, I try to preserve something like proportion, the virtue of which I preach constantly, mostly to Jill—it's a ridiculous habit, since she has a lot more proportion than I do. The point, in her case, is that she has too much.

"Bo Brimmer's long, unrequited passion for Miss Bisset is probably the best-known non–love affair of our times," I said. "Think about it. It's one of the best-known facts of Western civilization. Why should that be? People in Africa know it. People in Australia know it. Even people in Antarctica know it. I repeat, why should that be?"

"I think it's a very healthy sign," Jill said. "Bo's a man who makes news by not getting fucked. Usually the only way a woman can make news is by doing the opposite."

"Oh, horseshit," I said. "Don't bore me with your polemics. Women make enough news. I've never even met Jacqueline Bisset, come to think of it."

"She's fully pretty enough for you," Jill said. "She's world class, in the looks department, but you just stay away from her. She has enough trouble, and so do you."

"Hasn't it ever occurred to you what a convenience that non–love affair is to Bo?" I asked. "He could be in love with a secretary, and the secretary could be just as beautiful, and it could be just as unrequited, but there would be no publicity. Without the publicity there's no psychic kick."

"On the other hand, he could really love her, and it could be painful," she said. "He had a few dates with her—maybe it's real. After all, Bo *is* human. It could happen to him."

"All Southerners are human," I said. "You don't need to remind me of that. I still say it's convenient. It gives him something of the dignity of passion, plus it leaves him free to run his studio."

Jill got up and disappeared. I picked up the L.A. *Times*, which was on the floor by the couch. The lead story was about the capture of a ring of poodle-nappers, who had been kidnapping poodles in Beverly Hills and making them into poodle stew. The poodle-nappers were a small band of American Indians who had holed up somewhere in Coldwater Canyon. Their leader, though captured, was not cowed. His name was Jimmy Thunder. "If we cannot consume our enemy, we will consume his poodles," Jimmy Thunder said. So far the gang had eaten sixty poodles, a few Shih Tzus, and a Great Pyrenees.

The L.A. *Times* was about the height of a small stool, and I decided I would rather have it for a stool than to read it, so I put my feet on it. Jill came back with a pitcher of bloody Marys and some more celery.

"I hope you put in the vodka," I said. "That last one was mostly tomato juice."

"Have you always been this churlish on Sundays?" she asked.

"Since infancy. I don't like days when the stores are closed."

"Bo asked me to do a picture," she said.

"So why'd you put him off?"

She shrugged. "Maybe he should just stay in love with

Jacqueline Bisset," she said. "He might get her someday, if he keeps at it. You can't tell."

"In a pig's ear," I said, and went in and sloshed some more vodka into the pitcher.

Jill was in her studio, digging in a pile of scripts. She came back with a fat green script and pitched it on the couch. I glanced at the title, which was *Ladies' Night.*

"Bo likes this script," she said. "It was written by a woman in St. Louis."

"I don't think you should do it," I said. "I've worked on several movies about St. Louis, and they were all flops. I think you should make a movie about me."

She smiled. "That'd be sweet," she said. "Would it be funny or tragic?"

"Tragi-funny," I said. "There's never been a good movie about a screenwriter. With luck it could gross in the thousands. Actually I heard my story the other day, done as a hillbilly song. It was called 'Popcorn and Diamonds.' I was the popcorn, needless to say."

"Sing it for me."

"Can't, I only heard it once," I said. "I was stuck in a traffic jam on the Ventura Freeway—I didn't realize I was hearing the story of my life until it was almost over. It was sort of bittersweet."

I set my bloody Mary down and she reached over and took a swallow of it. "Too much vodka," she said.

"Oh, well," I said. "Maybe I will stay in your suite at the Sherry. That way I can watch your metamorphosis at close range. So I miss out on a few debutantes, so what?"

She gave a little nod and handed me back the glass. Nothing more was said, but Jill looked happy. I drank the pitcher of bloody Marys while she reread the script that had been written by a woman in St. Louis. We kept the radio tuned to a hillbilly station all afternoon, hoping to hear my song again, but it didn't come on.

CHAPTER 5

At my age—sixty-three—any decision is only a kind of reckless prelude to the obstacles it creates. I make decisions easily, but only because I know I can double back behind nine out of ten of them, if I need to. So few things are fixed in my life that I seldom have to reckon with the pinchers of finality—pinchers not unlike those that blacksmiths and torturers use.

The decision to go to New York with Jill was not a decision that permitted waffling. As a contract writer at Warners —one of a vanishing, bilious breed—I deal with equivocators every day, if not every hour. The studio equivocates about deals, producers equivocate about projects, directors equivocate about stories, agents equivocate about terms, unions equivocate about payoffs, actors and actresses equivocate about interpretations, cameramen equivocate about where to put the camera, writers equivocate about dialogue, and so on down the line to gofers, who probably equivocate about routes to the cigarette machines. The whole industry only moves in fits and starts, and I've never seen any reason to try and be better than my peers.

At some point during the afternoon, to celebrate my decision, Jill marched over to her drawing board and did a cartoon of our arrival in New York. "I can't imagine you going anyplace without your Morgan," she said, so she drew a sketch of a potbellied man helping a car the height of a dachshund out of a limousine. I seemed to be leading the Morgan on a dog leash, while holding hands with a thin woman who was balancing several cans of film on her head. We were both being regarded with disdain by the doorman of a ritzy hotel.

"That's how it will be, too," I said, and when I finished the bloody Marys I took the sketch and went along home—fortunately I only lived about two hundred yards up the hill. I put the sketch with the thirty or forty others I've managed to accumulate, over the years, and then I sat on my patio most of the afternoon, thinking up lies to tell Page. I had about twenty-four hours in which to assemble an assortment of lies, from which, hopefully, I would then pick out the best.

"You could just tell her the truth," Jill said, when I mentioned that I had to get home and think up some lies.

"I cannot just tell her the truth," I said. "The truth would cause hurt and confusion—not to mention anger."

"Why do you see her if you're scared of her?" she asked.

I stood with my mouth open. "Are you crazy?" I said. "I've never met a woman I wasn't scared of. Aren't you ever scared of the men you're involved with?"

"I can't remember," she said. "Mostly I've been involved with Europeans. They're not as scary as Americans."

She walked me halfway home while we talked. It was one of our rituals. When we got to a particular palm tree she stopped. It was sort of on a crest, so we could look across the city, as far as the haze permitted. Often I took a little rest at the palm, so we could continue whatever weighty conversation we had under way.

"Got yourself a new dress for the premiere?" I asked.

"No, but I have to," she said, looking worried. "I guess I have to buy a lot of clothes now. Maybe it's about time."

"I figured out the real difference between you and me," I said. "You're compulsively honest and I'm compulsively dishonest. Who do you suppose does the most harm?"

"Oh, I do," she said. "All your ladies seem to sail right off into the sunset, fat and happy." She looked straight at the palm tree, as if she might climb it.

"You're too balanced," she added, as if it had just occurred to her. "Everything you say is balanced. I couldn't live with it." She gave me a kiss anyhow, and started back down the hill.

Early Monday morning, while I was making coffee and sorting through lies, I heard the phone ring. It was Marta Lundsgaarde, old Aaron's hatchet-woman. Her official title was publicist, but, first and last, she was a hatchet-woman.

"I guess they let you sleep late at Warners," she said. It was seven-thirty. Her voice would have clipped fingernails.

"Hello, Marta," I said. "You're right. Things are slower over in the Valley."

"Why can't my life be that relaxed?" she said. "Miss Peel says you're staying with her, in New York. Mr. Mond don't think that looks so nice."

"She's a little nervous," I said. "I'm an old friend. I'm sort of the equivalent of a tranquilizer."

"We'll get her some Valium," she said. "Mr. Mond thinks maybe you should stay somewhere else."

"Like at home, you mean?"

"Whatever," Marta said.

"Marta, my breakfast is burning," I said. "I think I'll just let you take it up with Jill."

There was silence on the other end. Marta was sorting through her hatchets, the way I had been sorting through lies.

"You're older," she said. "You could give her some good advice. She doesn't understand PR."

"Oops, got to get to my eggs," I said.

I was on my second cup of coffee when Jill walked in. Her hair was brushed nicely and she had on a blue sweater with white bands around it. She looked fresh and unperturbed.

"Marta's in a snit," she said. She poured herself some coffee and took my last grapefruit out of the refrigerator.

"I don't want grapefruit," I said, but she set half of one in front of me anyway. Then she ate the other half.

"So what did you tell her?"

"I told her anyone can have a roommate," she said. "There's not much she can do to me at this point. If the picture flops I could room with King Kong and nobody would care. If it's a success nobody will dare complain, for a while. I might as well do what I want to."

She had figured it perfectly. Hatchet-persons don't throw at directors when the directors are on their way up. It's when they falter and start to descend that the hatchets start thonking in. Marta would just have to bide her time, which was precisely what she would do. Twenty years with Aaron Mondschiem had made her the perfect extension of her boss. She lived for combat, and she never forgot.

"All right," I said. "We'll be roomies. But if the picture does well, I hope you change studios. I don't want to worry about Marta Lundsgaarde every day of my life."

Jill was unfolding my morning paper. "We'll see," she said.

Page liked to put her car in my garage, out of sight. Her car was a maroon Mercedes convertible. My car was a Morgan, with righthand steering, ancient but still vigorous enough to get me over the hill to Burbank every day. At the moment, I was working on an episode for a TV show called *Lineman*, a not-very-promising series based on a ballad by Glen Campbell. It dealt with a stout fellow who worked for the telephone company, repairing breaks in the lines. This required a lot of climbing, and a good many near-electrocutions.

In the episode I was at work on, the victim threatened with electrocution was a lovable black bear cub. I had worked the cub into a ticklish spot and was trying to think of a way to get him out. Obviously all the children in America would have brain spasms if a bear cub got fried by an electric wire, right in the middle of the family hour. I was beginning to wish the bear-cub episode were over, so I could start on one in which a bunch of phone freaks kidnap the lineman and hold him for ransom. Their demand is that the phone company give everyone in America free phone service for one week—otherwise the lineman dies. It was a desperate act, and I seemed to think better when desperate acts were involved. Bear cubs didn't really stimulate me creatively.

The Morgan and I meandered over the hill from Warners and pulled into the deep garage that slants down under my house. Once there, out of the sun, I decided to sit in the car and wait for Page. I could go in and have a drink and wait, but if I sat in the car perhaps I could force myself to think about the bear cub a little while longer. An ideal solution would be a friendly bird, one big enough to swoop the cub off the wire and drop it in a lake or something. The trouble with that was that the only birds big enough to fly off with bear cubs were condors and eagles, neither of them too friendly.

Still, the idea had possibilities. Condors were topical at the moment, thanks to their impending extinction. Perhaps it could be a friendly condor, one that had been hit by a car at some point and rescued and nursed back to health by a little old lady from Encino—something like that. It might want to show civilization that it was grateful for such little old ladies, even though big businessmen were out to build condos in its nesting grounds. In fact, if we used a condor, we could probably get a condo builder to sponsor the segment. Condor Condominiums wouldn't be a bad name for a condo company.

On the whole, I felt the idea had promise. Who's to say but that a condor might take it into his head to rescue a bear cub from an electric wire? It was incongruous, of course, but no more so than what I hoped was about to happen to me.

While I was mulling over the condor solution, Page drove in. A maroon Mercedes convertible stopped alongside the Morgan. I hit my remote-control button and the garage doors slid down behind us, leaving us safe from detection, more or less. It also left us in the dark. Since I was on the right side of my car and Page on the left side of hers, we were not far apart. I put out my hand and she took it. The garage was no darker than the inside of a movie theater, and when my eyes adjusted a little I looked over.

"Why are you always so calm?" she said. "You always are." She was wearing tennis clothes.

"Because I've done a lot of things," I said. "I really have done a great many things, and none of them have killed me. Maybe it's given me serenity."

"Let's fuck in the car," she said, changing the subject.

"What a thing to say," I said, momentarily appalled by my own handiwork. After all, I had taught the girl her vulgarity—at one time she needed it as one needs a tonic. Her painter hadn't taught her much about language, and Preston, having no language of his own, had contributed even less. It was left to me to show her how words can add tone to acts.

"No, I mean it," she said. "I just got this car—I don't know if the seats will always smell this good."

The convertible was indeed just a week old—a birthday gift from Preston to celebrate the fact that a comic horror picture of his called *Ghoul's Gardenia* had astonished everyone by its first month's gross. The expensive leather seats did smell good and, of course, so did Page. Her smell was compounded of sun, sweat, and clean skin.

"Page, I'm a fat man," I said.

"Yeah, but the back seat's really roomy," she said. "We can just leave the doors open." And, to my amusement, she stood right up on the front seat and began to peel out of her tennis outfit, which I had found more than sexy enough to tolerate. But Page peeled as the young seem to now, with a few practical motions, done with impatience—done, certainly, without the slightest awareness that it used to be considered that there was something romantic about undressing. But then that was when it had been considered that there was something romantic about sex. Page and her young friends approached sex in the casual spirit that I might adopt toward a warm bath. It was just another of the day-to-day sensual experiences of life. Candle-light and flowers didn't interest them. Guilt and remorse didn't titillate them. They took it straight, the way I took good whiskey, and were downright surprised when a little tenderness was offered them, as a mixer.

"Come on, I mean it," she said, putting one foot on the door of the car in order to peel off a tennis sock. "It'll be perfect."

That was her favorite word: "perfect." Every time it crossed her mind to want something she said it: "That'd be perfect, wouldn't it?" She was as unself-conscious about her desires as she was about her young body. Things were either perfect, or they were disgusting. She was not old enough to have observed that a lot of life lies somewhere in between.

Her intimations of the perfect kept striking me as poignant, for some reason, and I hustled to try and help her sustain this one. Once her mind sketched out a fantasy, her body accommodatingly drew within those bold lines, I guess. I wedged in the back seat with her, and the good-smelling leather seats immediately became so slippery with sweat that if there had been room we would have slid right out onto the cold cement floor of the garage. From my point of view it was not perfect, but Page bucked around intently, one leg hooked over the front seat. In the dim garage, her eyes were luminous.

"See, I told you," she said, locking hands and legs behind me, to see that I kept still. My balance was too precarious to permit me the liberty of conversation, but somehow I felt a little sad. Page was wonderful, really—innocent and unmalicious. She should get to fuck in the back seat whenever she wanted to. For a while her body nipped at me, fishlike, so I guess perfection of a sort had been achieved. Watching her at rest, I decided I was sad for her, not me. I had Keatsian feelings. Page at twenty-five was more perfect than anything that would ever happen to her, and she should never have to change, grow up, grow old, grow pale, or tired, or bitter. It was the thought that those states would come to her too that made me sad. I wanted, this once, for life to make an exception.

When I managed to unwedge myself I discovered that in my haste to be obliging I had kicked one of my shoes so far under the Mercedes that I couldn't reach it. I stood barefooted and pantless in my own garage, feeling too old for such foolishness.

Page got out, sweaty and nonchalant, and peeked under at the shoe. "You can just wait," she said. "After all, I won't run over it." She shook her hair loose from her damp neck and went up the steps to my kitchen, carrying her bikini briefs in one hand. When I got to the kitchen she was sitting on a stool, eating peanut butter on a cracker and calling her maid to check on her year-old son. A couple of my gray hairs were stuck to her young breasts, and she casually picked them off as she talked, smiling happily at me when I straggled in, shoeless and unzippered.

"I think he said a word today," she said, when she hung up. "It was a Spanish word, though. I ought to spend more time with him."

"Now's your chance," I said. "I have to go to New York this week."

She looked at me over the jar of peanut butter—it was something Jill had foisted on me.

"I don't want you to," she said. "Preston's going to be gone." Then she frowned, as if it had just occurred to her to question something.

"You never go anywhere," she said.

I put my arm around her, thinking a physical gesture might get me out of a lie, but Page casually shrugged off my arm and just as casually stuck a hand in my pants and caught my cock. Her look, as she continued to eat her peanut butter and cracker, was contemplative—so was her fondling, for that matter. Both things suggested a mood of light investigation.

"Do you ever hear from that woman?" she asked.

"Which woman?" I said, thinking she meant Jill.

"That woman who gave the party where I met you," she said. "You used to sleep in her house at night, when you got too drunk. Patsy something."

She meant Patsy Fairchild, an old, old friend of mine whose husband—former husband now—was *the* movie stars' architect. It was at her house that I had met not only Page but most of Page's predecessors.

"Oh, Patsy," I said. "She left her husband. She's living in Mendocino now, with her girls."

I was so relieved that she hadn't meant Jill that all of a sudden her fondling had a happy effect. There was no reason it shouldn't have, since I hadn't gotten any rocks off in the car. Page, who seemed to have experienced a good deal of premature ejaculation in her life, had never really perceived that the reason I was able to keep up with her, more or less, was because I only occasionally actually dropped any rocks. In the Mercedes I had concentrated on not falling into the crevice between the seats. At about the time Page's bucking had reached its peak, my mind, rising free both of emotion and of desire, had returned unbeckoned to the problem of the bear cub, though still inconclusively.

Age can be a godsend. The seed slows in the stem, but the stem still quickens. Page's cool tongue tasted of peanut butter. She put her elbows back against the edge of Claudia's ancient dishwasher, a Maytag, probably one of the first models made, and wrapped her sunny legs around my fat old hips, and lifted her haunches and squeezed and grunted and squealed and sighed. Since a saltshaker lay to hand I salted her nipples lightly and licked it off, causing them to turn the color of raspberries. "Oh, that's perfect," she said. "That's perfect."

Above her shivering breasts, out my kitchen window, I could see the milky hills. I did love her, some—enough to want to see her there again, digging carelessly into Jill's jar of peanut butter. When she left, a half hour later than she meant to, she didn't seem to need to talk about New York. I mentioned—vaguely—some narration I had to write; just as vaguely, she thought she might go to Tahoe, to visit a friend. We parted in easy peace, Page sucking a lemon she found in the fridge.

CHAPTER 6

JILL had actually bought herself a white pantsuit. I couldn't believe it, and said as much. "I can't believe you bought that pantsuit," I said.

"Shut up, I don't want to talk about it," she said. She was standing on the sidewalk, looking despairingly at her bungalow, as if she might never see it again. A driver was holding the door of a big black limo for us. Jill looked inside the car as one might look into an abyss. Of course, the inside of the limo was not much smaller than an abyss. Being in it was like being in a leathery blue cave.

Jill was obviously more nervous than ever. "That's a very attractive pantsuit," I said, for emphasis.

"I told you to shut up about it," she said. "I hate to talk about clothes."

She was too nervous to tease, and I couldn't think of anything serious to say, so we stopped talking and let ourselves be driven to the airport. Jill's tension infected me and I became nervous, too. I decided my houndstooth sports coat was all wrong, my new red tie also all wrong.

After a long silence we eventually boarded a 747. We were in first class, which was like being in an elegant living room, with gracious maids serving drinks and salted almonds. After a while the elegant living room roared a little and rose into the air, above the smog. The blue Pacific lay below us. Jill clutched my hand.

"I always expect them to crash," she said. "This is when they crash, if they're going to."

"If we're not going to talk about clothes, let's not talk about disaster," I said.

I was not used to traveling first class on a huge plane, or, for that matter, any class on any plane, having been Hollywood-bound for the last several years. Fortunately I can quickly accustom myself to almost any degree of luxury. I put down three vodka martinis before we crossed the Grand Canyon and after that was in the mood to appreciate what was happening to me.

"*Variety* isn't going to get many names for its boxes off this airplane," I said, looking around. The other guests were tastefully spaced out around the perimeter of the living room. The only movie person I spotted was Marilyn Monroe's manager's former wife.

"A lot you know," Jill said. "Bertolucci's behind us."

She had gained a certain amount of confidence in the plane, I guess—enough to allow her to read magazines. At the moment, she was leafing through a copy of *Sports Illustrated* that I had managed to grab at the airport newsstand. I had plenty of books to read in my little satchel, but I wasn't reading. I was drinking vodka martinis and watching America pass beneath me.

"I don't think that's Bertolucci," I said, taking a squint at the guy behind us, who had on Levis. "I think that's a dope lawyer."

"A lot you know," she repeated. "Do you know anything about athletes?"

"Married one," I said. "I eventually got to know her a little. Why?"

"It must be different from being like me," she said. "The body must have the upper hand, instead of the mind. It even shows in these pictures."

I was soon in the process of eating the surprisingly good meal that began to arrive over Arizona and was not really finished until we were nearly across Ohio. Caviar over the Canyon, duck à l'orange as we crossed the Rockies, baked Alaska just east of the Mississippi. I tried without much success to remember if Claudia's body had had the upper hand, or her mind. Both of them had always had the upper hand over me, so I don't know that it mattered.

"Of course it's true that you think too much," I remarked, over dessert.

"Is that supposed to be a helpful remark?" she asked.

By the time the land darkened beneath us and lights began to wink on in what I guess were little Allegheny towns, Jill was relaxed and I was nervous and a little depressed, despite all I'd drunk and eaten and the brandy I was even then drinking.

Dusk has always accentuated my innate tendency to self-pity. Sometimes, without the slightest reason, I plunge into self-pity as if it were a swimming pool, or the running surf.

Jill registered the self-pity on her radar. She woke from a little nap she was having and said, "What's the matter with you?"

"Go back to sleep," I said, swirling the brandy in my glass in what I fancied was a cheerfully enigmatic way.

"Don't waste those Casablanca gestures on me," she said. "I never responded to Humphrey Bogart anyway. You wish you'd stayed home with your girl, don't you?"

"Not so much with my girl," I said. "After all, I'm with my girl. I guess I've just been a guest at the party too many times."

"But this is *my* party," she said, looking slightly hurt. "I would have thought you might want to be a guest, at my party."

"Oh, I do," I said. "Sometimes I just get to wondering why I never give the party."

"You always talk bullshit when you drink brandy," she said. "Two sips of brandy and you start making up categories and popping yourself into them. The only thing that's wrong with you is that you've moped around Hollywood too long, pretending it's the world. I'm the same way. This trip is long overdue, for both of us.

"I'll be glad when we land," she added. "Maybe you'll get out and meet a debutante. Anything is better than watching you mope."

Soon the night got deeper, beneath us, and we stopped bickering and waited for New York to arrive. We passed over unseen hills and descended until we could see the lights of Jersey. I had not exactly recovered my equanimity.

"You see, we lost most of a day," I said. "We got on at noon and now it's night. We got cheated out of an afternoon."

"I can spare an afternoon," Jill said. "It's worth it to see you with a tie on, for once."

Then our living room landed and rolled up to an unloading dock. We were ushered out with great courtesy. The fellow Jill claimed was Bertolucci was met by a gang of diminutive Italians. About half the people in our compartment were met by drivers, including us. A driver popped up at us before we were off the plane good.

"Miss Peel," he said. "I'm Sam. You just follow me. I'll have you back to your hotel in no time."

Sam took our baggage stubs and got our baggage with wonderful dispatch. They were the first bags up the chute, as if Sam had arranged it that way. A number of well-dressed people, no doubt more important than us, frowned when they noticed that their bags weren't first up the chute.

We followed Sam to a limo and got in, like obedient children getting on a school bus. No sooner had Sam pulled out than taxi drivers began to honk at us. Sam ignored them, safe in the knowledge that his limo was impregnable, superior to any number of taxis. They might nip at its bumpers, but they would never be able to bring it down. We drove along a freeway and over a vast bridge. Manhattan loomed before us, as it had in so many movies.

Jill was mute, but with excitement. Manhattan was something new, something she knew scarcely a thing about. It was a fantastic new world. Her eyes were full of lights, like Page's eyes after sex.

"Look at it," she said. "Let's stay a month."

I tried not to let on what a provincial I felt. After all, I spent most of my time pretending to be a man of the world. I was the man who had been everywhere and seen everything —or so I allowed. Since I am just enough of a writer to be able to convince myself with my own lies, I had easily managed to take myself in. I really considered myself a man of the world. It took a jolt like the sight of Manhattan to remind me that I was only a middle-class resident of the Hollywood hills—a man of Burbank in the daytime, and of two or three familiar bars at night. I hadn't been to Europe since World War II, or to New York for almost that long, and my memory of earlier visits was foggy at best.

My trouble was that I was in daily contact with people who went places, so naturally I came to assume that I went places, too. The people I worked with were always jetting off to Paris or London, to New York or Rome—sometimes even to Lisbon or Morocco or Copenhagen. I caught the backwash of their travel, meanwhile jetting off myself mostly only to Vegas. I had been to Houston once or twice, to Omaha, to Spokane, to Point Barrow, Alaska, and a few other unlikely places, but most of my cosmopolitanism was reflected off people who scarcely knew they had it and passed on to people who never realized I didn't. In that respect, I even had Jill fooled. She had never actually known me to be more than two blocks out of orbit, but I had her convinced that I knew the world like the palm of my hand.

In order to sustain that impression for as long as possible, I assumed a knowing expression as we rode in. I was even able to point out Park Avenue when we zoomed across it. "Oh," Jill said, "Park Avenue." For a moment she may even have had delusions of worldliness herself, probably because in Hollywood there are a lot of people with foreign accents —talking to people with foreign accents is a good way to become convinced of your own savoir faire.

Clearly, though, the staff of our hotel knew the world. There was steel in their formality. The doorman got to the door of the limo even before Sam could, which bespoke a real pro. I offered Sam a tip anyway, but he looked sternly at me and I retreated. Then I forgot to offer to tip the doorman, who looked sternly at me too. Jill tried to carry a suitcase in, a clear breach of established practice. A bellboy rushed out and appropriated all the luggage.

By the time we reached the desk, we had forgotten why we were there. We had to be prompted to sign the register. Then we shot up in an elevator and were deposited in a suite of large rooms. The bellboy rapidly instructed us in how to work the air conditioner, the heater, and the television set. I guess he assumed we could manage the water faucets for ourselves. Mastering a semblance of suavity, I tipped him.

Two minutes later, the doorbell rang. It was the bellboy. "The lady didn't get her messages," he said, handing me a brown manila envelope. I offered him another tip, but he brushed it aside. "It was our mistake, for godsakes," he said.

"I thought you knew when to tip, at least," Jill said. She perched on a windowsill and looked across at the park.

"Are you accusing me of lack of polish?" I asked. "Read your messages. You're probably missing an important party, right now."

She turned the envelope upside down and about thirty messages fluttered down onto the rug. Most of them were from magazines or TV stations, wanting interviews. There was also a typed itinerary of the places she had to appear the next day.

"I don't want to look at this now," she said. "We're wasting New York. Can't we go to a night spot?"

"A what?"

"Someplace impressive," she said. "Or just for a walk or something."

I went to the bathroom and checked my tie, which was, as near as I could judge, adequately tied. "I thought you'd gone to sleep," she said when I returned.

We discovered that we didn't have to go far for a night spot, since there was a fairly inviting one right in our hotel. I had a double scotch. Jill, in what for her was wild abandon, had a Campari and soda. Her eyes were still alight—she was drinking in the scene. The night spot, which is to say the hotel bar, was full of well-dressed people, all of them talking rapidly to one another. I was happy to think that my tie was adequately tied.

"New York seems to have deprived you of your usual insouciance," she said.

I made no defense. Jack Lemmon was a few tables away, talking to the son of O. B. O'Connor. O.B. had been an uncommonly smart producer, in my day. His son had no particular flair. Farther back, at a corner table, I noticed Maxine Nutip, undoubtedly one of the meanest women in the world. In her day, she had been *the* agent—had it not been for Maxine, someone like Lulu Dickey would not have been possible. But Maxine's day had passed, and she had returned to New York to piddle around a little with Broadway people. I had never had much to do with her personally, but I knew stories. She was with a couple of blue-suited junior agents. Her profile was like that of a saw.

"Maxine Nutip's over there," I said. She was a rarer sight than Jack Lemmon, at least.

Jill looked. "Trust you to spot an oldie," she said. "What do you suppose all these men do?"

"They arrange the world's economy, for one thing," I said.

"I'm not sure about them," she said. "Let's go for a walk before you get any drunker."

We paid up and proceeded down Fifth Avenue at a slow pace, zigzagging back and forth across the street so Jill could look in windows. At about the fourth I lost my patience. I was freezing, which is never good for my patience.

"This is absurd," I said. "You could see all this stuff right in Beverly Hills, you know. I can't believe we've crossed the fucking continent just to window-shop in Bonwit's."

"I don't get to Beverly Hills very often," Jill said. "You know how expensive stuff is there."

Rather than abandon her, I let her have her way. We proceeded willy-nilly until we fetched up at Rockefeller Center. I dragged her down to see if anybody was skating on the ice rink, but the ice was white and empty. A wind had come up and it was getting colder by the minute. Jill looked so snazzy in her pantsuit that I concluded we would probably be mugged. I had forgotten about muggers on our walk down the avenue, but as we meandered over toward Broadway the street got darker and I became acutely conscious of all we had read about them.

"There's a high incidence of mugging in this city," I said. She meandered on, several paces ahead of me.

"When in Rome," she said, meaning, I guess, that we should welcome our muggers. Without them we would not be having a true New York experience. Despite her nonchalance I scrutinized all approaching persons carefully. We encountered several youths who looked to me fully capable of mugging us, but happily they didn't. Perhaps, like lions, they had eaten their fill for the evening and were apathetic. I was anything but apathetic. Eventually we emerged onto Broadway and were sucked into a maelstrom of obviously unreliable humanity. I would have felt more comfortable in Africa, but Jill was oblivious to danger. She even went into a penny arcade, where pock-marked youths were restlessly toying with strange, loud machines of various kinds. The scene around us was like the scene around the bus stations in downtown Los Angeles, only raised by a factor of about ten thousand. "Now I realize what a sheltered life I've been leading," I said.

"Right, you and your rich girls," Jill said.

We walked on up the Great White Way, past the theater district. A black man suddenly clapped his hands and did a little dance in front of Jill. He was wearing an almost identical white pantsuit. "Hey, that's a nice cut," he said, and moved on.

As we moved on up Broadway the crowds gradually thinned out, and most of the shop windows seemed to be filled with cameras or cheap luggage. I became mugger-conscious again, particularly when we found ourselves alone on a traffic island beneath the Gulf & Western building. Down 59th Street the bright entrances to a line of hotels seemed to promise safety, but my companion was looking at the deep, dangerous park.

"Couldn't we just walk across it?" she asked. "You're not tired yet, are you?"

"No, nor insane, either," I said. "I have my future to think about. If I let you get killed before your picture opens, old Aaron will hunt me down."

I got her down the street, nearly to our hotel, and then when I relaxed my guard she jumped in a horse cab and forced me to come with her. Soon we were clip-clopping through the park, behind a speckled horse. The driver, a gnarled little man, was telling Jill how much worse New York was than it used to be. Apparently he had long since despaired of his life, which was why he dared to go through the park at night. As we approached the West Side we could see a pale, pear-white moon above the towers of great, dark, cathedral-like apartment buildings.

Later, back in the safety of the hotel bar, I drank too fast, out of relief. Jack Lemmon was gone, and Maxine Nutip as well. I attempted to impress on Jill that we were in a dangerous city, a city filled with random, arbitrary violence, but she was beyond my influence.

"The only bad thing that will ever happen to me is that I'll outlive everybody I know," she said, yawning.

"Yeah, but what about me?" I said. "I'm one of the people you'll outlive. Must I be murdered in Central Park just so you can get started on your fate?"

When we got back to our suite she spent some time testing the mattresses. Being a firm person, she believed implicitly in firm mattresses. I went to sleep in a chair while she was making her choice, and she had quite a time getting me awake enough to stumble to the bed I had been relegated to. She seemed to be wearing a peach velour bathrobe, which was so much more voluptuous than anything I associated her with that for a second I thought she was Page, or some other woman.

"It's a good thing I've known you for a long time," she said as she was trying to tug my pants off. I had fallen into bed with them on, a vice I'm prone to. She was so persistent in her efforts to tidy me up for bed that I had a hard time getting back to sleep. A peach velour bathrobe kept moving around my room, putting clothes on hangers and taking change out of pockets, not necessarily in that order. Then it turned out the light but refused to go away. It sat on the edge of my bed for a while, and the woman in it, Jill, watched New York out my window for as long or longer than I can remember. Near dawn, when my bladder tugged me up briefly, she was not there.

CHAPTER 7

"AREN'T you even going to eat breakfast with me?" she asked, the next morning. She was in the doorway of my bedroom, wearing a red dress. At that hour—whatever hour it was—I was only used to seeing her in jeans and her sweat shirt. I had to take a second look at the red dress.

"Was I drunk or were you wearing a peach velour bathrobe last night?" I asked. "Fame's certainly done a lot for your image."

"You were more than normally drunk," she said. "Get up. Your food's getting cold."

"I didn't want any food," I said. "I can't sleep when I'm in a strange place. I need a warm body beside me."

"It's not going to be mine," she said.

She disappeared, so in hopes of seeing more of her in her fresh, stylish incarnation, I got up and managed to drag on my own bathrobe, a disreputable white terry cloth on which, through the years, a great many substances have been spilled. In my view a bathrobe is a garment whose only virtue is that it can be flung off hastily, if one is in the heat of passion. So far, though, my personal terry cloth has had an unromantic career. I never seemed to be wearing it when the heat of passion took me. Mostly, I wore it while carrying out the garbage.

Jill sat at a table spread with food, eating a frugal piece of brown toast. She was also having some tea. Evidently the rest of the food, which included a poached egg, was meant for me. *The Times* was on the table but Jill wasn't reading it. I glanced at the headlines and couldn't see them.

"I'm going blind," I said. "I can't see the headlines."

"This is *The New York Times*," she said. "The headlines aren't a foot high. You have to make a little cultural adjustment."

Besides the poached egg there were some buckwheat cakes. A rich array of syrups and marmalades had been provided. Why Jill had decided I would be in the mood for buckwheat cakes and a poached egg, I don't know, but as it turned out she was right.

"What am I supposed to do all day while you get interviewed?" I asked.

"Go to museums and improve your mind."

"No, thanks," I said. "My mind's totally full. It's like an elevator. It can go up or down, but nobody else gets in."

The doorbell rang and Jill got up to get it. Marta Lundsgaarde strode in, in an iron-gray suit that went well with her disposition. Her coal-black hair had been somewhat extravagantly streaked. My own unkind thought was that she was wearing a skunk wig.

"Good dress," she said to Jill.

"You know Joe," Jill said.

"From years back," Marta said, favoring me with perhaps a tenth of a second of her attention.

"Hi, Marta," I said ebulliently.

"I hope you're ready," she said to Jill.

It looked to me like she was ready. Her eyes were still

bright. She gave me a nice kiss before she left. "You can come to the press conference," she said. "It's at the Plaza at four."

They hurried out the door, and I was left to contemplate my own enviable prospect: a free day in New York. In certain moods I might have wished for Page, but I didn't seem to be in any of those moods. My heart was in a mood to relax, not to contend, and even an unquestioning innocent like Page required a good deal of contending. I doubt that I've ever spent a day with a woman without becoming aware, at some point during it, that the bottom could drop out any second. Neither the secure routine nor the ecstatic moment altered that basic fact: the bottom could always drop out.

For once, I didn't feel the need of such a stimulant. I had only one errand to accomplish all day, which was to buy Jill a jewel. It was not an errand for the morning hours, so I had several cups of coffee and tried, with little success, to work my way into *The Times*. All the news in *The Times* was probably fit to print, but that did not mean that I was fit to read it. I would have had to read thousands of words, all of them closely marshaled in long gray columns, just to assure myself that I knew where matters stood in the world, as of that moment. It didn't seem worth it. With no effort at all, I could assure myself that I didn't much care. By the time I could have finished *The Times*, things would have rearranged themselves anyway. There is really no keeping up, as Claudia used to say. Claudia had zero interest in the world at large. "It's better to keep your eyes forward than your eyes backward," she said. The past—in the phrase of the day—was not her bag.

Then, abruptly, the past swallowed her, and sentiments that we had contested all our lives became my favorite sentiments. My normal procedure with sentiments is to intone them in bed, for the benefit of whoever I'm in bed with. If that person won't listen, then I intone them while lunching or dining. Jill had heard a great many sentiments intoned and had paid them no heed, but even so, I meant to buy her a modest jewel. She usually got involved with tightwads, men who never bought her anything.

About lunchtime I got dressed and wandered out on Fifth Avenue, ready for a little sight-seeing. It seemed remarkably cold. Leaves were blowing off the trees in the park; they blew along the sidewalks and into the street, crunched by pedestrians and taxicabs. No one but me seemed to think it was at all cold. Most of the people on Fifth Avenue seemed actually to be enjoying the weather. They looked strong, smart, and indestructible. Their faces were sharp. They all seemed to be talking to others of their kind, and for some reason they reminded me of Indians—American Indians, those that had apparently existed in the nineteenth century. Like them, the New Yorkers seemed total masters of their environment. They knew when to step off the curb and when not to step off the curb. They knew where to buy the best salami and how to avoid muggers and other evils of the wilderness. The wind didn't bother them. New York was their desert, their plains, their Canyon de Chelly. They were as tough as the Indians in good Indian movies—as tough as Burt Lancaster in *Apache*.

I was not of the Manhattan tribe, however. I was simply freezing. It occurred to me that I must be up against autumn, something I had never really had to deal with. It had been colder in Point Barrow, Alaska, when we were making *Igloo*, but I had never been required to go outside. I sat in a quonset hut all day, rewriting the grunts that were supposed to represent Eskimo dialect. All movie crews drink to excess, but the crew of *Igloo* set records in that respect that may never be equaled, and I certainly pulled my weight.

There were no quonset huts on Fifth Avenue, so I hurried along, pushed by the wind, until I came to the St. Regis Hotel. There I found a bar, installed myself, and ordered a Scotch.

"You look cold," the bartender said. "I guess you must be from California."

"Why California? There are other warm places in this country. I could be from Florida."

"Not a chance," the bartender said. "I *been* to Florida."

I refused to admit to being from California, though the bartender badgered me through two or three drinks. As I drank I had a conversation with him that could have fit right into any of about fifty movies from the '40s and '50s, some of which I had probably worked on. The bartender was stock—I knew twenty character actors, some of them gone to their graves, who could have played him better than he played himself. He was short and pugnacious. Since I was seeing Manhattan in terms of Indians, I decided he was either a Digger or a Ute. Probably a Digger.

"Then you're a writer, if you ain't from California," he concluded.

"What makes you think so?" I asked.

"You drink like a writer," he said. "They got thin blood, you know—them and Californians."

If I had been willing to play the role he assigned to me I would have soon been tipping him lavishly and calling him "my good man," but in fact I thought he was a pugnacious little turd and I didn't want to tip him lavishly. When he figured out that his witty analyses weren't going to make him rich he left me to nurse my drink for twenty minutes.

After a while I became depressed. My depressions are like thick cloud covers: not a ray of light gets through. It seemed to me I had reached a strange stage. Life wasn't really life any more—it was just a straight imitation of bad art. Nine-tenths of the time I found myself playing the roles I was type-cast for: the jovial drunk, the versatile hack. I didn't seem to have the energy to play against the roles any more—it was easier just to play them.

No one would have thought to cast me as a proficient adulterer, which is what I have been for several years, but for some reason coming to New York had given me sudden doubts about my proficiency. I had been too content to sit around the hotel room all morning, making no effort to get anything going. One could argue that at my age I could safely allow myself a vacation, but such an argument would be wrong. It is the young who can afford vacations. At my age any lapse into inertia might well prove permanent. Up until about a year ago I was a fine handball player—my handball balanced my drinking, in some way. Then my favorite opponent retired and moved to La Jolla, and I dragged my feet about finding another one until it was too late. Within weeks, I lost handball—I am no longer capable of a really hard game, and if I tried to force myself to it, it would probably kill me.

Compared to adultery, handball is relaxing. The heart doctors are right about adultery being the most demanding sport. It's faster than squash, and it goes on longer. It requires range, energy, and great shiftiness—not to mention peripheral vision. The more directions one can see in, the better it goes. The right touch is hard to get and easy to lose.

In my depression, it seemed to me I was losing it, right there in the St. Regis bar. I should have been in a phone booth, calling Page. Women love to be called from odd places. If I exerted myself, I might keep things in synch until I got home; but an unfamiliar fatalism was weighing me down, and I didn't much want to exert myself. The season outside and the season inside were one, and that season was autumn. I had flown east and aged, otherwise I wouldn't have felt so tranquil that morning, in a womanless room.

"Where's the warmest jewelry store?" I asked the bartender when he finally showed up again.

"What you need ain't jewels," he said. "What you need is a coat. This ain't California you're sitting in. You don't see no palm trees, do you?"

"No, but I see a wiseass," I said.

"I knew you was a writer," he said. "Writers can't take jokes. You better run over to Bloomingdale's and buy you a coat. Get one of them kinds with the fur collars."

He then directed me to a jeweler's in the hotel. The wind had deposited me more or less where I needed to be. A short Italian who moved like a leopard showed me some jewels. He slipped noiselessly from case to case. There had always been a leopard or two around the set of the jungle serials I worked on, but I hadn't thought of one in years. The carpet in the jeweler's was so deep that anyone would have moved like a leopard, with it underfoot. Even so, the man was liquid and sure. Brilliants hung from his deft paws, and he scattered them like entrails on a black velvet cloth.

I chose a sapphire, dark as blood, a pendant on a gold chain. It took half my savings, but then I was tired of saving my savings. I had never meant to save them, particularly—they had just accumulated faster than I could spend them. One of the things I almost never spent them on was presents for women. The women I kept company with had usually received so many presents that they had forgotten that there is a difference between presents and love. I reminded them of the difference. I made myself the present. It took them by surprise, and most of them were delighted to have a man for a while, instead of just more presents. They could always go back to getting presents, once they were through with me.

The leopard man looked at my check a long time before he let me take the sapphire. The check was for $4000, so I couldn't blame him. He took the check with him to another room, for several minutes. Probably he was examining it under microscopes, or running it through chemical tests. Fortunately I had so many forms of identification that I would be no trouble to track, if such were necessary. He and other leopard men could creep through the Hollywood hills in Fiats and swarm over me in my hut.

That was more or less what leopard men had done in the jungle flicks, when someone made off with a jewel or a beautiful princess. I once had a neighbor named Max Maryland, a professional extra, who had a particular fondness for leopard-man roles. He used to hang around Columbia and Republic all the time, hoping to get to put on some claws and creep through the jungle. He could have made more money at Fox, carrying spears, but he preferred claws to spears. Once he even got to play a Crocodile Man, in some serial or other, and it was the high point of his life. It would have made some people wonder about his sex life, but not me. I knew perfectly well he didn't have one. His wife Belinda ran an insurance office over on Highland—it was a lot more profitable than being an extra. Since Belinda was supporting Max's fantasies, she considered that she had a right to her own, and her own ran heavily to rodeo cowboys. She spent her weekends roving around the Valley, looking for rodeos, and Max spent his drinking in low dives, sometimes with me. The end of it was that Max got too drunk one week night, went to sleep in the street, near a curve, and was run over by a school bus, early the next morning. It made Belinda pretty sad; despite her need for rodeo hands she really loved old Max.

That was in the early '50s. I comforted Belinda as best I could by pointing out that Max wasn't really happy at his work any more, what with the death of the serials and the decline of jungle pictures. There were no longer any paws to don, or even many spears to carry. That and other things broke Max's heart. The last I heard of Belinda, she was living in Oregon with a stock contractor.

I hate it when people take too long to okay my checks—it makes a break in the dike of activity, through which all the wrong memories are apt to flood. I had had a big soft spot for old Max Maryland. He was one of the sweet innocents of Hollywood. At one time there were so many of them that no one could have kept count: people who weren't meant to grow up and live in marriages, or work at jobs. I guess they had come to Hollywood because pictures had seemed to them the answer to their need, which was to make a life of the games of childhood. Unfortunately, most of them weren't able to stay true to their obsessions. They embarked on sloppy attempts at normalcy, and only a few of them—those with the madness of monks—refused to be teased by reality, or love, or anything else.

Old Max was not one of those. He couldn't act and he couldn't grow up, but he lacked the madness of monks. He was just a big kid from East St. Louis, who liked to play jungle.

The leopard man was unable to find anything wrong with my check, so he was forced to let me have the sapphire. He put it in a black felt box and handed it over, suddenly languid with disinterest.

I hurried right up the windy avenue and put the sapphire in the hotel safe. Then I went up and had a club sandwich in our suite. The potato chips that came with the club sandwich didn't seem to me to have quite the freshness and spring of the potato chips in the major L.A. hotels, but then probably potato chips are not such an important part of life in the East. In the East there were autumn leaves to crunch, something the major hotels of L.A. have never so much as seen.

When I finished my sandwich it was nearly time to go to Jill's press conference, so I went to the closet and stared at my wardrobe for a bit, wondering if I ought to change. The bartender had made me acutely conscious of being from California, and I suspected that my attire had given me away. Unfortunately, the closet held nothing cheering—everything I owned, or at least everything I had brought, seemed to have checks in it. Travel suddenly gave me a new perspective on my wardrobe: it was checked. I didn't seem to own anything in solid colors. Here I was on the one day in the last several years when I needed to dress soberly, and I had nothing but silly clothes. They hadn't looked silly in Los Angeles, but in New York I could hardly bear to contemplate them, even as they hung in a closet.

After a time I decided that the best way to handle the matter would be to put on my overcoat. Fortunately some fleeting memory of cold weather had prompted me to pack it. It was a solid color at least, namely green. I had had it for about thirty-five years, a relic of a week in Chicago when I was briefly involved with an ill-fated attempt to film Upton Sinclair's *The Jungle*. The project went nowhere, because the director, a little Britisher named Morris Seton, developed a paranoid fear of being locked in a meat freezer. The jolly Poles who worked in the slaughterhouse we were using as a set were full of stories about frozen people, and Morris heard one too many. As a result he decided to change the setting and shoot the picture on the lake front, which upset

Upton Sinclair so much that he threatened lawsuits. In those days projects were abandoned with abandon, more or less—I barely had time to buy an overcoat before I was back on the train to L.A.

The overcoat had never been worn, so it looked almost as good as it had the day I carried it out of Marshall Field's. I put it on and brushed what remained of my gray locks, most of which were gathered in fuzzy tufts over my ears and on the back of my neck. I decided the overcoat made me look a little bit like a Central European director, so many of whom are even now ending their days in little houses off Melrose Avenue or Sepulveda Boulevard. The overcoat bolstered my confidence a bit, but I still took my time getting across to the Plaza, making sure I went with the lights. I had my own days to think about, and I didn't want them to end on Fifth Avenue.

CHAPTER 8

DESPITE my impersonation of a Central European director, no one at the Plaza was anxious to rush me up to the press conference. I asked several bellboys where it might be and they curtly referred me to the bulletin board. Ten minutes of aimless wandering failed to bring me to the bulletin board, and when I asked where *that* was, I was more or less brushed aside. I don't know what I would have done if I hadn't spotted Abe Mondschiem's gofer buying some Lifesavers. He was a mousy little wretch named Folsom, but I was glad to see him. If dandruff were considered desirable in our culture, Folsom could have made millions doing commercials. He even had dandruff in his cuffs.

"Hi, Folsom," I said. "Has the press conference started yet?"

"Mr. Mondschiem sent me down to get Lifesavers," Folsom replied. He took life one thing at a time. Dandruff was his only indulgence.

"Good, I'll follow you," I said.

Folsom made it clear that I was irrelevant to his mission by hastening up some stairs. I didn't take it personally. A gofer's job hangs by a thread. If Abe didn't get the Lifesavers quick, Folsom would probably have to walk back to California. Abe Mondschiem was a Head of Production, which meant that waiting was unthinkable. To think Lifesavers was to have Lifesavers appear. If they didn't, Folsom would disappear. Abe's whims had the weight of moral imperatives, at least to those who served him. Folsom was wise not to linger.

I got to the room just as Abe was making his opening remarks. He was a big boy, nicely dressed in a dark blue suit and a white shirt, with amber cufflinks, a more subdued touch than I would have expected of Abe, considering his fondness for Las Vegas. Jill sat at his left, Pete Sweet and Anna Lyle on his right. Marta stood in one corner. Pete looked flushed, Anna softly distracted, and Jill nervous but poised.

"Ladies and gentlemen," Abe said, "here we are and we just hope you love the picture as much as we do. We're very very proud of these people. Very very proud. We've arranged this little get-together so you can ask them any questions you might have."

He sat down and took his dark glasses out of his pocket, but he didn't put them on. I think he felt better just having them in his hand.

The speech had been delivered to a roomful of people in trench coats. Most of the trench coats were worn by men who looked like they might be middle-aged professors in small state teacher's colleges. Some stood and some sat, but all had little oblong reporters' notebooks. They were a poorly barbered lot—no doubt the rush of their profession left them little time for tending to their hair. Most of them looked like they had combed their hair at the beginning of the week—since it was Thursday, the results were beginning to fray. The women among them just looked grateful to be off their feet.

A tall man with an intense sweaty face rose to his feet, looking around the room to see if anyone had been quicker. Several people smiled fatigued smiles at the sight of him still so eager.

"I have a question for Miss Peel," he said. "Miss Peel, in the press sheet it refers to *Womanly Ways* as your directorial debut. That leaves me wondering about *Chili-Dog*. Didn't you actually do the major part of the direction on that picture?"

Jill blushed. I don't think she had expected that to be the first question. She looked quite sweet. *Chili-Dog* was a 25-minute home movie she and some of her chums at U.C.L.A. had made about Pink's, the world-famous hotdog stand at Melrose and La Brea.

"Well," Jill said, "I don't think *Chili-Dog* was really directed. It was just sort of a class project. I held the camera a lot, too."

The man's face became so sweaty that he was forced to mop it.

"Miss Peel, Miss Peel, how can you say that?" he said. "Those of us who maintain a commitment to documentary *revere Chili-Dog*. It was acute! It was biting!"

A number of people nodded, looking intently at Jill. It was obvious that they all maintained a commitment to documentary—cheaper than maintaining a mistress or a lover, I suppose.

A man in the front row chuckled sardonically. He had kinky hair and he was reading a book even as he chuckled. "Harris is being simpleminded again," he said. "He thinks that because people were biting things in the film—namely chili-dogs—that the film itself was biting."

"Pardon me, but it was my question, my question," Harris said.

"I thought the lady answered it, Harris," a third man said. He was portly, not unlike myself, and his shirt had come unbuttoned across his belly, exposing an undershirt.

A very young man in the middle of the crowd became agitated. "I thought the panel was supposed to talk," he said, standing up. "I want to hear the panel, not you fucking reviewers."

A dumpy little woman in the front row looked at Jill with an auntielike smile.

"Miss Peel," she said, "is it true that you plan to insist on an all-woman crew for your next picture?"

"I don't think so, no," Jill said. "I have no definite plans for a next picture. It would be premature to start choosing a crew."

"But don't you consider that you have a duty to your sisters in the industry?" the little woman said. "How long are they to suffer?"

The agitated young man was on his feet again, even more agitated. "What a crock this is!" he said. "How does she know how long they are to suffer?"

"I was just trying to elicit her views on feminism," the lady said, somewhat taken aback.

"Well, I've got a question for Miss Lyle," the young man said. He hesitated a moment, as if he suspected he might be arrested before he could get the question out of his mouth. His fears were totally ungrounded. The crowd paid him practically no attention. They were either reading the press sheets or staring fixedly at panelists.

"Uh, Miss Lyle, what was your favorite scene in the movie?" the young man asked quietly.

Anna looked dreamily around the room. "Oh, when I put on the wig and talked to the salesman," she said. "Just before I run over Pete."

Jill and Pete both looked uncomfortable. Anna had been away, doing television work in Toronto, and didn't know that the scene she referred to had been drastically cut, mostly because she had overacted so badly.

No sooner had the young man sat down than a thin little man popped up. He wore the most rumpled trench coat of all, and he too was sweating. It was obvious to me that we could have used this whole gang on the crew of *Igloo*. They would have welcomed the cold.

"Miss Peel, one quick question," he said. "Do you think it's quite fair to choose a car salesman as a symbol of post-industrial man? Don't you think you might have gone after bigger fish? After all, he doesn't make the cars. The cars come from Detroit, ya know. I mean, to just put it very simply, what about the higher-ups? I mean, I saw the poor guy as a victim, I really did. All that pressure, my god!"

The sardonic man in the front row, still reading, said, "Sidney, you probably consider Attila the Hun the victim of Mongolian itch."

The little rumpled man was outraged. "Pardon me, Victor, it's all very well for you to sit there and read," he said. "You're a symptom, if you want to know the truth. A symptom."

Then, having apparently forgotten that he had asked Jill a question, he sat down. The young man had already risen to his feet again, in outrage, but the fact that the little man had already plopped down took him aback. It was clear that the little man's question had been its own answer, because he was hurriedly taking notes on it. Abashed, the young man sat down.

The reading man looked up briefly. He had a bemused, English-gentry manner, which contrasted a bit with his kinky hair. "Miss Peel," he said, "are you conversant with the theories of Kracauer, Bazin, and Bela Balazcs?" He pronounced the last name in which I judged to be faultless Czech.

"No, I'm not," Jill said. Abe Mondschiem abruptly put on his dark glasses.

"Well now, that won't do, will it," the man said, and went back to his reading.

Abe decided to throw a little weight around. "Ladies and gentlemen, you're neglecting our stars," he said. "Our *stars* are here."

Silence fell on the room. It lasted for about a minute. Pete Sweet began to get red in the face, I guess from embarrassment.

"*I'm* conversant with the theories of Kracauer, Bazin, and Bela Balazcs," Anna said. She too pronounced the last name in faultless Czech, if that was what it was.

"Blow them out your ass," the reader said, unperturbed. "I didn't ask you."

"All right, that's outa line, that's really out of line," Abe said, getting to his feet.

The young man was on his feet again too. "Jesus, is this a hype!" he said. "Is this all I'm going to get to hear? I came all the way from the Village. I rode the *subway*!"

"Ladies and gentlemen, I find this perplexing," Abe said. He had begun to sweat. "We set up the screening, you saw the picture, and this is what you come up with in terms of questions? Ladies and gentlemen, I'm embarrassed."

"I have a question for Mr. Sweet," a new voice said. The new voice came from a young woman with long lank hair, who stood at the very back of the room. She had a long face, wore a trench coat like everyone else, and looked expressionless.

"My question is about the portrayal of sexuality on the screen," the woman said, her eyes quite blank. "Would you perform a sex act before the camera, Mr. Sweet?"

"Oh, Athené, for god's sake," someone said.

"Well, I've been photographed biting an ear, if I remember right," Pete said. "I guess that's a sex act."

"You bit mine once," Anna said, smiling pleasantly.

"I do not think your answer funny," the young woman said. "I didn't mean foreplay, I meant the *sex* act. Sexual intercourse, in other words.

"I was not speaking of mere performance," she added, in a noncommittal voice.

"Oh, his performances are never mere," Anna said with a little laugh. Pete said nothing. I could tell that he was wishing he had gone to the races.

"We should all be glad we didn't go to Radcliffe," the reader said. He got up, slipped his book into his trench coat, and walked out.

"I am speaking of integrity," the woman said. "Could you perform with integrity, if the script called for it?"

"More likely with nervousness, ma'am," Pete said nervously.

Abe decided he had had enough. "This has been interesting," he said, "but our time is about up. We have time for one more question for Miss Peel."

To everyone's dismay, Jaime Pratto stood up. He had been sitting over near a pillar, nursing his failure like it was the last drink before the bar closed. I hadn't noticed him and neither had anyone else, but the minute he surfaced we all knew what we were in for. The Phantom of the Press Conference had suddenly swung down from the balcony, to hector those who had disfigured him.

"Miss Peel, do you consider yourself a sellout?" he asked, the archetypal New York director returning once again to challenge the philistines of Hollywood.

"No," Jill said.

"Oh, you don't consider yourself a sellout?" he asked, phrasing it another way. His skin was the color a bruise is, after the bruise has stopped being purple and become a sick yellow. Like the bruise, he had a greenish tinge, particularly around his bitter little mouth.

"No," Jill said again. "I don't, Mr. Pratto."

"Oh," he said. "You know me. I'm amazed. I wouldn't think those cocksuckers you work for would talk about me much. If they had a decent bone in them, they'd be too ashamed, knowing what they did to my picture. But they do it to so many pictures they've probably forgotten mine by now."

Abe was only a growing boy—he had not been programmed to take much abuse. He grabbed the mike like it was Jaime's throat.

"We remember you, you little prick," he yelled. "We remember you made the worst piece of crap ever released over our name." Someone accidentally turned up the P.A. system, no doubt meaning to turn it off. His words deafened half of us.

Marta rushed on stage and grabbed Abe's arm, but evidently more or less to anchor him, in case he started after Jaime.

"My grandfather nearly had a heart attack, right at the screening, when he seen how bad it was," Abe spluttered.

"Your grandfather wouldn't know art from a baloney

sandwich," Jaime said. "Neither would you, you fuckin' butcher. That was a lamb of a film and you butchered it. Nobody who wasn't a sellout would sit on the same stage with you!"

"Aw yeah? Listen, we could buy you tomorrow!" Abe yelled, "only we ain't going to because you can't direct your ass going out a door."

Just as he said it, Jaime went out the door, and by common consent the press conference was at an end. A crowd of trench coats immediately surged toward Jill. Folsom, miserable as ever, began gathering up unused press kits.

"I asked for security, just a little security, and I get that cocksuckin' little motherfucker," Abe said, muddling his perversions. His round, oily face was so wet with sweat that he reminded me of a young hippo, rising from a tank. Marta was getting into her coat—in her life, tirades were no big news.

"All right, we fire everybody," Abe said, causing Folsom to drop several press kits.

"We can't," Marta said. "The security men work for the hotel."

"So what?" Abe said. "They know us at this hotel. Believe me, they know us. Tell them it was not satisfactory, not fucking satisfactory at all. An' how'd that kid get in? We don't need no kids. Where was Canby? Where was Pauline Kael?"

"Miss Peel's having lunch with Mr. Canby tomorrow," Marta said. "Miss Kael we still don't know about. Maybe Saturday."

"We never should have brought this fucking picture," Abe raved. "These fucking highbrow pictures always get you into shit like this. We should have brought *Baby-Killer*, if we had to come at all."

"Oh, well, it don't hurt to make a picture for the kooks now and then," Marta said soothingly.

"Folsom, is the car here?" Abe asked. "You didn't get no Wint-O-Green Lifesavers, like I told you, either. Is the car here?"

Folsom by this time was carrying so many press kits that he looked like a pack animal, and a desperate one at that—one that might dash over a cliff, load and all, the way pack animals sometimes did in trek movies. The desperation resulted from the fact that Folsom had been asked two questions but only had a one-question-at-a-time brain.

"They was out of Wint-O-Green," Folsom said, meekly offering his neck to the axe.

"So, was that the only newsstand in the world?" Abe asked. "Did I tell you to refrain from setting your feet on the sidewalk or something? Instead of lookin' around—you know, being resourceful—you brought me these fuckin' cherry-flavoreds. I'd like to shove 'em right up Jaime Pratto's ass. Give him a cherry suppository, how's that?"

This notion amused him; a pleased light came into his eyes just before he put his sunglasses back on. Then, evidently, his eye fell on me. The sunglasses focused on me unwaveringly, like gun barrels in Western movies. Gun barrels never waver, and neither do Mondschiems.

"Don't look so glum, Abe," I said. "Press conferences don't mean anything. You got a winner."

"Are we speaking to him?" Abe said, turning to Marta. "Why should we be? He ain't with us."

"You may not remember it, young fellow, but I went to your first birthday party," I said. "You were about three."

"It don't mean you ain't a nobody," he said. "It don't mean we're speaking to you."

"You're the nobody, you young puppy," I said, in my best Sydney Greenstreet manner.

The notion that he was a nobody bounced off Abe like birdshot off a barrel. A sense of the arch of history and the puniness of man is not common among Heads of Production. My impudence did cause him to register mild surprise—the surprise a shark might feel at being attacked by a perch.

"Listen at this one," he said to Marta, but vaguely. His mind, insofar as it could be called a mind, was already elsewhere.

Folsom, who had just left, reappeared, his face twisted

into what I would have called a grimace. Evidently, though, it was a smile of triumph.

"Car's ready, Mr. Abe," he said. "So's the elevator. I'm holding it for you."

It was a bold effort at rehabilitation on Folsom's part. Abe took it as a matter of course. "How about the Wint-O-Green?" he asked as they left.

I walked over to Pete Sweet, who was nervously lighting a cigarette.

"Well, famous at last," I said. "Congratulations."

"Oh, fuck," Pete said. "I wish I'd gone to the track.

"I guess it beats television," he added, with some melancholy. No one had ever quite fathomed the sorrow in Pete, but it was there. It slowed his walk and caused him to stare into space a lot; it also led him to gamble inexpertly. A sad, big man, he was irresistible to women, but he had a penchant for nondescript ladies, whom he quickly married and just as quickly divorced.

Anna came over and gave me a kiss. "Isn't he cute when he's moody?" she said, putting her arm around Pete. She looked flouncy and ready to rhumba, and Pete tucked her under his large arm, where she seemed right at home. The two of them had had an on-again off-again romance going back so many years that we had all lost count.

Jill was soberly and dutifully listening to the questions of two earnest students. Somehow they had managed to infiltrate the press conference, and they were pouring out long-pent-up needs: namely the need to talk to someone professional who would actually listen. Pete and Anna and I looked on as parents might, watching a favorite daughter. Anna was very maternal toward Jill, and Pete sort of gloomily paternal. He was convinced Jill had no judgment about men and would end up with the worst possible person. I agreed she had no judgment, but I was placing no bets on how she'd end up—much less with whom.

When the students finally left, Jill came over to us, looking a little blank. Pete tucked her under his other arm.

"Have you really read Bela Balazcs, or whoever he is?" she asked Anna.

Anna laughed. "I was just mimicking," she said.

Outside, on a windy streetcorner, we split up, and Jill and I stood on the curb, watching a yellow river of taxicabs flow down Fifth Avenue.

"It's not much like Malibu, is it?" she said, looking up at the great greenish towers of the hotels. Nearby, a pretzel vendor stoked his coals, and smoke billowed up. The smell of salty bread wafted past us. Up the sidewalks came the tribesmen of Manhattan, their breaths as smoky as the charcoal. Tribeswomen too, the young ones tall and elegant and serene, the old ones twisted and squat.

"I said that because it started on Malibu," Jill said. "I wrote the first ten pages of the script sitting on the floor while Pete and Anna smoked pot. I didn't realize this would be where it would end."

Her hair was short, but the wind had still managed to whip it into a sexy disarray. Her cheeks were reddening, and she no longer looked blank. She looked vivid: a woman enjoying the fullness of the moment.

"No one sees the end in the beginning," I said. "Not even me."

"Shit," she said, jabbing me with her elbow and tugging me off the curb. "I might have known you'd croak out a pronouncement before I could even get you across the street."

The river of taxis had become a yellow log jam. In high good spirits, we picked our way across it.

CHAPTER 9

JILL was combing her hair when I casually laid the jewel-case on her dressing table. We were to leave in five minutes, which is how I'd planned it. "Uh-oh," she said. She was wearing a white dress that only covered one shoulder, an unusually daring exposure for her.

When she saw the sapphire, with its subdued lights, she picked it up and held it against her bosom. She sighed and looked at me gratefully. "We'll speak of this later," she said, and put the necklace on.

"You should have been a maître d'," Marta said when she saw me in my tux. I decided she was warming toward me a little. The ride to Lincoln Center was made in total silence. Jill and I, who had talked in all manner of situations, found that in limousines we had nothing at all to say to one another.

As we were walking into Lincoln Center, toward a line of

photographers, Marta made a very professional move. She took my arm suddenly, linking it with hers, and bore me slightly to the left. Abe, in a violet tuxedo, materialized out of nowhere and took Jill's arm. Although mildly surprised to find myself arm in arm with Marta, I was not irked. Publicity is publicity. Marta and I circled the gauntlet of photographers and made our way unnoticed into the great red-carpeted entrance hall.

The moment we were inside the building Marta released my arm. She spotted Pauline Kael far across the hall and made for her like an arrow released from a bow. At once I spotted Mayor Lindsay, and Andy Warhol, ghostlike near the draperies. Like many of my kind, my appetite for the sight of famous people has never abated. All I like to do is look at them, though. Talking to them usually aborts the fantasy.

A feast of famous people lay before me, so I sort of nibbled my way around the edges of the table, secure in my anonymity. Even the few of them who knew me wouldn't think it was me, if they saw me so far from my customary haunts. If I had bothered to bring myself to their attention, it would have registered as a minor shock, like a pothole in the highway—nothing more.

Jilly Legendre was standing near the banisters. He resembled the Goodyear Blimp, painted black and come to earth. Bo Brimmer stood on the steps leading up to the balcony—Bo had a genius for finding steps to stand on. Since it took steps to make him appear to be a normal-sized human, no one could dislodge him once he found some. He was wearing a bow tie that dwarfed his head, a rare sartorial gaffe. Both he and Jilly were listening to a little fellow who could only be Jean Joris-Mallet, the renowned French documentarian. Joris-Mallet had just emerged from the rain forest with another of his renowned documentaries. Both Bo and Jilly wore the glazed looks of men who were enduring a boring monologue by someone too prominent to be ignored. Joris-Mallet wore a suede tuxedo, more Hollywood than Hollywood.

"Ah don't know about the Seychelles," Bo said with a touch of gloom, causing no break in the stream of French.

"Je ne connais pas," Jilly echoed, passing a finger back and forth across his mustache as if he were trying to rub it off.

I could tell they both wished Monsieur Joris-Mallet had had the ill fortune to be eaten by an anaconda. Before they could proceed with the conversation, Bo and Joris-Mallet were crushed against the banister by the sudden arrival of enough Italians to fill a Fellini movie. At their center, radiant, one golden breast almost pushed out of its cup by the crush, was Antonella Pisa, the star of the Italian entry in the Festival. She was something. Even Bo, oblivious as he was to the beauty of everyone but Jacqueline Bisset, could not restrain himself. He hopped boldly into the stream of Italians, was carried up a few steps, and made it to Antonella, who stooped, serenely, so he could kiss her. Joris-Mallet, who clearly thought she was a pig, abandoned Jilly without another word and trotted down the steps. He darted off in the general direction of the always sympathetic Leon O'Reilly, who was twirling his Phi Beta Kappa key and talking to a tall woman who, from a distance, I took to be Mrs. Kissinger. Later in the evening I discovered she was Alexandra Schlesinger, wife of Leon's old professor.

Jilly, prevented by his bulk from getting anywhere near La Pisa, blew her a kiss. She favored him with a shrug of resignation and was swept away, even as the sparks fly upward.

I secured another drink and stood around with it, feeling like Dr. Brydon, the lone survivor of the British retreat from Kabul. There is a famous picture—called "Remnant of an Army"—which all students of the Afghan campaign know well. It shows Dr. Brydon—the last of 15,000—straggling into Jalalabad on his exhausted horse, to inform the garrison that 14,999 of his colleagues lay dead in the Afghan passes.

It was looking around the glittering crowd in the entranceway to Lincoln Center that made me feel like Dr. Brydon. I saw so many new faces that I began to miss all the old faces: the ones that weren't there, never had been, and never would be. No artist was likely to paint my picture, standing with my drink, on the rich red carpet, but I was the last of 15,000 nonetheless—maybe even the last of 16,000. My companions had been slaughtered in passes, too—the passes of Benedict Canyon, Laurel Canyon, Topanga Canyon, and all the other canyons. They had not fallen to Afghan hordes exactly, but they had all fallen, one way or another. One couldn't even blame Goldwyn or Mondschiem or Harry Cohn or any of the other moguls—not really. We had been our own Afghan hordes, cutting ourselves down ruthlessly out of childish disappointment at our own inadequacies and the stubborn intractability of life. It was just not like the movies—life, I mean: not Gary Cooper's grin, not Paulette Goddard, not dancing in the rain. The direction was poor, the staging hasty, and there was no one competent in the editing room. Life was like pictures only in that it hardly ever managed to be as exciting as its previews.

I guess what I have never been sure about is whether other places engender the same intensities of hope as Hollywood. Do people in Ogallala and Far Rockaway keep on expecting the golden moment—or, perhaps, living so far from all forethought of stardom, do they accommodate themselves more happily to the humdrum days?

That one I couldn't answer, but I had begun to feel, looking about me at all the glamour, that it had been a mistake to come. I was a working man, from a working man's guild. What had I to do with all this fanciness? The camaraderie of crews had made pictures worth it, if they had been worth it: all that yakking, those tales of girl friends and wives, the fuck-ups, the loneliness of locations, the pettiness of the petty and the pettiness of the great. I was lonely for all those light-foot lads and rose-lipped girls—sunk in sentiment, a wobbly old Wobbly. Absurd, the turnings of the heart, not to mention the ironies of station: for crews are the most star-struck people of all; that's why they're crews. And I had never been a real Wobbly, or black-listed, or even very poor: yet the sight of all those monkey suits and trailing gowns caused me to pulse with resentment. Frippery, pretense, indulgence, overconspicuous overconsumption: that too was what Hollywood was all about, only in a workaday life one tends to forget it. Eight hours' work, Jell-O in the commissary, and an occasional trip to Vegas do not prepare one for a film festival. I had the mad urge to run up the stairs singing the Internationale.

Fortunately, while on the third drink, my mood passed. I forgot the 15,000, of which I was probably the last. It occurred to me that probably nobody in the hall would recognize the Internationale, except possibly young Bertolucci, who had shambled in with Shirley MacLaine and a crowd of people with trench coats over their tuxes—reporters, no doubt.

I waved at Jill as she was going up the stairs, and she waved back. Marta, across the room, motioned for me to come with her. Before I could move, the whole place was brought to a halt by the entrance of Lulu Dickey, all six three of her, dressed, essentially, in some gauze and a large ruby.

The ruby was in her navel, of course. If the ruby was intended to draw one's eye away from her somewhat inadequate bosom, it succeeded brilliantly. It easily overshadowed her bosom, and everything else she had except her wild, kinky hair and peregrine features.

Her escort for the evening was none other than Mr. Swan Bunting, Sherry Solaré's boyfriend and, as the papers always said, "a celebrity in his own right." Swan wore a denim tux, an unusual concession on his part. As Sherry's lover he was, in effect, the Prince of filmland, and he could have come in wearing sandals and a beach towel and no one would have said him nay. His shoulder-length black hair was nicely combed, no doubt by Sherry's hairdresser, and he and Lulu moved right on up the staircase, as if they were just coming in from walking the dog. They gave no more than an offhand nod to the people lining the way.

Swan's disdain was Olympian—though to say so is to malign the Greeks. The expression "could have cared less" might have been coined for him. For a while, before Sherry seduced him, his name had been Boggs-Bunting—Dr. Boggs-Bunting, in fact. He was the very successful practitioner of a sex therapy that would have caught on only in California. He called it "psychic gynecology," but it was really only a cheap spin-off of the talk-to-your-plants movement. In this case, what you talked to was your privities. The idea was worthy of Diderot, which is probably where Swan got it: he had passed through the Sorbonne on his way to becoming a punk.

In good old whacked-out California talking to cocks and cunts seemed like a spacy thing to do, and Swan got rich enough instructing lonely ladies and not-quite-gay young men in how to reassure themselves to be able to start a line of health-food vaginal products: douches in such basic scents as wheat germ, wild rice, and barley. For a while he even had a talk show, for which he dressed in a wheat-colored shirt and corduroys and explained psychic gynecology to the masses of Westwood, Santa Monica, and Bel Air.

Sherry Solaré broke up with somebody at about that time. Feeling down and out, she hired Swan at a fabulous fee to come and teach her to talk to her pussy. Everyone assumed that Swan was basically gay, but evidently Sherry's pussy did some fast talking. In no time at all he was established at the absolute pinnacle, as the lover of the only love goddess left. To celebrate, he took the confident step of dropping the Boggs from his name. He gave up his TV show, sold his health douche company, and was soon devoting himself full-time to Sherry. Of course, full-time devotion was the only kind Sherry tolerated. In her view, she alone was keeping superstardom alive, and her designated consort had numerous, maybe even onerous, responsibilities.

The fact that Sherry had not bothered to come to the opening of the Festival surprised no one, since an account of her latest illness, a raging nose-cold, had been carried on the front page of the evening *Post*. As everyone knew (since *The Times* and the *Post* had both informed them), Sherry was only pausing in New York en route to London, where she was to attend an auction of Victorian hat-pin holders.

Regularly, when Sotheby's Belgravia held its annual auction of these increasingly rare objects, Sherry flew over and bought wildly. She did not, however, hold undisputed sway among collectors of Victorian hat-pin holders—a source of great bitterness to her. An aged Swiss collector, as rich as she was, hotly contested her bid for dominance, and in fact only last year had broken her resolution and taken the prize of the auction, a rose-tinted hat-pin holder belonging to Lord Curzon's wife. The price had been a staggering £18,000. That auction had almost been the ruin of Swan Bunting. Unable, temporarily, to forget his humble origins in Carne-on-Sea, Swan had persuaded her she didn't really need Lord Curzon's wife's hat-pin holder. Sherry, whose own origins were Teaneck, New Jersey, momentarily forgot that she could buy the world, and the aged Swiss collector carried off the prize.

It had been a rare and nearly intolerable defeat, and Sherry meant to see that it didn't happen again. She was holed up in a wing of the Carlyle, studying the catalogue and taking saunas.

Swan and Lulu paused on their way upstairs only long enough for Lulu to bend double and kiss Bo Brimmer. Bo might be little, but he had teeth in his head, and even Swan was politic enough to smile at him. Then the whole crowd of them vanished through the balcony door, leaving me, Marta, and a few straggling socialites to make our way to the bleachers, as it were.

"What's the delay, never seen a movie star before?" Marta asked.

Our seats were low and outside, so far to the right in fact that I could see only a small corner of the screen. That was fine with me. I had seen the movie and only wanted to watch the crowd, but it annoyed Marta.

"Thirty years, and this is where I'm sitting?" she said. "Mr. Mond's gonna hear about this."

"With his big heart, he'll probably buy you the theater," I said.

The people nearby looked at us strangely—responding, I

guess, to foreign tones of voice. There was not a movie person in sight. We had ended up with two of the half-dozen worst seats in the house—seats that no one with the slightest real status would have accepted. It followed that the people around us hadn't the slightest real status. They looked good, though, from what I could see of them. It was like sitting in on a class reunion at Harvard or Princeton or Yale. The men all looked like they should have been holding martinis with olives in them. The women should have been having Dubonnet. Every woman in sight could have been Page's mother—it was a sobering thought, but in all likelihood Page's mother *was* somewhere in sight.

While Marta savored her own bile, I watched the people around us, these Easterners who hadn't left home, to see if they were any different from their look-alikes who *had* left home. Those—the Easterners of the West—I was long familiar with, from visits to San Marino and Hillsboro, Atherton and Marin County. Fortunately they hadn't turned off the lights in the theater yet—it is hard to make these distinctions in a dark theater—and I was able to conclude that the Eastern Easterners had been cut with a somewhat finer chisel. Western Easterners, once out of reach of the winds of Cape Cod or the rocky shores of Maine, tend to puff up, not much, but just noticeably, as people will who have lost their purity. The skin over their cheekbones becomes a shade less taut, the lines around the men's mouths not quite so deep and aristocratic. It was sort of like the difference between a carbon and an original. The words are the same, but the effect of the original is a little crisper.

Of course, it was the same tribe, east or west, but it was nice to get a look at the bucks and squaws who held the original hunting grounds. It was clear from the set of their mouths that they meant to hold them forever, and perhaps they would, unless a Jacobin-Zionist army arose in the suburbs and carried them kicking and shrieking to the guillotines. The thought of all those waxen ladies and granitic gentlemen, kicking and shrieking in the tumbrils of Jews, being pelted with bagels and patties of cream cheese, amused me so that I nodded blissfully off in the early moments of the film and didn't awaken until there was a clatter of applause. The clatter became nearer a frenzy, at least as much of a frenzy as such an audience could manage, and I looked up and saw the spotlight shining on Jill, in the front row of the balcony.

All the elegant people turned, craning their necks inelegantly, to see her. I felt apprehensions of loss. I was the father whose daughter had just married a boy he couldn't stand; the lover who finally has to admit his woman is going to find another; the friend who had begun to miss his friend even before the friend has gone away.

"They liked it, nobody whispered," Marta said. "Usually you get whispers from this kind of crowd."

Marta and I parted company—for good, we both hoped—and I stumbled into the foyer, feeling lost as a baby. Jill was up there with all the celebs, as they are now called. I wanted to take her right home and put her back in her bungalow and tell her to get back to her drawing.

Before I could even go to the men's room Leon O'Reilly tugged at my arm.

"This picture will make fifteen to eighteen million," he said. He had evidently arrived at that calculation while in the men's room toward which I had been headed. I was the first person he saw when he emerged, so he laid it on me. One thing about Leon, he was no snob. He wasn't normal enough to be a snob. He was twirling his Phi Beta Kappa key, and the old, mad light was in his eyes.

"Yeah, but what if it ruins her?" I asked.

Leon could not quite grasp the concept of ruin. Having—evidently—emotion only for his profession, he couldn't understand its more prosaic manifestations. He was convinced, for example, that Juney tripped and fell to her death because she insisted on wearing high heels. Tell him Juney killed herself because he married a woman who later left him, and his bullet-proof psyche would deflect the comment and cause it to ricochet back and pierce whoever uttered it.

"Fifteen-eighteen million won't ruin her," he said. "All she needs to do now is make a Western."

"A Western?"

"Certainly—the first Western to be directed by a woman," he said. "All the men in America will be outraged, as well they might. A woman will be invading the last domain of the male. Or next to last—penultimate."

"What's the very last?" I asked.

"Gas stations," Leon said, with no hesitation whatever. "Gas stations are the ultimate domain of the male, strictly speaking."

Leon's posture was perfect, his pinstripes exactly vertical. He was the most perfectly preserved Western Easterner I'd ever seen. Preston Sibley III, husband of Page—he too was undoubtedly somewhere in the lobby—was a slouch when compared to Leon.

"Outrage is excellent for box-office," Leon said.

"What could she make a Western about? Invent me a plot."

"Why should I?" Leon said. "This is a cutthroat profession. You'll just sell it to Warners. I'll invent it tomorrow and sell it to them myself."

"The real truth is that you don't have a plot," I said, to goad him.

"Oh, the plot is easy," Leon said, forgetting that I was going to sell it to Warners. "It's about a gang of frontier housewives. They are fed up with domesticity and the slavery of the kitchen. Male chauvinism disgusts them. Stealthily, they organize. No one suspects them. By day they sew and cook and scrub, and by night they rob stagecoaches. Sometimes trains. They invent the device of the silk stocking over the head. For a while no one even knows they're women."

"Beautiful," I muttered. The mad light was dancing in Leon's eyes. Juney would have loved it.

"Beautiful," Leon echoed. "Of *course* some of them are beautiful, though some of them must be plain. Their leader is Katharine Hepburn, wife of the revered local sheriff, who is of course John Wayne."

"Of course," I said.

"Then one of the women tears her shirt during an escape

and some breasts pop out," Leon went on. "So they know they're women. This sets the stage for the climax, which is that John Wayne discovers a silk stocking in his front yard one night after a raid. His wife, Kate Hepburn, has dropped it coming home. Naturally he puts two and two together."

"Can't she allay his suspicions, for a while?" I asked. "Can't she fuck him or something?"

"Are you serious?" Leon asked. "They're much too old for that. They are in their twilight years."

"You haven't kept up with the latest research," I said. "Sex sometimes happens even in the twilight years."

"Not in this picture," Leon said. "This is a family picture —we'll go for PG. As the plot thickens, more and more men get suspicious. The women realize this. They decide to pull off one last big job. The men find out. A posse is formed, consisting of the husbands of the gang. The posse ambushes the gang. There is a big chase. The men chase the women."

"Terrific suspense," I said.

"There's not much more," Leon said. "The men have better horses, obviously. All the women get caught. It's a trauma for the possemen. What do they do, hang their wives? It's worst of all for John Wayne, since his wife is the ringleader. There's a bounty on her head. He's torn between love and duty, as you can well appreciate."

"I hope love wins," I said.

"You must be atypical," Leon said mildly. "Obviously he has to do his duty, otherwise Kate Hepburn won't respect him."

"Then how do the women get off?"

"They make an impassioned plea," Leon said. "They point out about the drudgery of their lives, and the judge is moved. I think they get suspended sentences."

"But what about justice?" I said. "These women committed crimes. Somebody ought to go to the slammer for a year or two, at least."

"The writers can work that out," Leon said. "We'll call it *The Silk-Stocking Gang*."

I was almost respectful. Leon had become a real producer,

in spite of everything. For an off-the-cuff plot, his was not bad. It was probably one of the two or three best plots going around the room.

"Allow me to make a small contribution," I said. "You have no heavy. Get Lee Marvin for the heavy. Make him a bounty hunter. He finds out about the women first. Probably one of them is Catherine Deneuve, and he rapes her."

"Lee Marvin's not a bad idea, but what would Catherine Deneuve be doing in Kansas?"

"I didn't know we were in Kansas," I said. "I assumed we were in the Dakotas, or Montana, maybe."

"Even so," Leon said.

"Very simple," I said. "She's in love with the Marquis de Mores, a French nobleman, but he's tied up fighting the beef lobby. He has no time for love. She is forced to teach school. Cowboys come by and make passes at her."

"Could Steve McQueen come by and make a pass at her?" he asked.

"McQueen, whoever," I said. "The rest of the plot is simple. Lee Marvin shoots down a few ladies, but he only wings Katharine Hepburn. John Wayne's horse has fallen on him, so he can't shoot, but fortunately Jimmy Stewart, the local druggist, gets Marvin with a ten-gauge shotgun."

"Fortnum and Mason!" Leon said. It was the strongest language he allowed himself.

"I like that," he said, tucking his key back into his lapel. "I think I'll go try it on Alexandra."

In a twinkling, he was off.

I could see Jill across the room, surrounded by a hedge of tuxedos. While I was watching her, Folsom appeared out of nowhere and grabbed my sleeve.

"Hey, don't grab my sleeve," I said.

"Didn't wanta lose you," Folsom said, positioning himself a few steps away. His dandruff had not improved. While I was trying to figure out what he thought he was up to, Jill suddenly appeared.

"I'm in over my depth," she said. "Will you come to Elaine's? There's going to be a party there. Then we can go home together."

She looked at me a little defensively, as if I would probably be mad at her for having this new status. Being so new to status, she exaggerated its moral significance. I certainly didn't care that she had it.

"Of course I want to come to the party," I said. "Am I supposed to go with you, or what?"

"You can if you want to ride in the limo with Abe," she said, which settled that.

"No, thanks," I said. "I'll get a cab and beat you there."

She suddenly gave me a big hug. It was strange to feel her cheek against mine—I guess I still like to think of her as a girl, but her cheek smelled like a woman's cheek. Then she went away, causing the hedge of tuxedos to take to its feet and double back in her wake.

CHAPTER 10

I was of half a mind not to go to Elaine's, despite my promise. It would be more relaxing to go to the hotel, send Jill a message, and get sleepy drunk. She would be too surrounded to miss me, anyway.

But then there was no telling when I'd get back to New York, and it *was* the most famous literary bar in America, a kind of descendant, I gathered, of the Closerie de Lilas. I might as well see it, even if it was full of Hollywooders.

First, though, I went over to the coatroom and amused myself for a few minutes by watching ladies put on fur coats. Some of the older ladies were very meek and proper, in relation to their furs. They put them on circumspectly, making sure that the skins hung right. Others, mostly the younger ladies, just shrugged them on and strode off. Their casualness bordered on recklessness, which bordered on sexiness, in my book. I could have watched the ladies putting on their fur coats all night, but of course the pleasure was ephemeral. In a few minutes there was nothing in the coatroom but a few overcoats whose owners had been too drunk to remember them. They may well have hung there for years.

I had been too proud to put my old green overcoat on over my tux, so when I finally stepped out of Lincoln Center I became a flash-frozen screenwriter. The curb lay across an Arctic waste of sidewalk. Ladies in furs were walking merrily across it, arm in arm with gentlemen no more warmly dressed than myself—the sight made me feel silly, but no less cold.

Fortunately there was a taxi waiting, warm as an igloo or warmer. "Elaine's," I said to the driver. He was young, brown, and apparently scared. He started at once. I was vague as to the actual location of Elaine's but assumed all taxi drivers knew it.

"Elaine's," I repeated, for good measure.

"Egypt," the driver said cryptically, racing along. Before I knew it we were headed down Broadway. Vague as I was, I was pretty sure Elaine's wasn't on Broadway. Also, I didn't know what the driver might have meant when he said *Egypt*. For all I knew he had set off to drive to Cairo. The inside of the cab was plastered with signs exempting him from every imaginable responsibility.

"Elaine's," I said a third time, and added "Upper East Side." I felt sure that was right.

The driver paid no attention at all. Clearly he had a destination fixed in his mind. I sat back and tried to enjoy the ride. After all, I was having an adventure in a New York taxi, a common theme in movies of my era. Life was taking in after art again.

The adventure went on for quite some time. We passed through what I felt sure was the Village, but the driver showed no signs of stopping. When he did finally stop we were in front of an immense building. The driver looked back at me and smiled—his brown eyes shone with triumph.

"Whirl' Trade Center," he said proudly.

Obviously he had concluded it was where persons in tuxedos belonged. Not wanting to disappoint him, I got out. Seconds later, I caught an uptown cab.

"Elaine's?" I said hopefully.

"Eighty-eighth and Second," the driver said. "You're lucky you found me. There's been a decline in da profession." The cabbie was so gnarled he looked like a root.

"I was beginning to suspect that," I said.

"Yeah, these Vietnams," he said. "Get in the car with one of them an' you're lucky not to end up in Jersey.

"Being from California, you probably don't know da tricks," he said. "I'll show you da tricks."

He had me uptown in something like eight and a half minutes, a dazzling display of virtuosity, particularly coming from a root with a green cap on. At the slightest sign of sluggishness on the part of the traffic he hit his horn, wiggling through several near-jams with no use of the brake at all. Pedestrians seemed to sense that something implacable was bearing down on them. Wary as Mohicans, they hung back.

"Geez, da limos are here tonight," the cabbie said, when he screeched to a stop. "Do you woik in da movies?"

"When I woik at all," I said. I had handed him a bill, but he hadn't handed me back my change. Instead, he fixed me with a hard eye.

"Got a favor," he said. "My wife, she's bored, you see. Why is she bored? That I don't know. After all, every day, who knows what can happen? She could get raped, she could get moidered, but it don't help, you see. The thrill's worn off. So she's a typist, you know—retired. What do you think she does, to get herself less bored?"

"She probably writes screenplays," I said. "Either that or she plays canasta."

His little rootlike face twisted into a smile. I saw a couple of teeth.

"No canasta," he said, and without further ado he plopped a fat green screenplay into my hand.

"She wants it to be a movie, you see," he said. "You woik out there, maybe you can help. Just take it with ya, maybe pass it around. Let some of da big shots see it."

"Oh, well," I said. "What's it about?"

"She don't want me to read it," he said, a little sadly. "She's afraid I'll be ashamed of her if it don't read so good. All I know is it's about da Bronx. I don't guess nobody'd want to see a movie about da Bronx, but I ain't in da business. All she wants is for somebody in da business to give it a look."

I glanced at the title page. The screenplay was called *The Rosebud of Love*. That the wife of a root could think in terms of rosebuds was kind of touching. I liked it. Maybe it was just the property for Leon O'Reilly.

"Fine," I said. "I'll take it along. Just don't get her hopes up too high."

"Maybe just high enough that she don't trip over them," he said, handing me my change. We shook hands, and he was off.

Elaine's seemed to be a maelstrom. A lot of people were bunched around the bar, looking anxious. They looked like the people you see in ticket lines, trying to get tickets for sold-out football games. At the sight of me in my tuxedo, with a big fat screenplay under my arm, they melted away. Probably they had been forced to melt away several times during the evening. It seemed clearly recognized that screen persons should have rapid access.

Before I was really prepared for it, I found myself face to face with Elaine herself, *mater aeternitatis* of the New York, if not the international, literary scene. She seemed benign—perhaps concluding at a glance that I would hardly be likely to cause her trouble. When I told her I was with Miss Peel's party she led me right along. I didn't see any writers, but then writers photograph terribly and never really look like their pictures. I could have tripped over one and not known it.

Elaine led me to a room where the movie party was being held. Again leopards came to mind—not because Elaine was much like a leopard, and I am not much like Dante, either, but I had only to glance into the room to know that it was the sort of place where one would get more respectful attention if one were being led by a leopard. Elaine declined the role, and vanished. I stepped into the party and vanished too. A few eyes looked up when I entered, but they did not light up with recognition. I felt a little spectral, or astral, or both.

Jill sat with her back to me, between Abe Mondschiem and Bo Brimmer. She was talking to a man who squatted by her chair—I couldn't see his face, but he was big. Jilly was at the table, listening to Lulu Dickey. Swan Bunting stood behind her, waiting for her to finish her anecdote so he could rush home to Sherry. Preston Sibley, of all people, was sitting next to Lulu. Peter Falk got up just as I entered and moved over to a table from which issued a wild babble—the fun table, clearly. Around it were Bertolucci, Antonella Pisa, some unidentified girls, Andy Warhol, a number of young men who looked like well-barbered rats, Jean Joris-Mallet, and Romy Schneider.

The space between the tables—not that there was much of it—was filled with a Sargasso Sea of wavy people, invisibles like myself. There were minor actors, PR men, lawyers-cum-producers, reporters, editors, editors' girl friends, reporters' girl friends, and, I judged, anyone who could slip in on the coattails of someone legitimately famous. Through this swamp of safari jackets slipped the waiters, skillful as Cajuns in pirogues, carrying food to the tables. Why they bothered I don't know: the scene was far too hectic to eat in, unless one were Jilly Legendre, who could eat anywhere, anytime. Maybe the food was all for him.

When Peter Falk got up I started for his chair, but long before I got there a girl not unlike Page sat down in it and began talking to Preston Sibley III.

To my horror, I saw that it *was* Page, taking a seat by her husband. She had been mixed in with the mob of editors' girl friends, and I hadn't noticed her. Preston looked a little tight and Page very lit up. Page was physical as a puppy, and immediately started to play hands with Preston, only Preston wouldn't play.

She hadn't spotted me, so I stepped back a few steps to try

and decide if I wanted to be spotted. I felt outraged at the lack of justice in this world, the almost total absence of order, stability, and appropriateness. In my imagination Page had been at Tahoe for the last two days. In a properly ordered world she would be, in fact, where she was in my imagination—not in a New York bar with both her husband and her lover.

While I was absorbing that shock, the man Jill was talking to pivoted a little in his squat and I saw that it was Owen Oarson, and ex–All American-cum-producer. That was bad news. I knew Owen a little, from some poker games we had both attended. He had come to Hollywood as a PR man and ended up a gambler, but probably he still harbored delusions about producing pictures. He had a smart lip and he knew his poker, but nobody I knew had ever taken him seriously as a producer. Or as anything else, except an ex-All American, from Texas Tech, I think. I saw that he was looking up at Jill gravely and intently, ignored by everyone at the table except her. He had no status whatever, and had zeroed in on the one person in the room who was likely to treat him like a human being. Jill was talking rapidly. She might be the woman of the moment, but it was clear that the moment had already chewed her up and spat her back. At a table with egos around it the size of Lulu's and Bo's, Jill would be lucky to get someone to bring her a glass of water.

The sight of Page had affected me like a car wreck—adrenaline rushed out from whatever glands were keeping it. That was one shock. The sight of Jill in rapid, intense conversation with Owen Oarson was another. I hardly knew what I felt, beyond a far-reaching apprehension. In order to collect my wits I went back out to the bar and got a Jack Daniel's, my worry drink. Then I returned to the party and lurked in the general vicinity of the ladies' room for a while, hoping Page would come by on her way to powder her nose. It was a vain hope—Page had no need to powder her nose. While I was waiting, Anna Lyle came out.

"Hey, Joe," she said.

"Hey," I said. "Where's Pete?"

"In the sack, probably. He met someone he took to."

"Who are you with?"

"I believe I'm unescorted," she said. "I'm not being mobbed, either."

"Let's pretend we're together," I said. "If anybody asks who I am, tell them I'm Saxe Gotha."

"Who's he, some stunt man?" Anna asked, not very interested in my subterfuges.

"Look at *those* people," she said, pointing to a table in the rear. Five or six men and two or three young girls were sitting at it.

"None of their heads are shaped right," Anna said, going to the heart of the matter, as she perceived it.

Indeed, the males of the group did seem strangely off-plane. They were dressed in Levis or fatigues and wore cowboy boots or sneakers, and managed to look, collectively, as if they were waiting for Fritz Lang or somebody to pop them into an Expressionist film, something full of shadows and tilts and mirror shots. They were drinking rhythmically and glaring at the Hollywood tables as if their mere presence was an affront.

"Oh," I said, recognition dawning. "It's obvious. Those are the writers. I knew they were here somewhere. The one with the teenager licking his ear is Wagner Baxter."

Anna dreamily scanned the group again. "They look like they had difficult births," she said, dragging me over to the head table.

By the time we got there the composition of the table had changed somewhat for the better. Abe had moved to a corner table, with one or two publicity people and a Frenchman in a mink coat who was probably his coke connection. He was winking at a young TV actress named Mercy Merker, who was at the next table—Mercy wasn't winking back, though.

Anna took Abe's chair, which put me right next to Page. If you're going to be reckless, be reckless, I decided. She turned from playing hands with Preston, took one look at me, and began to giggle. She had a kind of husky giggle, very affecting. Obviously she had been smoking pot all afternoon with some of her friends and hadn't the slightest self-consciousness about being sandwiched between her husband and her lover.

"I didn't know you were here," she said happily. "You look wonderful in that tuxedo. You look like my uncle in Philadelphia."

"Christ, you've got forty-two uncles in Philadelphia," Preston said, shaking my hand. He probably supposed he knew me from somewhere, and I let him suppose it.

"Oh, Uncle Farjeon," Page said.

Jill turned briefly and took note of my proximity to Page. Owen Oarson was still looking up at her, waves of yearning radiating from his face like heat from an electric heater. It was embarrassing to be near somebody who wanted to be accepted that badly. But Jill wasn't embarrassed. Anna, who had probably never heard of Owen, asked him to pull up a chair.

"Thank you, Miss Lyle," he said. He got a chair. Bo Brimmer glanced around irritably, conscious of an alien presence within his aura. He ignored Owen but extended a small hand to me.

"Hi, Joe Percy," I said. I decided not to try to pretend to be someone named Saxe Gotha, although I could have fooled everybody but Bo.

"He lives in the Hollywood Hills," Anna said, as if that would identify me.

Page emitted what would have been peals of giggles, if her giggles hadn't been so husky. Preston looked annoyed, at having a wife who couldn't hold her marijuana. Jill wore my sapphire as if it had belonged to her forever. After one look, to see if I was in one piece, she decided to observe strict neutrality—probably because she was more interested in Owen than in whatever trouble I had gotten myself into. She turned back and resumed her conversation.

"Ah, yes," Bo said, when I mentioned my name. "You wrote *Neilsen's Hope*. Lovely film. And didn't you work on *Long Trail A-Winding*?"

"Sure, Maureen O'Sullivan," I said, as if that meant something.

Lulu Dickey, who was on my left, was strangely silent, and even the usually loquacious Jilly, with his fine idiomatic grasp of several languages, was not talking much. The two of them were hunched together, hogging the tablecloth. It occurred to me suddenly that Jilly had a finger up her. None of the other tables even had a tablecloth. I considered dropping my lighter so I could look under the table and confirm my suspicions, but I didn't smoke, or have a lighter.

"My goodness, they favored us with a tablecloth," I said.

"Ah insisted," Bo said.

"We *are* drinking champagne," Preston said.

Page drank what champagne was left in his glass and casually held up the glass, her head tilted back and her wet little teeth shining. A waiter deftly filled the glass.

"Me," Lulu said suddenly, holding up her glass too. I would never know about my suspicions.

"I thought Swan was very low tonight," she added, after a sip of champagne. Jilly evidently had no interest in Swan, or in us either, because he hiked his chair around so he could become part of the continental table.

"Swan hardly spoke to me," Preston said. "I can't be sure Swan likes me. I mean, we're doing their picture—I hope he likes me."

He excused himself and went to the men's room. He had hardly disappeared into the crowd before Page began purring like a kitten against my neck. No one took the slightest notice.

"I think Swan *was* very low," Lulu repeated. Obviously, she wanted the matter discussed.

Bo's little rabbit face turned her direction briefly, but he didn't say a word.

"You're not fair to him," Lulu said. "He's really very insecure."

"Swan Bunting is about as insecure as a bronze statue of Cecil Rhodes," Bo said crisply. Having been a Rhodes scholar, he was in a position to know how insecure such statues were. His Southern accent vanished, as it sometimes would, to be replaced by something more Oxbridge.

Jilly Legendre looked over his shoulder at us all. "Swan's just pussy-whipped," he said.

"I wish she'd smother him," Bo said. "Plot her twat over his nose and smother him."

"Oh, you're all so hard on Swan," Lulu said. "Hard, hard, hard."

Page, meanwhile, was breathing into my ear. "No wonder it always works," she said.

"What are you talking about?" I said.

"Fucking you," she said. "I always wanted to fuck my Uncle Farjeon. Why don't we go?"

I was a good mind to take her up. I lacked the ego to make a splash at such a table, but in fact all the real egos seemed flat, for some reason. Only Owen Oarson was really enjoying himself, and that was solely because of Jill. Bo and Lulu and Jilly seemed to be stuck in an obligatory occasion, for which they had no real taste. Probably they were all sick of one another. Only Bo seemed to have any real energy, and it wasn't radiating outward. Bo was working at his thoughts. He had suddenly noticed an antipasto and was nibbling a carrot like a savage rabbit.

Jilly got up and came around the table and kissed Jill. "My darling, I salute you," he said. "*Très beau, très clair, très fidèle.*" Then he went and installed himself by Antonella Pisa. Jill looked embarrassed, and turned back to her conversation.

Try as I might, I couldn't overhear what she was saying to that big slob. His face was long and rectangular, like a shoe box.

Page kept breathing, near my ear. The scene at the table, which had never really engaged my full attention, began to fade from it altogether, as in a dissolve. I was a little concerned about Jill, but after all, she was thirty-seven years old. She knew how to take care of the Owen Oarsons of the world—and if she didn't, it was time she learned. If she would only have met my eye for a moment, I would have felt better—we had always maintained our sense of one another through frequent eye contact, but for the moment she was too engrossed to give me a real look. Something—Owen Oarson, or Elaine's, or the whole evening—had jammed our system of mutual awareness, and it seemed to me I might as well leave.

Anyway, it was hard to imagine a more detached group of people than sat around that table—detached not only from one another but from what any ordinary person would describe as reality. Yet many of them had been ordinary persons once. Bo had run a paper route in Little Rock, Jill had grown up normal in Santa Maria, and Lulu had emerged from a ministerial household in Wisconsin. Preston and Page had gone to the right schools, and Anna to junior high in a Phoenix suburb before she ran away to Hollywood. Jilly was the only one whose life had been abnormal from birth, and he was getting more normal all the time. Of course the reason for the flatness might just be that I hadn't drunk enough. Liquor is like a fine lens to me. The right amount of it always sharpens my focus.

"I think I'll split," I said to Anna, as Page got up to go to the ladies' room.

"I'd go with you, but my feet hurt," Anna said.

I got up and tapped Jill on the shoulder. She looked up, startled.

"See you at the Sherry," I said. "I'm bushed. Too many museums."

"Oh, right," she said. "I guess I'll stay and talk some more."

On my way out I passed the table full of writers. They were still pouring down drinks. Suddenly I felt emboldened and decided to put my invisibility to the test.

"Aren't you Wagner Baxter?" I asked Wagner Baxter. The girl who had been licking his ear was asleep in his lap. The writers all looked up, surprised to hear a voice come out of the air. Wagner Baxter had a head the shape of a light bulb—shaved, of course. His head had been shaved even before Yul Brynner's, much less Telly Savalas'. His cheeks looked like a mule had amused himself for a few years by kicking gravel at them.

"Of course," Wagner Baxter said, looking down at the girl asleep in his lap. He seemed surprised that she was asleep. Probably she was supposed to be giving him a blow job.

"I knew your uncle, Boswell Baxter," I said.

Wagner Baxter took this news calmly.

"Do you butcher novels, like he did?" he asked.

All the writers opened their mouths at that, but they didn't laugh. They just opened their mouths. Maybe they were breathing germs at me. Their mouths stayed open, as if the difficult births Anna had ascribed to them had affected the hinges of their jaws. Perhaps they wouldn't be able to close their mouths until Wagner Baxter made another remark.

"Only literary horsemeat, like your stuff," I said.

I expected immediate attack, and was sort of half-hoping for it. Getting beat up might have made life seem a little more real. But the writers reacted in a strange way. They stood up instantly, as if my rejoinder had been the signal they had been waiting for.

"Uncle Boswell was a Hollywood fink!" Wagner Baxter said as he went past me. The rest of them grabbed their fur-lined Levis and goose-down windbreakers, kicked at the table once or twice, and then trooped out, glowering at the Hollywood party as they went. Wagner Baxter had managed to shake the girl in his lap into a semblance of wakefulness, and was dragging her after him.

"Hey, Wagner, don't be *rough*!" she said, sleepily, trying to get the hair out of her eyes.

I followed them out into the other room. They were all clustered around Elaine, struggling into their jackets even as they raised loud complaints. Elaine suffered it all with matriarchal calm. Since nobody had punched me in the nose yet, I walked up to Wagner and put in another two cents' worth.

"Your Uncle Boswell was an honest craftsman," I said. "I feel obliged to defend him."

It was a counterfeit two cents, actually. Boswell Baxter had been one of the worst snobs in Hollywood. For years he wouldn't speak to anyone but Ronald Colman. At least he didn't wear a green fatigue jacket, though.

Wagner Baxter ignored me, but turned to glare at Elaine. "I hate your mayonnaise!" he said vehemently, and left, abandoning the girl with long hair, who soon began to cry. Elaine took her over and deposited her like a lost kitten at a table full of convivial Broadway types.

I found Page by the ladies' room, idly picking lint off her sweater. Despite being rich, she always seemed to wear tacky sweaters that picked up lint.

"Any sign of your husband?" I asked.

"I didn't look," she said. "Was I supposed to look for Preston?"

The confusion around us seemed to be increasing. More and more people were crowding in, and even the skillful waiters were beginning to find themselves boxed behind tables. There were signs of exasperation everywhere. One of the most dramatic occurred just to our left: a little short man with a spike beard surprised everybody by picking up a lady twice his size and flinging her onto a neighboring table.

"Lie in your swill, you cunt!" he yelled, and rushed out. The lady calmly climbed off the table and began to pick linguine out of her hair.

"I don't think we'll be missed," I said. "Do you have a coat?"

"Oh, yeah, my fur," Page said. She slipped through the crowd like it wasn't there and emerged with a silver mink. She shrugged it on like it might have cost a nickel, and we went out into the icy wind, only to find that we were blocked from the taxis by a wall of black limos.

"We can take Preston's," she said. "I'm sure one of them's his."

"I've got a better idea," I said. "Let's take Abe's." I had spotted Folsom walking back and forth in front of a limo like a dog in a run. I grabbed Page by her deeply furred arm and strode right over.

"Open the door," I said to Folsom, hoping he would respond on reflex. The sight of a tuxedo and a woman in furs is like a Pavlovian stimulus to a gofer. Before Folsom realized it was us, we were sitting in the warm limo.

"Say," he said, sticking his head in. It had dawned on him that neither of us was Abe.

"Don't talk," I said. "Just tell the driver to get us to the Algonquin quick. Mrs. Sibley has a coccyx. Of course Mr. Mondschiem wanted to help."

"Aw," Folsom said, deeply confused.

"Oh, god, my coccyx," Page said in her huskiest tones.

Folsom couldn't muster his resistance fast enough. He glanced longingly at the restaurant, and then got in and slowly shut the door. The driver, an impassive fellow of Mediterranean origin, eased away. Folsom looked at the restaurant again, this time with a touch of despair. He realized that the die was cast. Maybe he would be back before Abe emerged, and maybe he wouldn't.

"Think how it would be to fuck in a limo," Page whispered, against my neck. For a girl who was completely careless about what she ate, she had remarkably sweet breath. At the moment it was flavored slightly with marijuana.

"Listen, don't get a thing about cars," I said. "I'm no acrobat."

Page didn't answer. Her eyes were bright. Under the streetlights they shone like her fur. The fur added its smell to the smell of Page. It was a contradictory smell, suggestive of great cold—the cold where the minks lived—and also great warmth. Page partook a little of the same contradictoriness; her lips were always cool in a kiss, but the rest of her was warm as a stove.

I looked down at her again and the eyes that had shone with excitement a few blocks before were closed. She was asleep, a state she passed into more easily than most babies. A little grass, a little sex, a little wine—a little of almost anything would put Page to sleep.

Probably she was the happiest person in the limo, unless the Sicilian driver was concealing euphoria beneath his olive exterior. Folsom certainly wasn't concealing euphoria; panic maybe, but not euphoria. He lowered the glass between the seats and looked at Page.

"Is she dead?" he asked hopefully. In his view a death would legitimize the undertaking.

"I suspect it's a coma," I said.

I was not quite clear as to why I had asked for the Algonquin. The name had sprung to my tongue unbidden, like the situation. Before I could order my thoughts—something I have not really managed to do in sixty-three years—we were there. Page walked in, but she could not be said to be awake. The gentleman at the desk very civilly made a room available, and Page, propped against me, snored faintly as I signed the register.

Instead of a key, I was given a strange little card, which fit in a slot in our door. The room it let us into seemed to be the shape of a slice of pie, but I was not inclined to quibble. I managed to slip Page's fur off as she pitched in a heap onto the bed. Since I wasn't drunk and I wasn't sleepy, I decided to let her nap a bit while I removed myself to the lobby, to weigh alternatives, as it were.

The lobby was just the sort of place I had once imagined I would spend my life in, as soon as I got famous. A smattering of after-theater people were sipping green liqueurs and weighing the merits of plays. The lobby was so comfortable that several brandies went by before I remembered that I was supposed to be weighing alternatives, even as my companions were weighing merits.

On about the fourth brandy, the focus that had been missing from the evening finally materialized, and it occurred to me that I didn't really need to weigh alternatives. It seemed to me that, in my tux, I was the perfect person to sit in the Algonquin lobby and drink brandy. I was, after all, from the world of entertainment. Except for the green liqueurs, everything was as I had expected it to be, long ago, in my fantasies: a gracious lobby, nice paneling, comfortable chairs, and a few well-preserved night owls like myself either sitting alone and contemplating life, or else conversing vivaciously about art and life. For once I felt appropriate. Even in my vast wardrobe of checked suits, vests, scarves, sport coats, slacks, and socks I would have looked appropriate in the Algonquin lobby. Perhaps I could take the rest of my savings and rent a corner there, for my declining years.

The only thing of mine that wouldn't have looked very appropriate in the Algonquin lobby was the very best thing—old Claudia. She had looked right at home in her spotted loincloth, sitting around the jungle sets with a few leopards and some fake vines and a couple of stunt men to yak with. With no vines to swing on and no stunt men to amuse her, she might have gotten too restless. She wouldn't have been content, as I was, to sit in a corner in evening clothes, smoothly consuming brandy.

I guess Claudia and I had belonged where we lived, in the Hollywood Hills. I couldn't quite squeeze her into my fantasy of old age in the Algonquin lobby.

Then, as often happened when I remembered Claudia, I remembered Stravinsky too, and Vera, his large, calm wife. I had to wipe my eyes on my French cuff. The Stravinskys had lived not far from where I live, and I had sometimes seen them taking walks. I loved seeing that bony, irritable little man, in his baggy khakis. He was always stopping on curbs to glare myopically at the racketing, rocketing skateboarders, who often narrowly missed smacking right into him. If one *had* smacked into him, I had the feeling Stravinsky would have bitten him, as a ferret bites a rat. Vera, majestic as a galleon, sailed right on. The composer's hand was always reaching for hers, and always found hers, after a search. That was my dream of love in old age, I guess.

Like a lot of mediocre artisans, I was corny about the great. My work was only a harmless kind of garbage. There was no chance that I could ever have done anything much better, and perhaps because of that I revered the great ones and would through all my days. I even had dreams of the Stravinskys—dreams of them flying over Hollywood, firebirds of the sunset, a quarrelsome jay and a great calm owl—at least as romantic as my dreams of Claudia. When she showed up in a dream she was usually over at Columbia, in one of those big hangars they used to have, a fake vine clasped between her athletic thighs, practicing her swinging.

My little lapse into reverie was interrupted by a waiter, who informed me that I could have one more brandy. I took him up on it, and then made my way a bit unsteadily back to the pie-shaped room. It was exhaustion, not drink, that made me unsteady. Being in New York was as tiring as walking around with weights on the legs. It was obvious, even after one day, that living there required training. Making it through a month in New York would be the equivalent, for a person of my age and disposition, of competing in the decathlon, in the Olympics of city life. In earlier years, the event could have been interesting, but I knew that for me it had come a little late.

CHAPTER 11

PAGE, of course, was still in a heap. As I got out of my tuxedo it occurred to me that getting back into it in the morning was going to seem pretty silly. If I had been a man of good sense I would have gone back to the Sherry, kept the peace with Jill—assuming she was around to keep peace with—and had some nice checked clothes to step into in the morning. It wouldn't matter much to Page. She would just wake up, shrug on her silver mink, and be back in her life in two minutes.

Instead of pursuing that sensible course, I began to try and undress Page, so she wouldn't be so wrinkled when she woke up. It was no easy task. While I was struggling with her tacky sweater she suddenly sat up and shucked it. For a moment it looked as if she might be going to rise to consciousness. She stretched out her arms, lifting her young breasts, but then fell back and resumed her warm slumber.

Despite the weight of New York, which seemed to have settled on my shoulders and calves, I only slept a few hours. I woke with Page cuddled against me, warm as coals and snoring faintly. There was a window near my head. I parted the curtain, to see how the smog was, and found myself staring at a grimy brick wall, perhaps six feet away. There was no sign of California, and I remembered that I was on the wrong side of the continent.

In order to restore my sense of reality, I watched some television. The set was ingeniously tucked away in a bureau drawer. The *Today* show was almost over before Page showed any signs of life.

"Are you watching the *Today* show?" she said with disbelief, sitting up and pushing back her abundant if somewhat frizzy hair.

"That's disgusting," she added. I made no defense, even though I knew that in her vocabulary disgusting was the opposite of perfect.

Without further comment, she stretched out on top of me—not for sexual purposes, as I momentarily supposed, but because she evidently preferred me to the mattress. She was soon asleep again, her hair between me and the television set. I accepted that, and for half an hour listened to television and watched Page's hair. Then she woke up and began to sneeze.

"It's your mustache," she said. "I'm allergic to it."

"You're not allergic to it," I said. "You just shouldn't go to sleep with your nose in it."

"I don't agree," she said, looking at me as if I had made a totally stupid remark. Then she got out of bed and went to the bathroom. When she emerged she yawned, bent over her pile of clothes, extracted panty hose, and yawned again.

"What are we in, a hotel?" she asked vaguely. The minute I saw the curls on her little pubis disappearing from view I began to feel sexy; but when I put out a hand Page looked at me as if I were a person with very curious ideas about life.

"It's too late to fuck," she said, with a touch of petulance.

"I was supposed to go back to Long Island last night. Preston's mother is giving a brunch.

"I bet the limo's not still around," she said when she was dressed. "You better give me some money. This means a taxi."

I gave her fifty dollars and she put on the silver mink and fell back on top of me. Her petulance had vanished and she looked wide-eyed and solemn, as children look when they haven't really had their nap out.

"I could come back in the afternoon, if you want to hang around," she said.

"Just name an hour," I said.

She named 3 P.M. and arrived at 4:45. At the Sherry, where I went to leave my tux, I found a note from Jill:

> All right, I'm busy all day. Do *something* new—why would a museum be so bad? I knew this would happen.
>
> JILL
>
> p.s. I wanted to thank you for my sapphire, but you weren't here.

At the sight of the note—a perfectly normal Jill note—I felt a quiet paranoia growing in me. Perhaps Jill and I weren't going to talk any more, or know one another any more. We had started across a glacier and a crevasse had opened between us. This had happened years before, but it had only been a hairline crevasse, about the width of a small brook, and we had been jumping back and forth across it for years, confident (indeed, overconfident) of our ability to leap crevasses, and outwit the glacier. But a crevasse that is only the width of a brook one day can be the width of Fifth Avenue the next, and the width of the Grand Canyon in a week or two. Soon we might only see one another as specks in the distance.

In order to drive the notion away, I sat down and wrote a self-justificatory note:

Dear Jill:

In your absence I will do my best to have an intellectually fulfilling time. I will undoubtedly devote many hours to museums, parceling my time out judiciously.

Be careful. I mean it.

Love, JOE

It seemed silly, so I threw it in the wastebasket. I have never been a good note writer.

Jill had a rave review in *The Times*, naturally. It was obvious to me that everyone would overrate her movie. In ten years' time those who had overrated it wouldn't be able to remember it, but the damage would have been done.

I lunched alone and got tipsy enough to distract myself from the sense that everything was slipping away. In the afternoon I went back to the Algonquin and saw Page. In the evening I drank for a bit in the bar at the Sherry and went to bed early, hoping Jill would show up; but she didn't come in that night, and there were no more notes.

The next morning I stayed in bed so late that I began to get bedsores. Jill and I were to catch a plane to the Coast late in the afternoon. The phone didn't ring even once, which meant that all calls were being caught at the switchboard. Finally I got up and fuddled around a bit, thinking about T. S. Eliot, or at least about his famous line to the effect that there would be time to murder and create. In my case there was no longer time to create, and probably not time to murder either, since the latter probably takes as much passion as the former, though perhaps only passion of a momentary, inconsistent nature.

I put on some checks and my old green overcoat and went out on Fifth Avenue, which was just as cold as ever and just as crowded with ruddy New Yorkers. Somewhere up the avenue there were undoubtedly great museums, filled with the imperishable efforts of those who had found time to create, but I cheerfully turned my back on intellectual improvement and went bouncing down to the Algonquin in a

Checker cab, where Page and I had lunch and sought, once again, the fulfilling fuck.

"I like it at your house better," Page said later, a little glumly. We were both staring at the brick wall out the window. It was a chill, gray day, and we had had an unusual amount of difficulty with the covers on the bed, a new thing for us. At home covers were seldom involved. Page had a point, even if she hadn't quite bothered to think it through. If we had been fresh to adultery, or a little more driven, the neutrality of a hotel room in New York would have been fine. But Page and I were casual—there had never been anything resembling a barricade put in our path. A sawhorse now and then, maybe, but nothing more serious.

"Some folks need their rituals," I said. Page stared at me blankly.

All I had meant was that we were both homesick. We missed the smell of California: open windows, sunshine on the sheets, my plants in their pots, the dusty hills above us.

"Don't you remember?" I said. "We have rituals. We meet in my garage, where it's cool. Then we sometimes make it upstairs and have fun in the sun. Then we have a swim in the world's smallest swimming pool, and you eat half my peanut butter and go home."

"Yeah?" Page said, her face brightening a bit at the memory of such a pleasant routine.

"Yeah, that was perfect," she added. I began to feel better just from hearing her utter her magic word. I tipped her back in the pillows and indulged myself in what in her view was a perfect thing, which was to lick her pale little cunt for ten or fifteen minutes. It may have been longer—I've never been a man who could lick a cunt and keep up with the time—but however long it was, we both enjoyed it. Page clasped her arms tightly over her eyes, and the muscles of her flat little stomach jerked and quivered. As for me, I tried to summon some smidgin of self-reproach, inasmuch as I could have been looking at Giotto or somebody instead of getting my nose wet, but Page came a couple of times, and self-reproach didn't. Her cunt was as alkaline and slippery as a mussel, and rose-pink, like the color inside the curl of a shell. After a time, I rested my cheek on her springy gold fleece and picked some of the nap out of my teeth while she, for her part, took another snooze.

That was about it for New York. When I got back to the other hotel Jill's bags were packed, but she wasn't there. As I was packing mine the doorbell rang and Folsom marched in and began to gather up suitcases.

"We go," he said, as if he were Tonto delivering a message to the Lone Ranger.

"Would you mind sitting on my suitcase?" I asked.

Folsom frowned—it was an unconventional request. "Why?" he wanted to know.

"Because otherwise it won't close."

"Naw, I almost got fired," Folsom said, retreating to the hall. I decided that that meant Abe had found out about my using the limo. I sat on my own suitcase.

I watched the gray buildings of Manhattan as we departed—watched the hurrying people on the sidewalk, some of them tilted slightly as they stood just off the curb, waiting for the length of the limo to slide past. I regretted, almost, that I didn't have another life to live—it would take that long, I figured, to become a real citizen of New York.

The driver, another Mediterranean, decided that reason dictated a route through Queens, which didn't help my mood any. Certain surroundings force one to imagine the lives of the people who have to live in them. Queens was probably not much different from Van Nuys, just colder and less neat, but on the other hand it was sort of the diametric opposite of Beverly Hills. Instead of smooth streets and green lawns and new cars, Queens offered cracked streets, no lawns, buildings as badly painted as old whores, and cars that all seemed to have competed in demolition derbies.

Folsom was in the front seat, chewing his lip. He was always chewing his lip. I was alone in the vast back seat. I could have been a cadaver in a hearse, for all the human contact available. I decided never to go anywhere again: it stirred me up too much. To go somewhere is to edge out of one life and into another. Some people probably found that stimulating, but I just found it confusing. It multiplied my choices, and I had too many choices as it was.

As I approached my flight gate I could see a vast white 747 out a window, waiting for me and a few hundred other people. Just as I was steeling myself to try and be nice to Owen Oarson, I saw Jill standing with Marta by a kind of velvet rope. Jill was wearing the white pantsuit she had worn when we flew to New York.

"Look, he's goin' back," Marta said when I walked up. "We thought maybe you'd found work in the East."

The way she sounded was worse than what she said. Also, she was squinting, which eliminated her eyes but exposed her turquoise eye makeup. I had almost forgotten how awful she was, but the sight of her skunk wig, turquoise eyelids, and liverish lipstick brought me back to reality.

"Go fuck yourself, Marta," I said, reverting to basic California speech before I even stepped on the plane.

Hate was not too strong a word for what I felt looking at her—nor for what she clearly felt looking at me.

Jill looked at us both, shook her head with quick impatience, and took my arm. "Bye, Marta, thanks," she said, and walked me onto the plane.

CHAPTER 12

ONCE again we were in a gracious living room. Once again we were offered nuts, and I received the first of several vodka martinis—this before a word was uttered. Jill was totally silent, obviously offended by my rudeness to Marta.

"All right, I'm sorry," I said. "I hate her. If she could she'd not only get me fired, she'd see that I starved. I've always hated her. You don't know her like I do."

"You could be big enough just to ignore her," Jill said. "After all, she's not happy."

"Oh, dear," I said. "Oh, god in heaven. You mean I've been boorish to an unhappy person? Of course it is true that some people retain their manners and decency even when they're unhappy, but those are usually people with manners to retain."

Jill made a little fist, but she didn't hit me with it. She just looked hurt. "It doesn't surprise me that you're rude to her, but I didn't think you'd be so rude to me," she said.

I watched her for a minute. She didn't seem so changed. All that I had been imagining about her was probably just paranoia. Maybe she wasn't slipping away.

"I'm sorry," I said.

We looked at one another a long time, without piling any more words on the situation. I believe she was grateful for my apology. Just as a weak sun was going down into the Eastern clouds, our great white plane took off. I caught one last glimpse of the gray towers of New York. Then we shot upward, into bright crystalline air. The bottoms of the clouds had been grimy, but the tops were a brilliant shining white, whiter even than the plane itself. The bright blue air made me feel friendlier.

Jill was looking out the window. For all her frequent bluntness, she was an extremely refined woman; so refined —when one thought about it—that it was almost impossible to deal with her. The cast of her eye, the set of her mouth, had so much mentality, so much consciousness, so much checked emotion behind them that sometimes, when I caught her looking a certain way, I was filled with both love and trepidation.

She offered me her eyes from time to time but spoke no words, and her eyes said, All right, say something, don't wait for me. People who think friendship is the stablest condition or relation or whatever haven't been friends with Jill Peel. Here we were, acquaintances for fifteen years and good friends for eight or nine; I was sixty-three, she was thirty-seven; we might have been judged to be mature people, stable, all that, and yet for a time both of us were afraid to say a word. Friendship, too, is ruinable, and can be destroyed as quickly and as absolutely as love. Neither of us wanted to ruin ours. A lot of emotion coursed beneath our silence, as the plane coursed over the brilliant clouds. A tall, surefooted stewardess began to a lay a cart with caviar, crackers, and pâté.

Fortunately, the bright air eased us. I had some caviar, Jill some pâté. Beyond the Allegheny the clouds began to thin, and I saw that we were mated to the sunset, our speed evidently equal to the turn of the earth. Far below I caught glimpses of orange-and-gold forest—evening on the autumn land.

"Why'd we suddenly lose track of one another?" I ventured finally.

Jill shrugged. "I was busy and you were busy," she said. "Neither of us wanted to hang around."

"It's all right—we can blame it on your premiere," I said. "It's not every day we experience a world premiere."

"Right," Jill said. "I'm sure my premiere quite justifies you keeping your nose in a cunt for three days."

I thought that one over for a bit. In a way, it was a brilliant shot, but a shot of a sort that most women produce routinely, out of the small change of their instincts. She went on eating her pâté, calmly.

"For god's sake," I said. "Why are you so hostile to me? You've never been this hostile to me!"

"Why, it's just my premiere," she said coolly. "We famous are known for our cruelty. However, you're just as hostile to me, and you're not famous. Maybe you can explain that."

"I'm not hostile," I said, though I was getting hostile. Her tone was infuriating.

"You could have told me you brought your girl friend to New York," she said. "I might have known you would, but I didn't. You don't have to keep reminding me of how naive I am."

I felt a certain sense of relief. Men sometimes stop being men and become neuters for a while, but women never stop being women. I would think it would tire them, being women constantly, but if it does, they don't show it.

"Is that all you're mad about?" I asked. "I didn't arrange that. I still don't know how Preston got her to come. She was going to Tahoe. I didn't know she was here until I walked into Elaine's. Seeing her at that table was a big shock, believe me."

"You absorbed it smoothly enough," she said. "Some shock."

My relief had been premature. I thought that what was bothering her was a misunderstanding. Explain it away and all would be harmony and affection again, right?

Not right. Wrong. Women are like lawyers and torturers, more interested in process than in result. Explanations may be part of the process, but they seldom affect the result.

"Jill, this is ruining my digestion," I said. "I didn't plan anything. Page turned up, that's all. Frankly, you seemed to be occupied, and it never occurred to me that I would be missed. Until this minute I had no idea that I *was* missed."

She shook her head. "You gave me the nicest present anyone's ever given me in my life, and you didn't think I'd want to come home and thank you for it? Just because I was talking to Owen didn't mean I'd forgotten *that.* I wasn't going to talk all night, and I wasn't going to dash right out and fuck him either—which is obviously what you thought."

"I guess the firing squad is what I deserve," I said. "Irony of ironies. Page zonked out and all I did was sit in the Algonquin lobby and drink brandy. You could have come. It's a great place to drink brandy."

"Good. You only had your nose in a cunt for two and a half days," she said. "It's not as bad as I thought."

But she said it companionably. I guess she had extracted her pound of flesh. She was even looking at me fondly. Awkwardly, I turned to kiss her. Our embrace was spoiled only by the fact that the seatbelt was crushing my nuts.

There had been some long, hostile pauses in our approach to a rapprochement. The plane was almost to the Mississippi. The sun was not much lower than it had been when we left the ground, but it was larger and more golden.

"What possessed you to buy me that sapphire?" she asked. "You're not rich."

"It was the hour for it," I said, and we argued companionably about the propriety of my action across most of the West—literally the Golden West in this case, thanks to the sun. It seemed to hang immobile in the lower quadrant of the sky, coloring the snowy Rockies and the mauve-and-crimson desert beyond them. I ate a lot, and Jill ate a little. Our companions in the first-class cabin strolled around looking thoughtful. They talked about Las Vegas, Baja, Acapulco, Mazatlán, and points south.

We were happy for an hour. Jill told me about her lunches, her offers, her adventures, but she never mentioned Owen Oarson or referred to the night she hadn't been in the hotel. No reason she should have, of course. I didn't say much about my activities with Page, either. Jill and I had left together, and we were returning together—more or less—and not too much else mattered.

Actually, though, it was less rather than more. Jill had secrets, and I had none. People in our profession are always saying "more or less," or "in some sense," or simply "whatever." I sometimes think "whatever" should be the true motto of Hollywood. I think they ought to letter it on the Goodyear Blimp and anchor the damn thing to the Beverly Hills Hotel, as a reminder to us all of how vague we are.

As the plane began to descend, I descended too, in spirit. Jill became very quiet. We had not kept up with the sun after all. It beat us over the coastal mountains, so that when we finally eased over them ourselves the Basin was smoky with dusk, purple in the foothills and up the Valley. People like myself, who are on the lip of age, get paranoid about slipping over. I never had worried about it much, but that was because I was in the habit of fantasizing myself a sudden, freakishly accidental, and painless end. I had been expecting a totally unexpected death since I was about sixteen, and the fact that in all those years I had seldom so much as cut my finger did nothing to dim the expectation. I'd be carried off some way, someday: a wave would smash me against a rock and knock me cuckoo, or a ball bearing would fly out of a skateboard and hit me right between the eyes, killing me instantly. Stravinsky had escaped the skateboards, but I wouldn't be so lucky. Naturally, I would feel nothing. Something would happen pretty soon, sparing me impotence, senility, loneliness, arthritis, and bad breath.

As we descended into the smoky, rushing L.A. dusk, with the reptilian coil of freeways rippling like golden boas underneath us, I momentarily stopped believing in my own fantasy. Maybe I was not going to die suddenly. Maybe I was just going to get old.

Going to New York had been a mistake. Lots of people go away for a week and come home and step right back into their lives. That was the normally normal way. Having once been normal, I had even done it that way myself; but not this time. My life had no more permanence than a movie set. Turn your back for two minutes and someone would hitch it to a tractor and pull it to another part of the lot. It was a collapsible, storefront life, because it was without hope, the brick and mortar of any life.

I don't mean to say that I lived in despair, like the victims of tragedy. No—my life was without despair, too. I had no pain, and not even a specific sadness, but somewhere along the way I had lost the habit of hope. Everything I did was a repeat; I hadn't the energy for anything new. Page would waltz off soon. I wouldn't be able to stop her, and probably wouldn't even try. In all likelihood she would be the last. She was perfect, though she would never believe it, and I doubted that I could accommodate myself to anyone who wasn't. *Basta*! Enough of fucking. Let the stem droop.

Then we roared over the back of one of the golden boas, half hidden in its swamp of dusk and smog, and touched down. We were home, what was left of us. Jill was very quiet, and so was I, possessed all of a sudden by the sense of age. It seemed we would never get through the egg-white tunnel that led to the lobby. A driver met us, bags were secured, and we became one of the scales on the serpent of cars.

"There's something I want to ask you," Jill said as we turned onto the San Diego Freeway. "How come you're always fucking other men's wives?"

I was surprised. "Are you planning to come to the defense of the nuclear family?" I asked.

"No, I just want to understand that one thing about you," she said.

"I wasn't that way my whole life, you know. I came to it late."

"That doesn't tell me why," she said.

"Because I don't want all of anybody any more," I said. "I only want the parts that nobody else is using. Most married women are half unused—maybe more than half, I don't know. The unused parts usually turn out to be the most interesting parts, for some reason."

We rode for a while.

"Anyway, part of somebody is really more interesting than all of somebody," I said. "Certainly part of me is enough for anyone. I'm fun for two hours but a week of me is damn boring."

Jill listened, but I couldn't tell what she was thinking. We were cruising up La Brea.

"I don't know why we're talking like this," I said. "This is your town, for the time being, you know. I hope you plan to enjoy it while it's yours."

"How long will it be mine?" she asked.

"About six weeks. If you're lucky you'll get an office with its own bathroom."

"Lulu Dickey asked me to do a picture," she said. "Leon O'Reilly's producing it. A Western of some kind."

"Oh, yeah," I said. "I know about it. With Duke Wayne and Kate Hepburn. I can do better than that. I can offer you an actual script."

I opened my briefcase and pulled out *The Rosebud of Love*. Despite good intentions, I had yet to crack its covers. I handed it to Jill.

"Where'd you get that?" she asked.

"It's a by-product of your premiere," I said.

"Oh. What's it about?"

"Da Bronx," I said.

It was only early evening as we made our way up into the hills. The sight of the purple sky over the familiar palms reminded me that we were in California again, California where autumn never comes. We put the windows down. Instead of the chill wind, whirling like a saw, there was the swish of sprinklers from the warm lawns.

"I guess he better let me off at my house first," Jill said. "I have to meet somebody."

There was in her eyes that look—I'd seen it a thousand times—of a woman with a new prospect. It brought a sharpness, a touch of incipience, not merely carnal but not wholly of the spirit either. Most of all, it was self-pleased. To see it in Jill, who had spent her life dissatisfied with herself, was very gratifying, much as I disapproved of the slob who had prompted the look. Her eyes shone the way Page's did when things were perfect. She was coming home keen about something, and for once it wasn't just more work. I had never seen her look so expectant.

I put no questions to the look. Whatever had happened or was about to, she was concentrating on it hungrily, assuredly, inscrutably. I had a feeling that I had better scoot on out of the way.

I helped the driver carry her bags up the steps, waited for her to extract her keys, and gave her a hug before scooting.

"Oh, Joe," she said, managing to focus on me for just a moment. "I'm sorry I was so cutting. I'm very grateful you went. I'm not sure I would have gone if you hadn't."

"Fiddle," I said, and went to the car.

The skinny little driver, who hadn't said a word once he introduced himself, suddenly said a word.

"Know da lady long?" he asked.

"Yeah, quite a while," I said.

"A nice lady," he said. "Believe me, I know a nice lady when I see one come down da pike. Real nice, this one. She never criticized da drivin' once. Jesus, I drove for Miss Solaré when they made *Fancy Pants* and I got this bleeding ulcer. Fuckin' thing bled for a year, all because of her. You think she's got consideration?—forget it. Not her and not that punk she's goin' to bed with. I miss a light takin' her home an' that punk would call me names, Jesus."

"Where you from, buddy?" I asked.

"Da Bronx, originally," he said. "I was Mr. Mond's driver in New Yoik, in da old days. You know, the forties, you know. He was there a lot, in the forties. Pretty soon he wouldn't let nobody else drive him, because I was so smooth, ya know, no bumps. Mr. Mond don't like da bumps. So one day, forty-seven it was, he says, 'Bernie, go pack da bags, you're goin' west.' My missus was game, so dat was dat. I been his poisonal driver ever since. Of course it took me some time to learn da town."

Instead of looking like a root he looked like a fence post, that thin and straight in his black suit. There should have been wires running out of his ears. But he knew the town. He put me at my doorstep, and I live in a one-block cul-de-sac.

"How is Mr. Mond these days?" I asked as I was unloading.

"I worry about him," Bernie said. "He sits in da sun. Don't go to da office no more. Sits in da sun, and he's already too brown. So I don't have much driving to do. Mostly just like tonight—trips to da airport to pick up da dignitaries.

"But he ain't slippin'," Bernie added, as if worried that he might have given the appearance of disloyalty. "Mr. Mond, he keeps up. He reads da trades, ya know, an' all day by da pool he's gettin' calls. Still got his hearing, too. He can hear a pin drop."

"My name's Percy," I said. "I used to write for him once in a while. Give him my best."

"Poicy, when was that?" he asked.

"In the old days," I said. "He'll remember."

"Aw, Mr. Mond, does he have a memory," Bernie said. " 'Bernie, maybe we'll take a trip to the East an' just drive around, da both of us,' he said the other day. 'Da pastrami ain't so good out here. I'd like a real sandwich before I die.' Gives me the shivers to hear it, ya know? I mean, New Yoik, I've forgotten da town. I'd get lost comin' in from da airport. But Mr. Mond, he's still got in mind a place on Eighth Avenue where he likes da pickles. Dat's a memory."

He tipped his hat, and the long dark car slid away into the night.

I had never thought to hear myself send salutations to Aaron Mondschiem—either age had mellowed me, or the melancholy of homecoming had weakened me. His house was only about a mile above mine—he was probably sitting up there under a sunlamp, getting littler and littler and browner and browner as he peered at the trades, the telegrams, the reports from the studio, trying to hang on to it all for a little longer.

I dumped my bags on the living room floor and got a drink and took it out on my patio. My conviction, which had been slipping for three thousand miles, continued to slip. Jill was about to get involved, Page would soon be on the wing, and my old chum Patsy Fairchild had divorced and moved to the north. Most of my drinking buddies were either dead already or so busy trying to hang on to the woman of the moment that they had no time to drink.

Probably I should go look for a woman my own age and make a companionable marriage, but I wasn't going to. In the last few years I had fallen into bad habits, such as making out with young women, all of them absurdly easy to impress. I probably couldn't impress a mature woman any more, and what's more, I didn't care. The daily sparring, jockeying, redressing, the little advances and setbacks of marriage, the necessity of dealing with a person when one barely felt like dealing with a game of solitaire, the Saturday night fuck and the Sunday afternoon drives to the beach: I just didn't want it. Solitude was like the winds of New York: it might singe the cheeks but it also quickened the blood, mine anyway. Pump a little alcohol into solitude and it could make one witty and wry.

As I sat by my midget pool, a pale-blue kidney bean in my back yard—two strokes got you across it—I felt like I had floated free of everything, or that everything had dropped away from me, even memory, the last thing to go. I didn't want to die, but I had to admit to a diminished interest in living. Not for me either ebb or flood—I was living in a kind of midness, kept going mostly by curiosity about my friends.

The house no longer even reminded me of Claudia: of her movements, her confident voice and even more confident ways. Fourteen years had passed, time enough for even those memories to leak out under the door. Old Claudia, my tiger woman, my jungle queen, only visited me in dreams now and then—I didn't hear her in the bedroom, modestly changing clothes behind the closet door, any more. Her ghost, like the ghosts of the Stravinskys, was a rare visitor now, good only for a drippy hour of drinking and snuffling in front of the TV late at night. I did remember how her eyes used to cut sideways whenever the name of one of her boyfriends—two of them stunt men, one a grip—came up at parties.

But then, eyes are always the easiest things to remember, eyes and smells—if one is speaking of women, that is, because the smells of women are as individual as sauces: some smell cool as crocks, others as hot as bricks in the sun or babies in fever; some chaste women always smell slightly musky, and some constant and incontinent fuckers have odorless bodies but somehow manage to leave the covers smelling of milkweed and damp sponges.

I used to imagine that I would sit down someday and write a book called *Remembering Women*, or *Women Remembered*, or *For the Love of Ladies*, or something like that, but despite my frequent fantasizing about it, I was never able to come up with a really good title, much less the book itself. Anyway, I had stopped wanting to be a Proust of women. I didn't even particularly want to remember them, not any more. As memory atrophies, so does desire. Homecoming is heart-hurting, and it was easier and just as much fun to remember the men I had known—those guys whose boyish laughter, in a hundred or a thousand bars, had been the background music for my life in Hollywood. It had been punctuated often, I admit, interrupted by sighings and shriekings, sobbing, querulousness and teeth-clicking—the general incessancies of women—but eventually, after the interruption, there remained the men and the bars.

It came to me that I could always call that old one-eyed fucker Bruno Himmel and get him out this very night, to drink and talk over the old days, when both of us had done much of our work for the terrible Tony Maury. In those days there was nothing we had to take seriously. Like many a man who doesn't know what to do with himself after work except womanize, Bruno was always happy to be invited to escape the ladies for a little while.

But even after three drinks I still felt disquiet. Staring into the blue-green water of my little pool didn't hypnotize me, and drinking good Scotch didn't fuzz me much. For a while a grainy moon was visible above the crest of the hill, a moon the color of oatmeal, probably dulled by high-lying smog. I couldn't get Jill out of mind—my daughter, neighbor, pet, chum, conscience, and last love. I liked to think of her, with her headshakes, her clear eyes, and her abruptness, as the most lucid of women. Maybe she was lucid, but she was also talent-cursed. All of us are born to die, but only a few are born to work, and Jill was one of the few. I wasn't, and so I had never had to try to balance work with love. What I was good at was chases: Nazis after gallant Resistance fighters, posses after horse thieves, leopards after lost white maidens whose planes, fortunately, had crashed near Tarzan's tree house. Now I was down to stalwart linemen and endangered bear cubs, but the quality of the product, and of the effort, had not really changed.

But Jill was the real thing. She wasn't great, but neither was she cheap. Hers *was* the madness of monks. How had I let that Goth get into her life? Of course she would rush to exchange her lonely madness and lovely lines for something cheaper and more common. Nothing was more natural. Probably all those who live for work imagine that love will someday arrive and save them from it. Jill should get to feel like a woman for a while, even if it didn't work out—and how could it work out, with Owen Oarson?

I felt a poor guardian, which was totally irrational but a hard feeling to shake. After living with the feeling for three-quarters of an hour, I went in and called Anna Lyle, thinking she might be home and bored, but nope, not home, so for the hell of it I called Bruno. The phone rang a few times and then he answered. In his brusque, continental way, he merely said "Who?" Then he breathed loudly into the receiver. "Moon Over Miami" was on his phonograph, probably his idea of seduction music. Bruno was even more dated than me—the thought cheered me up a little.

"Poked out your other eye yet?" I said, knowing that he liked it—as he always said—"straight from the elbow."

Effort to explain that the phrase was "straight from the shoulder" got nowhere with Bruno.

"Ah, Joey," he said. "Straight from the elbow. How many balls you still got?"

"It's not the motor, it's the spark plugs," I said elliptically. "Let's go have a drink."

"Oh, my old friend," Bruno said. I sensed a dilemma, and listened to "Moon Over Miami" for a bit as he pondered it.

"But of course, Joey," he said, smoothly and confidently, a moment later. "After all, you move to Rome, I don't get to Rome, so how long has it been, ten year, twelve year, I only get news from Tony Maury, and you know he is crazy. I will come—half an hour maybe. Where you want to meet?"

"The Honeysuckle," I said.

"Of course, Joey," he said. "Ah, the old days. Dietrich—where you got sick on the Pernod. You could never drink, Joey."

His little act must not have been too convincing, because I heard a girlish voice say, "Fucker," not softly either, before I hung up the phone. I guess it takes more than an eye patch to fool the young these days.

I opened a bag, but I didn't want to unpack. I just took out my trusty green overcoat and hung it back out to pasture in the closet; with any luck it would never have to work again. Then I put on some checks: sport coat, houndstooth pants, polka-dot shirt, blue neckerchief, and a tweedy little hat John Ford had given me because it didn't fit him. I lingered on my porch a minute, smelling the night. The kids next door had the stereo turned up and music floated over the hedge:

> Everybody's gone a-waay,
> Says they're movin' to L.A.aa . . . aa . . . a . . .

It was about a good-time Charlie who had the blues. After I listened to it for a while I dragged my hose out of the garage and turned on my sprinklers. The water fell gently on the sunburned grass, and the sweet smell of dust and wet grass rose from my lawn.

> My ol' heart keeps tellin' me,
> Not a kid at thirty-three . . .

Make that sixty-three. I set the sprinkler near the hedges and turned the hose down low, then set off along the bluish street, the worldly screenwriter returning from a casual jaunt to New York. The melancholy song had cheered me somehow. I was a good-time Charlie myself, and I was already in L.A., so whoever had left wherever the song was about ought to arrive pretty soon and keep me company.

Meanwhile, I would frequent my old haunts. One light was on at Jill's, the one she always left on, over her forsaken drawing board. Bruno and I would sit in the Honeysuckle, actually a horseplayer's bar on North Wilcox—it had never seen Dietrich, and they wouldn't know Pernod from shoe polish. We would drain many a glass, Bruno and I. We would pretend it was London, the Blitz; I should have worn my ascot. Bruno, of course, would be pretending he was overhead in a Messerschmitt, helping to bomb the Limeys—he had once, in fact, thrown a defused grenade at Carol Reed and gotten fired for his trouble—and while he was pretending to be having it out with the R.A.F. I would pretend to be in a bunker with a pretty nurse, someone on the order of Anna Neagle or Virginia McKenna.

The blue street curved downward under the silent palms—an empty desert river: Lee Marvin should have been dragging a mule across it, with a wounded comrade, or maybe Claudia Cardinale, tied to the mule. I strolled cheerily on downhill, expecting at any moment the fatal skateboard, the one going ninety around a curve with no lights; or, if not that, then the leopard, the Nazi, the kamikaze diving for the aircraft carrier through clouds of flak; or the bullet, ricocheting off the boulder; or the quicksand; or the croc that could swim faster than anybody but Johnny Weissmuller (since I was the faithful gunbearer, not the pretty girl, no danger of my getting saved); or the sudden loss of balance, the waving arms, the long fall over the cliff; or the school bus careening downhill (someone had cut the brake-lines), smushed like old Max Maryland; or, most likely of all, the evil teenager, the dope freak, sniper, or psycho, crouched in a eucalyptus tree with his slingshot and his poison pellets. It was all right—I wasn't worried. It's a fast town, never long at a loss for an ending. The oatmeal moon had disappeared, probably to go shine over Miami. Bruno was probably already there, already drunk. I didn't care. Everyone was busy now. All it would take was a gimmick—Hollywood would think of something. The guest at the party, though he had loved the party—those toothy girls, those puzzled drunks—really sort of felt like getting home.

Book II

CHAPTER 1

JILL was idiotic about the past. She had a thing about old men, fucking bores, most of them, big drinkers and big talkers. I couldn't stand any of them. The cameraman on *Womanly Ways*, old Henley Bowditch, was one of the worst.

The morning after the Oscars she woke up and started moaning about him. The picture had won three Oscars, which would have satisfied most people, but of course old Henley didn't get one, so it didn't satisfy her. "He's too old," she kept saying. "He won't get another chance. They should have given it to him. My god, think of the pictures he's done!"

I couldn't have named two of Henley Bowditch's pictures if my ass had depended on it, but of course Jill remembered about thirty. She sat up in bed and went on talking about it. "He *needed* it!" she said. "I didn't need it, I already had one.

They gave me a *writing* award, for god's sake. I'm not a writer!"

"Will you fuck off?" I said. "He didn't get an Oscar because he's mediocre. He's always been mediocre, or he would have had one by now. He ought to be out where I came from, making demonstration films for Massey-Harris tractors."

She stopped talking and looked at me.

"So far as I'm concerned, you can hang Henley Bowditch and Joe Percy on the same clothesline," I said. "And seven or eight others to boot. None of them were ever any good."

Her face turned red. "You're telling me about filmmaking?" she said. "You *were* selling tractors three years ago, as I remember. How'd you learn it all so quick?"

"I don't know it all," I said. "I just know a hack when I see one."

She got redder. "Henley Bowditch is not a hack," she said. "You owe me an apology."

She got out of bed and picked up her party dress and party shoes. She held them in front of her, waiting. I didn't say a word. She knew my views on apologies. When she saw I wasn't going to say anything, she yanked off her nightgown, yanked on her party dress, stuffed the nightgown in her purse, and looked around the apartment like she might have been thinking of gathering up all her belongings, but of course she didn't. She started for the door, not looking at me at all.

"Don't forget your Oscar," I said. "It's too bad you can't fuck it."

She grabbed it off the bureau and threw it at me, an awkward throw. Oscar hit the wall about three yards from the bed. Jill was too mad to talk. She went on out, her blue nightgown hanging out of her purse.

I guess I have a bad mouth. I always go too far. I just never feel like stopping where most people would stop.

It *was* kind of a surprise that Jill and Pete Sweet won the writing Oscar. Toole Peters, the most hot-shit screenwriter in town, was really pissed, because he had actually done a partial rewrite for them, out of friendship for Pete. That had been years ago, when he wasn't so hot-shit, so he got no credit and not much money. His adaptation of *Momma Sang Bass* was nominated in the other writing category, but it didn't win either, which was fine with me. Toole was one of the worst little pricks in Hollywood, him and his fucking suede jacket. He thought he knew everything, and he was fucking a girl named Raven Dexter who was just as snotty as he was. She had worked for the *New Yorker* once, so she knew everything, too. She came to the Oscars dressed in squaw clothes, because she and Toole were trying to help Marlon Brando drum up some interest in the plight of the American Indian. Raven drummed and drummed but the only thing she could get anybody interested in was fucking her.

I got up and walked over to the window in time to see Jill come out of my apartment building and start walking up Sunset. Her gown looked like it was going to fall out of her purse. While I was watching her the phone rang. Naturally it was Lulu.

"Any progress?" she asked. "Or have I called at a bad time? Eek. I bet she's still there."

"Nope," I said.

"What's that mean?"

"Nope, she's not here, and nope, there's been no progress."

"You're a slow sonofabitch," she said. "I want to know why the fuck you haven't pushed it. When do you mean to put in a word for me?"

I told her once that maybe I'd talk Jill into using her, but I hadn't bothered. I didn't bother to answer either.

"Listen, Owen, you're not any fuckin' Irving Thalberg yet," she said. "Just because your girl friend made a small winner don't mean you own Hollywood. I can get her a nice deal right now, with maybe a job in it for you, but if you fuck around much longer, I dunno. These things are liquid, you know. They can evaporate."

I let her rant for a while. When she finally hung up I put the phone on the hook and it rang before I could get my hand off it. This time it was old Mondschiem.

"Good morning, Mr. Mondschiem," I said. "I bet you're feeling good today."

"I got a liver that's not so good," he said in that growl of his. He sounded like a sick bulldog.

"I dunno, I think a rat bit it," he said. "Fucking liver. May I have a word with my sweethoit?"

"Mr. Mondschiem, she just left," I said. "You just missed her. She just went out the door."

"Sonny, it ain't my ear the rat bit," he said. "Do I need a message three times? She's gone, she's gone! Where's a nice girl like my sweethoit at this time of the morning?"

"She runs," I said. "Jogs. Likes to keep in shape." The old fucker always made me nervous.

"Jogs?" he said. The bulldog sounded sicker. "My sweethoit? With no security men? And what the hell do you do, lay on your ass? She could meet a rapist, you know. I know it ain't bad here like New Yoik, but that don't mean it's a good rural place, if you know what I mean."

He grumbled for a while and I was nice as pie. "I thought you was some kind of foimer," he said. "Texas or someplace. I thought foimers get up early."

When he got through grumbling I went in to shave and Bo Brimmer called. "Ah'm just callin' to express my congratulations," he said. "Ah was hoping for a word with Miss Jill."

"She took off a few minutes ago," I said. "Anything I can do for you?"

"You can come to lunch if you're free," he said.

That surprised me. "Just me?" I asked.

"Just you. I'll catch up with Miss Jill later."

"I'm free."

"Fine," he said. "Come about one. We'll slip off somewhere an' gnaw a bone."

Maybe he heard that I was going to be working with Jill for a while, or maybe he was scared of her or something and wanted to get me to help him with her, like Lulu did. I told the answering service to take the rest of the calls. Every agent in town would be calling up to tout their scripts, and all Jill's washed-out friends would be wanting to rattle off their latest story ideas. Let the service deal with it.

I got dressed and strolled off to Schwab's to have some pineapple and read the trades. I know it was old-fashioned, but it was handy, and the pineapple was good. When I sold my stock in the tractor company and left Lubbock I had about forty thousand dollars, and I had been in Hollywood two years and still had thirty thousand of them. The ten had gone for options on two screenplays. One of them still might pan out, if I could get Jill to work on it a little. Mostly I lived off poker, which is easy to do in a town full of people who think they're hot-shit gamblers. I didn't have an office or a secretary, but I had the classiest Mercedes in town, '59 coupé, butter-colored, also thanks to poker.

While I was eating my pineapple a girl came in and sat down a few stools away. When I glanced at her, her face was turned away from me and all I could see was her hair. Her hair was done like Farrah Fawcett-Majors', but I knew right away she wasn't Farrah. Too big. I could tell from the way her back looked, under her T-shirt. Also her hair was a little too orange. Then she turned to speak to the waitress and I saw that her nose was as crooked as a corkscrew. It's amazing the number of gorgeous backs that walk around Hollywood, attached to crooked noses and ugly chins. You can stand on Hollywood Boulevard any day of the week, and if you just watch the asses and the legs, you'll think you're in ass heaven. The mistake is ever looking at the faces.

Even with the crooks in her nose the girl at the counter wasn't so bad. She was big, at least, and sort of steaming with health. It comes off these big California girls like vapor. This one glugged down three glasses of orange juice, which meant she wasn't too worried about money. They don't give away orange juice out here in the land of the orange. I guess she felt me looking at her, because she turned and gave me a pretty direct once-over. Maybe, if I'd tried, I could have worked out a little sex-brunch, but I let it slide. I knew a lot of women like her: fresh, full of health food and vitamins. She probably spent half her time backpacking, and she probably did a hundred push-ups a day. Those big California girls had an athletic attitude toward everything, particularly fucking. No quickies for them. If they weren't going to jog three or four miles, or surf for hours, or bicycle out to Malibu and back, then they wanted to work it all off in the sack. It was like fucking lady gym teachers. If you don't do enough push-ups to suit them you're in trouble.

That was fine. Those big rangy girls were one reason for living in California, but this time I had other things to do. I had to get my suit pressed, for one thing, but I still kept looking at all that body. I also liked the remote, dumb look in the girl's eyes. Jill was too skinny and too smart, and she had been horny too long. She fell in love with me before I could stop her. It was all too personal, with her. I would have appreciated a little stupidity, or a little boredom or something, but I never got it. She was too keyed in—I couldn't fart without her wanting to know what the fart meant. After six months of that, fucking a big brainless beach baby would be relaxing.

When I stepped behind the big orange-haired girl she was leaning over the counter, whispering something to the waitress. Her T-shirt had pulled out of her jeans, exposing some nice bumpy vertebrae. I could see right down her jeans to the hollow of her ass. Hollywood *is* ass heaven. Asses like volleyballs, with just the right bounce. Up in the Midwest women have asses like feedsacks. Probably why I never could stand the Midwest.

I went home and got my gray suit and took it to the corner laundry and stood around while they pressed it. It wouldn't do to have a meeting with Bo Brimmer in a wrinkled suit. Even so, I didn't put the girl at the lunch counter out of my mind. Maybe she'd show up someday when I didn't have a meeting. It was pleasant to give that possibility some thought. There's no better time to think about fucking than when you've got a chance to make a little money, and I guess Bo Brimmer meant to offer me a chance to make a little money. Otherwise he would just have left a message for Jill and hung up the phone.

CHAPTER 2

STUDIO gate men are usually either toothpicks or sides of beef. The one at Universal was a side of beef. He was friendly and respectful—they always are—and he soon found my name on his list and let me in, but I would have enjoyed running over his fat ass, to tell the truth. It's easy to develop a hate thing for gate men if you deal with them every day. They have minds like prison guards, and in their eyes the very fact that you want to enter the fucking studio grounds makes you guilty until some secretary or some asshole executive proves you innocent. They look at you like you were probably a fucking terrorist. The studio is theirs, not yours, and they never let you forget it.

If I had a studio, I'd hire ex-cons to be gate men—give them a chance to get their own back.

It was a nice day in the Valley. For once the smog had gone somewhere else. I got past a couple of receptionists and made it to checkpoint three, which was Bo's secretary, a big Georgia girl named Carly something. There were a lot of stories about her being black belt in karate and all that. If some thug went after little Bo, Carly would chop him into hamburger. She was also smooth as cream. She gave me one glance and sent me right on in.

"He's expecting you, Mr. Oarson," she said. She had the build of a Bourbon Street stripper—her tits probably outweighed her boss.

"I hope I'm not early," I said politely. No stud numbers today.

Bo Brimmer was on the phone when I went in. His eyes were bright as buttons and his desk was so big he could have taken a nap in any one of its drawers. He reached up a tiny hand, shook mine, and pointed to the bar. I got some Scotch. The office was full of contemporary California art, most of which was creepo junk. There was a realistic mud puddle, evidently some kind of sculpture, right in the middle of the floor. That was bad enough, but there was also a big woolly wall hanging, some bread sculpture, and a strange scaly aluminum thing sort of stacked in one corner. I preferred to look out of the big plate-glass windows. Some helicopters were buzzing around the tops of the mountains. Probably cops chasing down a freak of some kind.

"Sorry 'bout that, Owen," Bo said, when he finally hung up. "Little problem over in Rome. Elephant went berserk and smashed up a cinemobile."

"An elephant?"

"Yep," Bo said. "The I-talian army's after him. He's been smashing up monuments left and right."

He picked up a pencil and thoughtfully chewed the eraser off it. Evidently it was his relaxation, because his desk top was littered with pencils he had done it to. He even had a little china bowl where he spit the erasers.

"You know Tony Maury, don't you?" he asked. "I wish the fuckin' elephant had trampled *him*. I don't know who the fuck is gonna want to see a movie called *The Doom of Rome*, anyway. It's gonna be the doom of Universal if we don't do something quick. They started this one while ah was still at Metro—ah nevah did think it had a chance."

"I'll go see it," I said. "I like that kind of stuff."

"Universal is grateful for your support," he said, flipping a dead pencil into a wastebasket. He pressed a button and spoke into a box.

"Carly, deah, get us a car," he said. Then he picked a red pencil out of a glass of pencils and nipped the eraser off it. He gathered up the eraserless pencils and dumped them in the wastebasket.

"Ah don't care, honey," he said into the box. "Just a car. One of them things that runs down the street."

Then he looked at me, selected another pencil, and drummed it on the edge of his desk. "Chewin' up pencils, what have ah come to?" he said.

"Well, you do a good Southern accent," I said, thinking that might be what he wanted to hear.

"Sure do," he said, with no accent. "Of course, I wanted to be an actor, you know. If I had just kept on growing, I would have been an actor, but it was not my ambition to be the Mickey Rooney of my generation."

The phone jingled. Instead of just ringing, it started playing the theme from *Burning Deck*. Bo grabbed it like it was hot, said "Yup," and slammed it down again.

"Not my idea," he said, meaning the theme. "Let's go eat."

The car that was waiting for us was a green Plymouth, and the driver was old and bald-headed. He looked like a Slav.

"Claude-Edmonde's," Bo said to the baldhead.

"I apologize for not taking the Rolls," he said. "When I do that the young execs follow me. Then they pretend they just happened to show up at the same place. I can't enjoy my vittles with a lot of ass-lickers around."

The bald-headed driver, who had not said a word, drove straight out of the gate without slowing down. Evidently he hated gate men too. Bo nearly swallowed a pencil he was so surprised.

"Did you see that?" he said. "He didn't stop at the gate."

"Too much stop signs," the driver said. He didn't sound like he was apologizing.

Claude-Edmonde's turned out to be a yellow French restaurant on Ventura Boulevard. The napkins were the color of mustard. A lot of TV people were there, all of them wearing three-piece suits. They all looked nervous—probably some big job shuffle was in progress. If I had been running a network I would have farmed them all out in a minute to places like Biloxi and Utica.

Bo had reserved a semi-private room for our little talk. The table was laid for five. Before I had my knees under it good, Lulu Dickey sauntered in, with Toole Peters and Swan Bunting tagging along behind her. The maître d' bobbed along in their wake, like a fucking penguin. Lulu had a kind of horsey sense of fashion—she was wearing some puffed-up peasant stuff. Toole and Swan were in the usual celebrity sloppy. Toole had on his suede jacket and Swan wore a Wonder Wart Hog T-shirt and dirty jeans.

"Man, why are we eating here?" Swan said as soon as he got in earshot of Bo. "I *told* you about this place. The escargot sucks, believe me. Sherry didn't like them at all. I think they contributed to her stomach problems."

Bo was unimpressed. "For youah informashun, Swan, we own this restaurant," Bo said. "That's how come it's sitting heah on Venturah Boulevard instead of bein' in Ly-on, where it belongs. We bought it so we'd have some place to feed those of ouah guests who have an appreciashun of fine cuisine. If you don't like it you can haul youah sloppy ass off to the taco stand of youah choice."

"Fuck, don't be Southern with me," Swan said. He took a chair and flicked his napkin open expertly. He didn't give me so much as a glance.

"You boys, you boys," Lulu said. "You have to be nice. I can't eat a bite if there's animosity around me. I get so worried my throat contracts an' nothing'll go through."

"You'll be lucky not to starve to death, then," Bo said.

"I didn't know we were eating here," Toole said. "I could have brought Raven. Raven loves French food." He took off his sunglasses and put them in his coat. His eyes were the color of soapy water.

"This gentleman is Owen Oarson," Bo said. "Swan Bunting, Toole Peters. Lulu you know."

Toole unfolded his napkin so carefully that he might have been doing a fucking ballet. He knew me from some poker games, so he nodded. Swan didn't bother.

"They better have watercress," Swan said. "If they don't have watercress, I'm kicking some ass."

"Your refinement astonishes us all," Bo said. "I do wish I'd got to go to the fucking Sorbonne."

"Listen, Bo, you better watch it," Swan said. "Sherry's never going through the Universal gate again unless you shut that up."

"Oh, you boys," Lulu said. "Swan just got up on the wrong side of the bed this morning. He's just a little down."

"Fucking the top cunt must be tiring," I said. My evil mouth got the best of me. Swan—who hadn't given me a second glance—gave me a second glance.

"What kind of punk remark is that?" he asked.

Bo Brimmer grinned over his bow tie. Maybe my remark had surprised him pleasantly. Maybe he *would* give me a job. It was high time somebody did. I had been showing up at big-deal events and eating shit for about as long as I meant to. Bumping into Jill when I did had been my first piece of luck, but that had been nearly six months ago. It was time for something else to happen. If insulting Swan Bunting was the way to make it happen, that was fine with me. There was nobody in town I'd rather insult.

"Who does this sonofabitch think he's talking to?" Swan said, addressing himself to Bo. "Who said you could invite him? Did Sherry say it? Did I say it? We said you could invite Jill, not him!"

"Be a shade less imperial, if you don't mind, Mr. Bunting," Bo said. "You're not my social arbiter. I still retain the privilege of chosing my own luncheon guests."

"Not if you want to make a deal with us," Swan said. "I don't go for this shit, not at all. I don't even like the restaurant, much less *this* asshole. What the fuck kind of thinking went into this?"

Toole Peters grinned. "Ever since he learned how to talk to pricks and pussies he's been a little vulgar," he said.

"You keep the fuck out of this, Toole," Lulu said. "I can't stand such animosity. My throat is closing up already. I won't be able to eat a bite."

"Maybe Swan will spoon you some gruel," Toole said, blinking his soapy little eyes.

Swan snapped his fingers loudly and the maître d' came bobbing over. "Phone," Swan said. "Sherry's gonna hear about this right now."

"No phones, Monsieur," the maître d' said nervously.

"No phones?" Swan said. It was the worst shock yet.

"There's a pay phone in the men's room," the maître d' said.

Swan shook his head is disbelief. "Man, this is the worst," he said. "You brought me to a place where I can't even get a *phone*? Sherry's not going to believe this."

"*Merci*, Jean," Bo said, waving the maître d' away.

"That's it, we're leaving," Swan said, getting up. "Universal can fuckin' kiss ass."

He stalked off without a backward glance and was all the way across the restaurant before he realized that Lulu and Toole were still sitting at the table. "Hey, you two, let's move it!" he yelled, startling the TV types almost out of their vests.

"I hate it when he's loud," Lulu said. "I just hate it."

Toole Peters simply ignored Swan and continued to study his menu. He blinked while he studied it. Maybe that was why I didn't like him. He was always blinking.

"Isn't it about time Sherry got a new boyfriend?" Bo asked. I had been thinking along that line myself.

"Oh, she likes 'em loud," Lulu said. "If they're not loud, she forgets they're there, and you know she can't stand to be alone."

Swan went out the door but in about two minutes he came stalking back to the table.

"You probably hired this goon to insult me so you could work out the deal with Lulu," he said. "Your little trick isn't going to work."

"If your problem's cab fare, I'll loan it to you," I said.

He looked like he wanted to hit me, but I'm very big and he didn't. "ARE YOU COMING?" he yelled at Lulu, and stalked out again.

"I think I'll have the trout almondine and have them scrape off the fuckin' almonds," Toole said. "I can't stand almonds."

The restaurant had gotten very quiet while Swan was roaming around, but in a few minutes, when it became obvious that he wasn't coming back, everybody started talking again. The maître d' approached Bo. He looked a little guilty.

"Monsieur Brimmer, there *is* a phone in the men's room," he said.

"*Ce n'est rien,* Jean," Bo said. "*Ce n'est rien.*"

After that, we all had a nice meal. There was some general talk about Jill directing a picture written by Toole and starring Sherry Solaré, and I made agreeable sounds, but it was all just general talk. Toole said he *might* write it, and Lulu said Sherry *might* star in it if she could get about three million up front, and I said Jill *might* be interested. Bo even said he *might* know just the story. Lulu managed to put down a healthy chunk of veal, despite her throat, and Toole picked around on a trout for about an hour.

On the drive back to the studio Bo was quiet. I guess he was out of pencils, because he nibbled on the earpiece of his glasses. The bald-headed Slav once again went through the studio gate without touching his brake pedal.

"Come up for a minute," Bo said. Carly was still there, alone with her bosom.

"Switch that driver to the lawnmower crew or something," Bo told her. "We can't have drivers just ignoring the sentries like that."

"Oh, hell, you must have got Gregor," she said. "I told them not to give you Gregor. He was a stunt driver, you know. He's the one who drove the car off the building, in *Scrap Happy*."

Bo's swivel chair had a motor in it that raised him to whatever height he wanted to be. He raised himself about a foot and looked me in the eye.

"We come and go, we men of ambition," he said. "We make mistakes and fail, or we get too rich and atrophy. Between the two, failure and atrophy, I think I would prefer failure, but maybe not. One thing I do know is that I'd hate to end up with my immediate peers as my sole companions. How would you like to go to Rome?"

"Why?" I asked.

"You're from Texas. You know those two Texans, don't you? Elmo and Winfield?"

He meant Elmo Buckle and Winfield Gohagen, a supposedly crack screenwriting team. They lived out in Tujunga Canyon, with a retinue of rodeo hands, jocks, dope people, guitar-pickers, and stringy-haired ladies. The retinue was so large that the area they lived in had come to be known as Little Austin. I had known them for years, not well, but well enough. They spent money like water and were very genial, except when they got violent.

"I know them," I said. "I get along with them fine."

"Well, they aren't really the problem," Bo said, "although it wouldn't hurt if they'd finish the script. Tony Maury is the problem. That old turd is ineradicable, or unflushable, or something. He's over there wasting ten million dollars of our money because he likes to watch people chase one another around in chariots. He likes to see horses run and buildings fall down, and he likes to make people throw knives and have them jump through windows."

He thought about it for a minute. "Of course they're all just alike," he said, "all directors. That's what they all like. Shit, I don't care, Bergman, Truffaut, I don't care who you pick, give them unlimited money and they'll make *Ben Hur*."

"So what would I be supposed to do?"

He looked at me with his little head tilted to one side. I think he was about to feed me a line of bullshit but he changed his mind. "You're supposed to take Jill," he said. "She probably needs a vacation. Just lead her to him and turn them loose together. If anybody can persuade him to finish the picture, it would probably be her.

"You may not know it, but you're fortunate in your woman," he added.

"That's all?" I said.

"Not quite," he said. "I've thought of a little backup idea. I'm sending a couple of kids over there to do a little documentary on the shooting of this epic. Maybe just videotape, I don't know. That kind of thing is big right now and we could maybe use it as a trailer. You want to be a producer—start by producing that. Who knows? It might make more money than *The Doom of Rome*."

"The timing's a little funny," I said. "Now's the time Jill ought to be making a deal on her next picture."

"I'm not sending you to Rome to live," he said. "I very much hope to see that picture wrapped in no more than six weeks. You can nudge those Texans and oversee the kids, and Jill can work her magic on Tony Maury. I doubt either one of you has anything better to do.

"Besides, maybe I'll have something shaped up with Sherry by the time you get back," he added.

"I'll have to talk to Jill," I said. "I'll get back to you."

"Don't study it too hard," Bo said. "It's just a spot of work. I want you over there quick, before that runaway elephant gives old Tony any ideas. He'll make those Texans write in Hannibal, and haul ass for the Alps, if we don't hurry."

Five minutes later I paused respectfully at the studio exit, and the side of beef, as friendly or friendlier than my grandad, waved me out.

CHAPTER 3

I drove through Laurel Canyon and went down to Hollywood Boulevard and had a couple of slow drinks. Hollywood Boulevard is a strip of sleaze, but I found it ideal for relaxing. Nobody from movies ever shows up there any more, which makes it a good place to have a drink.

I don't think Bo Brimmer gave a shit about movies—it was the brain game he enjoyed. He loved to set up those deals. I couldn't blame him. As a profession, what he did was about as precarious as wheat farming. He might raise a great crop of films, over there at Universal, and then watch them all wither in the theaters. My grandad shot himself because he finally got tired of watching wheat crops wither in the Texas sun, but Bo was a lot quicker on his feet than Grandad.

His offer was about the first thing in the way of a break that I'd had since I left the tractor company. So what if I only got it because I happened to be fucking Jill—or because I knew Elmo and Winfield? At least it was better than selling tractors. Being a PR man for a tractor company means going to every fucking county fair in the Midwest—for six years that was all I did. I hated the ugly, square-headed, shapeless people, in their poor clothes. There must be more shiny green suits in the Midwest than anywhere else in the world. I hated the airports too—all of them full of fish-faced salesmen drinking coffee out of styrofoam cups. If it hadn't been for a bad tendon, I could have spent those years in the pros. All the time I was bouncing around in the air, from ugly airport to ugly airport, wishing I hadn't had the injury, I was reading magazines. Magazines are always full of good-looking people, nothing like the boneheads you run into selling tractors. All Lubbock did for me was sharpen my poker. At least some real poker playing gets done in West Texas.

Now maybe I was finally going to get somewhere. All I had to do was talk Jill into going to Rome. It wouldn't hurt her, and after that she wouldn't have to do anything else for me, if she didn't want to. After that I could make my own breaks. I paid for my drinks and left.

Naturally she wasn't to be found. She had been to her bungalow—her purse was on the couch, with the nightgown still sticking out of it—but she wasn't there. I got myself a drink and looked through some of the scripts piled on the floor, but I soon got bored with that. Probably she was up at old Percy's, telling him what a prick I was. I suppose I should be grateful to the old fart, for drawing off so much of her yapping, but I wasn't. The better thing would be for her to learn to shut up. It was a little revolting, all that talk. I hate people telling me what they feel. All that squirming is sickening to hear. Squirming for money is one thing, money or recognition, but squirming for love is stupid. Nearly anybody can have love, only they don't know what to do with it once they get it. It's a worse waste of energy than jogging, or some tooty game like racquet ball.

I walked up the street. Old Joe was sitting on his front

porch, looking at one of his shoes. He had taken it off his smelly old foot. It was one of those shoes with the big gum soles.

"I thought these damn shoes would be good for my arches," he said. "God, they're ugly."

"Seen Jill?"

"Saw her on the tube last night," he said. "I guess she's been too drunk with success to make it up the hill."

"Aw, she probably went out to Anna's," I said. I went back down the hill and looked through the scripts some more. They were all rotten scripts. About eight, she finally came in. She was wearing tennis shoes—I didn't hear her until the front door shut.

"You certainly took your time," I said.

She came into the study without answering and sat on the window ledge.

"Owen, do you think you could not be belligerent just this once?" she said.

"But I am belligerent," I said. "It suits me. I like it and you like it."

"Don't tell me I like it," she said. "It's cute once in a while, but you're not just belligerent once in a while. You're always belligerent. It's childish and I hate it."

"Where were you?" I asked.

"Walking," she said. "Where would I be?"

I didn't care to get into where she might have been. Whatever she said was the truth, so there was no point. Jill was brainwashed about honesty. She made a fetish of it. I don't think it ever occurred to her that honesty can be just as bad as dishonesty.

"Lulu called to say I should hustle your ass over there and put you in her stable," I said.

"I don't want to be in her stable," she said.

"No, you want to be stubborn. You want to be the one who doesn't compromise. You're the girl who intends to beat the system, only you won't because you're not good enough."

She left the room, went out the back door. In a few minutes I went out and found her on her patio, looking at the sky. When I reached for her hand she yanked it away.

"I might surprise you, Owen," she said. "I might be good enough."

"Nope," I said. "You'll be the girl who made one picture and was never heard from again. The feminists will write stories in all their magazines about what happened to you."

She shook her head quickly. "If the feminists knew I was sleeping with a prick like you, they wouldn't come within a mile of me," she said. "My only use to them would be as a bad example."

Some women are always dying to forgive you. You don't even need to apologize. Just give them any kind of opportunity to forgive you and they will, and then fuck like crazy. Not Jill, though—it was one of the things I admired about her. She didn't make herself easy, not even with me—and she was in love with me. She couldn't be tricked. When she was angry every move had to be gradual. She kept her head too well, even after she got back in the groove sexually. Normally I hate having to take the kind of pains I took with her, but I guess in a way she was worth it. Being up against her was like being up against Bo Brimmer—interesting. She would make ten of a cunt like Sherry Solaré.

"On the other hand, you're getting a no-bullshit relationship," I said. "Ain't that what liberation's all about?"

She took my hand and put it on her knee. "I don't know what it's all about," she said. "I don't know why I let you in my life, or what I'm going to do next. I don't expect any real help from my sisters, nor do I expect any real help from you."

"Bo wants us to go to Rome," I said. A little of her kind of talk goes a long way. Better to talk about business.

"Why?"

"To straighten out the Tony Maury picture. I'm supposed to produce a documentary about it, and you're supposed to make old Tony shape up."

"No one can make him shape up," she said, "but it would be nice to go to Rome. I lived there once, with Carl. I don't know why Bo would send you, though. You can't have charmed him because you don't have any charm."

I didn't rush her. We played hands for a while. It got

dark. The sky to the west was orange with the lights of the Basin.

"I feel sorry for Swan Bunting," she said, after I told her about the lunch. "I know he's awful, but the thing nobody understands is that he *needs* to be somebody so badly. He *needs* position, just like you do. It's going to be hard for him to go back to being nobody again, after she dumps him. He'll probably kill himself."

"That's bullshit," I said.

"No," she said. "It's true. Some people can't stand to lose. They can only stand to win. It's almost sadder when bad winners like Swan start to lose, because nobody feels the least bit sorry for them. Everybody will say 'Well, the sonofabitch deserved it and now he's got it, ha ha!' "

"He does deserve it."

"That's not the point, Owen," she said. "We all deserve worse than we get. But when good people get hurt they still have their goodness. When someone like Swan gets hurt he has nothing to preserve him, no virtue, no character, no nothing. It's just the end. Don't you understand that?"

"So what about me?" I asked. "I'm just like him, you know. We're both self-made punks. Is it going to be the end when I lose?"

"Maybe you won't lose," she said, keeping hold of my hand. "Maybe I won't let you. Let's go eat."

CHAPTER 4

JILL couldn't keep her hands off scripts, if there were any around. It didn't matter that *The Doom of Rome* was just a garbagy spectacle movie: it was still a script. She spent most of the long flight to Rome reading it and worrying about it. I tried to read it but gave up. It read like pure garbage. Universal had paid Elmo and Winfield $300,000 to write it, and to my way of thinking it wasn't worth eighteen cents.

When we landed Jill insisted on going to a part of town called Trastevere. The gofer assigned to meet us was so relieved to be able to recognize us that he practically pissed in his pants. He had missed some dignitary the week before and almost lost his job. He was so nervous that Jill made him eat lunch with us, which made him more nervous, and me angry.

The restaurant was in a little piazza—a lot of scruffy kids

rode a motorbike around and around a statute in the center of the piazza while we ate. The fish was okay, but the noise was deafening. I would rather have eaten inside.

"What'd we do, come to Italy to listen to motorbikes?" I said.

But she was looking at the buildings. I don't think she even heard the sound. She had a happy look, being there—it made her prettier. In her way she was a good-looking woman, just too skinny.

"It's that color that makes this city so beautiful," she said. "The color of the wall of that building—sort of umber."

All the buildings were a kind of dirty yellow, except the church, which was gray. The gofer, a kid named Van, was trying to calm himself by gobbling some kind of green pasta.

"I'm glad you're esthetic," I said. "Just don't talk to me about buildings. Talk to me about how to get the script straightened out. I might want to keep this job."

When we got to the Hilton it looked like the Texans had taken over. A couple of saddles were stacked inside the door, and a cowboy with a big belt buckle was standing guard over them. Some kind of touring rodeo was in town, which didn't really surprise me. There's no getting away from cowboys, no place I've ever been.

"What are they gonna ride?" I said. "Wild Hondas?"

The cowboy heard it and looked like he might have liked to pop me one. He was probably getting restive around so much civilization.

We were given a room that looked out over the top of some skinny cedar trees. Jill took a bath and contemplated the city for a while, and I went to find the production manager.

"You be respectful to Tony Maury if you bump into him," Jill said.

"Far be it from me to be rude to a Hollywood legend," I said.

Buckle and Gohagen were the Mutt and Jeff of screenwriters, you could say. Buckle was a long tall drink of water with shoulder-length yellow hair and a face that looked like it had absorbed a smallpox epidemic all by itself, with seventeen or eighteen years of hard drinking as a chaser. Gohagen was fatter than he was tall and no one had ever seen him without a can of beer in his hand. In fact he was waving around a bottle of German brew when I found the bunch of them in Tony Maury's suite.

"Hell, it's ol' Owen Oarson, rhymes with whoreson and Orson and fuckin' what-all," Elmo said when he opened the door.

"Shit on the Pope, then," Winfield said. "He's the sonofabitch that's been sent to straighten out our ass, an' just when I was gettin' a taste for this miserable German brew. How you, Owen?"

I let them good-old-boy me for a little. I can be as good an old boy as the next asshole, when it's convenient.

Tony Maury was in another room, on the phone, so we went up to the Buckle and Gohagen suite for a while. It was on the top floor of the Hilton, with a sort of cinerama view of the Eternal City, but the suite itself was pretty much like their living room in Tujunga Canyon. Two or three silent, totally obedient, stringy-haired girls were sitting around smoking pot and looking spacy. Their only chore, so far as I could observe, was to keep rotating Willie Nelson records on the stereo. Now and then they threw in Waylon Jennings, for variety. Gohagen had an icebox full of beer. He amused himself by drinking beer and eating potato chips while he played footsy with one of his zombies. Elmo and I had a drink. Elmo at least had good taste in whisky.

"Shit, my buddy, this picture is shaping up disastrous," Elmo said. He was wearing a sheepskin jacket, although it wasn't cold.

"Why?"

"Because nobody can do anything with that old fucker," Winfield said.

"Oh, boy," Elmo said. "Even if Winfield and I could sober up, which we ain't done for some years, it wouldn't make a hell of a lot of difference. Have you ever worked with old T.M.?"

"Not until tomorrow," I said.

"He's got a will of high-grade steel," Elmo said. "Once in a while I make an effort to talk about the script with him—I mean I *am* a professional, an' so's old Winfield, though what he's a professional of is his big secret."

"Professional booger-picker," Winfield said, picking one.

"Well, however," Elmo said. "I had a go at T.M. just yesterday. I said, 'Tony, how the hell are we gonna work out this Brutus business? Fuck, we got to do *something* with Brutus. We can't just let the motherfucker stand there with a knife in his hand and anguish in his eyes for very long.' "

"Might be a good way to end the picture," I said.

"That was my very idea," Winfield said. "Have the little fucker stab himself out of remorse, you know."

"Anyway, that ain't the point," Elmo said. "All Tony said was, 'I don't see why I can't have another elephant.' That's all he's said for the last four days."

After a while the phone rang and we were informed that Tony Maury was off the phone. We went back down to his suite only to find that he had gone to the bathroom, which seemed to depress Buckle and Gohagen.

"Takes T.M. the better part of the day to piss," Winfield said. "I hope that miserable fate don't befall me when I get old."

"Winfield, I'll see to it that the goddamn Lone Star beer company installs you a silver kidney, for when you get old," Elmo said. "They owe you that. A two-hundred-horsepower kidney, for your retirement. Shit, it'll squirt that recycled beer out of you like your cock was a damn firehose."

While we were waiting, the production manager came in. He was a large, worried man named Roscoe.

"I don't know, Owen," he said. "I just wish we could have done it on the back lot. We could buy a country for what this is costing us."

Finally Tony Maury shuffled out, looking like some sweet, harmless old shoe clerk from someplace like Boston. He was a delicate little man, and he wore very clean khakis and a neat little blue scarf tied around his neck.

"My dear Owen," he said when we shook hands. "Have we met? I think we've met. Did you bring me an elephant?"

"Mr. Maury, I did better than that," I said. "I brought you Jill Peel."

"You did?" he said. His cold little gray eyes didn't flicker.

"My darling Jill," he said. "But she must be tired from her trip. I was tired from my trip. We won't wake her. I don't think we should."

He never stopped smiling his little pointless smile. I guess he had smiled it continuously for forty years. No one could remember a time when Tony Maury hadn't been smiling his smile.

"My dear Owen," he said. "So you didn't bring me an elephant?"

Then he shuffled off and stood in front of his picture window, looking out vaguely at Rome. I tried to talk to him, but all he would say was "My dear Owen," or, "My darling Jill." Then, once in a while, with a little well-bred pout, he would say, "All I want is one more elephant. I've tried to make that clear to our dear Bo."

Then he stared. I thought I was good at staring, but I was bush league compared to Tony Maury. He stared at nothing, smiling. He could do it for hours. Once in a great while he would mumble gently about an elephant. His little gray eyes were so empty it was hypnotic. He was like a snake who had found a new way to get his frog: he would bore it to death, stare at it until it fell asleep or just died of boredom. He made Buckle and Gohagen so nervous they drank like fish. Big Jim Roscoe was popping tranquilizers. All Tony Maury did was shuffle around a little, stare out the window, and mumble now and then.

Of course it was no surprise. Everyone in the industry knew that was how he managed to get his way. He just stood around and stared until whoever had to deal with him went mad and gave him everything he wanted. He was a shrewd old fart.

"Our dear Bo," he said, sighing. "The poor boy's a little paranoid about that elephant I want."

That night Buckle and Gohagen and a couple of their wenches—as they called them—took Jill and me to a restaurant filled with pictures of movie stars. Buckle and Gohagen were so popular there that they even got the waiters to sing "The Eyes of Texas."

"These Italians got the hoedown spirit, all right," Winfield said.

Naturally the two of them got the hots for Jill on the spot—or were reminded that they had had the hots for her for years. Of course, their own ladies hardly had the energy to wiggle their fucking toes. I had to listen to a lot of courtly compliments, which put me in a foul mood.

"You lead people on, you know," I said, when we were in bed.

"Not really," she said. "Those two just like to flirt. I've known them for years and neither one of them has ever tried anything."

Women always try to talk you out of jealousy, even though they know it's the one thing that always turns them on. The whole thing is a vicious circle. The more jealousy you work off fucking a woman, the more guys want her, because up to a point a lot of fucking just makes a woman more desirable. I was pumping beauty into Jill, no doubt of that. I wasn't so sure what she was doing for me. She held my arm for a long time, stroking the muscle.

"There are times when I almost think you like me," she said. "The fact that I make you nervous is my only clue."

"Is that some kind of asshole psychological comment?" I said. "Don't talk to me about the color of buildings and don't talk to me about psychology. Nobody knows why people do things."

The longer I thought about it, the more it irritated me. "I don't travel with women I don't like," I said. "Why do you want to come out with some kind of back-ass put-down?"

"It wasn't a put-down, Owen. I was just being fond. You have to allow me to express my feelings now and then.

"After all, I do love you," she added.

I let that one float out of the room, off the balcony, out

over Rome. She had some need to say it, I don't know why. I never meant to make her love me. Every time I hear somebody say they love me I think of a tag line people used to quote about old Mondschiem: All he wants is all you've got. A woman in love is like that—a mogul of the emotions.

After a while Jill sat up in bed and looked out the window, running her hand up and down my belly.

"You don't have to clam up just because I said I loved you," she said. "You think I'm going to cost you something, but I'm not. You don't understand what a bonus this is for me. I was practically past relationships when I met you. I didn't have any feelings at all, except for a few old friends and for my work. It's so good to feel all the things you feel at the beginning of something, and it's so rare, for a person my age. You're younger—you don't know that yet. At my age you're too damn smart, too mature, too all-seeing. Even when you meet somebody new and you let a little something happen you see those old limitations, bright as day, and you sort of direct how things will go and settle for little experiences in order to avoid big disasters. It's a bad thing. You plan how things are going to die before you even let them be born."

I started to doze off, but she shook my arm. "Listen to me for two minutes," she said. "I'm the only person in Hollywood who even thinks you're a human being. You may think you're just using me to get some kind of start, but you're not. Everybody else thinks that too, but they're wrong. It's not just what I can do for you that you need—it's what I *am*, and you need it as much as I need what you are. That makes it real, even if it doesn't last another two weeks. It's not as absolutely businesslike as you pretend."

"Turn me loose, I'm sleepy," I said. She did, but she was grinning. I guess she thought she'd made her point. When I woke up in the night she wasn't in bed, but I saw her silhouette outside on the balcony. She was standing out there looking: moonlight, Eternal City, all that. I went right back to sleep.

CHAPTER 5

THE next morning I found a note:

> Going early with Jim Roscoe to look at the sets. Come when you're rested.
>
> JILL

Since Jim Roscoe left about dawn, she probably didn't even sleep. I never knew anyone to sleep less. I think she resisted it, for some reason, as if she thought she'd lose something if she shut her eyes.

I got downstairs a couple of hours later, just in time to ride with Buckle and Gohagen, who were slumped in the back of their limo looking like dead men. Elmo was huddled in his peeling sheepskin jacket and Winfield had on Levis and a rodeo shirt. He had a can of beer in his hand, even though his eyes were shut.

"Ho, boy," Winfield said when the limo started.

"I thought I saw a rodeo hand here yesterday," I said. "Where did he go?"

"Ol' Casey Tibbs is in town," Elmo said, waking up a little. "That cocksucker was one of his hands."

"Not good to shovel shit," Winfield said.

"That means we don't like him even well enough to shovel shit with him," Elmo said. "Fuckin' Winfield has to have an interpreter in the morning, till about the fifth beer. He's too fuckin' stoned an' hung over even to enunciate."

"Motherfuckin' prick bastard and turd-plop," Winfield said, loud and clear.

Elmo didn't seem to think the remark referred to him. We rode out of town, over some dry hills. Except for the scrawny trees, the landscape didn't look too much different from Southern California. Also, the air was kind of oily.

"As it happens, that very cowboy made off with Winfield's top wench," Elmo said. "Old prissy Linda, that I'd been warning him about for the last six weeks."

"What he means is he's been fuckin' her himself," Winfield said, opening his eyes. "Elmo thinks that's a warnin', even though he did go to some lengths to conceal the whole squalid affair. I don't consider that a warnin', and I don't consider it very fuckin' neighborly either. I wish I was back in Austin so I could fuck his ex-wife."

"There's other wenches, Winfield," Elmo said. Evidently his conscience wasn't too clear. Why it should bother him I don't know. They had been fucking one another's women ever since I'd known them.

"Linda was not just a wench," Winfield said. He threw a beer can out the window and squinted at Italy as if he'd like to get a big eraser and erase it.

"Linda had done graduated from that category," he added. "She was the fuckin' love of my life, or of this month, anyway. I wish that goddamn Casey Tibbs would learn to stay home. Why should cowboys get to be fuckin' international celebrities like us?"

"I just got one word of advice for you, my buddy," Elmo said. "Don't you go dwelling on this emotional tragedy."

"Why not?—the love of my life," Winfield said.

"Because if you dwell on it, you're apt to get drunk and go challenge that bullrider, and then you'll be a dead motherfucker and I'll have to find a new partner, that's why."

They weren't any too amusing, in the morning, and they looked like warmed-over pizza. Winfield got carsick twice before we got where we were going, which was a sort of fragment of a town near some kind of monster garden.

"T.M.'s a nut," Elmo said as we eased our way through all the support vehicles that go with a movie production. There were several limos with Italian drivers snoring in them, and the usual sound trucks and vans full of props and stuff. The cinemobile that the elephant had kicked over was still lying on its side. Six or eight Italian kids in authentic rags were climbing around on it.

"This here's Bomarzo," Elmo went on. "A sickly little humpbacked Renaissance prince had some sculptor stick some monster statues back in the brush. Sort of his own little Disneyland, you could say. Now T.M.'s decided Nero did it, in spite of all the evidence."

"T.M. is not loath to wrench the facts of history," Winfield said.

It was obvious from one glance that Bo Brimmer had every reason to be worried. A fully equipped Roman army stood off in a little valley, doing nothing but drawing pay. There were extras everywhere, some of them stretched out on the ground with their capes over their heads, taking naps. It was the kind of big-budget, big-cast spectacle that hadn't been made since *Cleopatra*—a ten-million-dollar lollipop they were giving old Tony because he had helped them cash in on the disaster craze with a picture called *Crack*, in which three California coastal towns slid into the sea.

Probably *The Doom of Rome* had been around for ten or fifteen years, being blocked by studio head after studio head. Then the persistent old bastard had taken advantage of a temporary lapse of leadership to slip the project through.

I got out and wandered around in the confusion. Some tourists who had come to see the monsters were arguing with the security people, who didn't want them to. I passed a limo with Rosanna Podesta in it—she was playing Nero's mother. Tony Maury was standing on a bumpy hill, smiling his little smile. He had his arm linked in Jill's. She was frowning and talking rapidly to him. That was what we had come for, I guess: so she could put her touch with the old types to good use.

Of course, no matter how good she was, it wouldn't save the picture. The picture was some kind of afterthought of Tony Maury's that happened to be costing Universal a lot of money. All Jill could do would be to shorten everybody's agony.

I left it to her and spent the morning wandering around. The two kids from U.C.L.A. who were going to shoot the documentary weren't arriving until that afternoon, so I really had nothing to do but gawk at it all. We had decided to call our little documentary *Outtake*. The set was such a circus that I began to feel good about my part of the project for the first time. It might be a better picture than the picture, and all the film students in the world would probably flock to see it. I might even make a little money.

When I got tired of gawking I hung around with the guys with the walkie-talkies until a car came out that was going back to Rome. The car was taking in a little actor named Ellis Malki, who had let a camel step on his foot. Ellis was in intense pain. He was an aging fag who played some slimy functionary or other. He spent the whole drive sucking in his breath and suppressing screams of agony. As an act of consideration, Tony Maury had sent his personal driver to rush Ellis to the hospital.

"They bite too," the driver said, referring to camels. "My cousin had his ear bit off while he was at Warners."

The fact that Ellis Malki was in pain made no impression on the Roman traffic. We poked along like a black battleship, surrounded by Hondas and Fiats. Ellis got greener and greener, and I got tired of hearing him suck in his breath.

Later, while I was having a drink, Bo Brimmer called. It must have been about three A.M. where he was, but he sounded fresh as a daisy.

"What's your first impression?" he asked.

"That this is a stupid project," I said.

"That it undoubtedly is," he said. "Of course, stupid and unprofitable are not synonyms. What's Tony doing?"

"Standing on a hill grumbling because he wants another elephant," I said.

"Make me a good documentary, then," he said. "The more vulgar the better—*mondo bizzarro*, if you know what I mean. Shots of Winfield Gohagen taking a leak, and such as that. Let Jill help you and the kids if she wants to."

"No chance," I said. "She doesn't even think we ought to be doing the documentary."

"I know," he said. "Thinks we're out to mock old Tony, which of course we are. In this case mockery may be our only hope.

"Although," he added, "she may be right. It may not be in our long-term interest to show this trade for the sleazy business that it is. I do like the ring of that title, though. *Outtake*. One of my better ideas."

The kids he sent me—my interns, they were called—arrived while I was drinking: two bushy-haired movie brats who had evidently done nothing their whole lives except play with cameras. They were so excited you would have thought they had just arrived in heaven.

The next day I packed them out to Bomarzo and turned them loose. I didn't even have to point. For the next three weeks they were active as prairie dogs. Jill worked herself into a stupor on a picture she officially had nothing to do with, and came in so tired she hardly even yapped at me. With so little to distract us, Buckle and Gohagen and myself played a lot of poker. They knew some Riviera types who weren't too good, and I was soon averaging three, four thousand dollars a week, on the side. If the air hadn't been so oily, it wouldn't have been a bad life.

CHAPTER 6

TONY Maury choked to death at the wrap party for *The Doom of Rome*. He choked on a piece of fried squid, probably because he was trying to eat it and smile his little smile. Everybody was either drunk, stoned, or too tired to notice; he sat down behind a bush on the Hilton patio and turned black in the face. Elmo Buckle found him and yelled so loud that a little Italian policeman, thinking there was a robbery, accidently shot the bell captain in the leg.

Jill went into shock. She had worked at the old fart's side for four weeks, just because she can't resist working. Naturally she had convinced herself that he was someone to be admired. After he was carted off, still black in the face, I walked her around for an hour or two and then put her to bed.

"I know you think it's an awful movie, but there are some good things," she kept saying. "He knew how to shoot action —he really did. After all, he won those four Oscars."

I let her babble. Personally, I had no fondness for the old fucker. He was hard as nails and as selfish as a baby. Having him out of the way would just make his picture—and mine—easier to sell.

My two kids had got some wonderful footage of him shuffling around with his khakis and his little scarf on, looking at his new elephant. Our little documentary could even be considered an elegy to a Hollywood legend. Most of the footage was *mondo bizzarro*, all right. I had shots of Buckle and Gohagen and their wenches that were so revolting that an army of feminists would probably march on Tujunga Canyon and castrate them both as soon as the picture came out.

In the middle of the night it dawned on Jill that I wasn't particularly grief-stricken.

"You're not sad," she said. "He didn't even get to see his picture come out, and you don't care. I don't want to be with you."

She got out of bed and began grabbing clothes, which irritated me. She had a habit of running off, and I was tired of it. She had no intention of staying gone, of course. It was just her way of making trouble for a few days, maybe get herself a little extra attention.

"Look," I said, "I barely knew him. He was an old man, and he died working. I think that's lucky. You're the one who's always moaning about all the old directors who can't get hired. They sit on their asses in their mansions, if they haven't blown all their money and lost their mansions. Tony Maury got to work right up to the last day of his life, and he was too dumb to realize that people didn't care about his movies any more."

"*I* cared about them," Jill said. "He was just a little old-fashioned, that's all."

"Have it your way, but get back in bed. Where do you think you're running off to, anyway?"

"I don't know," she said. She was actually packing a suitcase.

Enough is enough. I got up and threw the suitcase back in

the closet, clothes flying everywhere. Then I wrestled her back to bed.

"I've had enough of your childishness," I said. "You don't need to run away because a man is dead. Lie down and try to get some sleep."

"I'm not upset about the death any more," she said. "Maybe you're right. Maybe Tony was lucky. What I'm upset about is you."

"I'm no different than I was yesterday," I said.

"That's right," she said. The minute I turned her loose she scooted away from me. "You're no different than you were the night I first laid eyes on you. You don't love this business, and you don't love me.

"I can forgive you for not loving me," she added. "I'm not particularly lovable, even if you were a loving man, which of course you aren't."

She looked at me, shook her head, and got up again. She began to gather up the clothes.

"I see," I said. "It's all right if I don't love you, but I'm supposed to love the fuckin' *movie* industry?"

"That's right," she said. "Or get out of it. There are too many cynics in it already. Maybe there always have been, maybe there always will be, but I don't think I want to be sleeping with one of them."

"Tony Maury was a joke!" I said. "Maybe he wasn't as much of a joke as your dear friend Joe Percy, or your chum Henley Bowditch, the half-witted cameraman, but he was still a joke. All he really had was a good head for business. Is all this because you think I'm crapping on some kind of *artist*?"

She sighed. "I don't guess he was an artist," she said. "Just a craftsman. But he was devoted to it, and he loved what he was doing. That's what's sad about you. You call yourself a producer but you have no craft. You can't even do the things those kids do, like focus a camera."

"Oh," I said. "Now it's a crime to be uncreative?"

"No," she said. "Maybe your craft was football and maybe you lost it because you got hurt, in which case all this is unfair. But be that as it may, it's still a shame not to respect craftsmen, and it's a worse shame to be like you are, gifted and cynical."

"I'm not gifted," I said. "That's the phoniest word in the language."

She had an armful of clothes, but I leaned out of bed and swatted them every which way. Jill shrugged and went to the bathroom. When she came back she had her robe on. She shook her head, a gesture I was getting to hate.

"I was just wrong about you," she said. "When I met you in New York I thought I had never met a person who wanted so much. That's what attracted me to you—how much you seemed to want everything—including me, I guess. All that yearning was very appealing."

"Only now the appeal's worn off," I said.

"Yeah, because you only want the easy things," she said. "The cheap things. It's fine to want to be a producer if you're going to try to be a great producer, like Mr. Mond. I wouldn't care if you wanted to be a great *anything*—tractor salesman, poker player, anything. You're just like too many other people: you want the quick winner, no matter how tacky."

She walked past me and opened the door.

"Mostly I want to get started," I said. "Do you have any idea how hard it is to get started in this business if all you've ever done is play football? I come from Plainview, Texas."

"Fine," she said, crying a little. "I come from Santa Maria, California. My dad sells lawn furniture. It's not where you come from. It's what you want. You just don't want enough. It hurts to love someone like you—it makes me feel that if you want me I must be cheap, too. That's why I'm leaving."

She started down the hotel corridor in her nightgown and bathrobe. It infuriated me. I ran into the hall after her and shoved her as hard as I could, which is hard. She went spinning off the wall and fell in the corridor.

"Where do you think you're going?" I yelled. "You don't even have a credit card."

She took her time getting up, holding one shoulder.

"Upstairs," she said. "Elmo and Winfield will take me in."
"Those slobs?" I said. "You'd go to those slobs?"
"In an hour of need, yes," she said. "They're human, unlike yourself. They'll lend me a couch."
She hobbled off, still holding her shoulder.

The dust from that one didn't settle for a while. I thought she'd be back the next morning, but she wasn't. One of Elmo's girl friends came down and got some of her clothes. Around noon I went down to the hotel restaurant. Elmo and Winfield were there, Elmo staring at an omelette and Winfield staring at a beer.
"Morning," I said. "Seen my roommate?"
"Your ex-roommate," Winfield said. "Inasmuch as we're leavin', we've ceded her our suite."
"Oh, well," I said. "Maybe I'll move in, too. It wasn't that bad a fight."
"If you give that lady any more trouble, you're going to have to whip about eighty Italians," Elmo said.
"And a couple of bad-ass Texans," Winfield added.
I had started to sit down with them, but I caught myself and took a table across the room. Naturally everyone on the crew would be on her side. Half of them probably fancied themselves in love with her. That had been a source of irritation ever since we arrived in Italy.
The more I thought about it, the madder I got. Elmo and Winfield had their gall, dragging around their doped-up little groupies and idealizing Jill. I hated the way she went around being nice to everyone on the crew: it was her cop-out, as far as I was concerned. As long as she had about fifty good old boys to flirt with, she didn't have to lay much on the line with me. There would always be another movie crew somewhere for her to charm. Since she had most of them too buffaloed even to make a pass, it was all free affection too. Maybe it was all she really needed.
I hated the whole business because all day it wasn't settled and all day I couldn't think. I just sat around feeling nervous and sort of blocked. That's exactly what's wrong

with love: it doesn't leave you yourself. You have to be on balance with somebody in order to think clearly.

Jill stayed gone and I stayed edgy, but I wasn't going looking for her. Eventually she'd come back and apologize. She'd decide that she'd been too hard on me, that I wasn't really as bad as all that. Also she'd come back because, good or bad, I was what she had going. It might be a shitty relationship but at least she was getting fucked. It might not be perfect, but it had some kick in it. She would show up, eventually.

The next day I spent the afternoon around the pool, watching a fat little French producer try to pick up teenagers. He was a ridiculous little turd, with his big cigar and his blue beret. I had sent my two interns to the airport to get some footage of old Tony's coffin being put on the plane. Also I wanted them to hang around and get some shots of the whole shabby gang straggling onto their jets to go home.

When I got back to the room Jill was there, talking on the phone. She had circles under her eyes. It didn't take much of a squabble to make her look her age. She finished her call just as I finished changing.

"What are you doing here?" I asked. "You don't want to be seen hanging around with a cheap bastard like me. Why don't you go marry James Joyce or somebody?"

"I would rather you didn't get nasty," she said. "I came to apologize, but if you get nasty, I may decide it's not worth it."

"It probably isn't," I said. "I don't appreciate you running off to spend the night with those two slobs, just because you got mad. You could stay and fight things out, for once. For all you know I might even change, if you stayed around long enough."

She sighed. "I know," she said. "It's just that we get so ugly to one another that I feel it's going to destroy everything. I run away because I don't want that to happen."

"I don't like your habits," I said. "I'm not some liberated creep. You don't see me rushing out to spend the night with other women just because I get my feelings hurt."

"Do you get your feelings hurt?" she asked, coming closer.

"Why wouldn't I?"

"I don't know," she said. "You never show anything but anger. I guess I don't think of you as being too vulnerable."

"That's another word I hate," I said. "*Vulnerable*. It's a phony word, like *gifted*. I don't want to be gifted and I sure as hell don't intend to be vulnerable to very much. Who was that on the phone?"

"That was Bo," she said. "He asked me if I'd handle post-production on Tony's picture."

"And what'd you say?"

"I said I would."

I went in and turned on the shower. She followed me. "Is something wrong?" she asked.

"You wouldn't bother to wait and ask my advice, would you?" I said. "Maybe I had other plans for us for the next six months. Maybe I hadn't planned to sit around while you help put this worthless picture together. You could at least have told him you'd think about it."

"But somebody had to do it," she said. "I was the logical choice."

Suddenly there were too many factors to consider. My brain was jerking around without a good hold on anything. Sometimes you have a sense of almost having things together, and then all the pieces start to slide around like the pieces of a jigsaw puzzle.

This time it was Jill's fault. She wouldn't wait—she just did things on her own, as if I didn't count. As if I had no plans. I felt tight, bursting. I was either going to hit her or leave. It was too confusing, that she had talked to Bo without my being there. I didn't like her talking to the little fucker anyway.

"Owen," she said, "stop looking like that. It's just six weeks' work, maybe two months'. It'll be all right."

I was a second from busting her, but she got inside and hugged me.

"Come on," she said. "Come on. God, you're more high-strung than me."

Maybe she sensed how close I was to throwing her at the wall. I don't know. She got a hand inside my bathing suit and before I could decide anything my cock was as tight as a cow's teat. I had about stopped caring whether I fucked her or not, but this time I let it go that way. Why not? We kept at it until we were both like dishrags, worn out. It was a way of postponing something, but why not? I didn't know what I wanted to do, and neither did she. I thought I might as well keep on. Maybe eventually the pieces would stop sliding and start to fit together again.

CHAPTER 7

ACTUALLY, having Jill help with the post-production work on old Tony's picture was the best thing that could have happened. I would have suggested it myself if I'd had time to think about it. For one thing, it kept her busy, and of course it got me free access to the cutting room. I carted off all kinds of discarded footage, some of which could be spliced into my own little film.

Bo had found a sharp kid for me to work with, a cutter named Jimmy Boyd. He went to work with the outtakes and the location documentary, putting them together in crazy sequences. He was a pale little mole who hardly ever came out into the light, but he knew what he was doing. The longer he worked with it, the funnier it all got, until it was the kind of documentary the Marx brothers might have made, if they had made documentaries. I just let Jimmy Boyd go to it. I believe in professionals, and he was very professional. I was the coach, he was the quarterback, and Bo Brimmer was the team owner, who checked in every few days. I was happy to have him snoop. I figured we'd have a very salable product by the time Jimmy got through.

While Jill put the finishing touches on Tony Maury's awful picture I had about a month's worth of affair with Lulu Dickey—a nice relief after seven or eight months of nobody but Jill.

One thing that made it nicer was that Lulu wasn't in love with me. She had one of the funniest bodies I'd ever grappled with: legs about twice as long as a normal woman's, no tits, frizzy hair, and a cunt the color of a plum. It looked like a plum with a short black wig.

"Where'd you get that?" I asked, referring to her cunt, the first time I had a chance to contemplate it. We were in her palatial mansion on a big pink bed, with a telephone with at least forty buttons on it right beside us. The buttons were constantly blinking, but Lulu let them blink. Up until a few minutes earlier her cunt had been blinking more rapidly than the telephone buttons.

"Lebanon," she said, swabbing herself with a Kleenex.

The nice thing about her was that she took nothing seriously except money. Her bedroom was full of huge blown-up pictures of her bombed-out boyfriend, Digby Buttons. "Where's old Digby?" I asked.

"In the dope hospital," she said. "Don't talk about him. I have a soft spot for him, even though he couldn't fuck if his life depended on it."

"Nobody's life depends on it," I said.

"Yeah, but it's not to be despised," she said.

She had cool, bright little black eyes and a sparrow face. Emotionally she was dry as a palm tree, which I liked.

"Impotence fascinates me," she said. "It's on the increase, you know. Over the last two years I must have tried to get it on with at least twenty guys who couldn't. Do you think it's because women are making more money now, or what?"

"Who cares?" I said. "I can't even get laid any more without having to discuss the role of women. Who cares about the role of women?"

"Yeah, but if you were impotent, you wouldn't be so

smug," she said. "Look at it. It's already sticking up again. So why should you worry? But maybe it's all connected to women's salaries."

"I only have to worry about one cock," I said, "and it doesn't give a shit about women's salaries. What's your number-one client doing these days?"

"Sherry? She's into meditation. She has a swami, and she doesn't talk to her cunt any more. She and Swan got bored with all that."

"Maybe it's time we got Sherry a new interest," I said.

"Christ, you fuck me and three minutes later you're talking about business," she said. "Good thing I'm not the romantic type. Are you in love with Jill?"

"Why does that matter?"

"Oh, well," she said. "I've just noticed that half the people in the world are fucking people they don't love. I love Digby, but here I am. I just want to know if you love Jill."

"She's nicer than most," I said, "but she doesn't have a purple cunt."

She got a laugh out of that. Her little bird face crinkled.

"I knew you didn't love her," she said. "Why are you always asking me about Sherry?"

"Just curious," I said.

She pointed at one of the buttons on the telephone console. It was red, unlike the others.

"That's her line," Lulu said. "When that line lights up I answer, no matter what I'm doing. The others can blink, but Sherry and I are very close. When she needs counsel I give it."

I rolled over between her long legs. "Suppose I shove it in you and wait for the red one to blink," I said. "I'd like to hear you give some business advice while you're getting fucked."

"I can handle that," Lulu said, opening her legs. It reminded me of a drawbridge going up, I don't know why. I socked it to the plum and we rolled around for a while, me feeling like I was glued to her, but the red button didn't blink. "She's probably with the swami," Lulu said.

"We have to be careful when Digby gets out of the hospital," she said later. "He's very sensitive to rivalry. He just can't deal with it. I guess being impotent makes him feel at a disadvantage. Let's not threaten him, okay? And let's not let Jill find out, either. I'd still like to handle her, even though I hate her."

"I'll have the little documentary ready to screen in about two weeks," I said. "Get Sherry to come and let me screen it for her. It's not long, and she might get a laugh out of it."

"Sure, but she'll probably bring Swan," Lulu said. "He doesn't let her attend screenings without him."

"Bring him," I said. "Bring the dogs, kids, her manicurist, whoever she wants. I just want her to see it."

Lulu was looking at me shrewdly, like she was playing chess and trying to look about seventeen moves ahead. It was ridiculous. I don't look that far ahead.

"You fucker," she said. "It's a good thing I define myself through my career. If I were dealing with this as a woman I wouldn't let you near her.

"There was a time when I was just a woman," she said, looking at me angrily, as if I was about to contradict her.

"So what?" I said. "There was a time when I was just the son of a wheat farmer who went broke. Obviously we've both gone on to bigger and better things."

"I guess that's why I keep Buttons," Lulu said, not listening. "He needs me. I can't do anything for his career because he's ruined it. He just needs me."

"Listen," I said. "I don't care about your love life. I think you're an exceptional businesswoman. I think we can help one another."

"How come you think you can help me?" she asked. "You're nobody, and I'm already on top. How can you help me?"

"I might get to the top, too," I said. "I might even take the elevator."

She shook her frizzy head. "I don't know why you want to be famous so bad," she said. "It's not that hot. I mean, I know everybody famous says that, but it's really true. I mean, look at me, I'm practically a queen and I'm lucky to get fucked once a month."

I laughed at that. "Your luck's changed," I said.

But she was still giving me her chess-player look when I left.

It's crazy, the way everybody in Hollywood wants to impress you with what a human being they still are. They all heard somewhere that fame and stardom reduces their humanity or something, and they worry about it constantly. Of course, it's true—most of them are only human about a tenth of the time, and then only through their greed and their egos. Nothing's more human than greed and ego.

That's why Jill was so exceptional. She had already decided she had stopped being human, somewhere up the road. "I'm a drone," she said. She had decided all she was good for was work, so she wasn't always dropping her humanity worries on me. She must have told me twenty times how surprised she was to be getting a little bit of a love affair again, after she had already given up on such things.

Of course, part of that was bullshit. When she was halfway happy she looked about twenty-four, and she still drew the guys. Most of them backed off from her, but she still drew them.

On the other hand, part of it wasn't bullshit. She was pretty resigned. The resigned look went away when she was feeling hopeful, but it always came back. She had sort of checked out on normal life, whatever that is. I don't think she really expected any long-term thing with me, although maybe she kidded herself once in a while, when we were at our best. When we were at our best we were all right. She was quick—had a mind. I didn't have to explain things to her. She understood things like a snap that most women wouldn't get if you talked to them for a week. I liked that, not having to labor the points. And she was pretty, at least when she was fresh.

The bad part was that she was too grateful. She acted like

I'd saved her from the old folk's home or something. People who are grateful expect you to be grateful back, and it's not part of me. I don't think I've been grateful since I was fourteen, when my Uncle Ellis gave me a .410 my folks didn't want me to have.

Lulu Dickey was a nice change, at least when I could get her to stop whining about her lost humanity. She was always apologizing for being famous, or else pretending that she wasn't. That was typical Hollywood. All the famous people have to act like their fame doesn't really belong to them. They treat it as if it had been planted on them while they weren't looking, by some publicity agent—the way narcotics agents plant pot in hippies' apartments.

If you ask me, most of them ought to consider themselves lucky to have something to distract them from their fucking humanity, which is all the same everywhere, as far as I know. Any idiot can feel. Anyone can have a baby, have someone die, fuck up a marriage, get lonesome, go broke, forget how to fuck, get bored with their situation, all that. Anyone can fall in love—I could do it, if I found the right face on the right body. Why movie people feel they have to keep the ability to suffer all that ordinary shit, I don't know.

Humanity just backs up on nothingness, of one kind or another. Maybe you build a routine and slog through it day after day, or maybe you fall out and stay drunk or take pills or something, but it doesn't change much. The same old boredom keeps sucking at your legs. I saw it all over the Midwest, when I was flying around. Bouncing up and down in those smoky little airplanes, I could look out the window and see nothingness for hundreds of miles in every direction.

Then when I got my office on the top floor of the tractor company I could look out toward New Mexico and see the same nothingness—fifteen hundred miles of it before you even came to an ocean.

When you first get to Hollywood you think it's different. You got the hills and the greenery, lots of fancy cars, women with some bounce in their asses, all sorts of pizzaz—but eventually it's just the same. You wake up some morning all smogged in—nothing but gray out the window, like fucking San Francisco. You don't feel like fucking, you don't feel like talking, and you know it's got you.

Fame has to be the answer—the big desmogger. It's the difference between having your plug pulled and having your plug in the socket. When you're famous you're always alive. The phones ring all day, the cars come when you want them, the money's in motion. You get invitations. Once you've got it you might have a problem keeping it, but that's not a bad problem. So it takes some smarts and some balls. It's not a bad problem to have. Without the kind of problems it brings you'd probably just be saving up to buy linoleum for some kitchen in some suburb, or else sucking wine bottles on some skid row.

Every time I hear people complain about fame I wish I could kick them out of an airplane in the middle of North Dakota or Nebraska or somewhere, or else fill one of their fucking swimming pools with fog and hold them under for about a week. If I ever produce a horror movie, I think I'll construct a fog chamber and throw a big party in it and then slip out and lock everybody in. Then I'll turn on the fog and let everybody wander around in it, getting back in touch with their humanity. That ought to get my name in the papers.

After Digby Buttons emerged from the dope hospital Lulu and I went out to her beach house to fuck. We were already sort of tired of one another, but somehow it just seemed to inspire us. After we knew it was all over we got pretty intense about it and didn't quite want to let it go. I guess once we figured we had gotten away with it we couldn't resist a last kick or two. We had an active time, there by the ocean-side, until Lulu finally decided enough was enough.

Her decisiveness really impressed me. Not one woman in a hundred will stop fucking somebody she likes to fuck just because she's decided it's time to stop. Most women will suffer five or six years of abuse and still not stop, but Lulu just wiped her cunt one day and stuck those long legs back in her prefaded jeans and called it off.

"I got this thing for Digby," she said. "Suppose we made the papers? It'd just be the end. He'd take about two pounds of dope and then he'd die.

"Besides," she said, "if we leave it nice we might get some time later on. Who knows? It could happen if you stick around."

"I'll probably stick around," I said.

"The trick is to avoid a lot of anger," she said. "I'm really not into anger. If I just go home and you just go home then what's to stop us from pickin' it up again later on, when I'm not so worried about Digby?"

"Nothing," I said. "Nothing's to stop us. Is Sherry coming to my screening?"

She looked at me shrewdly. "So what do you want to do, Owen, fuck her or produce her next picture or what?"

"I didn't say I wanted to do anything. I just think she'll like the picture."

"I don't know if you're too bright, Owen," she said. "You don't want to fool around with Sherry. She's too much for you—too much for everybody. She's even too much for herself. Even if you got rid of Swan and produced a picture of hers or something, it wouldn't matter. Sherry gets all the credit for everything she does. Her producers might as well not exist. All you'd be is her latest cocksman. A male sex object. In my opinion you'd do better to stick with Jill."

"I just asked a question," I said. "I don't particularly want your opinion."

Lulu sat and watched the waves for a while, frowning. "You don't know Sherry," she said. "She's not a pushover, like me. Sherry is tough."

"Maybe I just want a look at her," I said. "Maybe I'm as star-struck as the next asshole."

She stood up and pulled on the woolly coat that she always brought to the beach with her. It looked like it was made from an English sheepdog. I was just as glad to see the last of that coat. Every time I came near it, it shed all over me.

I guess it worried her, my future. She was still frowning when she got in her little brown Jag and drove away. But the next day, dry as a cactus, she called and said Sherry would come to the screening.

"Diggs and me want to come too, if that's all right," she said. "Diggs needs to get out more."

"Bring him, he's welcome," I said.

CHAPTER 8

OF course Bo would want to be at the screening. It was his studio, and he would naturally want to be on hand for any occasion involving Sherry Solaré. Sherry had walked straight off a picture he was producing once, and he had promptly sued her and won three million dollars in damages. The decision was still floating around in the appeals courts, but there was a good chance it would stick. Naturally the two of them hated one another. When I told him Sherry was coming his little eyes lit up.

"The top cunt," he said. "I've adopted that phrase, which I know you coined. Of course I'll be there. I don't want to breach protocol where the top cunt is concerned."

Outtake was about three times as good as I had figured it would be when we got back from Rome. Jimmy Boyd had done a great job. It was a funny movie about making movies.

In fact, the whole situation was funny. I was involved with a picture that even the critics might like, while Jill was helping to finish a total clunker, just because she was loyal to some notion she had about old Tony.

I was at the screening room twenty minutes early, wanting things to start. Lulu and Digby Buttons showed up first. It was my first look at Digby, except for those pictures in Lulu's bedroom—those had clearly been made in happier days. He was nearly as tall as Lulu and looked like he weighed about ninety pounds. He was shivering and wearing a shabby old overcoat, and his mouth hung open. It was hard to believe he had once been the idol of millions. They had a Chink bodyguard with them. I guess the Chink was supposed to pick Digby up if he fell down and started drooling in the aisles.

" 'Lo Owen," he said. Then he sat down, pulled some earphones out of his pocket, and began to listen to music and sort of jerk in his seat. Lulu sat down by him as if she was his little wife. It's amazing, the people women can love.

When Sherry came in she was wearing dark glasses so big and black that they could have been cut from the lid of a coffin. She didn't take them off, either. I would only have known it was her because her hair was the usual rat's nest.

Bo should have been there, but he wasn't, so I walked up and introduced myself. Swan didn't look at me.

"This is the one with a cunt for a mouth," he said to Sherry.

Then he looked at me. "One crack out of you an' we're leavin'," he said. "I'll take that fucking projector and wrap it around a flagpole."

I coldcocked him—hit him right in the mouth and knocked him flat. Bo Brimmer and one of his executives walked in just at that moment, which made it perfect. Hitting him was just what I needed to stop my nervousness. It had worked just that way in ball games, too. If I could lay somebody out on the opening kickoff I felt fine from then on.

Swan wasn't expecting to get coldcocked, of course, and I

hit him hard enough to stun him. I really knocked him flat down in the aisle, not to mention splitting his lip wide open. He lay there for a minute, bleeding into his beard.

Sherry Solaré sort of opened her mouth, she was so surprised. I couldn't tell what her eyes looked like, behind those coffin-lid sunglasses, but it could have been she was a little bit pleased at seeing her boyfriend get popped.

The executive that came in with Bo was certainly not pleased. He was absolutely aghast, and rushed over to Swan and knelt down by him.

"My god, what have you done?" he said, visions of lawsuits in his eyes. Swan did practically nothing but sue people, usually on Sherry's behalf.

"Kenneth, you do tend to miss the obvious," Bo said, coming up to Sherry. He nodded, she nodded.

"Hiya," she said, and then walked down to where Swan was lying. The black sunglasses swung my way for a second, but then they swung back. She had on a woolly coat that might have come off the same dog as Lulu's. I don't know why you see so many woolly coats in a place where it's never cold. Maybe they just go with woolly women.

Sherry looked down at the fallen warrior. "Now you know how it feels," she said. "It's not so sexy, is it?"

Swan's eyes had yet to clear, and he had quite a bit of blood in his beard. Sherry nudged his shoulder with her foot.

"Are you taking a nap, or what?" she said. "I'd hate to think I was fucking somebody who won't get up and fight."

Lulu was standing in the middle of a row of seats, watching it all from her great height.

Sherry nudged Swan again. "Come on," she said. "This is the first screening I've been to where there was a fight."

Swan shook his head a few times and his eyes cleared. He looked at Sherry furiously. Then he struggled to his feet and started toward me, but the executive, who was still worried about the legal implications of it all, got him in a hug and tried to restrain him. Swan ended up clipping him one, which caused Sherry to smile faintly.

"No, Swan," she said. "You hit the wrong one. Hit the big one."

At that point Bo strolled down the aisle, straightening his bow tie.

"Back in Arkansas we do our fighting in the great outdoors," he said. "We go outside, so as not to break the furniture or frighten the projectionists. Projectionists have enough anxiety as it is."

"Horseshit!" Swan yelled, shoving the poor executive, who was still trying to restrain him. "You fucker!" he yelled, pointing his finger at me. "I'll get even with you!"

But he didn't hit me. Instead he turned and stomped down to the front of the theater and dropped into a seat. He wiped his bloody beard on the sleeve of his corduroy coat.

"Ken, would you see if you can find him some Kleenex, or maybe some paper towels?" Bo asked. "He's bleeding like a stuck hawg. We don't want him bloodyin' up our seats."

The executive was very relieved to have something to do. He left, leaving Bo and Sherry and me standing in a clump. I wasn't sure what the next move was, but I felt relaxed again. Bo and Sherry appeared to be completely at ease with one another, despite their history.

"Can I sit between you two?" Sherry asked. "He's a vindictive little punk. He may come charging up here and try to strangle me, once he stops bleeding. I'd enjoy the picture more if I just felt secure."

"Honey, we'll have him put in jail if you say the word," Bo said. "We'll clap the motherfucker in irons."

"Don't call me honey, you peanut," she said, turning sour abruptly. Instead of waiting for us, she went and sat down by Lulu. Digby Buttons was still hunched over beneath his earphones.

"Look at him," Bo said. "I'd rather slosh through shit in my underwear than sleep with that. What *are* women, that they cohabit with such creatures?"

Then the light went off and the picture came on. The first shot was of Tony Maury standing on the very top row of the Colosseum, with a fat fag in an Australian bush hat standing beside him—the art director, actually. It was a fast little film. I couldn't tell what people were thinking, but once I heard Sherry say, "Lookit, it's Harvey. . . ." That was it until the end of the picture.

Usually there's an awkward silence at the end of a screening, while people try to think of something nice to say, but there was no problem about that this time. The minute the lights came on Swan jumped to his feet, walked up the aisle to where I was sitting, and motioned at Sherry.

"I hated it, let's go," he said.

Sherry had the black glasses back on. "Yes, Daddy," she said, standing up. I stepped out in the aisle as she passed by.

"Who told you you could hit him?" she said, as she went past me. That was it. No thank-you-for-asking-me, no comment on the film, nothing.

"See ya," she said to Bo as she went out.

Lulu was trying to get Digby to put away his earphones. The executive said, "Fine film, very fine film," and rushed off with a pained expression on his face, probably to try and placate Swan Bunting. Bo was still in his seat, nibbling on an eraser. He seemed in a thoughtful mood.

"Let's see it again," he said, waving at the projectionist. Lulu and the Chink had been trying to get Digby on his feet, but they sat back down. We saw it again.

"Goddamn, I've got good judgment," he said when the lights went on a second time. "I think it needs more tits, and maybe a little more cussin'. We might as well take our R and go for the college crowd."

Lulu and her gang came wandering up the aisle at that point.

"That was fun," she said. "Digby slept some, the second time around. We better haul it on home. He's just exhausted."

Her departure obviously didn't matter to Bo. He waved an eraserless pencil at her and went on talking. He monologued for a while about the various marketing options, but I didn't really listen. I was wishing I had hit Sherry Solaré instead of her boyfriend. I found it pretty galling that she hadn't bothered to say thank you. All I had wanted was a look at her, but she had been a better Indian than me. She had seen me and I had seen her sunglasses. I guess she had let me know my place, or what she thought was my place.

"How did you like Miss Sherry?" Bo asked, when he finally finished airing his thoughts on the film.

"She was damn rude," I said. "Doesn't she ever say thank you?"

"It's a power thang," he said. "The bigger you get, the less manners you need. When you're on top, one way to show it is by what one might call negative manners. The top cunt need never say please and thank you."

"How far down does she have to fall before she gets polite again?"

He looked at me as if I was dumber than shit. "I wouldn't wait around for please and thank you from Sherry," he said. "She's been up there so long she's forgotten about manners, if she ever knew. She's a desperate woman."

"Desperate? She didn't strike me that way."

"You haven't worked with her," he said. "You haven't watched her fight to get her way on every single point, every single day, for three or fo' months. Shit, I can remember havin' to reswing the door on her trailer, when we were making our little musical. The door swung from left to right, like so many doors do, and she decided she'd be more comfortable if it swung from right to left. We reswung the motherfucker."

"Why'd you do that?"

"Because we had six million in the picture," he said. "It don't cost six million to reswing a trailer door.

"Sherry's a worse addict than that shiverin' hulk with Lulu," he added, "only her dope is powah. Which is what ah call a desperate situation, with her getting older. Just don't you look for fine manners on her way down. You'll see bitterness, you'll see vitriol, you'll see folks gettin' scalded and fried all over the place."

"I thought you wanted to do a picture with her," I said.

"Oh, yeah, I do," he said. "Right now, before she begins the decline. Next week wouldn't be too soon to start."

"She doesn't look so bad," I said. "Maybe she's just lonely. Maybe she just needs lovin'."

He looked at me quickly. "Lovin' is a term that's somewhat ambiguous," he said. "Has Miss Jill seen the picture yet?"

"Nope," I said. "Tomorrow's her birthday. I've been saving it for a birthday present."

"Glad to know about the birthday," he said. "We owe her about a million roses for what she's done with Tony's picture. We think a lot of Miss Jill."

All I cared about was that he liked the picture. I was beginning to get a lucky feeling. I think from the way Bo kept looking at me that he had it in mind to tell me to stay away from Sherry, or to be nice to Jill, or some such brilliant advice, but if so, he didn't say it, which was just as well. I might have hit *him* too. It wouldn't have helped the picture, but I was getting pretty tired of his smart little eyes.

CHAPTER 9

An avid woman I can trust: someone who wants to lick every inch of skin, poke her tongue into every hole. That's fine. That's natural. That type of woman doesn't expect too much. Jill expected too much, and respected too much. She respected things that weren't even there, and she didn't seem to want to know every single thing about my past, like most women would. They always want to get control of your past—it's smart enough, I guess.

But Jill didn't go about things that way. She was too private, too discreet, and ten times too polite. She waited to be asked, which is no way to go about anything.

We got dressed up before the screening so we could go to dinner afterward. All during the picture she kept playing with a gold chain I had given her for her birthday, wrapping it around her fingers and then unwrapping it. I saw her smile a few times, but she didn't laugh out loud. It made me nervous. If she had giggled a few times, I would have felt better, but there were no giggles, and when it was over, there was the kind of awkward pause that you usually get when a screening ends.

The pause lasted about five seconds, which was long enough for me to begin to wish I hadn't met Jill. She wasn't going to lie. She thought it was crappy and she was going to say so. I knew it. I watched her. I don't know, I think I would have fallen in love with her if she'd lied at that point. It would have been as good as avidity. Anybody who won't lie for a lover is warped, somewhere. I was surprised at how much I wanted to hear her say it was a nice film. Then we could go eat, and go home and fuck, and who knows? Maybe I would have married her, who knows? She was pleasant to live with—a little strong on the health food, but pleasant. But if she wasn't going to tell me what I needed to hear, then fuck it. That's too basic.

"All right," I said. "You hate it. Fuck you. Do you want to go eat?"

"Yeah," she said, and tried to take my hand.

I shoved her hand away and got up and walked out. She caught up with me at the car.

"Owen, don't get that way," she said. "I don't respond quickly to films. You know that."

"Oh, fuck off," I said. "I don't want your explanations. I don't know what I'm doing with a woman your age anyway. People come to California for youth, not wrinkles."

She got in the car without a word. I shut up. She can ignore twenty minutes' worth of insults, so it was a waste of breath.

"Partly, I felt strange because it was Jimmy Boyd who cut it," she said. "Jimmy Boyd grew up with Johnny. I've known him since he was five."

Johnny was her son. She had such guilt hang-ups about him that I never brought him up, or encouraged any talk about him. He was nearly grown and off living in a commune somewhere in New Mexico. I guess the two of them had rejected one another, but I didn't really care. The last thing I needed was a teenage kid hanging around, hating me because I was fucking his mother.

"I mean, he's good," she said. "It's a good piece of editing, and I know you didn't do it because you don't have the patience. A little kid I used to make popcorn for did it. It made me feel strange, that's all."

"That's just a cop-out," I said. "I couldn't make a picture you'd like, and you know it."

I was so mad at her that I almost ran over the kid who parked cars at the restaurant. It was the yellow restaurant. At night it wasn't so full of uptight executives.

"You have no knack for saying the right thing at the right time," I said when we were seated. "I know you think your fucking integrity prevents it, but it's really just selfishness. You'd rather be right than make people feel good."

She played with her napkin, a faraway look in her eye.

"You still haven't told me what you thought about it, other than that you popped popcorn for the cutter," I said.

"I guess I just don't like satire that much," she said. "It only tells one side of the story, and that seems too easy. It's really easy to make Elmo and Winfield and the rest of us look like slobs. I could make you look like the cheapest hustler in town, if I handled the camera right."

"But it's true," I said. "I am a cheap hustler, and they are slobs. If you're so big on the truth, why don't you admit it?"

She shook her head. "There just has to be sympathy," she said. "Some satire's all right—we all deserve it. But you could show us with a little sympathy. A lot of people worked hard on that picture, and we're not all as ridiculous as you make us seem.

"It's why I respected Tony," she said. "He got a little sympathy into his pictures, at least."

"Well, I could never hope to equal a great like Tony Maury," I said. "I don't think I'm the right man for you. Every time I turn around I bump into some pedestal."

It wasn't a festive evening. I got depressed. Jill tried to

make light of it, to cheer me up. She even lied a little about the picture, but it was too late. Her timing was terrible. Everything she said sounded phony, and phony coming from her was worse than if it had been coming from a natural phony.

As soon as we got home I got drunk. She got drunk too, probably in an effort to keep me company. It didn't help matters, because she's as phony a drunk as she is a phony, and she was just going to be sick for about ten hours when it was all over. I felt disgusted with her and even more disgusted with myself for having gotten involved with her. It's hard to believe that knowing what I know I had hooked up with a woman whose opinion would make a difference to me. With millions of women in the world who wouldn't know a documentary from a pile of crap, I had tied on with one who knew something. What made it more stupid was that I didn't really need to have anything going with a woman. I could get what sex I needed off the streets—particularly the L.A. streets.

None of it made sense—I felt cornered. There's no easy backing away from a woman like Jill. You can't just say, "Whoa, ma'am, my mistake," and back out the door. A woman like her destroys all the simple appetites. I could still fuck around, but it just made me restless. I felt like things had been going up and down for months, like I was on some crazy ride at an amusement park.

The only thing to do was to start trying to get off. It would probably take months, but I was ready to start. Later on in the evening, when Jill crawled on top of me, expecting to get fucked, I kicked her out of bed. I got a foot in her stomach and shoved. She landed up against a chair halfway across the room. It seemed to surprise her.

"Why'd you do that?" she said.

"Because I have no sympathy," I said. "I'm just a hustler from West Texas. I don't give a shit about sympathy and I'm sick of you."

She thought she could change my mind. She eased back in bed. I grabbed her, rolled her over me, and dumped her on the floor on the other side of the bed. This time she hit a bookcase and about a dozen little pottery ducks fell off it. She couldn't stay away from pottery ducks.

"You're drunk," she said.

"So are you—happy birthday," I said. "I do it better than you, like almost everything else. I don't know what you can do, except sympathize."

She picked herself up and got some clothes on and left. I didn't pay any attention, and she didn't say another word. She looked like she might make it out of the building before getting sick, but I didn't care. It was just the beginning of something that would take a long time. I had done it before, twice. She might be back in the morning, or it might be a couple of days, but she'd be back. In the meantime she would talk to about twenty of her creaky old buddies, all of whom would tell her that I was a total shit. They would point out to her that I was completely wrong for her, that she was just being masochistic and self-destructive in seeing me, that it had no future, that I didn't love her, that I was just leeching off her reputation, and a lot of other things that were probably half true. Maybe they were *all* true: it wouldn't make a nickel's worth of difference, except maybe to them. They could congratulate themselves on having given good advice, and commiserate about the trouble Jill was in, and agree with one another about what a prick I was, and none of it would matter. Jill would be right back. She wasn't an organized woman, like Lulu. Lulu could turn it on and off like a faucet, but not Jill.

The big joke was that I wasn't an organized man. That's where I had them all fooled. I've always aspired to pure opportunism, but I never make it. If I'd been a pure opportunist, I'd have stayed with Lulu. In time I could have persuaded her to pack old Digby off to the dope farm, and I would have had it made. But I didn't like the taste of Lulu—not really—so I ended up being bossed around by my impulses, just like Jill. I hated Jill's style, but I still liked the taste of her. Long after I thought I wouldn't care if I never fucked her again, she kept turning me around. It kept happening, even after both of us had decided we might as well quit.

I guess it was a good thing for both of us that Hollywood is nowhere near as ruthlessly efficient as it likes to think it is. There were a couple of superhuman types like Bo around, but mostly the town consisted of half-assed opportunists much like myself. They dress like professionals, but most of them are just fuck-ups. Naturally most of them end up fucking the wrong people and making the wrong pictures. Jill was actually sort of right to hang out with the crews—the crews *have* to be professional or they get fired, or don't get hired.

Jill stayed away for three days. I didn't call her, she didn't call me. I played a little poker and got turned down flat by Carly Heseltine, Bo's secretary. It didn't surprise me—I knew she had a boss hang-up. I just thought I'd give it a shot.

Jill finally walked in just as I was thinking of driving to Vegas or somewhere. L.A. was beginning to get on my nerves. She was wearing a dress and carrying a script, so something must have been happening.

"Are you still mad?" she asked, a little hesitant.

"You could have called and asked if I was alone, before you came," I said. "You don't live here, you know."

"I know," she said.

"So call, like a normal person. This is not a public place."

"Owen, I think you're overdoing the snottiness," she said. "I'm sorry about the other night. I wasn't very nice about your picture and I realize your feelings were hurt. Can't we forget it? I have some news."

"Why would I need your news?" I said.

She ignored it. "I had lunch with Bo today," she said. "He really likes your picture. I think he's going to spend some money on it."

"So let him tell *me* if he likes it," I said. "You're not my wife, you know."

Of course he had probably tried to call. I had been letting the service take the calls, and I hadn't bothered to call in.

That hadn't been too brilliantly professional either, but that was the mood I was in.

Jill just shrugged.

"You're not much on nonverbal communication, are you?" I said. "What do I have to do besides kick you in the stomach. Most people would take that to mean they're not welcome."

"I took it to mean you were pissed off," Jill said. "Not to mention drunk. I didn't take it as a final statement."

"Why don't you go back home and pretend we had a great romance," I said. "Otherwise I'm apt to tell you about some of the ladies I've been fucking."

That shut her up for a minute. She thought it over.

"I don't think I could pretend it was a great one," she said. "I guess I just like to think it's *something*."

"It might have been, if you weren't so hipped on work," I said. "You're not too exciting when you're exhausted, you know."

She looked a little impatient.

"Name some ladies," she said.

"How about Lulu?"

She lifted her eyebrows, and waited. "Just one?" she said. "Aren't there any more names?"

"You wouldn't know the rest of them," I said. "They were what you might call casual fucks. One here, one there."

"I see," she said. "I guess that explains why you seemed a little worked down at times yourself. I knew it couldn't have anything to do with your arduous labors in the cutting room. You're not always exactly breathtaking, you know."

She tried but she didn't say it right. Some people can't insult. When it came to meanness, Jill was undersupplied, but she did have anger. Her jaw was trembling and she got up and paced around the room, looking for something to smash. If I had had anything to smash she would have smashed it, but I have no possessions to speak of. All she could do, when her anger burst, was to throw the script in my face. A script is hardly a satisfying weapon. Her face was red with anger.

"Why'd you quit her?" she said. "You're perfect for one another. Neither one of you knows anything, or cares to learn about anything, except your deals. If you teamed up the two of you could own Hollywood in a few years."

"I don't think I'd want to share it with a cunt like that," I said.

"Well, you won't get it without her," she said. "You aren't smart enough. Bo can think circles around you. Hell, *I* can think circles around you and I can hardly think at all. You want to know something? I'm glad you fucked her. It proves what I really already knew: how dumb you are. It will help me a lot, your doing that. Now I won't bother to count on us any more. I just won't bother . . . to pretend it's going to work."

Then she turned and left. She was about to burst into tears, but I wasn't going to get to see that.

I called the answering service and found a few calls from Bo and some from Lulu. But Jill had thrown my head off. I had no taste for business.

I got in my Mercedes and drove down to Redondo Beach, taking along the script Jill had thrown at me. I spent the afternoon reading the script and watching the little teenage truants in their mini-kinis flop around in the sand. About half of them had middle-aged lovers with gray hair and pot-bellies. It was a revolting sight, but I preferred Redondo Beach to the spiffier beaches. It was sort of the equivalent of my apartment, only with an ocean to look at.

I was mad at myself for not stopping Jill, making her cry, having a real fight, fucking her, something to take the edge out of the day. As it was, I was all edge. I couldn't tell what was happening, or what I wanted to happen. It was all crazy. At last I had what I had been looking for, a little start, and instead of being over at Universal, conning Bo up one side and down the other, I was sitting on Redondo Beach, getting sand in my asshole and watching the kiddies getting ready to fuck the grandads.

It was all because of Jill. For someone who was supposed to be leeching off her, I wasn't getting much. It was like she had broken my concentration. The same kind of thing had happened to me in high school, only then I had been lucky: the cunt jilted me for a fullback. If that hadn't happened, I'd still probably be back in Plainview, Texas, hoping it didn't hail out the fucking wheat.

It was a big irony, really. Joe Percy and Henley Bowditch and all those other old turds were sitting around commiserating about how I'd ruined Jill, and instead of me ruining her, she was ruining me. They thought I had her bewitched or something, which was horseshit. If I had left a mark on her anywhere, it didn't show. I could fuck her silly, but that wasn't a mark. I could act shitty and make her cry and walk out, but that only lasted a day or two. So far as I knew, she was an unchangeable woman. I didn't love her, I didn't know her. I just knew I was the one who was losing his bearings, not her. She had her bearings, okay. She wasn't sitting around Redondo Beach.

I was too disgusted with myself to be in the mood to do much of anything, but eventually I got through most of the script Jill had thrown at me. It was a Western, set in West Texas, about a frontier madam who gets hung because the big ranchers think she's helping the little ranchers rustle their cattle. The script was by somebody I had never heard of, and it was good: if it hadn't been good, I wouldn't have read ten pages of it, in the mood I was in.

Eventually it got to be twilight. The sky, the beach, and the ocean all got gray and gloomy—as gray and gloomy as the flats of the Panhandle on a March evening. It didn't drive the teenagers off, though. Some of them had on fluorescent bikinis—they flitted around on the beach like fireflies. Behind me I heard the roar of traffic on the San Diego Freeway, louder than the surf.

I got in the Mercedes and let the traffic suck me in. It carried me for a while, like a long wave, and threw me ashore in Hollywood. My mind started working a little bit again. I drove up to Jill's house. She was sitting at her drawing board, with a cup of tea on the window ledge beside her.

"Hi," she said. "Are you feeling any better?"

"I'm feeling dumb," I said. "I'd like to go someplace for a couple of days. Maybe out in the desert somewhere. You want to come?"

"Sure. Let's go," she said.

We were out past San Bernardino before we said two words. We didn't even look at one another. Somewhere near Riverside we stopped at a diner and ate. Jill ate some fried shrimp—she always ate shrimp if they were on the menu.

"You'd eat those things anywhere," I said. "Why do you want to eat shrimp in a desert?"

"I like them," she said.

We stared at one another for a while. At least she had a sense of humor. She knew what a big joke we were. She was happy to be chewing on shrimp in the desert, and began to smile at me.

"I don't know why you came," I said.

"You asked me," she said. "A lot of people respond to being asked. I'm glad you brought yourself to do that, though I have no idea why you did."

"Probably inertia," I said.

"I'm sure," she said. "Men are so goddamn lazy. Once they find someone who'll fuck them steady, they just go right on, click, clock, click, clock. I don't know why women are thought to be the passive sex."

We ended up in a motel in Glamis. I wanted to go on to Yuma, but Jill had been wanting to stop for an hour, so I stopped. It was a big deal for her, coming to the desert. The motel was crappy, not enough towels. Her legs were still damp when she came to bed.

"Someday I'll find out something about you," she said. "You can't hide forever."

It was crazy, being with a woman who would make a remark like that just when we were getting ready to fuck. I let it go. What was I supposed to say? She couldn't seem to shut up, even when she was excited. I had even got so I could sleep while she was talking, which is what I eventually did.

CHAPTER 10

THE next day I felt like I was going out of my skull, life was such a blank. I smoked some dope, which didn't help much, and we lay around in the crappy motel in Glamis until the middle of the afternoon. Jill was happy as a fucking lark, but I wasn't. It's depressing to look out the window of a third-rate motel and see a desert, particularly if you're in the motel fucking a woman you don't even know why you're involved with. We couldn't even get any fresh towels. The three we had got damper and damper.

In the middle of the afternoon I had a few minutes when I thought I might kill her if she said another word. I guess she sensed it, because she shut up. We had to go somewhere, so we went to San Diego. I didn't really feel like driving off into Arizona. Jill said we could go to the zoo, but actually I think she was just hoping for about a three-day fuck in a nice motel. I sure as hell meant to have a better motel, whatever else happened.

We got a great one in San Diego, and eventually I smoked enough dope to stop feeling depressed. We spent a couple of days ordering too much from room service, fucking too much, and watching too much television. We even went to the zoo at one point. I could tell it was a good zoo, but zoos bore me. Maybe I catch it from the animals.

When whatever mood we were in finally wore off, we dragged out the script of the Western—Bo had offered it to her—and went through it.

"I want to do it and I want you to help," she said. "We'll have to do it in Texas, so I'll get to see where you come from."

"That's a reason to do a movie?" I said.

"One reason," she said. "Of course he wants Sherry to play the madam."

We talked script for about a day, or rather she talked and I listened. On the third night we started back to L.A. Jill had had some pretty good ideas, such as that Sherry would have a youthful lover, the son of one of the big ranchers who wanted to kill her.

"I want you to work on it," she said. "Maybe you can produce it."

"I don't think so," I said. "I'm tired of being Mr. Jill."

She started looking depressed. I guess she thought a couple of days in a king-size bed had changed everything.

"I wish you wouldn't feel that way," she said.

"Don't start whining. I do feel that way. You make your pictures and I'll make mine."

"I wish you were the most famous person in the world," she said. "Then you wouldn't have to prove anything, and we could do something together."

I was tired of her being so nice to me. That always makes me nervous, when somebody's nice. We argued most of the way home, and when we got back to L.A. I asked her whether she wanted to go to her place or mine.

"I wish there was an our place," she said. "But you don't want that, do you?"

"I sure don't," I said. "We see enough of one another. Any more and we just fight."

"I don't mind fighting," she said. Then she fell into one of her silences. It wasn't exactly a hurt silence, but it was hard to live with. I could never think of a thing to say to her when she stopped talking. When I pulled into my garage she still hadn't spoken. She gave no sign of having noticed that the car had stopped. I finally got irritated.

"I'm going up," I said. "You can sit here and stare at the wall if you want to."

"I'm sorry," she said, trying to shake herself out of it. "Going away is always more fun than coming back, isn't it?"

For some of us it's just the same, but she didn't know that. She had natural highs, which I never get, not like hers anyway.

This time she couldn't really get out of her mood, even after we were in bed. Her eyes stayed open—it made me uncomfortable, having her there. I was too conscious of her. We were fucked out, or I was at least, but we didn't have anything to say to one another. We were just wide awake in the same bed.

"Maybe you can't really know someone unless you live with them," she said. "I guess that doesn't really bother you because you don't really want to know anyone. You certainly don't really want to know me. I've forced myself on you and insisted you have what knowledge you do have. I know you don't like it."

"Then why don't you stop it?" I said.

When I woke up the next morning she was sitting up in bed drawing pictures of my feet. She was using some old stationery I had that had the name of my so-called production company on it. Sunset Productions, it was called. She had made about forty sketches of one of my feet.

"You have extraordinary feet," she said. "If it wasn't for them maybe you could convince me that you had no character. I guess all your character just slid down to the bottom. They're Renaissance feet."

She was determined to look on the bright side. Probably half the assholes in the world had interesting feet. When she got tired of drawing mine she drew two or three pages full of breasts. "These are for you to fantasize about, since I don't have any," she said. She was always making tit jokes designed to get me to reassure her about being flat-chested.

"Not tits again," I said. "For god's sakes, I thought you were liberated. You don't fuck a tit."

She stretched and I rubbed her nipples for her. "All the same, a bosom ought to be bigger than an egg," she said.

We ate, and talked some more script. I changed my mind again. Maybe I would do the picture with her after all. When I sifted through all the pros and cons it seemed to make sense. At least Jill was on my side, and she had brains. Besides, if Bo and Sherry were going to team up again, it wouldn't hurt to be on the scene.

"Maybe we'll try it," I said.

"Try what?" she asked.

"Doing the picture together."

"Oh, yeah?" she said. "What made you change your mind?"

"It wasn't your tits," I said.

Then, for some reason, Bo Brimmer backed out. Not only did he change his mind and turn us down, he dropped his option on the script altogether. I was the one who got the news. *Outtake* had just had a very good preview in San Francisco, and I went in to receive congratulations and was told the Western was no go.

Of course the little fucker was looking smart and cheerful, as if he had just won a chess match.

"Why not?" I said. "I thought you liked the script."

"I do like the script," he said. "What I don't like is the mix. It needs to be either better or worse. It won't be a masterpiece, and it won't be a blockbuster either. What it'll be is a small winner, and we ain't hurtin' for small winners right now. What we'd like is a big winner."

"But you've got Sherry Solaré," I said. "That's not going to hurt you."

He looked a little irritated. "Sherry Solaré is a fact of life, like the common cold," he said. "Only she's more like walkin' pneumonia. I think we might do well to let this little opportunity pass. If you'll remember, I said I didn't like the mix."

"What mix?"

"You and Jill are a bad mix, to start with," he said. "Jill and Sherry are a bad mix, and you and Jill and Sherry are a worse mix."

"What's wrong with me and Jill?"

"I don't know," he said. "You probably know, but I doubt you'd come right out and tell me. I just know that I decline to get involved."

I was really upset. It had never occurred to me that he'd change his mind. Maybe I am more naive than Jill.

"You're not more naive," she said when she came in that night and found me. I was fairly drunk, from drinking all afternoon while I waited for her to get home.

"You just don't know Bo as well as I do," she said. "I'm not surprised he backed out."

"Hell, I thought he was in love with you once," I said.

"He was, but I never fucked him," she said. "If I had, it might have been okay, even if I'd only fucked him once. Sometimes it works that way. He's just one of those men who need to fuck a woman in order to forget her. Until he's done it the power is still hers."

"Why didn't you fuck him?" I said.

She just kicked my foot and went off to the bathroom to wash her face. She wasn't mad. It was all irritating. She must have kept her legs crossed for about ten years, before she met me. If she'd fucked him, she might have been able to disarm him, and I'd dearly love to see the little fucker disarmed.

"So why didn't you fuck him?" I asked when she came out of the bathroom.

"He really wanted Jacqueline Bisset," she said.

"You're too goddamn hard to get," I said.

"And you're drunk and upset and don't know what you're

talking about," she said. "*You* got me, so I must not be that hard."

She sat down on the couch and tried to take my hand, but I shoved her off.

"Look, you're overreacting," she said. "I tried to tell you Bo was tricky. He probably only offered me the script in order to be able to back out and upset our applecart. He's probably jealous of you, among other things."

"Who did you fuck, before I came along?" I asked.

She just looked at me. I was beginning to find her very irritating again.

"I'm not going to talk to you about things like that when you're drunk," she said. "If you can't be nice, then it's none of your business."

"It's my business if I want to know," I said.

She sighed and shook her head. "You should eat something," she said.

"Did you fuck any of those old guys?" I asked.

She got up and left the room. When she didn't come back I finally got up and found her in the bedroom, reading a script.

"It's all right if you fucked one," I said. "I guess senior citizens need groupies, too."

"Shut up, Owen," she said. "Go to your place if you want to get stewed. You don't have to bother showing me how obnoxious you can be because I already know."

"You're not helping," I said. "You're just sitting there reading some fucking script."

She looked up. "What did you have in mind?" she asked. "You're too drunk to drive, too drunk to eat, too drunk to talk rationally, and too drunk to fuck. That doesn't leave us too many options."

I wanted to kick the shit out of her, but I controlled it. I went out and walked up the hill. One nice thing about the plains, when you want to take a walk you don't have to go uphill. Old Percy was out squirting water on his bushes. I guess he had decided I wasn't going to axe murder his darling, because he offered me a drink. When we went in, an old one-eyed German of some kind came out of the kitchen, stirring his drink with his finger.

"Joey, see you later," he said, and went out the door.

"Bring the glass back," Joe said.

"Who's that?"

"Bruno Himmel," he said. "He's got a girl friend in the neighborhood. He just came to my house because he knows I stock Irish whisky."

I drank with him for a while, mostly because my head was swimming and I needed a place to sit down. I wasn't in the mood to puke in the gutter. Old Percy told me about his wife, the serial queen. I had heard about her already from Jill, but I heard it again.

"Quite a woman," he said. "Quite a woman."

We watched about three innings of a baseball game. He wasn't as bad to be with as he was to think about. "I don't know why we take this poison into our bodies," he said, meaning the whisky. He was drinking two to my one.

On the way downhill I puked in the gutter. It had been years since I'd drunk that much. I don't know why I did it, instead of going and fucking Lulu or something. Jill was still reading scripts, in her bed. I stood in the shower because I've discovered that if I run enough water on my head when I'm drunk, I don't have as bad a hangover. Maybe Jill thought I drowned in the shower, I don't know. She came and peeked in, wearing her nightgown. When she saw that I wasn't coming out, she slipped off her nightgown and got in with me.

"It's really amazing how much bigger you are than me," she said. "Your bones must be twice as thick as my bones."

I *was* twice as big as she was—maybe that was her turn-on, I don't know. We made a game of it when we first started out. She weighed 108, and I got down to 216 so I'd be exactly twice as big. But we had forgotten about the game and I was back up to about 225.

"In the morning we'll go to Mr. Mond," she said. "He trusts me and I bet he'll get the script for us."

I was too tired to think about it. I hated the whole business: having to carry around scripts to some asshole like Bo Brimmer or old Mondschiem. I was tired of being the one smiling the shit-eating grin. Jill kept playing with me while I was trying to get to sleep. I guess she had been a late starter, I don't know, but for once she was playing with the wrong cock. I went to sleep anyway and slept until my hangover woke me up.

The next day we drove up the hill to old Mondschiem's. He lay on a chaise by his pool, looking like a ninety-year-old french fry, white hairs on his old brown chest. He had a big head, all right, and a jaw like an axe handle. His grandson, little Abe the butterball, was playing a game of grab-ass in the pool with a couple of Cuban teenagers he had found somewhere. The teenagers were topless, which annoyed old Aaron.

"Get 'em out," he yelled when Jill and I walked up.

"I got no prudery, you see," he said to Jill, "but, I mean, a lady like you shouldn't have to see tits all over the place."

"This is business hours!" he yelled to Abe. Abe finally dragged his blubber out of the pool and the girls ran off giggling, their little tits bouncing.

"I mean, there's no respect," the old man said, fixing an eye on me. "Who's this, a foimer? Ain't he from Texas? Football or something?"

I would have liked to pitch him out in the pool and watch him sink, but I held my peace.

"You're da best," he said, patting Jill's knee. He took the script.

"If you say it's good, I won't even read it," he said. "Tell me who you want, we get started. Tell me how much, ya got it. I should be so lucky, at my age, getting to woik with you, my darlin'."

Jill was blushing. She couldn't take compliments. "Oh, now read it," she said.

I was glad to get out of there. What an old shitter he was. Of course, *Womanly Ways* had done about ten million better than anyone had thought it would. He could afford to buy himself a bigger tombstone.

"You ought to run a nursing home," I said as we were driving downhill. "You'd be da best."

She looked depressed. "Why does it make you so jealous that I'm nice to older people?" she said. "It doesn't take anything away from you."

I didn't answer. She just looked more depressed. "Maybe I ought to give all this up anyway," she said. "I don't really have any business directing movies. I just have a good sense of story, that's all. It's just an accident I got this far—I just had that script at the right time. All this success is just some kind of dirty trick that worked.

"I don't know why I let it become important to me," she said a little later.

We went to a restaurant on the Strip and I had some eggs Benedict while she ate a salad. She kept talking, a mile a minute.

"You never talk to me when I need it," she said, looking out the window. "It's going to be awful making a movie with you if you keep on being sullen. What have I done to make you sullen?"

I didn't explain it. Not that I knew, particularly, but even if I had known I wouldn't have explained it. If I knew anything, it's that you should never confess, never admit, and never explain, not with a woman. If you start doing any of that, they'll unravel you strand by strand.

While she was playing with her coffee cup, a girl I had been fucking about a year before came in and sat down in the next booth. She was with a guy I knew vaguely, a lighting director who mostly worked in TV. The girl didn't speak to me, I didn't speak to her, and eventually Jill stopped talking. The girl was beautiful enough to be in pictures or on the cover of magazines or the mistress of a studio head, but she wouldn't be any of those things. She was lazy and a dull fuck and half the time she chewed gum while she was having sex. She just forgot to get rid of it. A lighting director would be about tops for her, face or no face.

The next day old Mondschiem optioned the Western. Lulu Dickey got Sherry to agree to stay on it. *Outtake* opened in New York and got super reviews. Pauline Kael said it was the first honest movie about movie making. Vincent Canby saw it as an elegy to a Hollywood legend, and Judith Crist called it engaging. The kids flocked to it in droves.

Just as everybody had been about to forget us, Jill and I became news again. The Can't Lose Couple, they called us. *People* Magazine wanted to do a piece on our life style, but Jill wouldn't go along with it. The Western—we decided to call it *One Tree*, after the town where the madam gets hung—was budgeted at $7 million. It made Jill so nervous that she stayed up most of the night drawing pictures of my feet, or me sleeping, or whatever she could find to draw. Eventually it began to bug me. I got drunk one night and tore up all her sketches, and at that point we stopped fucking.

Old Mondschiem made us co-producers—I guess Jill talked him into it. What it meant was that we were both living under the shadow of the $7 million. In June we flew to Amarillo and drove down toward Clovis to look for locations. Jill was so scared and excited she squeezed my hand the whole flight.

We found some country down near the Palo Duro Canyon, as empty as plains can get, and six weeks from the time we picked the location we were on our way back to shoot. Anna Lyle went with us—she played a rancher's wife, the mother of Sherry's youthful lover.

Sherry was to arrive in three days, with Swan in tow. They had busted up, and stayed busted for a whole month, which was when she decided to do the picture. He had intended to produce her next picture, or maybe even direct it, but when he dragged himself back to her he found both jobs were filled. That wasn't going to sit well—not at all. I knew it, and Jill knew it, too.

In eastern New Mexico the wheat was still green. We flew over a lot of wheat, and then over the scalds and broken country up the Canadian River. It wouldn't be long before the combines rolled in from central Texas to start curling up that wheat. Once again Jill was nervous and kept squeezing my hand.

"I think I'd feel calmer if it was a war," she said.

For a day or two she walked around West Texas as if it were paradise, her eyes as wide as they were just after we fucked. New places affected her that way. We were staying in Amarillo and shooting out north of the Canyon, near a place called Adrian.

Jill walked around looking turned on, and the crew started falling for her, one good old boy after another. I kept out of it, laid back. Let them make fools of themselves. I had a lot of other things to think about.

Sherry Solaré sort of hung on the horizon. I could feel her coming, and so could a lot of others. She was like those great banks of clouds that roll down out of Canada in June and July, beautiful and white on top, but rumbling, always rumbling, and capable of suddenly turning black on the bottom. Maybe we'd get a nice rain, an afternoon shower, even a few rainbows, and then maybe one of those black bottoms would fall out, cut loose the wind, gut the wheat, and drown every fucking thing in sight, including me. There was that waiting feeling people get on the plains when the clouds are just sort of hanging there.

She turned out to be a week late for rehearsals, and all that time she hung there. We all stayed busy and ignored it, but it hung there.

Jill began to talk too much, so much that I was ready to get a separate room. She talked half the night sometimes. The air conditioning broke down and the nights were sultry. The sheets practically dripped when we fucked—we started again while we were waiting on Sherry. You have to do something on location, particularly if you're just sitting there, waiting for a cloud to make up its mind what it's going to dump on you. None of us could figure out why we were even in such a business. I couldn't even figure out why *I* was in it, and I had exactly the kind of job I had been hoping to get for three years.

Then she came, same coffin-lid glasses, same rat's nest of hair, same silence, and Swan Bunting looking like he wanted to take a dull machete to us all. The hicks in the Amarillo airport stared at her like she was Jesus.

"Listen," Swan said. "Our suite better be right, and I mean right."

Sherry turned her sunglasses his way. "Ho ho, Daddy's pissed," she said. "Where the fuck do you think you are, Switzerland?"

After that, clams couldn't have been more silent. Jill and I made conversation all the way back to the motel and then all the way to the set.

Book III

CHAPTER 1

I was sitting in one of the costume sheds, watching it drizzle and hating it, when Wynkyn Weil came in, his curly hair dripping. Wynkyn was Sherry's son by her second husband, Willy Weil, the producer who drowned when his yacht sank.

"Jill, can I sit with you?" Wynkyn asked. "I don't have my slicker."

"Sure, Wynkyn," I said. "Where's the slicker?"

He sat down by me and immediately took my hand.

"Let's hold hands," he said. "The rain got me wet."

I gave him a hug. Marie, one of the costume girls, was looking at him as if she'd like to brain him with a stick. Of course he took not the slightest notice of her. In regard to the crew, Wynkyn saw with his mother's eyes, automatically distinguishing between people who were high enough up to associate with and people who weren't. Naturally the crew hated him and denied him the affection they would have lavished on almost any other child—if only because they were bored, and homesick for their own kids. Wynkyn asked for nothing, and got nothing.

"I may have a fever already," he said. He had almost died of pneumonia once, and of course had learned to play on his frailness. I felt his forehead.

"Nope, no fever," I said. "All you are is wet. How come you don't have your slicker?"

We all had slickers, big floppy yellow ones. I was beginning to think we should forget about sunlight and shoot the picture in the rain.

"Oh, my slicker's in Sherry's trailer, but I can't go in and get it because she's fucking somebody," Wynkyn said plaintively.

Marie was so blasted that she almost knocked over a costume rack. She isn't as sophisticated as she likes to think. Wynkyn looked at her censoriously.

I felt my face getting hot, a reaction I hate.

"I tried to go in and get my slicker because I don't want to catch cold," Wynkyn said, drumming his fingers on the trunk where we were sitting. "Momma said I had to go back to Hollywood if I let myself catch cold. But when I tried to go in they yelled at me. That means they're fucking, don't you think?"

"Maybe not," I said. "There are lots of times when people don't want to be disturbed."

"Oh, but with Sherry it's usually fucking," Wynkyn said, examining a ring I had on. It was a small opal—I had bought it for myself, years before.

"Wynkyn, that's not a nice word," I said. "I don't want to hear you using that word again."

I meant it. The sound of it issuing from his severe little mouth made it all seem awful, everything.

"I think it was Mr. Oarson," he added, unnecessarily. There was no one else likely. Swan Bunting was in L.A., negotiating a TV special.

"If it stops raining, will you take me riding?" he asked.

"Can't," I said. "If it stops raining, I have to go back to work."

Wynkyn felt his own forehead, to see if perhaps I was wrong about his fever. "I don't care if she does send me back to Hollywood," he said. "Swan's there, and he's my only real friend."

"Oh, really?" I said. "That's interesting."

Wynkyn suddenly began to talk faster, as children will.

"Yeah, because Momma's mean to him," he said. "She makes him eat a lot of shit . . . I mean that's how Swan describes it. Not real shit that comes out of your ass but she talks mean and makes him cry. I've heard him. It's when she says, 'Oh, go jack off for all I care,' and things like that. She says that all the time. But I never let her make me cry any more. If I let her make me cry, then she feels guilty and bores me to death kissing me and stuff later on. You know?"

Marie looked like she was about to turn green. I just sat and listened.

"It's when she says, 'Oh, go jack off, you asshole,' or something like that, that Swan comes and plays with me. We play TV tennis, you know, where the little dot bounces around. Swan and I play that all the time. That's when he's my real friend."

Before I could sort anything out in myself, Jerry, the assistant director, came in. He had a setup he wanted me to look at, in case it ever stopped raining. Actually, that was just his excuse. Jerry had gotten in love with me, or thought he had. He had never said anything, but I could see it all coming from the choked looks he kept giving me. Gauldin Edwards, the head grip, was doing the same thing, and already, with nothing being said by anyone, Gauldin and Jerry were beginning to have squabbles that were really nothing more than suppressed jealousy.

Wynkyn was still holding my hand. He ignored Jerry, who didn't count in his system. I wish I could have ignored him, too, but I couldn't. I could feel his desire from about twenty feet. Men's eyes always seem to get bigger and more beseeching when that starts. Jerry's eyes were already pretty big. He wasn't going to be cool about it much longer.

"I can't come right now, I'm looking after Wynkyn," I said. "Sherry's busy. I'll be along in a few minutes."

From a distance, behind him through the drizzle, I saw Anna Lyle come out of her dressing room. She made straight for the costume shed. Of course she would: it's like my body contains a homing device, hooked into Anna, so she can always find me, particularly when I'm hoping not to have to deal with her.

The one thing Owen had been right about was that I shouldn't have used her. The Oscar had ruined her, in a way. It hadn't affected Pete Sweet much—he was still mostly hanging around Malibu, involved with the same hopeless women he seemed to like, but with Anna it was different. Champagne and roses had gone to her head and made her almost impossible to direct. All she had done since we got to Texas was niggle over her scenes. She kept finding subtleties in them that nobody else could sense. Of course what she was really doing was playing against Sherry. She kept trying to whittle down Sherry's scenes and build up her own. That, among other things, was wearing me down.

Before she reached the shed Sammy slipped in the door. Sammy was the cutter; he was sixty-five and I loved him. Of course Owen said he was just another of my old men, but I never thought of Sammy as old. He had more life in his eyes than Owen had, that's for sure. Owen's eyes were like clouds, except when he was mad. Sammy was full of happiness. He loved his wife, he loved his kids, he loved his grandkids, and he loved his work. Today he wasn't too joyous, though—the day before we had discovered that we had shot most of a morning with a hair in the lens. Sammy was trying to fix it, but there was still the possibility that we would have to reshoot.

But he hugged me and let me wear his cap, and we clowned a little. Wynkyn looked on solemnly. Then Anna tripped in, pretending to look dreamy. It was just an act. It bore no resemblance to her old genuine what-am-I-doing-in-this-world look.

"I just had a real good thought for the scene in the boardinghouse," she said. "Real good, for some time when you're not busy."

"That'll be Christmas Eve," I said, holding on to Sammy so he wouldn't leave me amid my problems. He had curly white hair, and freckles that were so old they gave him dignity. I was longing to put him in a scene, but he was too bashful.

"The missus wouldn't like it," he said. "Then all the women in the world would find out about me. She likes to think she's the only one that knows, you see?"

"I know, baby," I said. "I don't blame her a bit."

Anna plopped down on the trunk and gave Wynkyn a pat. He scooted away from her.

"Oh, Wynkyn, why can't I pat you?" she asked.

Wynkyn maintained total silence, as if no one had spoken.

Meanwhile, Jerry hadn't gone away. His face seemed to become slightly bulbous when he was around me. One of the prop men came up looking for him, and neither of them went away. Pretty soon the whole crew would be there. I think they clustered around me for security, laughable as that would have seemed if it hadn't been true. I was supposed to give them security, somehow—meanwhile, I hadn't even had a second in which to deal with the knowledge of Sherry and Owen. It was there in my chest, at the bottom of my windpipe, a knot the size of a golf ball.

I thought maybe I could escape for a few minutes by getting Sammy to take me to the lab to see the footage. We even started, Wynkyn tagging along as if it was his right. What could I do? If his mother was indeed fucking my boyfriend, I couldn't very well send her kid home to her. His highly paid nurse had disappeared. Sammy knew something was wrong with me, but Sammy is not a talker, he was just for playing with, flirting with, teasing; and anyway, we never even got to the car, much less the lab. While it was still drizzling the clouds broke and it suddenly looked like we might get to shoot. I went to deal with a problem in the sound unit that had come up yesterday but which, for some reason, no one had told me about. Someone had told Owen, who hadn't mentioned it, no doubt because of the new thing he had on his mind.

I dealt with that, and went to look at the shot, and then it became a glorious afternoon, during which the only problem was getting Anna settled down. It took half the afternoon to get her to stop overacting and just do her scene straight, and the only thing that saved us was that Anna is so forgetful that eventually she forgot to concentrate on her new existence as an international film celebrity and sort of nodded back into the role, as if she'd just noticed it.

But I was never alone; not a minute all day, and Wynkyn was at my elbow for two hours, until his nurse finally showed up and got him. Sherry never appeared, and I didn't see Owen until late afternoon, when I glimpsed him at a distance, talking to a wrangler.

Jerry and Gauldin stared at me all afternoon, love in their big eyes. I just had no airspace, not a bit, even though we were right in the middle of one of the biggest plains in the world. I had no time to feel, or to allow myself the slightest reflection. People noticed I was grim, I guess, but I'm always grim when I'm working, because I'm so scared.

As for the golf ball of feeling in my chest, there was just no chance to get it out. I was in a crowd, I had a decision to make about every twenty seconds, and there was no time for those feelings—not that I wanted to face them. I was grateful for the work, if not for the crowd. Several times I hoped it would cloud up and rain again, so I could just get a horse and ride away from the whole mess for a while: the trucks and trailers, the lights, wires, cables, work, love. The love was sort of like a big tangle of cables itself, none of them really plugged in any more—not so far as I was concerned.

But of course the sun shone like a million dollars all afternoon, and we worked until we were all dull with fatigue.

I concentrated like hell on the shooting—I always do, I have to, if I'm to make any sense of it at all—but even so, I was aware of a slight change in the atmosphere around me. Theroux Wickes, the cameraman, or director of photography, as he liked to style it, was actually nice to me, for the first time since production started. Theroux was a shit of the first water, a pompous little half-French, half-Upper-West-Side protégé of Jilly Legendre's. I didn't respect him as a person or as a craftsman, though Jilly, by bullying him constantly, had got fairly competent work out of him on *Burning Deck.* But I didn't like Theroux, and I only used him because the cameramen I would have preferred were all busy. We had rushed into production too quickly to have had much hope of putting together an ideal crew. Sherry's change of heart was responsible for that—Mr. Mond wanted to get the cameras rolling before she thought it over and backed out.

People were too nice to me, all afternoon. I noticed it, underneath the work. The old scrappy, brassy, fuck-you, don't-tell-me-how-to-do-my-job ambiance that makes a crew endearing, such a bunch of show-offy, soft-hearted, vulnerable overgrown boys, had shifted tone slightly, into something protective and subdued. It just meant everyone already knew that Owen was fucking Sherry, so they were being nice and cooperative out of sympathy. I guess I couldn't blame them, but it made my heart sink. I hate certain kinds of sympathy, most particularly that kind.

Finally it was evening. Big clouds were beginning to roll back in, meaning trouble for tomorrow. The crew piled into its bus and I waited as long as I could, hoping something nice would happen, something to convince me it had all been a mistake. Then Sherry and Owen got in her limousine, or rather Sherry did. Owen came over to where I was standing with Sammy. He looked sulky—not mad, just sulky, as if it annoyed him to be obliged to speak to me.

"Going with us?" he asked.

Wynkyn was having a fit of some kind—I could see his nurse dragging him toward the limo.

"No, go ahead," I said, as if I still had duties to attend to.

"I'll just ride in with the boys," I said. "Are you coming to rushes?"

"Sure," he said. He punched Sammy lightly on the shoulder, and left.

So I rode in with the boys. The road to town ran along a ridge—you could see for many miles across West Texas, probably into New Mexico. I loved the ride in—usually I could lose myself, staring at the plains and the sky; but not today. I had meant to sit by Sammy, to take comfort from his cheer, his good humor, his friendliness, from the mere fact that I knew a happy person, but it didn't work out that way. Theroux Wickes sat down by me while Sammy was joking with the driver.

"It was okay, it was okay," he said. He often said things twice. I guess he was referring to the day's shooting.

"You're a hell of a woman," he added, in his most intimate tones. He had told me that twenty or thirty times during the course of the production. Despite the fact that he didn't like me, couldn't stand me, and would go back and bad-mouth me around Hollywood for years, for the duration of the shooting he felt obliged to flirt.

"We should go out sometime," he said. "I mean it, Jill. I know some nice places."

It was a formality, what he was doing. I wanted to tell him I hated his mustache, but I held my tongue. Obviously, we knew the same places—which I also wanted to tell him. Finally, I wanted to tell him that I thought he was a third-rate cameraman. But I didn't tell him any of those things.

"We'll see," I said.

I guess he thought that was encouragement, because he put his hand on my leg and began to tell me why he had left his wife. Par for the course. I had heard why about ten other divorced men on the crew had left their wives, why not Theroux? The Texas dusk was heavy—I felt oppressed, as if I were crossing the Russian steppes with a busload of convicts, probably an image I'd kept from some forgotten film. Instead of feeling in tearing pain, I just felt flat. A big effort had failed—my effort with Owen—and the rope had suddenly gone slack, at least for the course of the bus ride.

I didn't tell Theroux to get his hand off my leg, but in my slackness I felt flickering, warring impulses. If I had had a machete handy, I would have reached down and cut his fucking hand off at the wrist, just to see him look surprised.

Of course Owen didn't come to the rushes. We were screening them in a big ballroom of the motel where we were all staying, and everybody was there who was supposed to be there except Owen and Sherry. Zack Kelly, the big kid who played Sherry's lover, had found a local girl friend; he was dancing around, sparring with one of the production people, showing off for his date. The little girl was overawed. She wouldn't have said a word if the ceiling had fallen in. Zack's high spirits cut the gloom a little, but not much. There was lots of tension in the room, all of it centered on me. How would I take it, how badly would I be hurt? I couldn't have clarified that for anyone. I didn't know. Like everyone else, I was sort of waiting for signals.

I gave them ten minutes, then called Sherry's room. After all, if I was anything, I was still the director. Up to me to give the signals, not wait for them, particularly with ten tired hungry people standing around, wanting to have the day over with. Maybe the two of them up there were on the threshold of a great romance, or even over the threshold: it still didn't justify inconsideration. It's the one thing I won't accept, because all the people I really admire manage to be considerate no matter what state their life is in. I had been exempting Owen from that standard for over a year, and it was time to quit, even though I knew that to judge him for being ill-mannered was mostly irrelevant. Manners hadn't occurred to Owen, and had no meaning for him. Maybe he had never been secure enough to approach life on that level, I don't know. He lived in his gut, not his head, but it didn't matter. I wasn't judging *him*, I was judging me, and I was tired of hearing myself make excuses for him.

Sherry's room was busy. I tried a few times and gave up. We saw the rushes, and later encountered Wynkyn and his nurse in the coffee shop, Wynkyn staring with infinite melancholy at an uneaten hamburger. If there's tragedy in Hollywood, it has to be the children. I sat down with them, perhaps to avoid having to eat with Jerry, who had not got three steps from me all day. I guess he saw this contretemps as his big chance.

"I'm going to sit with you and help you stare at that hamburger," I said to Wynkyn. "Then when mine comes you can help me stare at mine."

Wynkyn smiled wanly and took a small bite of the hamburger, only to spit it out. His nanny, a totally disoriented Englishwoman who always wore gray, made a bit of a flutter at that, but I think she was grateful for my company. Every time I looked up I caught Jerry looking at me.

"Do you think they have ratshit in them?" Wynkyn asked. "Swan says most hamburgers have ratshit in them."

"Why'd you order it, then?" I said. "There are other things to eat."

"It was Miss Solaré," the nanny said. "She did specify a hamburger."

"Oh, specify, specify," I said. "Would you like a grilled cheese sandwich, Wynkyn?"

"Could I?" he asked, looking at his nanny and back at me. "Even if Sherry said hamburger?"

"We directors have some authority," I said. A small revenge, getting her kid a grilled cheese sandwich, but not insignificant. Mrs. Hoops, the nanny, absented herself to the ladies' room, doubtless to escape responsibility.

Wynkyn ate all his grilled cheese, and I stared at a hamburger. Wynkyn got into the spirit of the thing and stared at it with me. I crossed my eyes and stared at it, which perked him up considerably. Mrs. Hoops came back, having freshened her makeup, but she still couldn't make any sense of the two of us.

"Do you really believe that about ratshit?" Wynkyn asked. "Swan really believes it.

"They don't have very good TV up here," he added sadly. "I've seen almost every one of the cartoons."

Seeing a sad child always makes me wonder if my own was ever that sad. A child whose best friend is Swan Bunting was in pretty sad shape, although if Sherry could abuse him to the point of tears, perhaps there was a human being there somewhere, after all. He was due back in two or three days, which was going to be interesting.

"I wish we could do something exciting," Wynkyn said.

"Oh, Wynkyn, don't sound like that," I said. "What would

you consider exciting? Think of something and I'll do it with you."

"Seeing the buffaloes," he said. "I can't get enough of them."

"Now, Wynkyn, you know your mother wants you in bed early," Mrs. Hoops began. Wynkyn's face immediately reflected defeat. I couldn't stand it. I made him look at me.

"Listen, buster, you've got to learn not to give up so easily," I said. "It's only eight. There's absolutely no reason why we can't sneak a look at the buffaloes. I'd like a look at them myself. Do you want some ice cream first?"

Mrs. Hoops, though she knew she was placing herself in peril, seemed relieved at not having to disappoint Wynkyn yet again. I borrowed Jerry's rented car, and Wynkyn and I drove out of town about twelve miles, to the ranch that had the buffalo we were using. There were about twenty of them. Wynkyn delivered an extensive critique of Texas television programming while I drove. I couldn't disagree with him because I hadn't had time to watch any.

"I guess you don't really care what Sherry thinks, do you?" he asked, out of the blue.

"No, Wynkyn, I don't," I said.

"I don't either, half the time," he said, rather proudly.

The dogs at the ranch barked like crazy, until they figured out it was me. The rancher, Mr. Debo, stepped out of the front door of his ranch house, but I guess he recognized the car because he went right back in. The buffalo were in a big pen, standing around a hayrack. Wynkyn and I climbed up on the board fence and sat and watched them. It was cool, and Wynkyn let me hug him. There was a moon, riding in and out of thinning clouds. One or two of the buffalo turned and looked at us, but mostly they just kept eating hay. Then, to Wynkyn's extreme delight, one of them got enough hay and came over near the fence. He grunted a few times, sighed the way everyone sighs when it's finally time to go to bed, and sank down. Wynkyn took my hand—at last something exciting was happening. We could have stepped off the fence onto the buffalo's back.

"Is he going to have a dream?" Wynkyn asked.

"What would a buffalo dream about?"

Wynkyn giggled, almost the first normal sound I had ever heard him make. "Maybe he'll dream he was going to be in a movie," he said. "Maybe he thinks that's exciting."

"On the other hand, maybe he'll dream we all dropped dead," I suggested. "Then he and his friends could have all these plains to themselves again, like they did in olden days.

"There were millions of them," I added. "Millions and millions. Think about that."

Wynkyn thought about it. We sat on the fence for half an hour, listening to the buffalo breathe. When the clouds hid the moon it would get so dark we could barely see the others, but we could hear them pulling hay out of the hayrack. Then the moon would come out again, very white, and we could see their horns and even their shadows, and could smell the dusty hair of the one underneath us. Wynkyn never moved. With the great sea of grass around us, the white moon, vast sky, and quiet beasts, we were both lifted out of our lives for a little time, and felt the breath of the immemorial—maybe the only time Wynkyn had ever had such an experience. I think he could have sat there all night, but eventually we both realized that we had had our fun. We were just sitting on the fence in order to postpone our lives.

"Let's go, kid," I said. "There's no point in getting your mother too outraged."

Wynkyn made a face. "I don't need half as much sleep as she thinks I do," he said.

The prairie was really nicer at night than it was in the daytime. We could see a red light high up on a radio tower as we drove back into town. For a few minutes I felt a sort of contentment—Wynkyn felt it, too. I felt almost tempted to kidnap him. Sherry probably wouldn't care, as long as I left a note. We could drive up to Wyoming, to the mountains, and do some more exciting things. Wynkyn might make a mother of me, and I might even show him how to be a child.

Instead, I delivered him to a worried—indeed, quietly

frantic—Mrs. Hoops. She had been growing more and more worried about what she would say if Sherry called.

I got my messages, found that the weather report was good and that we had a five-o'clock call, and managed to get to my room without meeting anyone sympathetic. The room was in an unbelievable state: I give up on order during a movie production, and the maids at the motel were so in awe of us and so afraid of doing something wrong that they never did much more than make the beds and replenish the towels. They had to do the latter, because Owen had a thing about towels. There couldn't be enough of them, not for him. The nicest he ever was to me was when we spent a weekend in San Francisco in a hotel that not only had a lot of towels but towel-warmers as well. To Owen, warm towels were really the last word. I never figured that out, except that it had to do with playing football and showering a lot.

Otherwise he was hardly a fastidious man. I had to clean his apartment about once a month or the litter would have buried him. He'd rather buy a new shirt than take one to the laundry—I found thirty in a closet in his bedroom, all worn once and all ugly. Of course he had that Mercedes that every homosexual in Hollywood wept at the sight of, but other than that, everything he had was tacky, and even the Mercedes didn't really fit with him. He would have looked more in place in a Buick, and been happier probably, only I don't think he ever realized that. Maybe the fact that he knew so little about himself was what made him interesting. I'd had too many men who were too self-aware, who knew too much about themselves and too much about me. Owen really knew next to nothing about either one of us—all he knew was what he called the basics, such as that he liked motels with lots of towels.

He hadn't cleared his stuff out of the room yet—I could see that just by turning on the bedside light, the only light I cared to risk. I wasn't in the room much in the daylight, and if I just turned on the bedside light, I didn't have to face the full evidence of the chaos of my existence: the ever-increasing confusion of clothes, books, suitcases, scripts, tapes, telexes, shoes, boots, Kleenex, pills, magazines, that the room contained. Owen was almost as compulsive about magazines as he was about towels. He read dozens, leafing through them petulantly and then dropping them on the floor. His fascination and disappointment with them was intriguing, another aspect of him that I never got to the bottom of. Probably he was just hoping to see a picture of a woman he'd like to fuck.

After a while I found myself sitting in the bathtub, with the water cold around my belly. It had been hot when I got in, so I must have fallen asleep sitting in the tub. I seemed to have reached a level of fatigue where there were spaces in my consciousness. I would wake in the midst of some action or other and have no memory or knowledge of how I'd gotten that far along in it. Probably I went around half-asleep all the time—at least I was always coming awake into a sense of limbo. Maybe I would be combing my hair and have no sense of having gotten out of bed and dressed.

I got from bath to bed, and just when it seemed I was getting firmly to sleep again, Jerry hit the door. The night had passed. Jerry knew I hated alarm clocks, and knocking on the door to wake me was just another way he could demonstrate his love.

"Jill?" he said. "Jill, are you ready?"

"Right, meet you in the coffee shop," I said, wondering if I even had a semi-clean pair of pants to put on.

CHAPTER 2

Owen didn't come to the set that day. I don't know what he was doing—it nagged at my mind all day that what he was doing was getting his things out of our suite so that maybe I wouldn't even get him to face me. But that was paranoia. He was co-producer—he would have to show up somewhere, sooner or later.

We were shooting a scene in which Sherry sent Zack, her youthful lover, off on an errand, to get him out of the way of the trouble that she knew was coming. He didn't know he'd never see her alive again, and neither did she, but she at least knew it was likely to be a rough day.

I guess Sherry thought she had me on the ropes emotionally, where she'd wanted me all the time. It had even crossed my mind that her interest in Owen was no more than that: a way of getting me on the ropes. Anyway, she chose the morning for a contest of wills.

To make matters worse, Abe Mondschiem was around. Mr.

Mond sent him up once in a while to check on things. It didn't matter much, since Abe couldn't be bothered to do any thorough checking, but it did involve a good deal of protocol: treating him like a king, in other words. He generally had two or three teenyboppers with him, and this time was no exception. They say he was into group balling, or at least group lolling around, but I don't know. Abe was always fairly nice to me, out of fear of his grandfather, and I didn't ordinarily mind his visits, since all he did was lie around the motel with the teenyboppers and eat a meal or two and maybe see some rushes. He hated sets and avoided them when he could, but for some reason he was there that morning when I arrived. Gauldin Edwards told me later that he was just passing through on his way in from an all-night binge in Lubbock. When it came to finding all-night binges, Abe was resourceful. He was wearing a Levi jacket and was drinking coffee with the rest of us when Bobbie, the woman who dresses Sherry, came over to the group.

Bobbie was all right—I think she sort of liked me, even—but she was a loyal factotum, and I knew there was trouble when I saw her approach.

"Hi, Jill," she said. "Sherry's asked me to tell you she's made a dress change. She doesn't want to wear the yellow dress. She wants to wear black."

It had to be just to irritate me. The lady she was playing certainly wouldn't be likely to wear black in the scene we were about to shoot. I just shook my head.

"Maybe she's got the scene mixed up," I said. "Black is out of the question. It has to be the yellow dress. That was all decided day before yesterday."

"I know it was," Bobbie said, "but Sherry's been rereading the scene and I guess she's changed her mind. She wants to be more somber."

"I'm sorry, Bobbie," I said. "Black is out of the question. She'll have to change again if that's what she's got on."

I guess when you make a profession of dealing with whims you become professional at it, just as you would about directing traffic if you became a traffic cop. Bobbie got a cup of coffee and made her way back to the dressing room, to deliver the news.

"You want me to see what I can do?" Jerry asked. He was bird-dogging me again, his face as bulbous as ever.

"Would you give it a try?" I said. "The black dress is ridiculous in this scene."

Abe was sitting on the fender of his limousine, drinking coffee. He took his dark glasses off when I came over, and I saw that his eyes were soon going to disappear in fat. He was already too fat to move his body naturally. Most of the time only his head moved—this way, that way—while his body sort of slumped there. His belly was trying to pop out of the silk shirt he wore under the Levi jacket. Folsom, his gofer, was standing off to one side, glum as usual.

"Hello, Abe, good morning, Folsom," I said.

Folsom twitched. Abe had started to yawn but stifled it.

"I don't know why we didn't film in Stockton," he said. "Ain't it flat around Stockton?"

"I don't want to know," I said. "It's too late to move."

Abe was not deeply curious. "Want some coke?" he asked. I didn't but he did. Folsom got the cocaine out of the limo and Abe snorted a little, sitting on the fender. It caused no immediate change in his disposition.

"Folsom's taking the rap if they bust us," Abe said, conversationally. "I told him he could keep drawing his salary. Be a nice change for ya, Folsom. Maybe they'll even send you to Folsom prison."

Abe got a laugh out of that. Folsom looked uncomfortable, probably because he realized that the part about continuing his salary was not likely to be true. While Folsom and I stood around uncomfortably, Jerry came up. His face was so anxious it had stopped bulging.

"She had a fit," he said. "She's still having it. She demands to wear the black dress."

"Sherry's mad?" Abe said. His face turned as pale as oil can turn. I had forgotten he was terrified of her. He had inadvertently crossed her once, long ago, and her fury had made a deep impression on him.

"Shit, let her wear fucking overalls if she wants to," he said when he found out what it was about. "We don't want no trouble with her. Trouble with her is real trouble. It usually costs a million, just to make peace."

"It won't cost a million this time," I said. "I'll go talk to her."

"She called me terrible names," Jerry said, which amused me. He was genuinely shocked. Name-calling of that sort, like robbery and murder, was supposed to happen to somebody else.

"Consider it a baptism of fire," I said, but I don't think he got the point, or knew what a baptism of fire was, for that matter.

"I wish I owned a truckin' company or somethin' simple," Abe said, looking more and more pained. "How many people in the world are going to know the dress is wrong? Five hundred? A thousand? It's Sherry they care about, not the dress."

By this time half the crew had wandered up, clustering, as usual, but also maybe hoping for a little early-morning drama, something to cut the boredom.

I was sorry they were bored, but in no mood for early-morning drama. I just turned and walked off, with Jerry stumbling after me.

"She's really in a fury," he said. "Maybe you better let her cool down."

"She was probably acting," I said.

I wasn't full of fury, but I felt a growing outrage. Not only was she fucking my boyfriend, she was trying to have her way about the picture too. I'm sure she was banking on the fact that Abe was around, because she knew she could bully him into anything. She would threaten to destroy the picture if necessary.

What she didn't know was that I didn't wholly care. I was ambivalent about the picture anyway, and always had been. I don't know that I would have done it if it hadn't been for Owen. I guess I saw it as representing our chance. If the picture worked out and he got a little more position and a little real confidence in himself, things might be a lot better. It might be just what we needed.

So in truth my motive was illegitimate and had nothing to do with art. The material itself was sort of borderline, and I had no deep confidence in it. There were some good things in it, but they needed to be built on skillfully, and I didn't know if I was doing that. At bottom, I guess I doubted myself too much—myself as a director, anyway. I was so seldom sure. I had to anguish over practically every decision and in the meanwhile had sort of lost focus on the whole. The picture had become as confused as my love affair, and also confused *with* my love affair, and I was proceeding with it, day by day, with very little real conviction.

Sherry was sitting there in the black dress, cool as ice, no sign of temper. I couldn't hate her—it's my limitation. Her compulsions were too naked, her needs too intense. It was a wonder she could live with them. Her face had a flat expression, not friendly, not quite sullen.

"Okay, what about it?" I said.

"I want to wear the black dress," she said. "That's all there is to it."

We stared at one another for a while. There was always a certain air of entreaty about Sherry, no matter how imperious she was being. Please let me, she was asking. Her son had picked up the habit.

"I'm glad you're not bothering to rationalize this esthetically," I said. "A woman who wants to give her lover a gay send-off wouldn't ordinarily choose widow's weeds, would she?"

She pouched her mouth, briefly. "I don't care," she said. "It's what I want. It's how I feel. I'll make it seem right."

"Nope," I said. "You have to wear the yellow dress."

"Don't boss," she said. "Even if I liked the yellow dress I couldn't wear it now."

"Why not?"

"Because everybody knows I wanted to wear the black dress," she said. "Everybody knows it. I just can't seem wrong. You know what I mean?"

"Sure," I said, "but you're being ridiculous. Not much loss of face is involved in changing dresses. So you changed your mind. The crew can put it down to a mood. Maybe you're getting your period, or something. You better hurry up and change. We're nearly ready for you."

"Do you want Swan?" she asked.

"What are you talking about?"

"He'll be back tomorrow," she said. "Take Swan. He's not so bad. He's even a pretty good fuck, when he feels okay. I just have to wear this dress."

For a moment I was too startled to know what to do. I guess Bobbie was, too. Swan and Sherry had been together four years. That's not to say they had been a love idyll for four years, but still. No wonder the poor bastard cried a lot.

What was terrible was that she was a greatly gifted woman, with talents far beyond mine. I felt embarrassed for a moment, that someone with so great a gift could be so small of heart.

I just shook my head. "You have to wear the yellow dress," I said—my one small certainty.

"Look, I have approval of everything," she said, sort of tonelessly. "I have approval of you, you know. Why should I do what you want?"

I was sick of thinking about Sherry and Owen. I reached down with both hands, caught the throat of the black dress, and ripped the whole front out of it. Buttons flew everywhere. Sherry's eyes flared—I guess she thought I was going to strangle her, but I turned aside as quickly as I could, because I didn't want to see what Owen was fucking. There were three other dresses hanging in the trailer, the yellow one and two others. I took two of them and left the yellow one. Sherry sat there with the torn front of the black dress in her lap, looking frightened. Or maybe she was acting, I'm not sure.

"Twenty minutes," I said, "and if you don't put that dress on I'm going to rewrite the scene and give it to Anna."

Then I left, feeling very depressed. Ripping the dress had

been momentarily satisfying, because I beat her and she knew it, but the thrill wore off immediately. It lasted about two hot seconds, and then I felt very twisted. Beating Sherry wasn't really any fun, no more so than beating Owen. Some people really need to win, and beating them, even when it's the only thing to do, just brings them a little closer to giving up. They manage not to let you enjoy your victory, somehow.

I took the other two dresses back to costume, ignoring the nervous cluster of men around Abe's limo.

She put on the yellow dress and played the scene like she had lead weights in her jaw, for eleven takes. She might have been a housewife acting for the first time in a detergent commercial. Then she changed. On the thirteenth take she was stunning, a woman taking leave of a boy she deeply loved, gaiety in her mouth and melancholy in an occasional cast of profile, in her eyes, in the way her long fingers toyed with the necklace she wore with the yellow dress.

I didn't direct it, she just did it, I think probably as a gesture of contempt, to show us how far above us she was when she cared to try. It was a wonderful, transcendent piece of acting. Everybody cried when they saw it in the rushes, and I cried, too, and felt hopeless, because it was no wonder he wanted her, a woman with gifts like that. More hopeless-making was that everyone gave me credit for making her do it. Bobbie had spread the story of the ripped dress, and I was hailed as a heroine for standing up to Sherry when in fact I had just remembered Owen at the right moment and had my own back in a small way. I never considered that my ripping the dress produced that moment of acting—the fact that it happened just emphasized to me that I wasn't strong enough or knowing enough to direct her.

I didn't see Owen for two more days—to this moment I don't know what he did during all that time. I had almost turned from raw to numb before I saw him, and I prepared and discarded—all in my head—speeches that would have rivaled the Gettysburg Address in eloquence. It wasn't just the matter of ourselves that I needed to talk to him about, either. Production problems were piling up, things I didn't really have the time to deal with, yet somehow I couldn't bring myself to call him, or actually track him down. My hand wouldn't pick up the phone. He would just have to come out from somewhere and make some acknowledgment about our former existence.

At night I kept falling asleep in the bathtub, or on the commode, or on the floor by my bed with the script on my lap or my address book open to addresses I couldn't later remember why I was looking up. Joe Percy was the only person I called, and he was so unrelenting in his self-righteousness about Owen that I got furious with him. He considered that he had predicted it all the moment he saw Owen squatting by my chair at Elaine's.

"I knew it from the first," he said, about twenty times. It was a safe bet that he was drunk.

"We all knew it," he went on. "Pete Sweet knew it. We knew he'd do this."

"Oh, shut up," I said. "I don't need to hear you be smug. Of course you and Pete never try to do anything in the present. It's too much easier to judge the past."

"We do things," he said, defensively.

"Right," I said. "You both fuck the easiest, most compliant women you can find. They're just sort of pillows with cunts. Watching me and Owen is like watching a football game, to you. You can't be a quarterback, but you always know what the quarterback's doing wrong."

We argued some more and I hung up and took the phone off the hook so he couldn't call back. Then I cried myself to sleep—tired as I was, it only took about two sobs.

A few hours later, when I woke up, I called back and apologized. It was unfair of me to be mad at Joe for failing to help me civilize Owen, when for all I knew it was the bad things about Owen that attracted me. It was all I could do just to keep him within the boundaries of the decent. I even lied to him, telling him he was gifted when he wasn't. He was a schemer, of course, but his schemes were immature and amateur. Even now he probably had some muddled scheme in the back of his mind: he would ball Sherry until she was batty and make her let him produce her next picture, or something. That was just stupidity. Swan Bunting, her lover for four years and supposedly her Svengali, had quickly been shown to have absolutely no influence with her when it came to pictures. Sherry walked right over him, and she would do the same with Owen when the time came. He would be the one with his brains fucked out, not her.

In fact, Swan got back to town before I even saw Owen again. I was standing in the lobby of the motel, trying to explain to Gauldin Edwards why I didn't think I could fall in love with him, a conversation some black humorist would have loved, considering the fragmented state of my emotions, our mutual affection, my total exhaustion, and the fact that Gauldin was such a nice man that not loving him a little bit was almost impossible. I guess I was just trying to explain to him that I couldn't sleep with him, ever, I didn't think. He of course was making patient sounds and not allowing anything to sound final—he knew he'd bring me around eventually. I was just trying to think of a way to unstick myself from the conversation so I could go up and fall asleep in the bathtub—the circles under my eyes by that time were so heavy I could almost feel them while I was standing talking—when all of a sudden Swan piled out of a limo and came rushing into the motel. He was wearing a striped Australian rugby shirt, dirty jeans, and sandals. He started to rush right to the elevator, but then he saw me and came over. His mouth was hanging open, and he was panting, as if he had run all the way from Hollywood.

"Jill, what the fuck's happening?" he said. "I can't believe any of this. Sherry's phone's been off the hook for three days. I've left about fifty messages and she hasn't called in. Is she sick or something?"

I sort of gave Gauldin the nudge—go away, Gauldin. He kissed me and went.

"No, she's fine, Swan," I said. "To tell the truth, I think she's having an affair with Owen."

Swan turned white. Obviously I had confirmed his worst

fears. He stopped panting and rubbed his face, which was unshaven.

"With Wynkyn here?" he asked. "How could she do that with Wynkyn here? Wynkyn loves me."

"Yeah, I know," I said. "He told me you were his best friend."

Swan stared out the door at the limo, as if uncertain whether to go and get back in it. Then he smiled at me.

"Fun and games," he said, and started for the elevator again. He actually pushed the up button, but he didn't really want to go up. The elevator opened, an old lady got out, and Swan just stood there. The elevator closed and he came back over to me.

"Do you think I should go fight him?" he said. "Do you think that would impress her?"

"It might if you won," I said, "but I don't think you could win."

"I don't either," he said, sort of reflectively. "I didn't the first time. Besides, it might upset Wynkyn. He's very easily upset. Sherry just has no understanding of that kid. Do you want to eat supper?

"I guess you don't," he added before I could answer.

I ate with him—what else to do? I didn't want to take him to my room, and it seemed wrong just to leave him there, vague and hurt in the lobby.

"Did you know she makes me pay rent?" he said. "She says it's her accountant that makes her do it, but her accountant doesn't make her do anything. She fucking makes me pay rent! Can you believe that? Since I gave up my show and my psychiatric practice all I've done is spend money on her. Shit, I was worth a half a million at one time, and now I'd be lucky to put my hands on five thousand. She soaks up money like fucking water. She says it would be bad for our dynamic for me to live off her, but you know what? She's just tight. She never spends a cent except on goddamn hat-pin holders."

"Maybe you should kidnap her collection and hold it for ransom," I said, so tired I felt like laughing and crying both. "Otherwise you'll be broke pretty soon."

"I'm broke now," he said. "I've been broke for months. She

could have given me a point or two on this picture, but she didn't.

"I don't think we're in love any more," he said, pulling on his beard. His eyes weren't focused on the room, but on some scene invisible to me, some scene with Sherry, past or future, who knows? What a movie it would make if someone could photograph the scenes people have with their loved ones, in their minds. I had been having them with Owen in my mind for three days, so many I couldn't even remember them. Of course, the scene I would eventually have with him face to face wouldn't resemble any of them. When it finally happened it would all get mixed up, and I wouldn't be so clearly in the right. In fact, it would all probably get turned around so that I was clearly in the wrong—he had been driven to Sherry because I wasn't a good enough lay, or something.

"But I guess you have your problems, too," Swan said. It had taken him a while to think of that, but it at least indicated that people weren't such total shits as you can make them in your mind. I had the impulse to leave the table, before I got really sympathetic to Swan and let myself forget all the brutally discourteous things I had seen him do, some of which he had done to me.

"In fact," he said, "I guess we're in the same boat, only you're a nice person and everybody will be on your side. Nobody will be on my side, not that I deserve it. I was a poor winner, you know. When you're a winner on the scale of Sherry something happens. You just think, Fuck it, why bother being nice, it takes too much time. It's fun to be able just to trample ass, particularly since most people deserve to be trampled."

"It's the other way around," I said. "Most people deserve to be treated nice."

"Not really," he said. "You're just sentimental. Most people will fuck you if you don't fuck them first, and the minute they get more power than you they trample your ass. I know, because I'm about to be the victim of a fucking stampede."

Evidence of that was all around us, in the stern disapproval of the crew, who came in twos and threes to eat and didn't stop to jolly me or make small talk. Swan had treated them all like shit, so how dare I eat with him? As the evening wore on, I had trouble explaining that to myself. For some foolish reason—probably hatred of the clutter and the silence in my room—I kept sitting there with him, long past the point when I could have made an excuse and left. Tired as I was, I wouldn't have even needed an excuse.

Even more foolishly, I got drunk. Not on very much liquor, I admit, but combined with fatigue and emotion it was enough. Then, to my total surprise and horror, Swan tried to seduce me. I had been with him for about three hours, which I guess is a long time, in our trade, but when I suddenly realized, outside the door of my room, that he was trying to kiss me, I could hardly speak or act. It was like the gears of my speech had jammed. I had the presence of mind to duck, but even that was slow, and his kiss landed somewhere near my eye; all I could think was, My god, doesn't he know this is just what she wants? But of course he didn't know that. He was only trying to seduce me because he was in Texas and his girl friend wasn't his girl friend any more and he didn't know what to do with himself.

As it was, I wasn't sober enough to see what he *did* do with himself—but then, why worry? The whole motel was full of restless, confused men, and Swan was no worse off than most of the rest of them. I guess he wandered off down the hall or maybe went and slept in the airport—I understand he left the next morning, after a wild argument with Sherry that took place through a door that she refused to open. I didn't see him again until months later, when I ran into him in the Polo Lounge.

There was a brief moment during the night when I woke up half undressed and with sexual feelings and thought, My god, did I sleep with Swan? I managed to assure myself that I hadn't only by remembering that I had carefully brushed my teeth after I came in, and while I was doing that there had been no one there. So I couldn't have slept with him, and the sexual feeling had to have come from a dream, though what or who I dreamed of, I couldn't remember.

I hadn't drunk enough to make me vomit, only enough to make me queasy in the morning; and it was in the morning, while I was standing in the bathroom contemplating my unwashed hair, that Owen returned.

CHAPTER 3

I had a late call that morning—we were moving the set—and when I heard the door open I just thought it was the maid. I was more interested in the deteriorating state of my health and looks—when I had left Hollywood five weeks before I was in excellent shape, and I looked like I had spent the five weeks being in a war. In fact, it had just crossed my mind that maybe Owen left me because I was working so hard I had let myself get ugly. Then I turned back to the bedroom, to look for a shirt, and there he was, looking for a shirt himself. He turned with one in his hand just as I came into the room, and we saw one another more or less at the same moment—in that moment I saw his face change from cheerful to surly, which was very discouraging. It was as if the sight of me had spoiled what might have been a perfect day. By being there at a time when I would normally be on the set, I had interfered with his perfectly innocent need for a clean shirt, and he didn't like it.

If his face was the mirror of his soul, then he had a pretty ungrateful soul. I felt a need to cover myself and stepped back into the bathroom and wrapped a big towel around me.

I contemplated not coming out of the bathroom at all. Why bother, if the mere sight of me was going to make him unhappy? He never had been particularly eager to be involved with me, except right at the first. Why drag at him?

But shit, I thought. We could at least talk. So I secured myself in the towel and went back out.

"I didn't know you were here," he said.

"If you took any interest in the production schedule, you would have known it," I said. "Are you going to keep working, or what?"

The sight of him had sort of paralyzed my feelings. I felt no urge at all to spill out the hundreds of bitter comments I had been stockpiling.

"Yeah," he said, in answer to my question. "Sure."

I felt the need to be immensely cautious—not to look him too much in the eye, not to ask blunt questions. Also, I was acutely conscious of what a mess the room was in. All the chairs were full of scripts or clothes or junk, not to mention most of the floor, so it was very difficult to know how to go about having a dignified conversation. There was no place very clean except the bed.

"Well, when do you mean to start coming to the set again?" I asked. What I wanted was for him to start talking, and hopefully issue precise statements. I didn't care how distasteful and final they were, just so long as they were precise and would leave me knowing what was what. Sometimes pulling words out of Owen was like pulling buckets of water out of a deep well. You have to wind the old windlass for many, many turns, and I didn't feel like winding right then. He was fucking the queen of America: surely that would give him enough juice to allow him to talk plainly to me.

But no. He just sort of stood there, with two ugly flowered shirts in his hand, as if my presence had confounded what otherwise would have been a simple decision about which ugly flowered shirt to wear. I felt, wistfully, like appealing to the Deity, to make this man before me talk, so I wouldn't have to do it. I felt like my vocal organs—in fact, all my organs—were numb. If one of us didn't speak, we would have to stand there all day, amid the messy residue of our life together. Finally I went and sat down on the edge of the bed.

"Aren't you going to talk?" I said. "I don't want you to apologize or violate Sherry's sacred trust in you or anything, I'd just like it if you could tell me what's happening. Maybe I could rearrange my life so it wouldn't be so painful."

He looked more sullen, as if he had known I would make just that kind of demand. I began to feel that I was probably crazy, or at least highly untypical. Maybe I was the only person who thought all the time. Maybe other people's brains went on and off, like stoplights.

"I was coming to the set," he said finally. "We broke up."

My dirty heart took hope. "Broke up?" I said. "After three days? What are you talking about?"

"Cunt," he said bitterly—a reference to Sherry, but hardly an explanation. Before I could ask him to be more explicit he was on top of me. At the feel of his breath on my face all my quelled feelings awoke, the hatred as well as the love. I was not about to be the answer to whatever rejection he had just received, but I was at a disadvantage. He was a lot bigger than me, and as recently as three days before, I had still been fucking him.

Still, if there is one thing I'm good at, it's balking. The fact that I had wrapped the large bath towel around me two or three times was also helpful. I hugged my arms to my sides and ducked my chin, which didn't give him a lot to get at. The fact that I was hunched within the protection of the tightly wrapped towel made him furious. He yanked at the top of the towel so hard that it snapped my head back.

"What's the matter with you?" he asked, as if it were evidence of the most extreme perversity on my part, that I was resisting him when he needed me. He had even managed to get his pants open and there his need was, plain to see—but the fact that he had felt that sure of me just made me set my brakes the harder. His eyes, above me, were blind, so far as any knowledge of my feelings went. When he figured out that he couldn't simply yank the towel off he just sort of sat there, waiting for the physical blessing I was expected to dispense. He kept trying to kiss me, if only to keep me from talking. He knew me well enough to know that if I ever started talking, I'd only get madder. He had that much instinct. If he could have brought it off, he would have had me too. The sex act would have amounted to forgiveness, would have wiped the slate clean. After that, complaint would only have been petty.

He tried to get his hand under the towel, but I caught it and hung on.

"No," I said. "I want to know what happened. Don't you know how cruel it is to leave people in the dark like that? I've been half out of my mind, and I have a picture to direct."

"Are you my wife?" he said. "Did we get married?"

He loved that comeback. He used it all the time. It was his way out of every tight corner. If we're not married, baby, you got no right to ask. It was such a trite line of defense that it usually threw me off stride for a second. In this case, just as he said it, the phone rang. That was annoying, because I had told the switchboard to hold my messages until 9 A.M., thinking by some miracle I might sleep late. It kept ringing, and finally I answered it.

"Is Owen there?" Sherry said.

"He's here," I said, annoyed that I hadn't realized it would be her. Nobody else would bully the switchboard into putting them through.

"Tell him to hurry, I'm hungry," she said. "Wait a minute, let me speak to him."

I hung up, took the receiver off, and covered it with two pillows.

Owen had lost his erection, but not his look of little-boy belligerence. I got off the bed and stood over him.

"I guess your friend doesn't regard the split as final," I said. "She informs me that she's hungry and wishes you to hurry up. She doesn't like to be kept waiting, as you certainly must know. You better stuff it back in your pants and get snapping."

Any sarcasm invariably made him insolent. "I was just letting you look," he said. "For old times' sake."

I almost laughed at him.

"Why'd you lie?" I said. "Why'd you say you'd broken up if you were about to go eat breakfast with her?"

He got off the bed and began to change shirts. "Because you crowded me," he said. "She crowds me. Both of you always want some answer. How the fuck would I know the answer? Maybe I will break up. She's just as bad as you."

His stomach bulged, paunchy, until he shrugged on the clean shirt and straightened himself to button it; then, briefly, it flattened. Owen stuffed his penis back in his underpants, treating it like it no longer belonged to him. It all seemed a shame. I had genuinely tender feelings for his body, only his dumb personality kept getting in the way. I should have fucked him—Sherry would have smelled it. Let him try to explain that. I never think fast enough, or feel truly enough, or something.

When he buttoned up he looked at me defensively; he had still not forgiven me for being in the room when I wasn't supposed to be, thus occasioning a conflict.

"You're not coming back to me if you go up there," I said, trying to make it sound like a resolution writ in stone. I meant it, of course, but Owen flicked off final statements like he flicked off sweat.

"If you're going, I want you to get your stuff out of here," I said. "At least it would reduce the mess. And I'd appreciate it if you'd come back to work. The picture has to get finished some way."

"She wants to fire you," he said. "She's talking to Abe about it. She says she can't work with you."

With that unsatisfactory statement, he left. Not a word about us. I would never know what was in the man's mind. Maybe I would just have to forget about knowing.

I felt ghastly, and looked worse than that. Then I accidentally saw the two of them getting into a limo to go to the set, which didn't help any. I found Sammy and made him stop work and drive me out. I needed the comfort of someone older. In fact, I was so jangled I was forced to broach my troubles. Sammy listened, and drove. He had on a sweater with a cow on it, bought in a local feed store.

Sammy acknowledged trouble reluctantly. "Everybody's on your side," he said. "Everybody. Not to say nothing against Owen, but we all know he's done you bad. And not to say nothing against Miss Solaré, but she ain't popular, you know. She's got no respect, so she's got no friends."

He gave my leg a pat. "We all love you," he said. "Even Theroux. He loves you."

"No, he doesn't, Sammy," I said. "Theroux dislikes me."

"Well, he's a hard guy to know," he conceded. "But we all love you."

Didn't I know it? I had more general love than anybody. I was their wronged darling, a role I was thoroughly tired of.

When we got to the set, Abe was there to put the fear of God in me. His approach to it was to put his arm around me, something he didn't do gracefully. He wasn't used to putting his arm around anyone older than sixteen. In the distance, Texas was as brown as a buffalo.

Folsom tagged along behind us, and when we got near the coffee machine he veered off and caught up with us a few steps later, bringing Abe his coffee.

"I tell you, I'm getting bad vibes," Abe said. "Sherry's not happy, and you know what that means."

"Just calm down, Abe," I said. "Sherry's been complaining for the last ten years. That's just her style. It doesn't mean anything."

"You're wrong, that's where you're wrong," he said, stepping back so he could point his finger at me. Somewhere he had learned to point his finger like a real executive.

"It means fights," he said. "It means money lost, trouble all down the line. It means I get a fuckin' ulcer. That's just some of the things it means."

I had a slight headache, from my drunkenness, and I wanted badly to be let alone for a few minutes, to look at the new set and talk to the boys about it. While I was considering how best to deal with Abe's anxiety Wynkyn came out of Sherry's dressing room and walked slowly across to where we were talking. He walked like an old man, not a seven-year-old. He walked right up and took my hand, standing there politely, so as not to interrupt. The sight of him disconcerted Abe; he immediately stopped talking.

"Abe, go on back to Hollywood and don't worry about it," I said. "We'll be done in two and a half weeks, maybe a little more. Nothing's going to go wrong."

Abe didn't listen. He was concentrating on the new problem, which was Wynkyn.

"Listen, Wynkyn," he said, "would you mind excusing us for a few minutes? I have to talk some grown-up talk with Jill."

Wynkyn simply ignored the sounds, in the maddening way he had. He stood there squeezing my hand, busy with his own thoughts. Abe couldn't stand it. He reached in his pocket, pulled out a wad of bills, and peeled off a twenty. He extended the bill to Wynkyn.

"Look, buddy, here's twenty bucks if you'll get lost for ten minutes," he said. "Go and make 'em let you look through the camera."

I was stunned by the gesture, Wynkyn merely contemptuous. "I've seen through the camera a million times," he said. "If you want to talk about fucking, go ahead. I know all about fucking."

Abe looked like he would like to stuff the twenty-dollar bill down Wynkyn's throat, but he restrained himself.

"All right," he said. "If he hears, he hears. Sherry says you're ruining her part because of Owen. She says you can't handle it and you're making her do everything wrong. She wants to take you off the picture."

"With two and a half weeks to go?"

"Listen, a lot of bad things can happen in two and a half weeks. I can tell you some stories."

"It's nonsense," I said. "Her scenes are fine. You've seen the rushes."

"Yeah, but that was before!" he said.

"I've got to go to work," I said. "We're wasting some great light. If you want to fire me go ahead, but I don't think your grandfather will like it much."

Of course, if he had not already known that, he would have disposed of me on the spot. He made a vague wave, which must have meant for Folsom to get the car. Folsom made a beeline for it and Wynkyn and I walked over to the set.

"Blubber-gut," Wynkyn said. "That's what Owen calls him."

Owen was standing by the boom, talking to Gauldin and Jerry and a couple of the light men. Theroux Wickes was flirting with Anna, who couldn't stand him. The tension in the group was so intense it almost gave off its own light. Only Owen was confident and at ease. It must give a man a great lift for everybody to know he's fucking a movie star, even if the movie star isn't particularly nice. As I approached the group I began to be disgusted with myself, for being such a masochist. Why didn't I just quit? I didn't want to have to talk to Owen with Gauldin and Jerry standing there. The movie wasn't worth it. Unspoken emotions are probably as deadly as X rays: if so, me and Wynkyn and Jerry and Gauldin were all being quietly fried to a crisp.

But I walked on into the group and pointed out what I didn't like about the set. Hearing my voice making more or less pertinent professional comments was a shock to me, as it often is. How can my voice keep talking and my head keep operating when the rest of me is such a mass of unsorted emotion? I've never understood it. I think I would respect myself more if the woman could obliterate the professional once in a while. Why should a man love me if I'm that mechanical about things? On the other hand, I would hate to be the kind of woman who flings her emotion at the world until she has nothing left to fling.

"Do you think I should have taken that man's twenty dollars?" Wynkyn asked me later, when we were watching them move the cameras.

"No, and I thought I told you not to use that bad word again," I said.

"Oh," he said. "I forgot."

When you disapproved of him, even mildly, Wynkyn looked like he was ready to commit suicide.

"Don't look that way," I said. "It's not *that* important. It's just not a word you should use."

They were positioning the buffalo on a nearby hill, and one of the wranglers, a tall cowboy named Jimbo, came and asked Wynkyn if he'd like to go over in a pickup and see them. Wynkyn was ecstatic, as much at getting to ride in a pickup with a cowboy as at getting to see the buffalo again. Jimbo had a fat wife—I had seen them eating at one of the local cafes several times. I tried to imagine my life if I had just married a nice man, a local of somewhere—would it all still be turmoil and churning inside, or would it be quietude and happiness, or would it just be boredom? Unanswerable.

That afternoon I was passing one of the pickups and looked in and saw Owen, slumped behind the wheel. At first I thought he had died, and I sort of went cold—but then I saw that he was just sleeping. The sun was blazing and he was really hot. He was leaning forward, with his head on his arms, and the back of his shirt was wet and stuck to his back. I couldn't just walk past—I had to stop and look, to see if I could pick up any clues at all from looking at him. Of course I couldn't, but my looking woke him up. He was sleeping with the pickup door open and suddenly there I was, three feet away, staring at him. I wasn't staring hostilely, either, though he probably thought so. Emotion wore him out—he often collapsed and slept for hours, after our fights. Three days, and she had worn him so that he could drop off in a blazing-hot pickup.

When he opened his eyes he seemed happy to see me, almost.

"I gotta see you tonight," he said, to my great surprise.

"That's a change," I said.

"Sherry's accountant's comin'," he said. "She doesn't want me to be there because she doesn't want me to know how rich she is."

"So you want to kill time while you're banished?" I said.

Then Jerry came running up. If it hadn't been him, it would have been someone else. Someone came running up every thirty seconds.

"I'll be at the rushes," Owen said.

He was. By that time I was tired. I had decided over and over again, all afternoon, that I wouldn't see him. What point? I ought to behave with pride, though I didn't know why. I had been lonely and proud for most of my thirty-seven years, and had come to think of the two states as mutually linked. The more proud, the more lonely. I had not found it to be true, in the long run, that my difficulty made men the more determined to win me. Most of them took my difficulty at face value and went elsewhere, to win easier women.

But then curiosity was working in me, as well as pride. I wanted to know what he thought was going on, between him and Sherry. I could at least try to find out.

Then when he showed up in the room he did the predictable thing and tried to fuck me. Even though it was perfectly predictable—having already happened once that day—it once again took me by surprise. I am the opposite of a good boy scout: I am never prepared.

But prepared or not, I was a wall of resistance. Right after work I had heard that Joe Percy had had a stroke—not a terribly bad one, evidently, but a stroke, and I felt blocked and frightened. The hospital wouldn't let me talk to Joe, and I thought, My god, what if he gets worse and dies before I can talk to him? That was really all I could think about, and when Owen came in and cornered me near my dresser I was really much more absent than I had been that morning.

I resisted mechanically, not very involved in what was happening—it was only because he was so big that he was even able to push and shove me into paying attention to him.

I got my head clear, for a little, and tried to look at him, really look at him, since I have the belief that if I can really look close at a man, I can always know what's true about him. There was no point in listening to Owen—he lied all the time, with his mouth and with his flesh too. I would have to find out what was true in my own way.

"Owen, please stop," I said. "Just stop for a little while. We can't fuck our way out of this, for god's sake."

"If you love me, we can," he said. "If you love me, why can't you show me?"

"Because there are some basic questions I need to have answered first," I said. "Such as why, if you still want me to love you, you're spending your nights with Sherry now. That's pretty damn basic."

"I don't *know*!" he said. "You think people know everything. If you love me, why don't you fight for me? Maybe I haven't decided yet."

Once again I had a strong impulse to laugh. This man who was trying to drag me into bed had a less sophisticated intelligence than Wynkyn Weil. He was telling me to fuck him so he could decide between me and another woman. Would any man really be dumb enough to say that?

Yet something very intense was working in him, because he had seldom pursued me so hard. Normally he preferred to lie back and be enticed, but this time there was something desperate in his single-mindedness. I told him I was just getting my period, but I don't think he even heard me, though he usually disdained me at such times, not from fastidiousness but because it gave him a convenient excuse to prowl.

My mind was more confused than my body, which was totally resistant. Owen was virtually a textbook case: a man who violated all the rules, who had shown zero consideration for me and my feelings; and yet I guess I still would have slept with him if my body hadn't been suddenly like a rock. All the feeling in it had been quelled, yet in my mind I felt the sort of tenderness for him that I usually feel bodily—a kind of pity that he was so desperate and I couldn't seem to help.

Finally he saw that nothing was working and stopped wrestling. He went and dropped in a chair and stared out the window of the motel, where there was nothing to see except an occasional truck passing on the highway.

I made him a drink. Until Sherry came along, all he had done at night was drink.

"Joe Percy had a stroke today," I said. "One reason I'm upset is because of that. He's really an old, old friend, though I know you disapprove."

"He's not so bad," he said. He took the drink and was silent. I turned off the light in the room, so we could see out the window better. I had a drink, too, to be friendly. I thought maybe if we drank for a while, something might get said. But we drank for quite a while, until I realized nothing was getting said, and nothing would, because Owen had no need for things to be said. We were totally unlike one another in that regard: I'm the one with a crazy need for words, descriptions, analyses, all things I don't particularly respect but which seem to be necessary to my relationships—or at least always had, until Owen came along.

Talk had been the center of my existence, but it was only something that occurred now and then, to little purpose, on the periphery of his.

After we had both been drinking for a while, Owen just sitting there, quite silent, I began to feel forgiving, not of what he had done with Sherry but of the fact that he wouldn't talk. He was not really to be blamed: I was just trying to force my way of being onto a man who had a way of being all his own. I went on and got drunk with him in order to try and wipe out my own craving for talk, to try and approach wordlessness in order to show him that I did care. We sat by the window for about four hours, drinking—I had the phone off the hook so Sherry couldn't summon him back.

The drunker I got, the more contemptuous I became of what everyone would say if they knew what I was doing. They would say I was letting an awful man walk all over me. But then it's so trite and shallow, so limited in intricacy, what people reason about other people's relationships. Owen could manifest only needs, not affections. He was manifesting one now, by sitting with me for hours and assuring himself of the wrath of a superabundantly wrathful woman. His need had something of love in it, not the nice outgoing parts but the harsher, more clutching parts. My habit had been to go where I was asked, but of course I had never expected to be asked to share anyone with Sherry Solaré. That was not quite the kind of demand I had hoped to answer.

I hung on to his hand and put my head against his leg as we watched the trucks, and then, since Owen was so silent, so lost in himself, my mind went back to Joe and I tried to figure out when I could go see him. I got very worried, imagining how it would be if Joe couldn't talk and I had to try and explain my life to him without him being able to answer. Horrible.

Owen slept with me. I got too sentimental, or too scared, and he got it after all, not one to remember, in the state we were in by that time.Watching those trucks had something to do with it. There was a red light opposite the exit to the motel; a lot of the trucks had to stop at it and when it changed they would grunt and start off slowly, like big funny buffalo, picking up speed as they disappeared into Texas. I got to thinking of the loneliness of those guys, those men who drive trucks. Owen was not unlike them. It was a miracle he was not out there, speeding down some road, with headlights and pills and hillbilly music to pass the night with instead of a strange woman like myself. I guess I just decided to give it one more night, in the hope that whatever had called us together in the first place would get stronger if I didn't give up on it.

Anyway, I didn't expect it to resolve anything, and it didn't. I had a five-thirty call, and was actually awake, listening to Owen breathe, when Jerry tapped on my door. It was just getting light—I couldn't see Owen's features, but when I looked across him I could see the light through the hairs on his chest, even see the little line of hair on his shoulder, which was near my face. For a moment I felt a childish yearning for the day not to come, and even when I forced myself up and got dressed I had the urge—it was more than fatigue—to sink back down.

I went away and left Owen sleeping, and the only time I saw him that day was from a distance, sitting in Sherry's limousine, a sight that upset me so I couldn't hold my hand steady. Obviously he had gotten away with me, somehow. Maybe she had fucked the accountant—not unlikely, since he was very good looking and also a financial genius of some kind, able to make her millions multiply like rabbits.

I didn't regret the night, exactly, but it was still a long, awful day, during which Theroux Wickes demonstrated once and for all that he was not competent to be the cameraman on a picture as costly as *One Tree*. I started hating him for his preening and his incompetence, and then late in the afternoon somebody told me that Anna Lyle was fucking him, which made me furious with her. For an hour or so I even regretted my casting: as I reasoned, if she could sleep with Theroux, after hating him for two months, then she must be a bad actress. Years later we laughed about it, but at the time I was so angry that I avoided her all day.

That night, when I got in, there was no Owen at the rushes and no Owen in my room. I ordered a cheese sandwich and some chicken soup and ate it in my room so I wouldn't have to make conversation with anyone. I sat in the chair where he had sat the night before, and watched some more trucks—not feeling sorry for myself at least, too tired for that, but feeling sort of temporarily out on my feet. Was this a life? And if so, how did I get to such a strange place in it?

I fell asleep over that one, woke up some time in the night, started for the bathroom, stepped on the tray I had put on the floor, broke the saucer the soup had been in, and almost cut my little toe off, something I didn't realize until the morning, when I woke up with my foot stuck to the bloody sheet. Jerry came in and tenderly peeled it off and took me to the hospital; fourteen stitches were taken, more than I would have thought a little toe was worth. To make up for my injury, the crew was all tenderness and cooperation that day, and we finished the hanging scene, Sherry's last. I was civil. She was no more than adequate in the scene, but we finished by midafternoon and she left.

That night, in a fight with Owen, using a gun nobody even knew she had, she accidentally shot Wynkyn dead. Nobody remembered hearing the shot, but everybody in the motel heard her scream. We were all in the coffee shop, and it was only a two-story motel. The scream rose like an aria above us and our wretched food—only it was more terrible than any aria: we all knew instantly that our minor troubles were as naught. Then Owen ran down the stairs with that poor dying child in his arms and rushed to the hospital where they had stitched my toe, but too late. Sherry never worked again. None of us who heard the scream expected that she would. She might not have known how to raise Wynkyn, but I guess she had loyalty enough not to want to outlive him. Eight months later, expertly and ingeniously, using a hose she had cut off her vacuum cleaner, she gassed herself in her custom-made BMW, with the radio on, in her seven-car garage in Beverly Hills.

CHAPTER 4

I don't know how we finished that picture. Of course, in a major sense we didn't, as the footage clearly shows, but when Wynkyn was killed we still had a certain number of pages to shoot, and we shot them. Gauldin Edwards, who tried gallantly to joke some of the gloom away, said we ought to retitle the picture and call it *Zombies of the Panhandle*—his effort didn't make anyone laugh.

I came to hate the media before they were finished with us. I mourned Wynkyn—we all did—but the publicity that followed his death was just despicable. It made it seem that what had happened could only have happened to a little boy who had grown up in Beverly Hills, the son of a superstar. That there is domestic violence elsewhere—in Ohio, for example—and that kids get blown away by it, was hardly dwelt on. It seemed to me that Wynkyn was an all-too-common kind of casualty, and I resented everything about the coverage.

Owen, of course, left when Sherry left. The local police made no real trouble for them, but then, two days later, they caught Zack with some cocaine and came down on him like he had invented drugs. I guess the local people had had about enough of us—the new had worn off and their minds had had time to dwell upon all the debauched and depraved things we probably did every night in that motel.

The bust was a pity: Zack only had a couple of scenes left to do. I don't think he was even into cocaine: having the drugs was just part of his image or something. Mr. Mond sent up some legal weight and we got him out of jail and finished his scenes and shipped him home to L.A., but that too had its effect on the picture. In his last two scenes he just wasn't the same Zack. The spring had gone out of his step, and his face had changed.

In the last ten days of the production I felt such a slippage of spirit, not just in myself but all around me, that I felt we weren't going to get through it. I hit Jerry one day, furious because I had heard him say for the tenth time that Wynkyn's life had been ruined anyway. Of course he was just saying it to make himself feel better, but I didn't think Wynkyn had been that totally ruined, and I hit out.

That same day, out of nothing but weakness, I started an affair with Gauldin. It was not fair to him, poor man—God knows he got me at my absolute worst. I quickly made his inadequacies—all of them quite normal—into the cause of all wrong in the world, but I couldn't face being alone and I did care for him, in a sort of motherly way. At least he was divorced at the time, so I wasn't breaking up any home by sleeping with him. But it was still a wrong thing to do.

When finally, on a smoggy day in August, we returned to Hollywood, I tried to break with Gauldin, tried to thank him, tried to explain what I had hoped he realized anyway, how desperately but temporarily I had needed him. I tried to explain that on the porch of my house, when we drove up to it and I realized—maybe faced just then—that I didn't want him to come in, didn't want him to bring his bags up on the porch, didn't want him getting his hopes rooted in me any deeper. If I let him bring those bags in, I would be months and years getting him out, during which time it would never be more than half right. I just couldn't: I had to stop it there; hard, for the man had treated me with great generosity. He had soft blue eyes and a face, like Sammy's, that would always be mostly boyish.

"Oh, Gauldin, you know what it was," I said. "You can't come in. But you have my love."

He was not a fighter. His blue eyes just looked hurt. "How do I have it?" he asked, with a little shrug, and picked up his bags and went down the hill. It was not the last of him, of course; he came back, we worked out some uneasy terms for a while, then I got him a job which he desperately needed to pay his alimony and child support, and when he came back from that he had a new girl; and I was able, through the years, to show him that he did have my love, some of it, a lot of it in fact—though always there was a touch of puzzlement in his eyes when he looked at me. Fortunately, Gauldin was too healthy a man to be able to convince me that he was really one of my victims.

The minute he left I went up the hill to see Joe. He had been home from the hospital about a week; I had talked to him, finally, and he hadn't sounded too bad. When I got to his house, I sneaked a look. I could see through his front window, peek through his plants. He was sitting in a chair, reading *Playboy*—not half so fat as he had been when I left.

"A lech to the end," I said, stepping through the door. It startled him greatly—all men hate to be caught reading *Playboy*. They hate to have it thought that their imaginations really operate at that level.

The flesh had begun to leave his face; he was almost gaunt —unimaginable, but there it was. I surprised him more than I knew. He was unable to come up with an immediate sassy reply: instead, he stood up, tears welling in his eyes. Probably none of his girls even knew he was ill. We embraced and I held him close, to calm my own feelings, for I had never thought of Joe as other than essentially jolly, despite having witnessed his many drunken depressions. Above all, he was jolly.

"Well, it's no joke, a stroke . . . if you'll forgive the rhyme," he said. At least he still had his voice, the sexiest old voice around, a baritone of which he was justly proud.

"But you don't want to hear about being sick," he said. "Everybody's illnesses are the same. They're only unique to the person they're happening to."

"Oh, I'm sure you managed to have a unique stroke," I said.

He was an altered man—frightened. For a time I didn't know what to do, because I had never seen him that way and hadn't expected to. He had always been cavalier—in fact had told me once that since his wife's death he had nourished a sort of mild death wish. I guess the stroke had changed that.

In a while we got a little more used to one another, and I stayed and made him dinner. Missing almost a year of a person is odd: even persons you know well don't stay exactly the same. When you come back together again a lot of fine adjustments have to be made. My old friend was clearly no longer a man who went around fucking everything young and rich. Until I walked into the room and saw him I had not realized how rapidly people can fade. A man whose sexiness has always been a fat sexiness can look awfully pathetic when he suddenly becomes thin. The spirit had changed, too, with the flesh. His old banter, when he tried it, sounded like a parody of its former self. I put up with the parody for a while, and then I began to find it distasteful.

"Listen, stop it," I said. "You don't really feel like joking. Why would think I'd want you to put on an act for me?"

"Why, because I always have," he said. "I've fooled you all these years. It wasn't me you loved, it was the clown I pretended to be."

I ignored that.

"All right, tell me about the man from Texas," he said.

"He was not just a man from Texas," I said. "He had a name."

I spoke more sharply than I had meant to. No one would call Owen by his name any more, or even mention him, around me. All my shoved-down feelings weren't shoved down very far—they were always ready to rise up. In my mind I was always defending him, against unspoken accusations. What did anyone know? What did I know, any more?

"Then tell me about your picture," he said.

"Oh, why?" I said. "It would be like talking about your illness. It's unique to me, but to anyone who's ever made one it would be an old story, except that this one cost Wynkyn Weil his life."

Our conversation, which for years had been a rapid, natural flow, impossible to check, seemed now to be full of stops. Not much more was said that evening. We sat on Joe's couch, looking out over Hollywood, and he held my hand. We had hugged a lot in the past, but he had never exactly held my hand, and when he took it I guess I looked up in surprise.

"Don't worry," he said. "I can no longer ejaculate."

"What?" I said. "What's that supposed to mean?"

He looked very embarrassed. Maybe he had chosen that means of calling attention to the area where he most wanted sympathy.

"It's a fact," he said.

"For god's sakes," I said. "You just had the stroke a month ago. I think you might give the old appetites a bit more time to recover, don't you? The debutantes of this world may not have seen the last of you yet."

A few minutes later I discovered that he was asleep, sitting at my side. He didn't have a fat neck any more; his chin had fallen onto his chest. I got him awake enough to walk him to his bed, and he showed me a little red bottle on his bedside table.

"Seconal," he said. "In case I feel another stroke coming on. I had to pay a lot for it, but if I feel one coming and I have time, I'm going to take it. I don't want to lie around staring at the ceiling for years. You'd have to deal with me, because no one else would bother."

"Oh, Joe," I said; but it was clear that having the Seconal gave him great security. He went right back to sleep.

I went home and unpacked, so that maybe all my clothes would stop smelling like the inside of a suitcase. Then I went and looked at my cups, to see if any of them had broken. I have a passion for nice cups. When the last earthquake hit I realized it the moment I heard my cups breaking. But my new cups were all still there, as perfect within their terms as anything could be.

While I was admiring them, the phone rang. I was as frightened for a moment as if it were an earthquake. Who would call me, my first night home? Of course my greatest fear was that it was Owen. If it was, what would I say? More likely it was probably just Gauldin, which would be bad enough, but handleable.

"The hunter home from the hill," Bo Brimmer said, when I snatched the receiver up.

"No, from the plain," I said. "How did you know I was here?"

"Only God has better intelligence than Universal," he said.

I was very glad it was him. He had such a crisp mind—it reminded me of cereal before you pour the milk in. For several months all the minds available to me had been like cereal about two hours after you pour the milk in. Not very flattering to my crew, but that was how it felt.

"I wish we were married," he said. "We'd both be less lonely."

He almost invariably proposed to me. I guess it was ritual, although if I'd said okay, let's try it, he probably would have.

"I won't say it couldn't happen," I said.

It could happen the day I got ready to marry a mind, but that I didn't say. It was a game we both got a little bit of a lift from playing. He was not to make his proposal too heavy, and I was not to make my rejection too absolute.

"I'm finally over Jackie," he said.

"I'm sorry to hear it," I said. "I believe in irrational passions, even if they mostly bring pain. They're more honorable than the common arrangements we all make.

"Excuse me," I added. "That most of us make."

"I wasn't always this above it," he said. "I had a pretty common arrangement with my wife. Since she lives in Little Rock, people forget that I actually had one. In fact I'm much more the married type than yourself. The purpose of marriage is order, and I respect order. I've even achieved it in my life, if at somewhat too great a cost."

We rattled on for more than an hour, to no real point, but quickly, rapidly. A talk with Bo was like verbal Ping-Pong: the ball came right back. It was refreshing.

To my surprise, he told me that Tony Maury's movie was making money. I had almost forgotten it, thanks to working so hard.

"It's logical," he said. "It's a summer movie. We've got it in every drive-in in America. People like to watch other people whack at one another with swords, in the summertime."

"How about Owen's movie?" I asked.

"We closed it," he said, and didn't elaborate.

I felt torn, a little. Poor thing. All he wanted was to make it to what he considered the Big Time. The concept was a little old-fashioned, but so was he. He didn't even need the substance, if he could just have the show: limousines, hotel suites, a few slaves, his name in the paper. It was the kind of thing thousands of people had, but not Owen. He kept falling off the curb. The limos kept driving away without him, or if he was on the inside, it was only by the grace of some woman—me, Sherry, or whoever took pity on him next.

"Well," Bo said, "the only reason I sent him to Rome in the first place was because I thought either Buckle or Gohagen would bash in his head. I needed you free. You're the only woman out here who understands me."

"I don't understand anybody," I said. "I certainly don't understand you."

The kick I got out of talking to him wore off a little once he forced me to consider how calculating he was. He was more feminine than any of us—or at least his brain was. Poor

Owen liked to think he was calculating, but his calculations had the consistency of pudding, compared to Bo's.

"The town is rife with rumors about *One Tree*," he said. "Sherry is said to be very concerned. I think you'll be lucky to get much say about the cut."

"I'm not sure the cut matters," I said. "I wasn't really up to that job. You were quite right to reject that picture."

"I was certainly right," he said.

"Bo," I said, "if you care for me, why didn't you try to talk me out of it?" I couldn't quite say "if you love me"—we had always avoided the word. A mark of good taste on both our parts.

"I wanted you to fail," he said, with no hesitation. "You can't be changed by abstract advice. My judgments are useless to you: you have to come to your own understandings. You have to sweat the sweat, bleed the blood, fuck the fuckers, and lose the money before you can agree with what I can figure out in my head in five seconds. I don't need experience, but you can't proceed without it. Now maybe you understand that you're not a director."

"I'm not?" I said—though I was more or less in agreement.

"No," he said. "You can do some of the things directors do, but you're not a director."

"Can you tell me what I am?" I asked. "If your head is so fucking good, why aren't you happy?"

He chuckled. "That's two questions," he said. "I'll take them in reverse order. I'm not happy because I can't attract the women I care about most. That's sad, but it's not a tragic or a particularly uncommon problem."

"Answer the first question," I said. Actually I was attracted to his voice. Somehow the sight of him sort of threw me off.

"Producer," he said. "You could be the best in Hollywood. You'd just be a whiz at it. I'd give you a picture to produce tomorrow, if you'd come over here. You'd be excellent, and we'd make a tremendous team."

I had fantasized about the same thing, a time or two. I probably would be a good producer, and we probably would be a good team, if he could stay out of love with me, or if I could get in love with him. Neither seemed likely.

Then I got worried about the line being tied up so long. Joe might have awakened and be trying to call. I made an excuse and hung up, and of course no one called. I opened my windows and listened to the distant traffic, to the airplanes that occasionally came over, to car doors shutting down the hill as people came home from parties. I had not slept in my own bed alone for a while, and it felt strange.

I woke up to a warm dawn, not a bit of mist in the hills. I put on some pants and a shirt and went right up to Joe's. Not only was he alive, he was sitting on his front steps, in his pajamas and disreputable old bathrobe, reading the paper.

"I've lost my touch with the horses too," he said, by way of greeting. In the morning light he didn't look quite so bad, although I was not yet used to seeing him gaunt.

"I'm already tired of your self-pity," I said.

He took my hand again, as soon as I sat down beside him on the porch. It seemed to be a new need. I think he had just been sitting there waiting for me to come.

But when I made him breakfast, he ate it. He had an appetite, and he was going back to work in a week. I began to feel better about him. After we ate I hustled down the hill, to go find out about the movie I was probably not going to be allowed to edit.

CHAPTER 5

THE people who are the hardest to deal with in Hollywood are I guess what you'd call middle management. Or maybe you'd call them upper management: junior executives, vice presidents in charge of some segment of production, or in some cases, vice presidents in charge of nothing whatever. Such people may have nothing of substance to do, but they are still liable for punishment if they do it—or don't do it—badly. It's at their level that insecurity bites the deepest. The top men generally have protection. If they get sacked, they're usually spared absolute humiliation. They retain some options, stock or otherwise; at the very worst, they can usually salvage a deal that makes it sound like they are becoming independent producers by choice. Sometimes it even *is* by choice.

The people one and two steps down the ladder don't have that cushion. They can be fired anytime anyone above them needs a scapegoat, which is often. They can be fired even if no scapegoat is required, just because the wind changes, or the tide turns, or whatever.

I knew something was fishy when I got to the studio and found that the only person I could persuade to talk to me was B. G. E. Filson. It's not accurate to say that I could persuade him to talk to me, either; it would be more accurate to say that I was unable to dissuade him *from* talking to me. Obviously—very obviously—Abe had assigned him to me, to divert me, get me out of the way, seduce me, anything.

It was a task for which Barry Filson was really ill-equipped, whichever way it went. He was one of the few people in Hollywood with three initials before his name—I believe he was from an old Connecticut family—and I did remember that the first initial stood for Barrett. Naturally everyone in Hollywood called him Barry, as a way of putting him down. I don't think he was a bad guy—he was just stiff and had too many manners and was a little weak—but he probably led a terrible life. Abe and the various other executives had no trouble rolling right over him. What he was doing in the movie business was a puzzle to everyone, I think including himself.

My problem with him wasn't that I disliked him—I scarcely knew him. I just didn't like the role he had been sent to play. I tried to sort of sidle around him and go directly to Mr. Mond, but that didn't work because Mr. Mond was sick. That was a surprise. So far as I knew, he had never been sick before.

"I think it's bronchial," B.G.E. said. He was wearing a beautiful gray suit, and it fit him and didn't look out of place on him the way fine suits do on a lot of junior executives out here.

"Well, if I can't talk to Mr. Mond, I guess I'll go talk to Sammy," I said. "I hear there are some problems with the cutting."

Barry—since we weren't in Connecticut, I called him that, too—looked very uncomfortable. He would never make a hatchet-man.

"I don't think Sammy's cutting it," he said.

"What are you talking about? He just left Texas three days ago. He was cutting it then."

"An emergency came up with that picture we're shooting down in Durango," he said. "I think Abe sent him down there."

We were in his office, which had a couple of Matisse lithographs on the wall—real Matisse lithographs. Every time I saw them I realized how limited I was. There was something mature and joyful about the drawings that I envied so much I couldn't stand to look at them. At the same time, I couldn't keep my eyes off them. Barrett Gordon Evarts Filson couldn't really hold my attention, with those drawings on the wall behind him, even when what he was saying seemed to be rather sinister.

"Barry, if Sherry is making trouble, why don't you say it?" I said. "I know she hates me. All I want is a straight answer."

"I think you'll have to talk to Abe," he said.

He had fine features, beautiful features, really, but the weakness was there. He wouldn't meet my eye. And he wasn't even on the make, particularly. I can forgive a man lying and cheating if he's driven by ambition, but Barry wasn't. I guess he was just a gentleman who liked to live where it was sunny, but was still a little too active for Palm Springs or Bermuda or the Bahamas, or wherever his peers lived.

I felt very tired of the failures of men. They were always failing in the most basic ways, like looking down or away at the moment when they should be gutsy enough to meet your eye.

"Why are you doing this?" I said—a terrible question to ask him. What could be worse than asking a man to account for his motives? In fact, I got very angry with him and said awful things, not vulgarly awful but subtly and cuttingly awful: things he would remember later, maybe months later.

He wouldn't fight back, though. He stuck with his manners, offered to see what he could find out, and suggested we have lunch. His embarrassed good manners just made me more irritable; I felt bound to counter with absolute bad manners, so I marched out and went to see Abe's secretary.

Her name was Wanda, and for my money she was the smartest person in the whole studio. She was a grizzled old girl who had lived her whole life in California—she had been through everything, and I think she liked me because she sensed that, at the rate I was going, I too would have been through everything in not too many years. She smoked constantly, drank all night, slept with God knows what kind of men, and dyed her hair a different color every few months. At the moment, she was living with a girl friend who was every bit as grizzled as she was; the girl friend was an executive secretary at Metro. They went on a cruise together once a year, to get away from it all.

I felt I could count on Wanda for a little bit of truth. She was really Mr. Mond's employee, not Abe's. Mr. Mond kept her on to see that Abe didn't do anything too wild. I think Abe hated her, but he didn't have the guts to fire her.

When I came in she was sitting in a cloud of smoke, typing. The page emerged perfectly typed from the typewriter, despite the little cloud that hung between Wanda and the machine.

"What have they done with Sammy?" I asked.

Wanda shrugged. "Did you look in the commissary?" she said.

"B.G.E. says they shipped him to Durango."

"Barry's beautiful, but he wouldn't know a turd from a fig," Wanda said. "It's just that you're about to get fired."

"Would Mr. Mond really let them fire me?" I asked. "Have you talked to him?"

"Not for a week," she said. "Usually it's every ten minutes. I think I'm about to get fired, too. I think the old man's given up.

"You know Hiram died," she added. "I think that did it."

Hiram was a friend of Mr. Mond's youth—the last such friend, I guess. He was an aged banker who had lived in Miami for thirty years or so. Besides being a friend from New York days, he had financed Mr. Mond in his early years at the studio. The two of them talked on the phone for hours, every day.

"Died about a month ago," Wanda said. "Hiram was the last link, you know. Everybody's got their links—even him. I think we all better get ready to move."

I was very taken aback. I had been blindly counting on Mr. Mond's support. If Wanda was right and he had stopped caring, there was no telling what would happen.

"Did he love you?" Wanda asked. It was strange to hear the word come out of such a face.

"Mr. Mond?"

"No, the big guy," she said. "The one that's with Miss Solaré."

"Oh, no," I said. "No, I don't think so."

"The way she's acting, he did."

I didn't try to discuss it. The suggestion stirred too many feelings—it just confused me. I went to the commisary, but I couldn't find Sammy, and our cutting room was locked, which was stupid. Finally I stopped looking for Sammy and left the studio. Wanda had mixed me up. Why would she ask if Owen loved me?

I drove aimlessly around Hollywood for a while. Maybe if I had known how to shop, I would have gone shopping, but I've always been terrible at it and as a means of getting my mind off other things it's no good to me.

Finally I drove down Western Avenue, to a section that had gone heavily to seed, where there was a big secondhand book shop I liked to poke around in. It was called the Past Tense and was in an old frame house that had somehow managed not to get knocked down. The owner was a huge man named Tub McDowell—I guess he fascinated me because he was so unlike anyone else I knew in Hollywood. He weighed about three hundred pounds, and wore fatigue pants and an old flannel shirt, the same fatigues and the same flannel shirt for months at a time, until they were absolutely black with book dust, as were his hands and sometimes his forehead and chin. He lived amid his books like a bear in a cave—in fact, poking around on the second floor one day, looking for some books on costume, I found the cave—a cubbyhole where he slept: just a mattress on a cot, no sheets, and a television set sitting on a whisky crate near the bed. The mattress was black, too—it was kind of awful—and as years passed and Tub and I got to know one another in a casual, shop-owner-to-more-or-less-regular-customer kind of way, I often wanted to ask him to at least turn the mattress over and sleep on the clean side for a while—or better yet, to burn it and get a new one from the Goodwill or somewhere. But he was very shy with me and I could never bring myself to mention it.

It was quite obvious how he had got the name Tub. He had an enormous belly, bulging over his fatigues and somehow never quite covered by his shirttails—the portion of it below his navel was always visible. A few drunks and bums occasionally came in, to panhandle, but I seldom encountered another customer. It seemed to me Tub only bought books, rather than sold them, but if so, it didn't seem to dampen his enthusiasm for the enterprise.

Despite his belly, which moved when he walked almost as if it were an independent thing—a kingdom of flesh bearing only a casual relation to the body it was attached to—I didn't find Tub gross. Mentally, he was a delicate person, far more so than most of the men I dealt with, and though his hands were big and fat, he handled books as lightly as if he were handling lace or fine porcelain. Also, though he himself was invariably filthy and begrimed, his books were immaculate, not dirty at all, the many thousands of them. It was as if somehow Tub had managed to absorb all their sins and soilings himself, as they passed into his possession.

At times of deep stress I sometimes used the book shop as my hiding place. Tub always left me alone, and I could sit on the floor and read, in an alley between the shelves, and feel quite safe. I suppose the shop was Tub's hiding place, too, though I had no idea what he might be hiding from; but another thing I loved about it was that if I really wanted a book, he seemed always to have it, unless it was a book he disapproved of or considered inferior. He seemed to have taken the proper measure of every book on every subject, and if I asked him for a worthless book, a frown would flicker briefly across his big face and he would get off his stool and pad off through his rows of shelves like a bear, the untied strings of his tennis shoes rattling on the floor like claws; in a moment he would pad back, smiling happily, and hand me the book I should, in his view, be looking for.

"This one's much better," he would say, a little apologetically, and if I decided actually to buy the book—something I did only once in a while, out of shame over all the free reading—Tub would frown and smile and manage to arrive at a figure much lower than the one he had marked in the book.

"Hi, Tub," I said when I came in, and he grinned and nodded shyly. I had almost overcome his inhibitions about talking to me—if I stayed around a while and he was in the right mood, he would talk to me freely about his life, much of which had been spent in the navy; but in this instance I was not much in the mood for talk myself, and I drifted on upstairs to where the costume books were, taking a quick peek to see if perhaps he had done anything about the mattress. Of course he hadn't.

I sat for an hour, looking at costume books and listening to the buses run on Western Avenue, and then went down to get some tea. Another of Tub's delicacies was that he drank tea all day. When I came down, a young man with very long hair was standing at the counter, showing Tub some books. The young man was overpale and dressed in Levis and an old tie-dyed shirt. I was struck by the reserve in his face. When I see men, I know right away whether they're going to try to speak to me, and this young man wasn't. He didn't even glance at me. There was something monastic about the scene: Tub was the big old monk, the young man the respectful novitiate. Tub was grimacing and looking anguished. There were three books before him, and he stared at them as if they were gems.

"I guess about three hundred dollars," he said.

The young man immediately nodded. Tub stood up, and his belly shook as he dug into his fatigues and came out with a wad of bills. The young man took the money and folded it carefully, then nodded at Tub and went out the door. Tub handed me my tea, evidently a little embarrassed that I had caught him actually conducting business.

"That was Doug," he said, by way of explanation. "He's a book scout."

"I've heard of boy scouts, but not book scouts," I said. "What does he do, camp out in book stores?"

"Oh, he travels," Tub said. "He makes the rounds—estate sales, junk shops, places I never get time to hit."

"Can I look?" I asked, setting my tea to one side of the books. Tub nodded. The first book I picked up was a brown leather-bound one.

"That's Mackenzie," he said, as if I would automatically know what he meant.

I had never heard of a Mackenzie. The title page said *Voyage From Montreal on the River St Lawrence Through the Continent of North America.* It had a big map in it, but I didn't unfold it. The name of the river caused a memory to snake through me, wriggling through the barriers of years and experience like the line of a river on a map, all the way back to a lover, my kindest lover, a boy named Danny Deck, who used to sit on a mattress with me in an apartment we shared briefly in San Francisco and read books about great rivers. It was such a soft memory, after the harshness of the last few weeks, that in a moment I found I was crying, without having consciously come to tears. I only knew it when I noticed that Tub McDowell seemed greatly disturbed: frightened to death, to be more accurate.

It was true. I was dripping on the book, which I think ordinarily would have appalled Tub, had he not been too disturbed to notice.

"Did we do something wrong?" he asked, as if posing the question to himself, trying to think what social error had caused such a calamity to happen.

"No, no, I'm fine," I said, and it was true. I felt much better.

"Wipe your book," I said. He was glad to have that to do, though I think I had made him almost not like the book, as if it were somehow at fault for such an outburst.

I don't cry much, never liked to. For one thing, it always

makes men feel so guilty and insecure that it's less trouble all around to suppress it. Such jags as I have are usually solitary. When I recovered from the memory of Danny I drank my tea, though to my embarrassment, spurts continued to wet my cheeks. I felt like my tear ducts were out of control, like the wash part of the windshield-wiping mechanism. Someone kept pushing the wash button, inside me. I was left with only the delicate problem of explaining myself to Tub.

"You mustn't take that personally," I said. "I once had a boyfriend who spent all his time reading about rivers. The book reminded me of him, that's all."

"I've got a lot of books about rivers," he said, as if it were the only comment he was qualified to make about such a situation.

"Actually, he was a writer—my boyfriend," I said. "He wrote a novel called *The Restless Grass.*"

Tub's huge face changed, became excited. "Danny Deck?" he said. "You knew him?"

He went padding off into the aisles. In a minute he came back, Danny's book in his hand.

"Doug found it in San Francisco," he said. "It's inscribed."

I had never really looked at the book—even now didn't entirely want to. Danny had disappeared only a few days after it was published—drowned in the Rio Grande, everyone assumed; at least they found his car parked near it. I never knew what I thought about that, except that whatever he had done with himself was partly my fault, for giving up on us—although I knew he understood that I couldn't help it. Still, I had never wanted to read the book. He had read most of it to me, sitting on the mattress in our apartment, and I was satisfied with that.

But when Tub put it before me, I opened it and there was Danny's large, hasty handwriting on the flyleaf: "To Wu, only man to beat me at Ping-Pong seventeen times running, in friendship, Danny."

"But I knew that man," I said. "I knew Wu. How could he sell this book?"

Tub shrugged. "Maybe he died and his widow sold it," he suggested. "It's worth some money."

"How much?"

"About a hundred dollars."

I turned the book over and looked at the picture. There he was, too dressed up and consequently stiff. So like me in some ways—no wonder we couldn't work out. Only he was infinitely more generous than me. I handed the book back to Tub. It was practically the one romance I didn't feel bad about, even though it had failed.

I even remembered when I was leaving him, early in the morning, with San Francisco fog all around us. I wanted to hit him for being so lovable and yet not holding me, but at the same time I was determined to go. It was the only one of my partings that hadn't been bitter and vengeful, yet if Danny had been bitter and vengeful and had accused me of the very things that were true, I probably would have stayed. A few weeks later I went to Europe with another man and didn't know for a long time that Danny had disappeared. By then my life was moving so fast that I never quite found time in which to feel a true sorrow, or even decide if I really believed he was dead.

"Do you want it?" Tub said. "I mean, since you knew him. You could just have it."

"What are you talking about?" I said. "You just said it was worth a hundred dollars."

He ducked his big head, embarrassed. "Well, technically," he said. "But books should belong to the people who need them."

Why do you need so many, Mr. McDowell? I might have asked, but I didn't. Let people have their needs. Why did I need an asshole like Owen Oarson?

"No thank you," I said. "It would mean more to someone who didn't know him, someone who just read it and loved it."

That night, after Joe was asleep, I went down the hill and poked in my closets, in my piles of drawings, trying to find the ones of Danny and the apartment in San Francisco, but I never managed to find them. They were there, but too many years of life, all unsorted, lay on top of them. I thought when I started the search that it might be fun to live in memories for a few days, since the present was so intractable, but I soon got impatient with it. All it did was make me miss my son, of whom there were drawings at every level. He was still in New Mexico.

While I was looking at drawings of him, Gauldin called, drunk. I don't know where he was. Despite the fact that it was totally pointless, we wrangled on the phone for nearly two hours. I felt like beating my head on the floor for having been such a fool as to let the whole thing start. In the end I told him he could come over, regretted it, and waited to repulse him, only to fall asleep on my couch. Next morning he wasn't there—I found out later from a mutual friend that he had been stopped for drunk driving, sassed the cop, and had had to spend the night in jail. The next time he called, three or four days later, he was so sheepish that I temporarily broke down. By then I had figured out that the thing to do about it was to get him a job for a while, and I was working on it.

Poor Gauldin got such a bad bargain with me, but then probably he never realized it. I guess it says something about the intimacy if I had to be the one to feel cheated for both of us, but that was where things had come to, and for a while that was where things stayed.

CHAPTER 6

It's an odd feeling to direct a picture and then return to Hollywood only to find that you've been removed from it. Odd, and confusing to the emotions, sort of like it would be to get married and divorced before you even made love. In my case it was even more confusing because no one would admit that anything unusual was happening. Most of the principals didn't have to admit anything, because they weren't there. Sherry was up at Tahoe, in one of her numerous retreats. Abe was in Mexico, and Mr. Mond was sick. I was left to get what I could out of the likes of Barry Filson.

Finally, in considerable confusion, I had dinner with Bo Brimmer. Of course I knew it would drive Gauldin up the wall, and it did. He even hit me, evidence of more fury than I would have expected of him. I didn't blame him for it a bit, since it was purely my weakness that had brought him to the point where he could be so goaded. He had the insecurity of the working man, always afraid of losing his woman to the boss, the brain guy. Who could blame him? I tried not to make Gauldin feel threatened, but then he had every right to feel threatened. There was nothing wrong with his heart, and nothing wrong with him as a man, and even though he went off cursing and crying and left his suitcase and had to send a friend back for it—he was so proud—I wasn't worried about him, or very upset. He would always find women to respect him.

Bo had his problems, of course: too little, too smart, no sexual confidence. He was seen around town with a lot of women, but I doubt if he ever slept with any of them. He took me to the Bistro, a very dressed-up place. It always startles me a little to come into a dressed-up place—makes me realize how odd I am, how blind to a lot of styles and ways of life. I hadn't dressed beautifully ten times in my life. I hated trying to make up my mind what to wear. I always postponed my decision until the last minute, and then I chose wrong. To conceal the fact that I was overawed, I told Bo that he should stop wearing bow ties, which he always wore and which I hated.

His eyes were methodically going over the room, to see if anyone important was there. "I wear them because they're disarming," he said. "People in bow ties look like rubes."

Although he seemed to be his normal, perfectly controlled self, I knew he was really very nervous. His face was tight with it, and he smiled too continually. Bo lived with an even higher charge of tension than I do—our charges had never quite gotten aligned, but his tension certainly gave off signals. It made me wonder if he was going to try to fuck me. He had always intrigued me, in a strange way, and I felt sort of curious as to what he would do. My curiosity had some sexual content. Not a lot, but some. I felt a breath or two of interest as he gave the waiter precise commands and got us some mussels and some white wine.

But his talk, perhaps because he was nervous, was all business. He told me about the books he had bought, about the projects he had available, ready for me to produce.

"Sherry hates you," he said, when *One Tree* came up.

"I know that, but we're not talking about that," I said. "We're talking about the picture, and Sherry can't possibly care about that. Not now. All I want is to see that the actors get a decent break."

Bo shrugged. "Hating you might be her way to handle the grief," he said. "Sometimes people stay alive that way."

"So what do I do?" I asked. "Some of those actors are hanging their hopes on that picture."

Instead of answering the question, he spun brilliant conversation around me for an hour, a lovely cocoon of words, observations, comments on food, criticisms of pictures currently playing, remarks about the nature of women, even a quick list of the painters my eyes reminded him of. Somehow he managed to eat without its affecting the rhythms of his sentences. I got a little fascinated with it—he had breath control like a singer.

The talk continued right up to my doorstep, and woven into it were a couple of subtle proposals of marriage. Each time he mentioned it, the little breaths of interest I felt in him died out. Nothing is more abstract than the concept of marriage apart from knowledge of a body—at least to me. He should have tried something first. On the other hand, he probably used the talk to ease himself past something he knew he didn't want. We retreated from one another smoothly enough, when we got to my house, but I felt a little disturbed anyway, because a small but interesting possibility kept advancing and receding and never coming to anything.

In the morning Mr. Mond called, his voice as different from the voice I knew as if he had moved to a different planet.

"Come up here, my da'lin'," he said, with an awful tonelessness.

"This dope I had to take, ya know," he said. "I didn't know what was happenin', not until yesterday. I want ya to come up."

I didn't feel much like seeing him fade out before my eyes, but of course I had to go.

When I got there he made them wheel him out to the poolside, by all the telephones, where he had spent the better part of the last fifteen years. The better part in every sense, I guess. That little blue pool of water, in the beautifully green lawn, with the trees hanging over it and the flowers and the grass always freshly watered, had been his real place ever since I'd known him.

Now the beautiful high place was the same and Mr. Mond was different. It was horrible to see the pallor of death so rapidly eat away the tan of a man who had done nothing but burn himself brown for fifteen years. The tan hadn't entirely left his skin, but the pallor spread underneath it, leaving him a shadowy color, with black splotches here and there on his arms. He took my hand absently and held it, almost as Joe did, and the flesh that was left on his fingers was soft, over the bone. Now that the flesh was sinking off his face, his skull was almost visible, and that enormous jawbone, that Joe was always claiming had actually knocked down a small actor once, was sunk down against his chest, his neck no longer powerful enough to move it, much less swing it. It lay there, propped on his chest, pulling his head to one side so that I had to tilt mine to really look him in the eye. Amazing. It reminded me of the jawbone of a horse I found in a field in Mendocino one time.

When Mr. Mond talked, it was slowly and tonelessly, I guess because the effort to really open his mouth was great. A number of attendants were around, at a respectful distance, but there was no sign of Abe, and no teenagers with bouncing breasts. The telephones with their panels of buttons were not ringing, not blinking, and the whole beautiful garden had a mortuary feel.

Yet, deep in his black eyes, Mr. Mond was still there. His eyes fastened on me more tightly than the hand that held mine, in a grip as toneless as his voice. The color was fading from the rest of him, as his life was fading, but there was still a mean glint in his eyes.

"Steal it," he said, and then wheezed for a while, rasped, tried to clear the bubble and froth of mucus from his voice.

"Steal da picture," he said, when he could.

"What do you mean?" I said. "What are you talking about?"

"Some mischief," he said. "I got nothin' to live for but some mischief. It's all been mischief, everything I done with you. I got away with it, ya see, because I kept my options. I'd a made too much trouble, so da board put up with me. And I'm da smartest anyway, so I made them money, ya see? I don't know how much, hundred million a year, even when I was ninety, ninety-one. None of them others done that, not no fuckin' Goldwyn, Harry Cohn, nobody."

He lifted his jaw a little, stirred by pride, and then let it fall back on his chest.

"But they're glad I'm sick," he said. "They been waitin' ten, twelve years for me to die. It's all right. Way of da woild. I'm old, I'll die. But I want ya to steal da picture foist."

"How can I do that, Mr. Mond?"

"Ya disappoint me, my da'lin'," he said. "How do I know how? Hire a burglar. Steal the keys to da lab. Get da negative. You can walk around, you figure it out. But steal it. Get everything you can find. Otherwise that whore that thinks she's such a big star is going to ruin it."

"To be honest, I'm not sure there's that much to ruin," I said.

"Not da point," he said. "Didn't I say mischief? We don't let 'em get their way, ya see? We don't let the big star get away with it. Why should they get their way? We done it, you an' me! So we see that they don't get their way!"

He was an amazing old man. He stared at me passionately —how many forms it takes. He wanted me to be his weapon, help him strike one last blow. I hadn't realized how resentful the old must get of the people underneath them—the younger people. Now he had accepted the inevitable, but he wanted one last shot, one final act of pride, the victims of which would be the men who would get to live once he was dead.

Only it wouldn't be *my* final act, just his. What was I supposed to do after stealing the film?

"You're famous," he said, when I asked him. "You're da

woman director. So ya steal your own film and what can they do? If they put you in jail the public won't stand for it. Abe don't care about the picture. He'd just as soon boin it. They'd get the insurance money and not have the problem of no release. Steal it. Make 'em pay a ransom. Make 'em give you da cut. You'll get publicity like nobody's ever seen, like if Garbo come back or somethin'. Da publicity will make da picture."

I didn't know what to say. It was a sickroom fantasy to end all sickroom fantasies.

"I'm not much of a criminal," I said.

"What criminal?" he said. "Listen, ya got moral rights. Ya made the picture."

Then his strength played out and he stopped talking. The life seemed to fade from his body. He was so weak he could barely mumble a goodbye, when they wheeled him in. Even his eyes faded, but they faded last, burning there in his ashen old face long after he had stopped talking.

I didn't know what to make of it. Even dying, he was capable of some deviousness. I thought he liked me, and had always thought so, but then, who knows what old men really feel about young women? Years before, ten years maybe, well before I had ever worked for him, he had exposed himself to me once. I was just visiting the house with a friend who was doing a script for him, and as I was coming out of the ladies' room he came out of a bedroom with his pants down, fumbling with a shirttail. I don't think it was accidental, either. I think he was lying in wait. What reminded me of it was his eyes, watching to see how I'd react when he suggested I steal the film. Later, when I thought about it, it was his eyes I remembered, not his cock, which looked like a piece of old cork.

The next day I almost had an encounter with Abe. He was walking down a corridor with Jilly Legendre, who was just back from shooting a picture in Turkey. Abe flinched at the sight of me and made some hasty excuse before I got in earshot. He turned and hurried back down the corridor.

Jilly, immense, dressed in white pants and some kind of red Greek shirt, watched Abe go with surprise.

"What have you got?" he said. "Swine flu? I've never seen Abe move that fast, and I grew up with the little prick."

Perhaps in a way that was Jilly's secret. He was a native of movies. He had grown up among movie people, in Hollywood, Paris, New York, and he knew the industry and its ways as a farmer knows his fields. He stood out in Hollywood because he loved it all: the deals, the indulgence, the confusion. To Jilly it was all just like walking around home.

It was a bright day, and since I had inadvertently blown his appointment, we decided to go to the beach and catch up on one another. Jilly had a new Rolls—he liked all the appurtenances—and when we got to Malibu he sent his driver off for food and wine and we settled ourselves on his beach. We were an odd sight: a very fat man and a very skinny woman.

Yet for all his self-indulgence and sophistication, Jilly was not world-weary, which was why I liked him. He looked at it fresh. When I told him about Wynkyn he shook his head.

"Hollywood oughtn't to try and propagate itself," he said. "It ought to die out at the end of every generation. Experience never gets passed on here anyway."

We had a pleasant day, good for me. Somehow I could always be at ease with Jilly—I guess we trusted one another not to get nonsensical. The notion of anyone so fat and anyone so skinny joined in the sexual act affronted our common sense of esthetics.

Besides, though Jilly shared Abe's taste for Latin teenagers, he had a great love, an aging French actress, very imperious, who had skillfully kept him on the string for years and might keep him there forever. It left us free to indulge our mutually insatiable curiosity about one another's life and work.

I told him about Mr. Mond's strange suggestion—he agreed it would get the picture unbelievable publicity—and then he told me about an affair he had had with Sherry years before.

"You have to remember how concentrated she is," he said. "Sherry has only one thing: herself. She needs nothing else, believes in nothing else, knows nothing else. But she absolutely has to be pleased with herself: nothing can be wrong, and in order for nothing to be wrong the whole world has to assume a certain shape. Everything she knows and relates to in any way has to help keep the world tilted so that it reflects Sherry in just the way she needs it to.

"She's good at shoving the world around," he added. "She puts the camera where she wants it, and society and friendship and love are like the camera. She puts everything where she wants it, and as long as she can do that she's fine."

"But she can't do that now," I said. "Wynkyn is dead."

"No," he said. "Death is not a camera."

The ocean rolled in, and rolled in, hypnotically. The sun was not too bad, so I took a little nap, lying on my stomach on the warm sand. When I woke up, Jilly was still drinking wine. Black hairs curled into his navel, from the vortex of that great belly.

"It wasn't much of a love affair," he said, as if the conversation hadn't lapsed. "A man isn't really a camera, either. They don't hold their focus that well."

The water turned steel color, before we left.

CHAPTER 7

THE next morning Abe called. He was characteristically direct.

"Hey," he said. "It's okay. It's okay. Come and cut the picture."

"Really? What happened?"

"We don't know and we don't care. Sherry's lost interest in making trouble. She's gone to Italy. So let's don't waste no more time.

"Did you hear what happened at Universal?" he asked, once the business was settled.

"No."

"It just happened," he said. "It's on television. A driver went berserk and killed eight people. Ran over them with a limo. The S.W.A.T. team's after him. Think what a movie! It would have to happen at fuckin' Universal."

By the time I turned on the television it was all over, and

various policemen and survivors were describing it to the television reporters. The man who went berserk had been a former stunt driver, a Central European who, according to the news, had been around Hollywood for thirty years. He was one of those people Joe would know all about. Everyone agreed he was a man of formidable driving skills, because he had smashed his limo into a studio gatehouse, killing two attendants, then wove around the studio until he got six more people, all of them unaware that anything was happening. Even after the police got there he had somehow rolled his car over an apparently impregnable police barricade and set off, only to lose control a few minutes later, screaming through Laurel Canyon with twenty police cars in pursuit. He smashed into the hill and was dead when the police got to him.

Bo was on the newscast briefly, expressing his shock and horror.

It was the kind of happening that conspires to make L.A. seem crazier than it really is. For the next few days the news stations ran clips of some of the man's great stunt drives, and unearthed a lot of old stills and such. What was haunting to me was not the man, or even his victims, but his fat, bewildered wife, also Central European. She was asked again and again for an explanation of the tragedy, only to grow more and more bewildered.

"Gregor was man . . . men have these moods . . . when he was angry nobody better stop him . . . I am sorry," she said, but then you could see it all become too much, and she faced the cameras silently, not sobbing, just retreating as deeply as she could into silence and stolidity.

We were halfway through the cutting when Mr. Mond died. It was something of a shock, because reports were that he was getting well. The Academy had even decided to stage a tribute on his ninety-second birthday—they went ahead and arranged a spectacular gala, and then he died. Some people thought it had been his last trick, getting the industry to plan a party and then popping off, so as to leave them holding the bag. The gala had to be hastily converted into a memorial tribute—awkward, because now that he was finally dead almost everyone in the industry was happy to forget him. Having to say nice things about a man they hated, with him not even there to hear them, stuck in a lot of craws.

I went with Bo. There was to be an immense party at Jilly's, later on—his French actress was in town. Bo was very cheerful. The black humor of the gala appealed to him, made him even wittier than usual.

Everyone was there—including Owen. It had never occurred to me that he would be there. I don't know why it hadn't, since it was well known that he hadn't gone to Europe with Sherry. Her distraught, sick face was in the papers almost every day. Usually she was at a night club with her new love, a Spanish millionaire. Somehow I just never expected Owen to be anywhere that I was again. It threw me off, even though we got no closer to one another than about fifty yards. He was with Raven Dexter, Toole Peters' old girl friend, a tall, vague New Yorker who had been in Hollywood seven or eight years and was still working on her first screenplay.

I caught glimpses of him throughout the evening, amid the swirl of conversation, the speeches, the film clips, the jokes, and Abe's predictable collapse into tears. Owen was never smiling, that was all I registered. Raven Dexter talked to Clint Eastwood all night. I had the funny sense—Joe Percy was always talking about it, but I had never felt it before—of being in a movie rather than a life. Of course, literally, I was in a movie: there were TV cameras everywhere. Emotionally, I was in a very trite role: jilted woman, going out with man she doesn't care about, suddenly sees man she does care about, with another woman. The sense that I was in a movie was almost comforting, because maybe if it felt that way, it would turn out like it turns out in movies, with me getting him back if, upon consideration, I really wanted him back.

To make it all more complicated, Truffaut was at the next

table, with Jacqueline Bisset. The sight of her drove Bo to a fever of brilliance. He even revealed a rich command of the French language, which up to that moment none of us knew he had.

Then at Jilly's party I got high—not on much, a little marijuana, but I was in a state to get high if I took anything at all into my system. Jilly had a pained, reserved look on his face all evening: his lady was very difficult. It was a good thing he had a beard. Large men with beards automatically take on dignity when they're unhappy. As for Bo, he could not have been higher, brighter, or more voluble—he was not for a moment going to let it into his consciousness that François Truffaut might have something he didn't.

While I was high I saw an amazing thing. Jilly had an immense and beautiful Dalmatian that wandered around the party looking as grave as his master. There was dancing around the pool, which had a kind of island made of mattresses in the center of it—of course everybody thought it was for fucking, but I think Jilly just lay on it and read scripts. Four or five beautiful young people were skinny-dipping, showing off their beauty, probably unaware that the sight of them in their healthy young glory was creating sinking feelings in all of us not-so-young and not-so-beautiful spectators.

The Dalmatian was just as beautiful as the skinny-dippers, but no one noticed him except me. Then a Mexican servant brought out a really huge block of caviar—two pounds maybe, probably the best you can get—and set it on a low table by the pool. No one noticed that either, except the Dalmatian and myself. The Dalmatian walked over gravely, sniffed it once, and then, within ten seconds, ate every bit of it. He didn't exactly wolf it—it just disappeared, as if it had been sucked into him. I was the only one who noticed. The Dalmatian walked away with about $800 worth of caviar in his belly, and no one even laughed. They were too busy wishing they were young enough and beautiful enough, not to mention uninhibited enough, to skinny-dip.

Later I sometimes wondered if seeing the Dalmatian eat

the caviar had anything to do with the fact that Bo and I ended up having a one-night stand that night. The sight of Owen, plus getting high, plus who knows what else—maybe all those body-proud young men at Jilly's, lingering on the diving board so everyone would be sure and see what nice young cocks they had—I guess it combined to detach me from my normal self. And probably the sight of his true love and permanent fantasy had stirred Bo up. Going home late—the mist was in the hills—I thought anyway I'd kiss him because I've always liked his mouth and it might be the only time ever that we'd both be out of our patterns enough for it to happen. But he kissed me first and sent his driver right on home when we got to my house. Of course those persistent Hollywood rumors about him being freakish or perverse or a breast-biter or just too little to do anything were all nonsense. He was an insistent lover, even a little desperate. Maybe that was because his sex drive was fueled by the thought of an impossible love, I don't know.

When I woke up the next morning Bo was dressed, drinking a cup of coffee. He was also on the phone to his house, telling them what clothes to bring him for the day. When his driver came and I followed him out on the sidewalk, he got me to step off the steps before he did. Then he kissed me.

"You're a darling," he said as he turned to leave.

I did like his mouth, but that was the last I got of it. For some reason, that night ruined our relationship. Bo never came back to pester me, like normal old Gauldin. A bit of an affair with me would have done his reputation a lot of good, but it didn't happen, and I don't believe he ever mentioned that I'd been a conquest. I don't understand why that one night distanced us so completely, but it did. After that, when we met at parties, we didn't chat. I did not go to Universal to become a producer. Bo didn't ask me to accompany him to the Oscar ceremonies, as he had for a number of years, and when he left Hollywood, scarcely more than a year later, to assume command of a national television network—probably the most powerful media position in the country—he didn't call to say goodbye.

And I didn't miss him, although he was one of the brightest men I knew, and gave the most intelligent advice. The little roads that lead people up to and then away from one another are the most mazelike roads of all. My road to Bo, Bo's road to me, who knows? Friends for years, lovers for a few hours, and then quits. Even a pseudo-sage like Joe Percy would have a hard time assigning causes in such a case.

A week later I saw Owen again. Foolishly, I had agreed to go up to Tujunga Canyon, to a party at Elmo Buckle's. Actually, I had even agreed to be Elmo's date for the evening—or in other words, the hostess of the party. Of course Gohagen was a co-host. I usually called him Gohagen because I knew he was shy, underneath his hardened manner, and he had a greatly exaggerated respect for me. So did Elmo, I guess. If I called Winfield Winfield, he got morbid and drunk and told me he loved me, despite the fact that he had three live-in women at the time, one of whom was pregnant.

As for Elmo, he claimed to be in love with a Canadian actress, who had evidently just left. Apparently she had managed to share the house with him for three weeks without ever consummating the act of love—as he delicately put it.

"We never consummated the act of love," he told me mournfully as he was driving me to his house in the Canyon. "That's why I'm forced to call on you to help me out. If she hears I have a respectable woman for a date, don't you reckon she'll want to take another look at it?"

I had followed Elmo and Winfield for years, through labyrinthine loves, seductions, and mate-swappings, without ever having been able to decide which group was the more masochistic: them, or their women. No woman who wasn't somewhat masochistic would have put up with their rather stereotypic chauvinism. On the other hand, no healthy man would have put up with their women, who were either totally passive zombies or else the meanest-spirited, most grasping, bitter-mouthed poor-white women I had ever seen.

It was as if they had a pipeline running from Tujunga Canyon to Austin, out of which crawled only those two kinds of women. That Elmo had branched out as far as a Canadian actress was a sign of some progress.

"I hope she comes and takes another look at it," Elmo said as we drove.

I had no comment. Underneath all their acts, Elmo and Winfield were likable, intelligent, perceptive and kindly men, and I could never understand or imagine what colossal uncertainties drove them to live as they did.

Their party was filled with the usual assortment of record producers, dope dealers, hip bankers, rock singers, a jet-set child or two, and many hillbilly musicians, plus a few very nervous younger executives from Beverly Hills who were seeing how far out they could get and still make it back. I made tacos and Elmo and Winfield cooked up a ferocious chili. They argued enough about its ingredients to cause a bystander to think that a five-star meal was in progress. Winfield brought all three of his girls, and Elmo, I think, managed to consummate the act of love with one of them before the evening was over—though I had told him specifically that if I was going to be his date, he would have to refrain from such a thing, at least until after he took me home. Theirs was a strange friendship—neither of them quite trusted a woman until she'd slept with them both.

A lot of marijuana was smoked, some coke sniffed, a lot of chili eaten, and some loud hillbilly played. I felt quite at home with Elmo and Winfield, although I didn't like a soul at their party except them and one seraphic young guitarist, who stood over me half the evening, trying to think of something to say. Whenever I asked him a question he called me ma'am.

"I lived out in Floydada until I went off with the band," he said. "It sure is crazy out here in L.A., ain't it, ma'am?" He was such a baby he reminded me of my son, who hadn't called home in weeks.

Somehow Elmo's house seemed like it ought to be in Appalachia, although the kitchen was all redwood, very expensive, and all the cars parked below it were Mercedes or Ferraris or something. I spent most of my evening in the kitchen, which smelled wonderful, partly of chili and partly of redwood. Once in a while Elmo came in, drunker and more stoned each time. Each time, he hugged me.

"Shit, the wenches of Texas have become a race of fuckin' harridans," he said on one such visit. "One of them's giving old Winfield a blow job, right out in the yard. I seen it. How much lower can a civilization sink?"

Then he insisted that the angelic young man play his guitar for the guests. I went out of the kitchen to listen and saw Owen. Once again he was with Raven Dexter, who was wearing a woolly coat of some kind, not because it was cold but because Lulu Dickey wore woolly coats. She had cornered one of the young executives and was promoting her screenplay, and Owen was standing by himself, looking out a plate-glass window. He hadn't seen me and didn't know I was there, so I got to study him a little. It was a rare opportunity for me to try and figure out what I'd seen in him to begin with, but I didn't do much with it. I got scared he'd see me and went back to the kitchen, only to sit there hating myself for my cowardice. Was I going to hide in the kitchen at every party he turned up at, for the rest of my life?

While I was hiding, Gohagen came in the back door. Although he was extremely drunk, he at once figured out what I was doing.

"Sittin' there hidin' from fuckin' old Owen," he said. "I wisht I had some room to talk, but hell, look at me. I just got sucked off by a woman I didn't even know, and me with three women here. Let's go for a ride before something else happens."

"You're too drunk," I said. "I'm scared to ride with you."

Gohagen was perhaps forty-two, and he looked like he had lived three lives. In fact he looked like he was even then living two or three, simultaneously, and probably he was.

"You want us to beat the piss out of him?" he asked, blinking at the suggestion that he was too drunk to drive. "Me and Elmo will take him on, if you say the word. I know we're drunk, but we're persistent."

I didn't want them to beat him up, and I didn't want him to see me, either. I *really* didn't want it. The only impression I had formed in my inspection was that he had a selfish mouth, which I already knew. While I was hiding I found a novel Elmo had written, and read about half of it. To my surprise, it was good. In Hollywood, when a screenwriter tells you he writes novels it makes as little impression as if a woman like my mother tells you she plays bridge. It never occurs to anyone that such novels could count, but it seemed to me that Elmo's almost counted.

My hiding worked. Owen and Raven went off, as did the young executives, the hip bankers, and the dope dealers. Only the musicians stayed, and I finally did go out and listen to the young guitarist. Gohagen was in intense conversation with his pregnant lady friend—the other two sat silent as statues nearby.

When Elmo came in and sat down by me, I asked if I could borrow his book. It was called *Fast Company*.

"You can have it," he said. "Shit, you can even have the remainder of it if you can think of something to do with it. I got twenty-three hundred copies stacked in the garage.

"I had a great theme that time," he added. Elmo had weary eyes. "My theme was that life is a mess. Undeniably great fuckin' theme. You want to run off with me and go live in Italy? We could just be friends."

"Not this year," I said. "Maybe next year."

"Your ex-feller was asking about you," he said. "Half the time I feel like whipping his ass, but I never get around to it."

"You boys are a little hard on him," I said.

"Yeah, maybe," Elmo said. "I guess anybody that's had to stick it in Sherry deserves some sympathy. You know what she told me one time? She said I looked like a Berkeley professor. An ordinary Berkeley professor, she said. Worst insult I've had since my first wife told me I didn't know how to fuck. Me and Winfield call her the Sphincter. That's our pet name for her."

"Who? Sherry, or your first wife?"

"Sherry. Winfield hates her worst than I do. She seen him

naked at an orgy or something and told him his cock was so little she thought he had three balls. That kind of remark carries a sting, let me tell you. Winfield keeps having fantasies of hitting her between the eyes with a ball-peen hammer.

"Do you know that I got a daughter that's married?" he said a little later. "Hell, *I* ain't even married. Makes me feel funny. Old Winfield's got kids older than mine. He's already a fuckin' grandpa, an' look at him. Three women, and he can't fuck often enough to do justice even to one. I don't know why I go on livin' in fuckin' L.A. If I could just quit spending money, I'd be rich in a week, at the rate I make it."

Gohagen came slouching over and plopped down in a chair, beer can in hand.

"I've been meaning to ask you a bold question," I said. "Do you set your beer can down when you make love?"

He grinned shyly. "Most times," he said. "Unless some wench slips up on me and humps me up against a tree or something. If I get to lie down in a bed, I usually set it down."

"Just wondered," I said.

Later, the two of them drove me home, leaving Winfield's three women sitting in front of a huge TV set. Winfield insisted on driving, to show me he could drive in any state, I guess. His driving didn't bother me, but it scared Elmo badly.

"This is two-lane traffic up here, I mean two-way traffic and a two-lane road, and this sure as hell ain't England," he said. "How come you're driving on the left?"

"Just giving myself a little advantage on these hairpin curves," Winfield insisted. He careened out of the Canyon at a speed so great that Elmo was silent with apprehension. I was unafraid. I didn't think I was going to be hurt in a car wreck. Subtler fates were in store for me.

They asked about Joe—Uncle Joe, they called him—and before I could finish telling them, we were at my house. Owen's butter-colored Mercedes was sitting in front of it. Winfield reacted quickly and drove right on past. We all caught a glimpse of Owen, sitting behind the wheel. Winfield rolled on, five or six blocks down the hill, and killed the motor. They both looked at me.

"Don't look at me," I said. "I didn't do anything."

"He smelled her," Elmo said. "I told you he would. This is your fault, Winfield. You just want to fuck that silly-ass New York wench, so you asked her to the party knowing full well who she was shacked up with."

"Well, I like to fuck silly women," Winfield said, defensively. "I'm silly myself, and the whole world knows it. I never asked her to bring a date."

They stopped talking and we were all silent.

"I consider it a sinister development," Elmo said.

"Oh, I don't," I said. "Let me out."

"But you don't live here," Winfield said. "You live up there."

"I know that," I said. "I think I'd like a little walk before I go home."

"Wonder what he did with Raven," Winfield said.

"Don't give it a thought," Elmo said. "Three women are waiting at my house, remember? I don't plan to go home and tell them I just happened to drop you off at Raven Dexter's."

I thanked them and got out and began to walk up the sidewalk. They began to follow me in the car. Winfield didn't even turn around. He just backed.

"Why are you following me?" I asked.

"Dangerous city," Elmo said. "We just want to make sure you get home safe. We owe you that. After all, you did make the tacos."

"Go away," I said. "This is my neighborhood. I walk here every night. I just want to be alone for a few minutes, if you don't mind."

Of course all men mind, even friendly men. They never want you to be alone—not unless they have plans of their own.

However, Elmo managed to be mature. "The reason chivalry is dead is because women won't put up with it no more," he said. "Ain't that right, Winfield?"

I walked on, and the car stayed where it was. When I was

two blocks up the hill I looked back and it was still there. I heard the sound of one of Winfield's beer cans hitting the street—even heard it roll down until it struck the curb.

After that I walked more slowly. At times, in fact, I stopped walking altogether and just stood there on the sidewalk, trying to decide what mood to be in when I finally arrived. It required decision, because I really was in no mood at all. The sight of the familiar car, sitting in front of my house, plus the glimpse of Owen sulking at the wheel, had caused a sort of surcease in my feeling processes. I certainly didn't feel excited, expectant, or angry. I didn't even feel apprehensive. I just felt blank—which I didn't like. I wasn't going to be a blackboard on which he could write whatever he had decided he felt.

It's odd that I should have tried to deal with actors, when I myself am such a bad actress—not even bad, just a nonactress. Hauteur would be appropriate for such a situation, but I couldn't act hauteur. Maybe I just felt a little vindicated: the power to make someone come back, for however illegitimate a reason or purpose, is still a satisfying power. After all, he had come back. The fact was more eloquent than he was likely to be.

Eventually I reached my block, and then the car. He was fatter in the face, unhealthily so. I was hoping he would be generous enough to come up with some first words, but it was a vain hope. He just looked.

"All right," I said. "Hello, if you won't say it."

"Didn't see you at the party," he said.

"I stayed in the kitchen. Didn't much like the crowd."

"That's their good crowd," he said. "You ought to see their bad crowd."

It made me impatient, really impatient. Did he think he had come to talk about Elmo's taste in people?

"Owen, what do you want?" I asked.

"Maybe just a cup of coffee," he said.

"If that's what you want, go get it at a diner," I said tersely.

"Go ahead and get mad," he said. "I wouldn't blame you."

"No reason you should."

He shrugged—his second shrug in a very short space of time. It was as close as he could come to penitence.

"Stop shrugging," I said. "No one's going to forgive you on the basis of a gesture that weak."

"Do you want to take a trip?" he asked brusquely.

"Is that why you came? A trip where?"

"I don't know," he said. "We could figure it out on the way. Tucson, maybe. Or maybe just San Diego. I liked that motel we had."

"Um, lots of towels," I said.

We stared at one another for a while.

"No," I said. "It's insolent of you to suggest it. Take your trip with Raven."

"I will if you don't get in," he said. "Come on. I'm tired of this town. Let's go somewhere else for three or four days."

"No," I said.

"You say no too much," he said. "You don't have the guts to do the things you really want to do."

I turned and went up my sidewalk and he started the car and was gone by the time I got to my steps. I sat on the steps for a while. Maybe I thought he might come back, try to argue, I don't know. He had never been a man to hammer at rejection—he just went away from it. I felt stirred up and horrible. I hated the arrogance of it all, and his absolute refusal to deal with the past. He didn't understand that I had to deal with the past before I could feel myself a present. We were a mismatch: he just wasn't that way. The past never got a hand on him, as he liked to put it.

I spent the rest of the night on my couch, drinking tea with lots of lemon. Probably I drank a quart, or maybe a gallon—trying to drown my antagonistic feelings in tea with lots of lemon. Half my antagonistic feelings were for Owen, and the other half were for myself. I didn't turn on the television, although I could have consoled myself with plenty of all-night movies. Having just rejected real life, I wasn't ready to lull myself with fantasies.

Probably he had nailed me. Probably I didn't have the

guts to do what I really wanted to do. The more I attended to principles, the lonelier I got. I should have gone off into the desert with him and fucked for a few days. It seemed incredible to me, once my first anger cooled, that I was still evidently holding out for some totally stereotyped version of the American dream. Did I really suppose that if I just stuck to my principles, someday Owen and I, or someone and I, would develop into a model American couple?

Probably the big secret I kept wanting to deny was that the essence of what Owen and I had was just cheap, not fine. It wasn't ideal, or progressive, or filled with social potential, or creative, or domestic. It boiled down to crude attraction: fucking in motels was about the best we had ever done, or would ever do—three or four days in some place we'd never see but once, with the sheets a tangle, the flicker of television, and the smell of sex. I would get ashamed to let the maids come in, at least until the towels ran out. Why I had to try and convert that into some recognizably normal domesticity was a question to which there was certainly no answer in the tea leaves.

I spent three days in a turmoil of regret, fantasizing about what might have happened if I hadn't been so cautious and so ordinary.

Then I heard that Raven Dexter had suddenly married Toole Peters. Their pictures were in all the magazines, Toole looking unusually sickly.

About two weeks later Owen called, sounding drunk and almost jolly. He was pretending things were easy between us. We talked about my picture for a bit. It was a Friday night, and I had just settled down to drink tea and read some scripts.

"Let's go to Nevada," he said. It was dusk. He had always felt better with evening to protect him. He knew it wouldn't do to approach me in the brightness of morning. Better to have a little weariness working for him. I was too prickly in the morning, too clearheaded. Better to drive along hypnotically for several hours, lulled by the night and the road. It helped us to stop being so individual.

I waited a moment to see if he was going to say anything else.

"I don't like Las Vegas," I said. "Never have."

"How about Tahoe?" he said. "Somewhere around there. I'm fresh. We could drive all night."

With Owen, waiting never got one much.

"Sure," I said. "Good idea. Let's drive all night."

CHAPTER 8

OWEN had eyes like a lion, amber, and empty when he was satisfied. At least in the shadows of bedrooms, with just a little light and my eyes only a few inches away, they seemed amber. In strong light they were light brown. The secret, I decided, was not to let strong light into our lives. Lower the shades. Make love in the light from the television. Get food from room service, or from some place that delivered. Stop trying to make it into a sunny relationship, with walks and beaches and balanced meals.

I tried it. Not only did I not raise the shades in the motel, I didn't try to raise the shades to Owen's mind either. I would keep the lion at rest except to mate, and if it took a lot of mating to keep those eyes empty, that was all right, too. It was hard for me to disconnect my curiosity, but in this case I made every effort. I didn't ask him about Sherry or Raven or much of anything. For once, I let him be the curious one. He wanted to know about Gauldin, and I told him. He wanted to know what picture I was doing next, and I said none.

Of course, I didn't get away with it. Owen didn't like my new uncaring ways. Sex had nothing to do with his dropping back into my life—for me, maybe, but not for him. He wanted my talk, after all. I guess he liked to hear it in his ear as he lay there daydreaming. In fact, he wanted all the things I had given up on—or rather, what he wanted was for me to keep wanting them, grasping for them. He didn't want the life I wanted: just the emotion that flowed from my wanting it. I guess it was richer and more involving than what he got from Sherry and Raven, both of whom were too self-centered to keep his resistance engaged. I kept it engaged and he liked it.

Of course everyone who knew us thought I was an utter fool. Everyone assumed that he'd probably murder me this time, and they didn't want to be implicated, so we were simply dropped. Rationally I couldn't blame people, but emotionally I blamed them a lot. Despite myself, I guess I entertained social hopes. I even went out and bought Owen some decent shirts. Probably he hasn't bothered to take the pins out of half of them.

In a town where the most bizarre couplings are commonplace, our rather ordinary mismating was somehow considered offensive. It was as if I were the homecoming queen, or the nice girl next door. I wasn't supposed to be fucking a thug.

One day I ran into Winfield, the first time I had seen him since the party. He was at a sidewalk Mexican restaurant on La Brea, staring moodily at some tacos.

"Hello, Gohagen," I said. "What's the matter with those tacos?"

He smiled faintly. "They look kind of rubbery, but that don't matter," he said. "I've eaten many a rubber taco. It's continual domestic crisis that's put me off my feed. Sit down and eat 'em for me."

I took him up on it. "What kind of domestic crisis?" I asked.

"Ol' Sheila's having her baby," he said. "She's in the throes of labor at this very minute."

"So what are you doing here?"

"Evading responsibility," he said. His hair was too long for a fat man, but there was still a certain spirit in his eyes, hard-pressed as he said he was.

"You mean no one's with her?"

"Elmo's with her," he said. "Elmo don't mind childbirth as long as he ain't the father. Besides, him and Sheila's in love now, so that makes it appropriate."

"Uh-oh," I said. "How long have they been in love?"

"That's a good question," Winfield said. "A very fucking good question. An even better question is when did they first fuck? If it was nine and a half months ago, then that's another can of worms. However, Elmo won't admit to more than three months, and Sheila will only admit to about three weeks ago, when she oughtn't to have been fucking anyhow. It's enough to make me want to go to Texas."

"Why?"

"I don't know," he said. "I guess I miss the bleakness."

I ate all his tacos while he contented himself with a pitcher of beer. He looked at me admiringly.

"Always like to see a woman with an appetite," he said. "How's your fuck-fest going?"

"My what?" I said, shocked for a moment.

Winfield grinned. "That's what I always call it when I find myself involved with someone without no smarts," he said. "A woman of the people, as it were. Ain't that what it amounts to?"

"Maybe so," I said.

Whatever it was, it ended that day. We were going to dinner, but Owen didn't come, nor did he call. At first I didn't give it a thought. He was probably gambling. It was not unusual for him to gamble for a day and a night, all engagements forgotten. If I mentioned to him later that he had had a dinner date with me, he would only look mildly surprised, not guilty or apologetic or even defensive. In fact, plans of any kind were less than useless with him. His planning was only rhetoric, having no connection with his real life. Perhaps he had the instinct to know that his only chance with people, particularly women, lay in catching them unawares. If they thought about it much, he wouldn't catch them. He depended on the sudden force of his presence. I could understand that, and I had even learned not to project, to entertain no visions of what tomorrow would be like, or this evening, or any particular time.

It was not until a day and a half after the broken date that I realized what had happened. Sherry had come back. I had known it, of course—her picture was in the paper—but I hadn't connected the two things. I was sitting on my porch, reading a script, when it dawned on me.

A few days later he was seen at a party with her. The longer I thought about it, the more indignant I became, not so much at the desertion—I knew that would happen sometime—but at his lack of manners. It was not quick anger I felt but a kind of deep, volcanic indignation. A few days later I let it erupt. He drank at a bar on Hollywood Boulevard, and it was simple to ambush him. When he came out, the late afternoon sun on Hollywood Boulevard was fairly blinding, and I stepped in front of him and slapped him just as he was putting on his sunglasses. It came as a complete surprise—I knocked his dark glasses flying.

"You should learn to use the telephone, Owen," I said.

Something, maybe my finger, maybe the earpiece of his glasses, must have hit him in the eye, because he immediately put his hand over it. It was too much of a surprise for him to react angrily. He just stood there, huge in his tacky sport coat and slick slacks and white shoes, one hand over an eye and the other eye looking at me without comprehension. I got in my car and left. Skateboarders were doing curlicues on the sidewalk, that slick, expensive sidewalk near Hollywood and Vine. On the Boulevard the incident had gone unnoticed. Girls with great legs, in hot pants that were about three years out of style, walked on the sidewalk, sipping Orange Julius or eating slices of pizza, and cocksmen and hustlers stood in the doorways of shops, looking at them.

Most of the hustlers were dressed more or less like Owen. I saw him pick his dark glasses out of the gutter, but he didn't put them on. He stood on the sidewalk, squinting in my direction, his glasses in one hand and the other hand over his eye.

Late that night, wakeful, watching the hands of my clock, I felt awful. It's sad to call a lover by his name for the last time. The name is part of the pith, after all, part of the luxury. If Owen showed up again, I wouldn't be calling him Owen. I would descend to pronouns and just call him *you*. His name was the first thing I got from him, when he squatted down by me in New York, and the last thing he got from me, there at Hollywood and Vine.

Indeed he did show up, about four months after Sherry's death—I just called him *you*.

The morning after I slapped him, Sherry Solaré decided I had to be punished for my trepass—the screwing, not the slap. She informed Abe that she wanted to recut the picture, which she had evidently seen a few days before. Abe, coward that he was, hadn't told me he was screening it for her, but I knew it would happen eventually.

I wasn't surprised by any of it, and I was calm as morning when Abe called, very nervous, and asked me to come in for a conference.

"I didn't think it would happen," he said, after telling me what had happened. "I thought she forgot it, you know. But I guess when she seen the cut she got ideas."

He was watching me closely, to see how high my resistance was going to mount.

"Calm down, Abe," I said. "I'm not going to make any trouble. Why should I make trouble, when you and your grandfather have been so nice to me? Stars are like that—we all know it. I can live with it. I don't want the studio to lose another cent over my differences with Sherry."

Abe could hardly believe it, which is some credit to him—it was hardly true. Still, he soon convinced himself that he was having unbelievable luck. No trauma, no lawsuits, no fits.

Overwhelmed, he walked me all the way out of the studio, to my car.

"Listen," he said, looking at me in a new way, "Grandpa was right. You're some lady. We're gonna get you another picture to do, one that bitch ain't in. You know, a quality picture."

"That'd be fine," I said. Having learned to slap, I was apparently even learning to act.

Abe kissed me goodbye, leaving sweat on my cheek, and started off, then turned and shuffled back to my car after I started the motor.

"An' hey, maybe we could even have dinner sometime," he said. "Talk over some projects—you know? Or whatever?"

"Why not?" I said.

"I'll call ya," he said, looking suddenly confident. He straightened his cuffs, as triumphant as if he'd already fucked me.

CHAPTER 9

In a light mood, very relaxed, I drove to Tujunga Canyon. I found Elmo and Winfield out in their yard with their shirts off, idly throwing a hunting knife at a tree.

"Shit, we could become goddamn urban guerrillas, Elmo, if we could ever get the hang of how to make this knife stick," Winfield said. "We could go throw knives at all the studio heads and destroy capitalism."

"I like capitalism," Elmo said. "I'm just out here trying to master the simple art of knife throwing."

Neither of them managed to get the knife to stick in the tree even once. I tried but missed the tree completely. Winfield got frustrated and threw the knife harder and harder, but it only whanged harmlessly off the tree trunk. Finally he got disgusted and threw it up on the roof of his house.

"It's a lemon, why keep it?" he said when Elmo looked pained.

"Because I paid a hundred and seventy-five dollars for it," Elmo said. "That was a handmade knife."

"Fuck, it wouldn't cut the hand that made it," Winfield said.

"How's the baby?" I asked. Both men looked uncomfortable.

"Sheila's mother come and got her and it both," Winfield said. "They decided to take it back to its roots."

"*Him* back to *his* roots," Elmo corrected. "The child was a boy. Little Winfield the second."

Winfield sighed. "Here I done accepted the paternity of the little tyke, even though not entirely satisfied in my own mind on that score, and now he's gone. I never even got to change a diaper."

Elmo went in and got some wine glasses and some wine, and he and I sat on the lawn and drank wine while Winfield drank beer. Most of the witticisms were about what an uncouth slob he was, but he ignored them. Actually he was not much less couth than Elmo, who had lost a couple of teeth since I had seen him last.

"Broke 'em on a toilet rim, one night when I went to puke," he said when I asked him about it. He seemed indifferent to their absence.

Then the two of them had an argument about whether a hairy belly was automatic evidence of sexual prowess. Winfield had a line of hair running from his crotch to his navel, while Elmo's torso was almost hairless and unappealingly white.

"I'm going to steal my film," I said, as a way of interrupting the argument. "If you really want to be urban guerrillas, here's your chance. You can help me."

"Steal a whole film?" Elmo said. It stunned them both.

"Enough of it to keep them from releasing it, at least."

"Is stealing a film a felonious act?" Winfield asked. "I'd lose my visitation rights to half my kids if I committed a felonious act."

"Aw, come on, Winfield," Elmo said. "Let's help the lady. You don't like your kids anyway. I don't blame you. They're the worst-mannered bunch of runts this side of North Dallas."

"I guess I'm game," Winfield said. "Can we take the hunting knife?"

"No, 'cause you threw it on the fucking roof just as I was about to get the hang of throwing it," Elmo said.

"What do we do with it after we steal it?" Winfield asked. "Ain't it going to be kinda heavy?"

I hadn't really given that significant question much thought, but the two of them, veterans of several caper movies, were quick to supply a number of possibilities.

"This is big-time stuff, you know," Winfield said. "Sherry Solaré's involved. That bitch will have the S.W.A.T. on us by morning."

"Just because she said you had a short cock don't mean she controls the S.W.A.T. team," Elmo said.

They continued to spin out plans, and I listened. I was determined to do it—for complex reasons. Owen was just a small part of it. For one thing, the film was bad enough as it was: I really didn't want her to recut it. Also, it sort of amused me to think of Mr. Mond getting his way beyond the grave.

Mainly, though, I think it was that I was just through, in some ways. Certainly through with directing. I had been lucky with *Womanly Ways*, but I really wasn't crazed enough to direct, or smart enough either, and I wasn't going to get any better. Somehow my stupid affair had left me obsessed, for the first time in years, and I felt no need to hang on to my chance to work. Maybe Elmo and Winfield would let me sit around and write scripts with them, when I felt like doing something again.

"I know," Winfield said finally. "We can just steal the film and take it to Texas."

"Why Texas?"

"Texas is the ultimate last resort," he said. "It's always a good idea to go to Texas, if you can't think of anything else to do. Me and Elmo got to go to Rome to write a Western for old Sergio Leone next month, and we was planning to go home first anyway. Besides, my baby boy's in Texas. Maybe I'd get to sit and watch him suck on a teat sometime."

"Why didn't I think of that?" Elmo said.

"Because you're drunk on the fruit of the grape," Winfield said. "You're not nice and mellow from drinking good brew, like I am. Good brew kinda detaches the brain, you know."

"I guess the fact that your brain's detached explains why you fuck so many worthless women," Elmo said.

Winfield took it mildly. "Same ones you fuck," he said.

"Let's steal the motherfucker and take it to the Blue Dog," Elmo said. The Blue Dog was the evidently fabulous estate the two of them owned outside of Austin.

"Naw, let's avoid the Blue Dog until we see how the S.W.A.T. team reacts," Winfield said. "We could go down to the Rio Chickpea and visit old Donny de Lorn."

"But Donny ain't our friend no more," Elmo said. "Remember, he fucked old Sarah? Or have you got so permissive you don't care about things like that?"

Donny de Lorn was a country singer, bigger in Texas than anywhere else, though he had made a kind of flash on the national scene thanks to a movie in which he played a psychopathic truck driver.

Before I left, an hour later, Elmo and Winfield were already packing for Texas—the packing consisted of putting an ice chest in the back of their pink Cadillac convertible.

"If I wasn't too old to handle drugs, we'd have a trip to make ol' Hunter Thompson eat his heart out," Winfield said. "We can always buy some Levis along the way if our clothes get dirty."

They followed me to my house and left the Cadillac. It was beginning to feel a little like an adventure. As we started for the studio in my car, Elmo at the wheel, wearing an immense leather cowboy hat he sometimes fancied, I thought of Joe. There was a man who needed an adventure. Maybe it would put a little life into him again.

"How about Uncle Joe?" I said. "Why don't we take him?"

"Happy to," Elmo said. "You an' him can cuddle up there in the back seat and keep us amused with civilized talk of the sort we don't often hear."

I left them in the car, drinking and talking about the possibility of doing a script about our forthcoming caper, and went up to see Joe. He was sitting on his couch with some racing forms in his hand, watching television and drinking a martini.

"All right," I said. "I'm tired of you sitting there, and us never talking or doing anything. Let's go see the world."

"Any particular part?" He was amused at me.

"Texas," I said. "We're going to steal my film and put it in Elmo's Cadillac and drive to Texas to a place called the Rio Chickpea. Are you so apathetic that you can resist that?"

"No," he said, killing the TV with his remote control button. "I'll go anywhere with you and those Texans, even to Texas, where I've had bitter experiences."

I think he was as happy as the rest of us, to be leaving. Some life came into his eyes. He brought a huge shaker of martinis, an overnight bag, and for some reason, a green overcoat.

"For the chill nights of the desert," he said, with a touch of the old melodrama.

Our caper was absurdly easy, so easy that it was almost a letdown. A movie about stealing a movie could be made complex and hilarious, but stealing mine was simple, and not even particularly amusing. Joe knew both of the night men, from the old days, and gave them some martinis in their coffee cups. Of course both of the night men trusted me as if I'd been the Virgin Mary, and when I told them I needed some of the film they didn't even ask me why. It would have been hard to convince them that a nice girl like me was pulling a caper. They sat around with Joe talking about minor actresses they had been in love with, while Winfield and I went in and stole some film. Elmo insisted that he was a wheel man, and refused to leave the car.

We ended up stealing the sound track and three or four miscellaneous reels of film, enough to cause a lot of confusion. Joe and the night men were out drinking martinis under the stars. I guess the night men thought I was taking the film to another lab. They even offered to help us carry it, but I wouldn't let them. The one thing I felt guilty about was the trouble they were probably going to be in.

Joe pooh-poohed my worries. "I know those men," he said. "They're resourceful. They'll lie their way out of it when the shit hits the fan."

We all fell silent as we drove back to my house. It was strange to have actually done something criminal and yet feel nothing. Up to the last minute it had seemed like a joke that probably wouldn't happen. Now it was done, and what made it the more strange was that I didn't really feel driven by an impulse to vengeance, not against Sherry or anybody, nor did I feel like the film was something of my own that I had to defend. Even before it was finished I had lost most of my feeling for the film—Wynkyn's death and my trouble with Owen had destroyed the passion of involvement I ordinarily would have had. If I had tried to tell a lawyer why I had just stolen a film, I wouldn't have really known what to say.

We changed cars at my house, and as we swung onto the Hollywood Freeway and sped past downtown L.A. and out toward San Bernardino and the desert, I felt momentarily euphoric. We were going at last. Everyone's spirits lifted. Elmo drove, his big hat cocked over one ear, and Winfield devoted his energies to popping the tops off beer cans and quaffing their contents. Even Joe had come alive. He sloshed his martini shaker from time to time, to see if there was any left. It must have been level full when we started, because there was a lot left. He leaned forward in his seat and talked to the boys about baseball. It was a side of all of them that I had never been invited to see. They managed to have a very serious conversation about baseball, with the Cadillac doing at least ninety on the San Bernardino Freeway.

Once the glow of L.A. faded behind us, I began to feel sleepy. I crawled under Joe's green overcoat and lay resting, my eyes still open. I saw the sign for Riverside and remembered all the times Owen and I had come this way at night. But there was no ache in the memory—no ache anywhere. I got cold, but none of the men seemed to feel it, and anyway I didn't want the top up because with it down I could lie back with my head against the leather seat and see the stars, thin little points all over the sky. It was interesting, how the men had suddenly forgotten everything but baseball—and how serious their voices were, well modulated, even scholarly. Joe looked at me fondly from time to time. He was happy, very happy, that we had included him, but his mind was on the conversation. I wouldn't have had it otherwise. I snuggled closer to him, under his overcoat, and went to sleep.

CHAPTER 10

I woke, warm as toast, into gray light. Instead of having Joe's overcoat over me, I had Elmo's sheepskin. No one was in the car, but the motor was running and the top was up—the fact that the heater was on accounted for my warmth.

I peered out the window and saw my three traveling companions lined up by the side of a very empty road, relieving themselves. Winfield was drinking beer, even as he pissed. With their backs to me, I was reminded of the three monkeys. Then Elmo and Winfield, almost simultaneously, made the funny little hunching motion that men make when they're stuffing themselves back in their pants. Joe continued to stand. There was an empty martini shaker on the floorboards near my feet.

Elmo spotted me watching, and looked abashed. They stood outside the car, shivering, until Joe came up and they all got in.

"Well, we done embarrassed ourselves before breakfast," Elmo said. Winfield said nothing—evidently he was not at his most cheerful. Joe didn't look so good either, although his condition was more ambiguous than Winfield's. Winfield looked like he was going to be sick for several hours.

"Good morning," I said. "Where are we?"

"Smurr," Winfield said.

"Beg pardon?"

"Smurr," he said again. "Fucking Smurr."

"Don't talk to Winfield this early," Elmo said. "It's a waste of breath. His brain won't come back on for three, four hours yet."

"Fucking lie," Winfield said. "She asked me where we were and I told her. It ain't my fault she don't know about Smurr, Arizona."

"Let me out again," Joe said. "I shouldn't have got back in."

They let him out and he went off behind the car to be sick.

"Uncle Joe can still drink," Elmo said. "If I drank that much gin it'd render me impotent for a month."

"Malt liquor would render you impotent," Winfield said.

Elmo grinned. "He's always been a sour companion in the morning," he said.

By the time Joe got back to the car, looking weak but relieved, the grayness had receded and the desert cleared and darkened just slightly, as the sky became light. It was as if someone were focusing the universe: first a gray blur, then an almost momentary darkening of the land in relation to the sky, then a beautiful clarity as light flowed down from the sky to the earth. Soon we could see the road stretching before us for many miles, through the still desert. The sunless sky had the brightness of ice. Then it turned deep orange at its lower rim.

"Well, no S.W.A.T. team, at least," Elmo said.

"Give 'em time," Winfield said. "Abe ain't figured out he's been robbed yet. It's only five A.M. The question is, Where do we want to be four or five hours from now?"

"Poor question," Elmo said. "Starting from Smurr, there's no place I can get to in five hours that I want to be."

Listening to them was like listening to old married people talk. They had been buddies for so long that they had their own codes.

"Ol' Winfield's paranoid," Elmo said. "He's wrote too much TV. He thinks we ought to skitter off into Mexico. This road we're on—which I only pulled off on so we'd have a private place to piss and puke and whatever—goes right down into Sonoita, which is one place the S.W.A.T. team don't go. Then we can bounce around in Sonora and Chihuahua for three or four days, and if we don't die of dysentery or get caught in a dope war, we could sort of back into Texas somewhere around El Paso."

"I don't want to bounce for three or four days," Joe said. "I say that frankly. I'm game for just about anything but bouncing."

"Well, I just thought we might take the scenic route," Winfield said. "I was hoping to see some Mexican villages and broaden my mind or something."

"I'll let you out and you can hitchhike," Elmo said. "I ain't eager to go into Mexico in my pink car—some big pusher might see us and covet it. Or else you'd buy some dope and we'd all get caught."

"Being in a Mexican jail wouldn't be much worse than working for Sergio," Winfield said. "I'm scared of that crazy fucker. Last time we worked for him he almost shot me, remember? He was showing off his damn six-guns."

"Maybe we oughta all go to Italy," Elmo said. "Joe and Jill could serve as our intermediaries. Hell, Joe knows Sergio's style as well as we do."

"I bet I do," Joe said. "I bet I do."

He had taken to repeating every statement he made—a small habit, but for some reason irritating to me. I don't know why, but after loving him for years everything he did sort of irritated me. I had made him my model in matters of spirit, and then he lost his spirit, leaving me without a model, more or less. Elmo and Winfield led such sloppy lives that I couldn't use them as a standard, although I did like the way they complemented one another. When one was down, the other could be counted on to be up. They were sometimes both up, but never both down. That's how friends should be, I felt.

"Well, if we ain't going to Mexico, let's at least go someplace before I have to get out and piss again," Winfield said.

"We could go visit my son," I said. "He's somewhere near Albuquerque."

"Too far north," Elmo said. "Besides, why would you want to get an innocent child involved with a gang of international film pirates?"

We drove all day, through Tucson and on into New Mexico, the men taking turns driving. Even Joe took a turn driving. He tied a little checked neckerchief around his throat and settled into the Cadillac as if he had been driving them all his life, although he had driven nothing except a small Morgan for as long as I'd known him.

Elmo and Winfield reminisced about the women they had loved and lost, and all three men drank beer continuously, all day. I mostly kept quiet and watched the undulating desert slip behind us. It seemed endless and monotonous. The men were solicitous of me, but even so, I felt a little left out, almost an interloper, despite being the cause of the trip. At times I wished I could be present but invisible, so I could hear what they *really* had to say about women—what they would say about them to one another if no woman was present to hear. My sense was that they would all reveal their fright, and perhaps their hostility to the creatures who had the power to frighten them.

Perhaps I was just being conventional again, to imagine that they were either frightened or hostile. Maybe they were neither: just sort of puzzled. I spent the day in an odd kind of reverie, watching the desert, keeping kind of half tuned in to the men's conversation and at the same time staying kind of half tuned out. When it warmed up, Elmo put the top down, and then at midday had to put it up again because the sun was so bright. In the afternoon, with the sun just edging downward, we drove across a barren, horrid part of New Mexico, a country without the purity of real desert but not fertile either.

Always, from girlhood, I had shaped futures with my mind, sculpting them as a sculptor shapes clay. Events always altered the imaginary shapes I made, but not totally. Enough of my construct survived that I could at least recognize it.

Now, suddenly, time was all around me, like the desert and the sky. It was flat, too, empty of ridges and mountains, valleys. When I looked down the road ahead, nothing at all came to mind.

"I think I went wrong," I said, startling everyone. It startled me too—I had thought out loud.

"Exactly the way I feel," Winfield said. "I went wrong, too. In my case it happened over in Rome, when I let myself get dependent on that expensive German beer. Thangs ain't been the same since."

Joe was looking a little tired. But when he caught me looking at him he smiled and it was really a friendly smile, not apologetically friendly, as he had been so often of late.

"You shouldn't have deserted your craft," he said. "Just because you've slopped around with movie crews for a long time doesn't mean you really know how to make movies."

"Nobody really knows how to make movies," Elmo said. "It's a matter of hoping the right accidents will happen."

"Jill was meant to draw," Joe said.

"I don't know why you say that," I said. "I drew for years and I wasn't really that good. I was just okay. Every time I saw a great drawing it made me feel like a dilettante."

"Craft, I said," he insisted. "Craft, not art. Art happens like love, but craft is loyalty, like marriage. To do it good is what's necessary, and that's all that's necessary. Maybe a few times in your life you get lucky and do it better than good, but that's irrelevant. Loyalty is what's necessary, if you want to get something good out of the union."

"Heavy words," Elmo said.

"I don't know what you're talking about," I said, but I sort of did. And he was sort of right. I dimly remembered what a clean satisfaction I used to feel when I did a good drawing. For a few years that feeling had been one of the mainstays of my life, and it irritated me unreasonably that Joe would continue to remind me of it.

"Maybe I got tired of being limited," I said. "Maybe I needed to try something else, so as not to be so limited."

He didn't answer. In fact, no one spoke, and I began to feel sad and oppressed. Part of it was the endless, dusty, toneless land we were driving across: how had I got trapped in it? The mere sight of it made me want to cry, as did my sense of being alone and without a future. I felt inexplicably, irrationally bitter toward Joe. He was my oldest and dearest friend, and yet I didn't feel that we were friends any more. My silly love affair had distanced us, though for no good reason. I felt he shouldn't have let it. It seemed a betrayal, and the longer the men were silent and I was left to contemplate the emptiness and the sky, the closer to tears I felt, yet I held back, knowing how badly men react to tears. If I cried, they'd probably throw me out of the car at the next town. Anyway, I didn't want to cry until I could be in private.

Even though all three men in the car had always been extremely considerate and generous in their dealings with me, I still felt they were my enemies. They didn't understand what needed to be understood, and I couldn't count on them just to be one-way. I missed Owen. He wasn't generous or considerate, and he didn't understand anything, but I could count on him to be a particular way. The men I counted on for complex things were too complex themselves. Right then, when it must have been obvious to them that I was unhappy and needed someone to talk to me, they were about as talkative as three clams. We must have driven thirty miles without a word being uttered.

Finally I couldn't help it. The landscape and the silence made me feel too lonely. I started to cry. All the men looked aghast, just as I had known they would, so I pulled Joe's coat over my head, in order to cry in private. After I had cried for a while I felt a great deal better. I couldn't see the saddening desert or the empty sky, and I felt protected and relieved. I knew the men were suffering, because I could hear them making meaningless conversation in stilted, awkward tones, but if they were suffering, that was fine with me. Let them suffer. They all had poor records with women, as far as I was concerned: they were far too content to sit around reliving the loves of the past—that kind of laziness. I stayed under the coat, partly for revenge and partly because I felt cozy. I had had too much space around me all day. I grew up with seascapes and little California hills, and I wasn't used to being a pinpoint in the universe.

When I came out, after twenty minutes or so, things were much nicer. The sun was beginning to set, spreading layers of color along the rims of the horizon for what seemed like hundreds of miles. All the men tried to ignore the fact that I had risen again. They sort of cut their eyes my way and went on talking somberly of baseball.

"All I've got to say is I'm glad I'm not married to any of you," I said cheerfully. "What a bunch of lowbrows. I never want to hear another word about baseball, okay?"

They were so relieved they all became drunk, on accumulated beer.

"Like having sixteen cobras loose in the car, having a cryin' woman," Winfield said. "Now I remember why I run away from home so many times."

The next thing I knew I was being made to drive. Joe got very drunk and began to pontificate, repeating each pontification two or three times, but I was tolerant. My fit was over and it was fun to drive a pink Cadillac and watch the sunset. By the time the sun was gone and the sky darkening, we were on the outskirts of El Paso.

"It's Texas, womb of my youth an' Winfield's too," Elmo said.

Now that we had safely skirted Mexico, nothing would do but that we go there. I was about to drive the Cadillac across the international bridge when Joe remembered the stolen film in the trunk. We had all forgotten about it. After some dispute, we parked the Cadillac and walked across the bridge. There was hardly any water in the river, just a lot of brown sand with a silver ribbon running through it. Elmo climbed up on the bridge and pretended he was planning a suicide leap, although it was only about thirty feet down. Some Mexican guards watched him without interest.

"There's not a whole lot of regard for human life in this part of the country," he said when we got him to come down. He was quite drunk.

"Hell," he said. "Those guards were gonna let me jump. Last time I tried to throw myself in the Tiber fifty Italians started praying to the saints."

Overhead, the sky had turned a rich purple. Finally we came to Mexico and walked along the street whose pavement was so full of holes it looked like someone had attacked it with a giant paper-punch.

We found a restaurant, and I tried not to drink because it was apparent that I was going to have to drive. The others drank margaritas like they were soda pop. Elmo said we should eat quail, and before I could think, an immense platter of them arrived. He had ordered two dozen, as if they were oysters. They were very good, but I kept thinking of little birds, running around the desert.

During the meal I decided not to go back to Hollywood. They would never trust me now, anyway. Maybe I'd draw, like Joe wanted me to. Or maybe I'd go to Europe. If there was a pull, that was it. Carl, my second husband, now a producer, didn't hate me, at least. He had a new, even younger wife, and if he felt secure, he might be generous, decide we were old friends, and give me a job on a picture, just enough so I could live. I wanted to hear Italian voices—the quiet Spanish of the waiters made me nostalgic. Maybe I could have a room in an umber building and sit and sketch clothes on clotheslines and gray piazzas and old women in black dresses holding hands.

Of course it had been silly to steal the film. It might as well go back, even if I didn't. Sherry couldn't totally ruin it, any more than I could make it a masterpiece. If it were shown, some of the good work that Anna had done, and Zack and some of the others, would be seen and admired so they could get other jobs. That was the real point. Anna needed to keep acting or she would just get fat or marry somebody awful, and Zack needed to keep working, too. Otherwise he'd just sit around and take dope.

After we ate the twenty-four quails Elmo and Winfield wandered off to see if they could find a whorehouse, and Joe and I stayed in the restaurant and bickered. I don't know why we bickered—it was all we could seem to do any more. Maybe we had idealized one another for too long, I don't know. Now the idealizations had sort of worn through, so we bickered. He drank brandy and got drunker, and finally the other two came back, looking sheepish, although I doubt they really did anything. I went ahead by myself across the bridge, and the three of them shambled after me.

Elmo stayed awake just long enough to guide me through El Paso, and then I had three sleeping drunks and a long road ahead of me. I had toyed with the idea of getting off at the airport and flying somewhere, but once the men went to sleep and weren't able to stimulate my hostility, I didn't feel like stopping. I had never driven such a powerful car, and the sense of speed and power it conveyed was exhilarating. The road was spotted with red taillights, mostly of trucks, and the sky overhead was filled with white stars. The road was four lane, so I didn't have to worry about traffic. It was like I was on a small freeway, crossing a vast desert.

The place where Elmo told me I had to turn in order to get to Austin was 120 miles away, so I got in the fast lane, feeling reckless, and let the big car fly. The trucks were big slow troglodytes, compared to me. I left them behind me in strings. By the time I had really settled into the thrill of the speed, and stopped worrying about collisions and traffic cops, I had covered the 120 miles to Elmo's turnoff. A mountain loomed behind the turnoff, with a thin white moon just over its crest. The new road seemed lonelier and more endless than the one I had been on. Behind me, the trucks didn't even sniff at it. They lumbered on past, like elephants in a circus parade.

The stars were white all night. I only had to stop twice, at little towns, for gas at all-night gas stations. Both times Winfield grunted, rolled out, went to pee, and came back, without having really opened his eyes. Elmo and Joe slept on. I felt a bit of tiredness in my shoulders and neck, but not much. I was temporarily in love with the night and the speed. Only the land near the road seemed really dark. The sky was pale with moonlight, and I could see dark ridges far across the white plateau. Several times I saw deer and, now and then, far off, the light from some lonely house. How amazing, to live so far from anything! What were the people in those isolated houses doing, with the lights still on in the middle of the night? I had no idea what kind of people would live in such emptiness—possibly people who were even stranger than Elmo and Winfield and Joe and myself.

The car ran all night, without complaint, its engine quiet and tireless. I seemed cut off from consciousness, absorbed by the curving, sometimes dipping road, and the pale light and the speed. Occasionally one of the men would grunt, wheeze, snore a little. When it began to get light I was sorry, for the first light was not as lovely as the moonlight. The land and the sky were the color of gray flannel. Then Elmo, who was in the front seat with me, began to thrash around uncomfortably. Suddenly he began to try and get the window open, and as soon as he did he hung himself out it and began to vomit. I braked gently, but before I got stopped he was through being sick.

"Couldn't keep down my quail," he said glumly, staring at the impending sunrise. It was just beginning to burn the horizon ahead and to deepen the blue of the upper sky. The men all woke up and began to groan from the fullness of their bladders, so I stopped at a small town called Roosevelt and took a walk by a little river while they attended to themselves. When I meandered back, thirty minutes later, they were all looking worried.

"Thought you'd left us to the tender mercies of the S.W.A.T. team," Winfield said when I came up.

"They ain't no harsher than the mercies of West Texas," Elmo said. "We're purt near the womb of my youth. This here's about the cervix. Let's get some breakfast to weigh us down. I feel kinda light on my feet, from all that tequila."

We ate breakfast in a small cafe, and were stared at by cowboys, and indeed by everyone who came into the cafe.

"If this is the womb of your youth, you must be illegitimate," Joe said. "I don't think they cotton to our kind."

"They better not sass me," Winfield said. "Dreaming about my first wife always makes me mean. It might take a good fight to get the spleen out of my system."

After breakfast we lazed around for a while, sitting on the banks of the cold little river until it was time for the post office to open. We had unanimously decided to mail back the film.

The postmistress was a rawboned woman who looked at the cans of film with no particular surprise.

"We ain't never had a show here," she said as she considered her instruction book. "Too close to Junction. Folks here don't feel like they're going no place unless they can drive a few miles."

After some research she advised us to send the film back by bus, which we did across the street at the grocery store that doubled as a bus station. Later that morning, from just outside of Austin, I called the studio and told Wanda, Abe's secretary, what time to have the film picked up at the bus station.

"Stolen film?" she said. "Who stole any film? I don't know anything about it. Abe's been gone, you know. He got married. It's his honeymoon he's gone on. Not too much has been happening around here. You mean you stole the film?

"That's the funniest thing I ever heard of," she said when I confirmed that I had. "Maybe we just won't tell Abe. I don't think we ought to confuse him, so soon after his wedding."

"Who would marry Abe?" I asked.

"Dunno, think she was from Vegas," Wanda said, and took another call.

CHAPTER 11

When I came out of the phone booth I found that the men had whiled away their time in a liquor store. They had tequila and limes and the ice chest out on the hood of the Cadillac and were making margaritas. Elmo had bought a hammer and was hammering some ice cubes he had wrapped in a towel.

"They don't even know we took the film," I said.

"You mean we wasted a gesture?" Winfield said.

"Who cares about a movie anyway?" Elmo said. "We should have kidnapped Abe and threatened to throw him out of the Goodyear Blimp unless we got final cut. These are violent times. Simple theft don't count no more."

They made a shaker of margaritas and spent the rest of the drive to Austin drinking them and licking salt off the backs of their hands. Joe had a white stubble on his cheeks and looked hollow under the eyes. The sun was hot and I soon got sleepy. The boys tried to show me some of the landmarks of Austin as we drove into town, but I felt sort of glazed and nothing registered except that there was a lake.

"I want to sleep," I said. "After all, I drove all night. You can just let me off at a motel and pick me up later."

"You don't need no motel," Elmo said. "Winfield and me have upwards of forty old girl friends in this town. Any one of them will let you use her apartment for a few hours. Hell, they ought to. We support most of them."

"Could get sticky, Elmo," Winfield said. "How are they going to know our relations are platonic?"

I insisted on a motel and they were forced to drop me at a big round Holiday Inn on the lake. I tried to get Joe to stay with me and get some rest, but he was too stubborn.

"Look, you're not as young as them," I said. "Can't you be sensible this once? You don't need to drink all day and all night just because they do."

He was already half drunk, and that curious, resentful light came in his eyes when I pointed it out to him. I guess it was the male need to be forever boyish, although the man was in his sixties. Any effort on my part to try and restrain him from being boyish only got me resentment. We almost had a fight in the lobby of the strange motel, only it was just an eye fight. The fact that I was suddenly so tired kept it from flaring out.

They drove off, to continue their drinking, and I went to my room and undressed and stood under a shower for a long time, then sat with a towel wrapped around me, looking out the window at the blue lake. The room was dim and the sky outside very bright. After a time I pulled back the bedspread and lay down on the cool sheets. I started to pick up the phone and tell the operator to hold my calls, but it suddenly occurred to me that there was no need. Not a soul in the world knew where I was except the three men in the Cadillac, and they were undoubtedly so relieved to escape my censorious presence that they would be unlikely to bother me for a while.

I was, I guess, free. That bondage to the telephone, which in Hollywood is as vital as blood, was broken. My agent didn't know where I was. No actor knew where I was: no producer, no writer, no director. Nor my mother, my son, nor any lover. There would be no calls while I slept, and none when I woke up—not unless I chose to put the plug back in by calling someone, somewhere.

I was too tired not to sleep, but it wasn't good sleep. I felt like I was floating. There seemed to be space between me and the bed, and more space between the bed and the floor. I felt feverish and uncomfortable and kept trying to get down to the cool sheets, but I couldn't make it. I was always a few inches above them.

When I woke up I was lying on sheets that were no longer particularly cool, and I had a headache from the concentration I had had to practice in my sleep, to keep from floating away.

The sky outside was still just as bright, but the sun had moved and now the room was bright, too. Eventually, despite the air conditioning, the sun warmed the sheets and me, and I felt a little more relaxed. Owen had ruined me for motels. I associated such bedrooms with his body, coming down to mine. I always got scooted up in bed, with Owen, until my head was right against the headboard. I could remember exactly how that felt, the moment when my head had gone as far as it could go and that pressure merged with all the other pressures. It even became a part of coming, after it had happened enough times.

I got up, in an effort to direct my thoughts into more constructive channels. While I was staring out the window I saw the pink Cadillac returning. It wheeled into the driveway of the motel, filled with people, some of them female. In a minute Winfield walked out on a little parapet over the lake, holding hands with a girl who was approximately twice his height. She had long, gorgeous blond hair and looked very young.

I expected the party to sweep in eventually, but it didn't, so I put on some clean pants and a blue T-shirt and went down. I found them out on the veranda. Joe was sitting with another of the large, healthy-looking girls.

Elmo, looking somewhat sour, had no girl. He was sitting with a brown, dried-up little man who managed nonetheless to look English, perhaps because of the way he combed his wisps of gray hair.

"That's the woman herself," Elmo said, when I walked out. "Our conscience, you might say."

"I'm not your fucking conscience," I said. I was getting tired of that line, and of all lines that elevated me in any way. The tireder I got, the less elevated my language became.

"This here's Godwin Lloyd-Jons," Elmo said. The man rose, took my hand in a steely grip, and more or less bowed.

"My dear, I'm extremely pleased to meet you," he said. "Though it's perhaps the dullest opening remark imaginable, I have to tell you that I admire your film profoundly.

"Profoundly," he repeated, pausing for effect. "Not only was it wonderful cinema, but it helped me in my work. I have a whole chapter on it in my forthcoming book."

"Godwin's the greatest living student of the fuckin' middle class," Elmo said. "We bought him right off the Oxford campus. Greatest living student."

"It's the truth," Winfield said. "If scholars could be as famous as screenwriters, old Godwin would be as famous as Elmo and me."

Godwin sighed and sat back down. "Isn't it ridiculous that these boys are so rich?" he said. "I have just one thing to say to you, Winfield."

"What?"

"Go stick your dick in a beer can," Godwin said.

One of the girls giggled, but she was ignored by all.

"Godwin's sharp-spoken when he's sober," Elmo said. "Then when he's drunk he loses control entirely and buggers students and such. It's a wonder he ain't been kicked out of this fair town of ours."

"Fair town?" Godwin said. "This place is as bad as Kabul. The cuisine is no less nauseating. But why should Miss Peel have to listen to this drunken twaddle of ours?"

I was wondering that myself. I wished they would all go

away, except Joe. Then maybe he and I could sit on the veranda by the quiet lake and become, again, the friends we had once been. That seemed to me to be the thing I wanted most, and maybe it would happen if we could be alone in a place where he could drink comfortably and relax. His girl looked big enough to pick him up and throw him in the lake if she wanted to. She had a broad face and in no way resembled the fine-featured, expensive women he was prone to. She was more Winfield's type, and indeed Winfield seemed a little uncertain as to which of the two girls he was interested in, holding hands with one and constantly making eyes at the other. Elmo seemed to have no interest in them—he drank steadily.

I asked Godwin what his book was about, a question that caused Buckle and Gohagen to look pained.

"Don't ask Godwin something like that," Winfield said. "Have you ever listened to an English sociologist before? Now he'll talk for seventeen hours."

Godwin smiled wearily. His eyes were a washed-out blue and his lower teeth crooked, as if some giant had taken his face and squeezed them loose from his jaw, but despite that, he was not entirely unappealing.

"I like to think that these men's brains have gradually assumed the shape of a local delicacy called a chicken-fried steak," he said. "That is, a thin, flat piece of meat. An interesting evolutionary development, if true. As for my book, there's not much to say, though it's kind of you to ask. I have the misfortune to be a sociologist with a prose style. Quite a good one too—Flaubertian, if I do say so myself. I writhe around on the floor of my study for days, searching for the *mot*. I even run a fever."

"Is that true?" one of the girls said. "I'd like to see *that*."

"Only way you'll see it is if you happen to be writhin' underneath him," Winfield said. "Or on top of him, as the case may be."

Godwin suddenly stood up and came over and took my hand. "Can you imagine how lonely it is for an ironist, in a land like this?" he said. "You're clearly very intelligent—the most intelligent woman I've met in years. Perhaps we should marry."

Joe Percy burst out laughing, which irritated me.

"In all likelihood," I said.

"Don't give him no encouragement," Winfield said. "Godwin will marry anything that walks, male, female, or chicken."

"Let's take a walk and get to know one another better," I said lightly to Godwin. "I didn't leave home to sit around among crazy people. I was among crazy people to begin with."

Godwin looked surprised. He let go of my hand, and drained his drink. "Your suggestion is so civilized it startled me," he said. "Walking isn't precisely a local custom. However, only the brave deserve the fair."

We left them and found a path down to the water. A few black women were fishing at the edge of the lake. Downtown Austin was lit by the setting sun.

"I say, that old man's seriously depressed," Godwin said. "Is he in love with you?"

"I hope so," I said. "We're such old friends we've forgotten how to be friends. Maybe we really aren't friends any more and just don't want to admit it."

"Nonsense. The man's dying and wants desperately for you to make it up to him," Godwin said. "He talked about you all afternoon, though from his talk I couldn't tell if you were his daughter or the love of his life. I'm not young myself, and I know what such talk means—also I went through something not unlike what you're describing with my first wife, and then again with a lover—a great gentleman many years older than me. It's love struggling in the grip of death. Stop fighting him and give him anything he wants, before he drops dead on you, as dear Alain did on me. Else you'll have terrible regrets."

It made my hair stand up. Even as I began to believe it, my voice disputed what he had said.

"He's not going to die," I said. "He's not that old."

Godwin smiled, showing his crooked teeth.

"Quite irrelevant," he said. "Some men are able to die when they stop being able to find a compelling reason to live. I'm of the opposite sort. I should have died in World War II, with my dearest friends, but I didn't and now I've flourished quite unjustifiably for three more decades, in defiance of a complete lack of significance. But your friend's different. He's lost his vanity. At his age, vanity is vital."

It was very upsetting, what he was saying, but we continued to walk down the brown path by the quiet lake, with the falling sun burnishing the water far ahead of us and throwing its golden light on the brown buildings of Austin.

"How can you say complete lack of significance?" I said. "You write books."

"I've never pretended to myself that they mattered," he said. "Not one middle-class heart will ever be moved by my analyses, or one pattern changed. My writing provides occasions for academic disputation, and it gets me a good living, but there it ends. I live for what used to be called love—now it seems to be called relationships. Unhappily, my colleagues and myself are largely responsible for that word change."

"Did you ever know Danny Deck?" I asked. I had just remembered my old love. Danny had talked of a professor named Godwin.

The question startled him. "Of course," he said. "He took my girl from me. She ruined him, ultimately, or so I like to think. Absolutely horrible woman."

"I think I met her once," I said.

"How extraordinary you should have known them," he said. "Sally's still around, you know. Married to a black legislator now, very rich. Dope dealer, actually. Elmo knows them. I may yet kill the woman, if I get the chance. Daniel's child is quite beautiful. I often see her in the park, near my house. I've even thought that when somebody finally kills Sally I might try and make her my ward. Such a fetching girl. Love to make her my ward."

And do what with her? I thought. His washed-out eyes were shining. He looked at me shrewdly.

"I remember him as vividly as if it were yesterday," he said. "We almost drowned together once, in the middle of a desert. Was he in love with you?"

I nodded.

"Perfect," he said. "Put that boy down in the middle of the Gobi and he would have contrived to find a woman like you, and then contrived to lose her. But one is foolish to feel sorry for writers. They're all fucking liars, and they fatten on pain. Also they invariably steal women, or men, or whomever one happens to be loving."

We walked on. I looked with different eyes for a few minutes. Some Mexicans went by in a boat. These were Danny's skies, his hills. It was a pity we had never come to Texas together. I didn't want to talk about him any more, but Godwin was wound up.

"Though he had a sympathetic heart," he said. "The boy understood some things. He threw a young sadist I happened to be in love with off a balcony, you know. Then just before he disappeared he sent me five thousand dollars in the mail, to get a young friend of his out of a dreadful jail. The job only cost a few hundred. Danny was never heard from again, and of course I fell in love with the boy. Kept him here in great comfort for three years and then the fool ran away and married. Dear Petey. I suppose he's aged beyond recognition now."

"You seem to fall in love a lot," I said as we walked back. The water was darkening, and the cars driving across the bridge began to turn their lights on.

"It's been my modus operandi," he said. "It's in my genes. I could easily fall in love with you, though I sense that would probably be silly."

I didn't answer, because I couldn't think of any answer to make. I didn't really want to rejoin the crowd—nicer to sit by the dark water, listening to its lappings. But then I didn't want to talk about love any more, either, and it seemed to be Godwin's favorite subject. Soon we heard the tinkle of glasses from the veranda above us. When we got to it, the group was just as we'd left it, only everyone was drunker.

"Ha, I win," Elmo said when he saw us. "I told you she wouldn't elope with him."

"Maybe she just stopped off to get her things," Winfield said.

"Thank you," Godwin said, to me. "That was a pleasant walk—though of course it wasn't much like punting on the Thames. There's hardly any foliage here."

Elmo stood up, stretched, and stepped up on the railing of the balcony. He seemed to be about to feign suicide again, or maybe he wasn't feigning. This time it was about forty feet down, which gave him a chance of sorts. It struck me that we were not a group with very solid attachments to life. The two young girls didn't count. They were just kibitzers. The rest of us were floating in a kind of middle space—floating as I had seemed to float in my superficial sleep. Elmo's fondness for teetering on bridges and parapets just dramatized a more widespread proclivity.

I had no reason in God's name to be in Austin, Texas, with a lot of half-crazed men, but there I was, and they seemed to be the only people left—at least the only ones with whom I had anything in common. Undoubtedly I had friends in other places, true friends, rooted friends, sane friends, stable friends: people who knew what to do about kids with measles and broken plumbing and groceries and in-laws and mortgages. But somehow—if I still had friends like that—I had forgotten their names and their addresses, and even if I could remember them and find them, it seemed doubtful that they would want to put up with my awkwardness and oversensitiveness, my penchant for big, stupid, slightly cruel men, my obsessive need to work, and my general unwillingness to make any of the sensible, mature compromises they had made. I couldn't make them. They wouldn't make. The man didn't exist who could trick me, excite me, or distract me into anything like a marriage now—not even the cautious, hedged play marriages of my living-together acquaintances. That was as clear as the moon, which had already risen and cast its white reflection onto the water below.

I drank a couple of margaritas and watched the moon, so clear and pearlike over the Texas hills, and listened to Godwin as he elegantly and expertly insulted Elmo and Winfield, and their various wives and girl friends, and Texas, and the university, and all universities, and America, and England, and everything else that lay in his mental path. It struck me as strange that a man who spoke so eloquently should have such bad teeth and wear clothes that made him seem so seedy, but then perhaps it was a continental thing: the sensibility having run so far ahead of its outward trappings as to be quite indifferent to them. Perhaps I would be that way eventually, an old lady with a fast mind, wearing awful clothes and the wrong jewels and a hairstyle that didn't suit me.

It was decided, while the moon shone cleanly in the sky and shimmered in the lake, that the time had come to make our departure for the legendary Rio Chickpea. The men went off to drain their bladders, and I was left with the girls, who seemed not altogether keen on making the trip.

"Last time we went down there we didn't get back for a week," the blonde said. "Shoot, I got exams. My folks will kill me if I flunk anythang."

"Makes me feel like a groupie anyhow," the other one said, a little morosely. " 'Course I guess I am a groupie"—she looked nervously at me. "If I ain't, what am I doin' here?"

I left them to work out their own dilemma. Joe was standing in the lobby when I went in. He was in front of a water fountain, sort of weaving. When he bent over to get a drink he hit the pedal on the fountain too hard and the stream of water hit him in the eyes. He was pretty drunk, and pretty old. Godwin's words came back to me, and I felt a pressure building in my chest. I had to do something. I took three or four deep breaths: it was what I had been taught to do in high school, when I was playing girls' basketball. Take three or four deep breaths before you shoot the free throw.

Joe just stood there, not even wiping the water off his face. He blinked to clear his vision. It was really time to shoot the free throw, as far as he and I were concerned. Though we had been friends for many years, this upstart, animosity, had overtaken our friendship and tied us up, with not much time left on the clock. I had no purse, no Kleenex, so I went over and dried his face on his own shirttail, since it was hanging out.

"I had a handkerchief," he said, pulling one out of his pocket. There was the spark of hostility in his eyes. Once again, it seemed, I had come as a reformer, attempting to do for him without waiting to be given permission.

When you stop talking to someone you love, really stop, it is like lifting weights to try and start again. I took a couple more deep breaths, feeling overdramatic but also feeling the weights dragging the words I wanted to say back inside me, back into the safe and formal depths so that all can remain conventional and polite.

"Look," I said—my voice broke and trembled, even on that one word. How can a voice break on a monosyllable?

"Look," I repeated, hearing it tremble again. "I still love you. I need you for a friend again. I can't take any more of this resentment."

Joe just looked at me, lowering his head a bit. His lashes still dripped.

"Let's don't go with them," I said. "We have to get out and stop sometime. We can't just follow Elmo and Winfield all the way to Rome. Let them go on. We can get a suite, like we had at the Sherry, and stay here a few days and rest."

Joe was staring across the lobby.

"I like the way that little Englishman talks," he said. "He reminds me of a lot of people I used to work with. I worked with Aldous Huxley, you know. I even met Evelyn Waugh. The English have a great way with insults. It amounts to a kind of poetry. I guess that's what they've got left. Inspired malice."

I felt very sad. He wasn't going to talk to me. He was going to slide right past me, into reminiscence.

But then, to my surprise, he put his arm around me. "Don't look so resigned," he said. "So I've been an asshole for a while, what can you expect?"

"What's that mean?"

"Well, after all, I haven't been getting any pussy," he said, with a tired grin.

"That's not my fault."

"It is, too," he said. "You withdrew the stimulus of your disapproval. Us old guys need every stimulus we can get."

"That's absolutely ridiculous," I said.

"Now I can't even handle a drinking fountain, much less a woman," he remarked cheerfully. "I like that idea about getting a suite. I'm not up to a rock ranch just now."

I guess it was only a modest rapprochement, but it was enough to make the weights drop off. I felt physically lighter, freshened by relief, and if Joe hadn't looked so very tired, I would have wanted to go to dinner. He kept his arm around me and we walked slowly across the lobby. Just as we got to the elevator, Elmo and Winfield and Godwin stepped out of it. At the sight of us standing there arm in arm, Godwin smiled, showing his bad teeth.

"There you are, Winfield, you fat fart," he said. "You bet on the wrong man. It's not me she means to elope with."

"Fuck, so what?" Winfield said. "If I hadn't been shit-faced drunk, I wouldn't have bet on what a woman would do anyhow. I'd have bet on something simple, like a horserace, or how long it will take Elmo to fall in love with an Italian whore, once we get to Rome."

"If you're implying that ol' Antonella was a whore, I ought to whip your butt," Elmo said, but he looked glassy and gave the words no force.

"Much as I hate to miss it, I think we'll pass on the Chick-pea," Joe said. "Jill's persuaded me to have a quiet old age."

"Oh, well, there won't be anybody there but dope dealers anyway," Winfield said. "You can see plenty of them when you get back to Hollywood."

"If you're still here when we return, perhaps you'll come to dinner at my house," Godwin said. "A rather amusing rabble seems to congregate there."

"Yeah, convicts mostly," Winfield said as they left.

We went up to my room and sat on my little balcony for a

while, looking down at the lake and watching cars drive across the bridge and off into the night. We were friends again—we even held hands as we watched the cars—but there were differences. Before, we had been loquacious friends. Joe had been my teacher, I guess. I had always rattled on obsessively about whatever problem was uppermost in my life, and he had pontificated about it, from the depths of his great experience, as it were. It had made a nice balance and provided a kind of dialogue, but we weren't that way any more. I was too grown-up, finally, to want to talk about my problems, and he was too bushed to pontificate. We just sat and looked, enjoying the cool, placid night. The only thing we could think of to argue about was whether to get a suite immediately, or wait until the next day. Joe was for immediately, and I was for the next day.

"I don't understand you," I said. "We've been estranged for a year and now we've almost made up and all you can think about is how to get more space between us. I have a bed the size of a living room. I can have half and you can have half. Anyway, I feel out of place in suites."

"But movie directors love suites," he said. "I suppose my fondness for them is envy. With a little luck I could have been a movie director. In my day almost anybody could end up directing a picture."

A little later I realized that one reason we were so silent was because Joe was asleep. Of course he was still drinking, and after a while I stopped hearing the ice tinkle against the glass. I looked over, and his head had fallen sideways, against his shoulder. I got him awake enough to walk to the bed, and got his shoes off, and his pants, but gave up on his shirt, which was a silk shirt anyway and quite good enough for pajamas. Then I went back and sat on the balcony a while, until the steady sound of motors from the highway made me sleepy, too.

I slept without floating. About dawn I awoke, aware that Joe had gotten out of bed. I saw him moving slowly across the room toward the bathroom. For a fat man, he had thin legs and not much of an ass. I dozed again, and when I awoke next there was thin sunlight in the room and the sound of cars from the bridge below.

Joe was propped up in bed, looking melancholy. He had a bit of white stubble on his cheeks, which looked out of place with his well-kept mustache. He smiled at me.

"Do you always wear those nightgowns?" he asked.

"What do you mean, *those*?" I said. "It's just a simple nightgown." It was plain cotton, the only one I had grabbed when we took off.

"What did you expect, something with sequins?"

"I guess something less chaste," he said. "Though don't ask me why. You know what's really depressing about old age?"

"You don't get any pussy," I said.

"Oh, well, no," he said. "Pussy's in the nature of an accidental blessing—always was. What's really depressing about old age is not getting erections in the morning. That's hideously depressing.

"I realize this is an odd conversation to be having on our first morning in bed together," he added, looking at me quickly to see if I was embarrassed. I wasn't, particularly—I'm always curious to know what really goes on with men. Joe seemed to be my only immediate hope of finding out.

"All our conversations have been odd," I said. "Why is it more depressing not to get an erection in the morning than not to get one in the evening, or the afternoon?"

"I always got them in the morning, up until my stroke," he said. "At least I did unless I was sick or depressed or something. Waking up with a hard-on sort of set the tone for the day. It's an inducement to optimism. Even if you have a hundred erections and no pussy comes along, it's still an inducement. Even if it's your wife you're in bed with and she doesn't like to fuck in the morning, or maybe isn't fucking you for a while, a hard-on sort of reminds you that there's always hope.

"It could have to do with screenwriting," he added, frowning.

"Your not getting erections?" I said. "You're blaming that on screenwriting?"

"Oh, no," he said. "I blame that on age. What I blame on screenwriting is more of an overall condition. A way of thinking. I'm conditioned to think in terms of payoff. Life ought to be like a good script. The incidents ought to add up, and the characters ought to complement one another, and the story line ought to be clear, and after you've had the climax it ought to leave you with the feeling that it has all been worth it. But look at my case, just to take one. I passed the climax without even noticing it, and I've forgotten half the characters already. There was never a clear story line, and most of the incidents were just incidents. My life would have had a lot more coherence if I'd killed myself when Claudia was having her affairs. I often felt like it."

"All this you've decided because you don't have erections in the morning any more?" I said. "It sounds to me like ordinary self-pity."

"That's what a lack of erections will bring you to," he said. "I thought when I met that big girl yesterday that I might have a chance for one more, but I guess it didn't take. Nowadays the old body follows the supposedly ageless imagination, and I guess even my imagination is old. It passed that girl right on by."

"You mean you've been surly all this time because your penis doesn't stick up any more?" I asked.

He nodded. "Partly," he said. "Partly."

In truth, though some barrier had been broken during the evening, I had not recaptured my old loving feeling for him, because he was not his old, cheerful, iconoclastic self. There was too much defeat in him, too little bounce. I needed that bounce.

Also I was tired of letting ideas determine my behavior. Ideas had held me back all my life—mostly my own ideas, which just made it worse. I moved over a little closer to him, which made him look at me quizzically. Fortunately he didn't look hostile—I am easily rebuffed. He just looked quizzical, and we held hands for a while. I didn't want him to think I wanted to make love, because I didn't. That was unthinkable, with Joe. But if all it took to make him cheerful was for his cock to stick up, that was something else, and maybe worth a shot. Without looking at him, or asking permission, I slipped my free hand inside his underpants, thinking maybe just to take his penis in my hand—only I found that he was so shrunken away that there was practically nothing to hold. There was just the head, almost hidden in its little nest of hair. I touched it lightly, hoping it would immediately emerge, but it didn't.

"Not too commanding, is it?" Joe said—just the sort of thing he would say at such a time, when I was making a major effort to do something unlike myself.

"Shut up," I said. "If you want to be helpful, why don't you think about all those rich girls you used to fuck? You found them plenty stimulating."

"Can't remember anyone but Page," he said. "My memory's atrophied too."

I continued to stroke the head of his penis, which only seemed to draw farther down in its nest. All in all, I had gotten myself into a pretty pickle. Having started what I had started, I couldn't afford not to succeed, yet I wasn't succeeding. His penis was trying to vanish. What little experience I had had with impotence involved young men who were nervous, not old men who were tired. I knew that in theory I was supposed to take him into my mouth and resurrect him that way, but I was not about to do that. That was another idea I wasn't going to be guided by. Even with my lovers I had never been very adept at that, or very excited by it, either. I just didn't want to think about how sad and embarrassed Joe would feel if I failed, now that I had touched him. The fact that his penis stayed almost hidden in his pubic hair annoyed me, not so much with the stubborn little organ that it was, but with myself. Thirty-eight, and still awkward, still never quite knowing what to do.

"Silly things like this often happen to me in Texas," he said. "I once slept with a woman in Houston who asked me questions about Gregory Peck during the whole performance.

"You look so earnest, lying there," he added. "That's always been one of your problems. How can I get a hard-on when you're looking earnest?"

"I can't look like a debutante, not in this nightgown," I said. "I feel pretty damn earnest, if you want to know the truth."

He chuckled. "Oh, honey," he said. "I don't really need an erection. After all, I've had a million or two."

I stopped listening to him and lay numbly, stroking his balls. There was nothing else to stroke. Then he suddenly became garrulous and started telling a long story about Ben Hecht and a whorehouse in Burbank. At least he was talking again. Actually I didn't really listen—I was thinking of my son. I had begun to miss him acutely, and it wasn't guilt, either. I just wanted to go see him. I wanted to find him and sneak into his room while he was asleep and just look at him for a bit. Also I wanted to hear him talking to me, although, since he only talked to me about guitars, my mind always wandered during our conversations. My ignorance irritated him slightly. But I had a very clear vision of him in New Mexico, and if Joe and I ever got out of bed and went on with life, that was where I meant to go, to see Johnny.

While I was thinking about it the sun shone into the room and onto the foot of the bed. It warmed my legs. Then I noticed that Joe's penis had come out of its nest a little. It wasn't hard, but it had lengthened some. It was no longer just a head. Joe was still talking about whores in Burbank. I had lived in Burbank and had never known there were any there, or much of anything else there except Warner Brothers. As the sun got warmer on our legs I played with Joe's cock as delicately as I could. I didn't want it to go away again just yet.

"Flaubert knew about whores," Joe said. "He left some remarks in his letters. I used to know the best parts of his letters by heart."

Then, to my happiness, Joe's penis stopped being a sort of cool, floppy worm and became that thing that men are so devoted to. When I had first touched it, it had been only a tiny head, hardly thicker than my thumb, but it had thickened so that it and my hand didn't fit into the underpants any more and I had to lift them so it could straighten itself and lie up against the base of his belly. I could feel the pulse of a vein.

"There," I said. "That ought to make your morning."

Joe was delighted. Rather shyly, he lifted his underpants and stared at himself—I didn't want to look. I've not found them a visual treat, though some men seem to. Owen would stand in front of a mirror for minutes at a time, I guess to see if his was hanging in a manner to suit him.

When Joe got tired of admiring himself I put my hand back on it—it seemed a good idea to make it last.

I put my face down on the warm sheet and Joe gently ruffled my hair and stroked my cheek.

"You put that well," he said. "You really have made my morning."

"Not sure it was me," I said. "The memory of the whores of Burbank was probably what did it. I'm not sure I would have wanted to be married to you, Joe."

"You're very special," he said, still stroking my hair. "You're really somewhat unusual, you know."

At that—the inadequacy of it—we both laughed, a laugh that rang like bells in both of us, bringing back our friendship. It was like beginning together at the Warners commissary again, only better, because in those days I was too awed and inhibited to do much more than giggle. And in those days, no doubt, after awing me with his reading and his worldly wisdom, Joe had probably gone right out and got fucked by a Burbank whore.

I felt joined to him again, by the knowledge that we, at least, still saw the humor in our errant lives. I scooted a little nearer to him and got comfortable under his arm. In a few minutes, as Joe was dozing, his penis sank back through my fingers and I put it back in its soft nest and covered it with my hand. Then I dozed, too, slept until the sheets became so hot that Joe grumbled and got up and pulled the blinds.

We had learned our lesson, though neither of us could have recited it, and we were good to one another after that—though except in that one regard our habits didn't improve.

About three years later I came home from doing a picture in Europe, for Carl, and found Joe dead in his chair, with a girlie magazine in his lap. He had died the night I got home, which would seem like tragic timing but wasn't actually. We had straightened out our timing once and for all, in Austin, and I had talked to him from London a day before his death. He had seemed content and even told me he had a girl, someone more beautiful than Page, and richer. I never corroborated that—most likely that last debutante was a nice lie, something he could twit me with on the overseas telephone. I didn't go see him the night I got in because I had a lover tagging along—a ski instructor, of all classic things. He was from Mississippi and had had a minor part in Carl's picture. His name was Jackson, and he wouldn't be left in Europe. Jackson was a wonderful, graceful young man, all sweetness and Southern manners and uncertainty, whom I had said yes to because I had grown very very tired of saying no. Later, not long after Joe's death, Jackson decided he was more gay than not, and ended up selling underwear in San Diego.

I felt rather guilty for taking Jackson away from all that nice snow, but I didn't feel guilty about Joe. I don't think he would have rushed down the hill to my house if he had come home from Europe with a big insecure debutante.

I did, however, take it as my prerogative to remove the girlie magazine before I called the police. The cops who came were big boys, too, and while they were standing around staring at Joe's flowerpots I finally began to cry—crying just to keep from laughing, I think. They were so big and awkward and well-meaning and dumb—boys who should not have been sent to deal with such a delicate thing as the death of Joe Percy. They kept holding their helmets in their hands and looking at me and shuffling.

"How was he employed?" one asked.

"He wrote for the screen," I said.

Then, blushing before he even spoke, one of the cops—it was an Officer Harrison—came over to the couch where I was modestly weeping, and sat down beside me. He was so big I expected the couch to tilt like a seesaw, but it didn't.

"Uh, how were you connected with him, ma'am?" he asked.

We would have laughed at that question like we laughed that morning in Austin. Perhaps our lesson had been that we had learned to laugh at everything important that didn't make sense, which was almost everything important. From the look on his broad, solemnly anxious face, Officer Harrison hadn't learned that lesson yet.

"I don't know, Officer," I said. "I don't know. I never figured it out."